Tale of a Blackbird
By R.C.J. D...

CW00531159

To my mother, for all the books.

"We are all subject to the fates. But we must act as if we are not, or die of despair."

- Philip Pullman

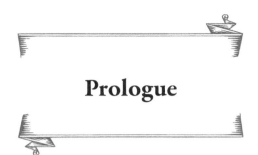

Prologue

The city of Mala was on fire.

Burning bodies fell from the spire like cinders from a flaming chimney, a high tower dominating over the layered districts of the city spat out its inhabitants like shooting stars in the night sky. Screams, smoke, clashing of metal, it all wafted along the air current into the Clerics Palace, where he watched his plan unfurling with a smile. By now the last of the Black family would be cornered in the upper spire, being put to the sword, and soon the other eleven cities would know of their downfall.

Let them be afraid, they will all meet the same fate.

"Master," a masked man announced himself. "I have bad news."

"What is it?"

"I'm afraid the Black heir wasn't found among the bodies."

He turned on the masked man. "Then find him, find Maddox. Seal the port. Do *not* let him escape!"

Outside of the palace the army amassed and were soon to be sent down to slaughter all uprising citizens in the lower districts. In the lower districts the loyal citizens to the Black family had put all local officials to the sword and hung the bodies from the lampposts. Beyond the high walls that enclosed the city of Mala and to the south was a port, where a man and woman hidden in a crate were lifted and stowed away in the hold of a ship bound for the mainland. In the woman's arms she cradled a bundle of rags that stirred, but the woman rocked the baby until it fell back to sleep. The ship cast off and waves rocked the sleeping child further, who dreamt of screaming shadows, safe in the arms of a woman who was not her mother.

The ship drifted away, leaving behind it a city without an identity. Leaving behind it a tower of death that had once been their home, with halls filled with corpses that had once been their family.

Mala was the past.

Days passed into weeks to months as the man and woman fled into the distant mountains, away from the clutches of their enemies. A house was built and became a home, where the child grew into a curious little girl who never shied away from the hard training placed upon her. Three years passed when the man received a piece of paper which arrived tied to the leg of a raven.

He left and never returned.

Chapter 1: The Unknown

"Wake up, my little blackbird," a sing-song voice merrily called from the distance, making the boat rock and landscape fade. Her throat was parched, skin slick with sweat, but even though she realized it was a dream, Birdie struggled to keep hold of it, to make sense of it. But it was gone, like a shadowy room when the curtains are thrown open—which was just what happened. Bella pulled them aside and let the daylight flood in, making Birdie moan and block the light from her eyes with her hands.

"Do you have to do that every morning, Bel? It's my birthday, let me sleep!" Birdie pulled the bedcovers back over her head and groaned as her aunt's footsteps came closer.

"And you think the evil in this world cares that it's your birthday? Evil creatures, demons, it's her birthday! Please wait until it's a time more suitable. Get real—or more importantly—get dressed!" A hand grabbed the blanket and Birdie kicked at it, but to no avail, as the blanket was ripped off and flung to the ground.

Birdie shielded her eyes by looking between her spread fingers, seeing if the blanket was a lost cause or not, but Bella had her hand on her hips, a sure giveaway. Birdie yawned and stretched, wiped the sleep from her eyes.

"Come on, I let you sleep past sunrise. Get dressed and meet me outside." Bella turned and left the room, taking the blanket with her and opening the window for good measure.

Using the wash-basin in the corner, Birdie washed and dressed into her training clothes, tying her tousled hair back into a tight braid. In the main room of the cottage a steaming pot of porridge hung over the fire, which she ladled into a cup along with a spoonful of honey and brought outside with her.

The surrounding woods were alive with activity, birds chirruped from the trees as they swayed, creaking and knocking against each other. Bella stood by one of the workbenches by the woodshed, sharpening her knives. Birdie ate the porridge as they set off along the trail, walking adjacent to the river where a lone beaver was once again making repairs to the dam, and entered the treeline, passing by the archery range and coming to the Knife Tree.

It didn't look anything like a knife, really, and was only called that due to the fact that it was a dead elm tree that they used for throwing blades at. It was situated just before a steep decline, and Birdie had spent many hours during her life searching those thorny bushes for misaimed weapons.

There were other trees they could have used. Hundreds, in fact. But that would be easy, and if there was one thing that Bella hated more than anything, it was doing things the *easy* way.

The first time Birdie had confronted her aunt over the Knife Tree's location—or more correctly the scratches and stings gained from searching through those bloody bushes—the only answer she'd gotten was '*It builds character*'. Builds bloody calluses, more like.

"You first," Bella said, putting her hands on her hips. Birdie took the three throwing knives from her belt and took position. They hit, the second *just* making the trunk.

"Not bad," Bella said sucked her teeth. "But you've been slacking lately. Try again."

Birdie pulled the blades out of the trunk and re-took her position, but hesitated.

"Is something the matter?" said Bella.

Birdie twirled the knife in her hand. "You'll never answer."

"Questions, is it? Go on, it being your birthday and all."

"I was dreaming of Maddox last night, his face was hazy after so long, in shadow. You know the dream I told you about before, when you fled in the boat?" Bella nodded and Birdie closed her eyes, trying to bring it up in her mind's eye. "But there was something else, before that. Something new, *someone* new."

Birdie peeked and saw Bella had lifted an eyebrow, a rare mark to show that she was intrigued.

"I didn't see a face, but he was looking at the spire. It was there in my dream, just like in the books, and he was... happy. He was *happy* about the people being killed, about the people that were jumping out of the spire. He was responsible for their deaths, and he didn't care."

"I wouldn't worry too much about it, Birdie. If it's who I think it is, he's a long way from us now."

"You know him?"

"I never *knew* him. But Nefaro was the ring-leader behind that night. He'd organized everything. I guess that must be who you're seeing."

Birdie didn't like the thought of the murderer of her family infiltrating her dreams.

They remained throwing knives for an hour before moving on to archery. An hour later they went back to the cottage and Bella dished out Birdie's favourite, trailhead soup. After she'd devoured three bowls of the spicy soup, Birdie didn't have to wash up and had a nap beside the fire.

She dreamed of tree-sized bushes that kept chasing her around the house, throwing knives at her.

Upon awaking, the fire was almost out and Birdie put a few logs onto the dying embers. Bella wasn't anywhere in or outside the cottage. Birdie noticed a package on the workbench outside. Picking it up, she read Bella's note on the parchment.

Happy sixteenth birthday, little Blackbird.

Birdie untied the ribbon and opened it.

Inside was a beautifully hand-crafted knife, with a hickory handle and polished steel blade. A bird had been carved into the hilt, which had been painted in a midnight black. While Birdie wasn't one-tenth as good at forging weapons as Bella—and that was being generous—she had been painstakingly put through the basic lessons, and at least could respect the time and effort the woman had put into her gift.

After checking outside for her aunt and finding a note by the woodpile it read '*patrolling area*'. Birdie decided to go fishing. Shouldering her rod, she set off down the path and followed the river until it joined a larger one.

It was unusual for her not to be on patrol with her aunt. Birdie often patrolled the south and eastern boundaries. Not many people ventured this deep into the forest, so far from civilisation, but Birdie knew they were still being hunted.

She felt a small bit guilty about shirking her duties, even if it was her birthday. But with the sun shining down on her face and the river gurgling by, the smell of fresh grass strong in her nose and the anticipation of catching a fish, she wasn't complaining.

Birdie sat by her favourite spot near the moss-covered boulders, and was about to cast, when something caught her eye. Not fifty paces downriver she found torn clothing, with blood stains covering the fabric, and more blood drops led away from the river and into the trees.

It looked like it was from her aunt's clothing.

Following the blood trail into the trees, a figure sat slumped against a pile of rocks. Birdie couldn't see its face, the figure facing away from her; only a bloodied hand that lay limp by its side. Steeling herself, she walked around to get a better look.

It was a man.

He had short cropped hair turned scarlet from the two gashes running down his scalp and forehead. Two familiar throwing knives stuck out from his chest, one of which looked like it had pierced his lung. She picked up a stick and poked him. Feeling braver, Birdie held a hand in front of his mouth. Not breathing, so she checked his pulse. Dead.

Birdie left the corpse and searched the area, finding another trail of blood that led away from the river. She found her aunt's body crumpled by a dead-fallen tree, its bark all rotted and covered in a sickly black fungus that smelled of puss. Her clothing had been ripped open, revealing her chest, and scratch marks covered her upper torso, neck and arms. Birdie's hands shook as she reached down to check her aunt's pulse.

"Thank the Gods, you're alive," cried Birdie, as Bella gave a choking cough, spitting out a mouthful of bloody spit.

"Birdie, is that you? Don't... Don't touch the man. He... He's diseased. Don't touch him, or you'll get it too." Bella cracked open one bruised eye, registering the panic rising in Birdie's face. Birdie frantically wiped her hand that'd touched the man on a moss-covered tree.

"You touched him?" Birdie nodded and Bella let her head drop. "Shit-balls."

On entering her aunt's room, the stench made Birdie gag. The incense did little to cover the putrid odour that crept over her aunt, like maggots to decay. For days now Bella's skin had been breaking out with more of the white spots. They ran down her neck and chest, leaking puss onto the stained sheets. Old spots were now surrounded with a dark and peeling rash, veins turned green and swollen, lips a dark, dry grey. For some reason the disease had not stricken Birdie ill, *yet*. It could only be a matter of time.

Steeling herself, Birdie soaked the cloth in a bucket of water and wet Bella's forehead, then threw the rag into the bucket and picked up the bowl. "Bella, I've made soup."

After some time, Bella's eyes opened. "Blackbird?" her voice was weak and croaking, like the toads by the river. Eyes dark shadows, sunken and tired.

"Yes aunt, I'm here. You need to eat some soup. You'll feel better, I promise."

"There's no time. You need to leave, before I fall back to sleep. They're coming, he was only a scout."

"Bella, you're ill. It's the fever. It will get better if you *please* just eat some of this s—"

A high-pitched scream cut off her pleading, it echoed through the woods outside. Bella grabbed Birdie's hand, nails digging into her flesh. "Get to the woods. Don't look back!"

"Come with me. We can make it out together."

"No, I'd only slow you down. Look for Maddox... in Mala. Don't trust anyone. Take this..." As Bella took off her necklace and handed it to Birdie, she began to cough a black froth that drooled down her chin. "Go," she rasped. "Run!"

"I'm not leaving! I'm not!"

But Bella pushed her away, still stronger even in her weakened state. Bella stumbled out of bed, forcing Birdie from the room, banging the door shut. Birdie tried to push the door open, but it didn't budge. She slipped the necklace over her head and ran from the room, deciding to get outside and see what was happening. The walls passed by in a blur, and as she left the cottage another scream echoed through the surrounding dark forest.

It sounded closer.

Her foot tripped on something and she tumbled into the log-pile in front of the woodshed.

"Run," Bella screamed from inside the cottage. "Don't look back!"

Birdie saw lights deep in the forest. She ran across the open meadow, away from the lights. Another scream pierced the night, making Birdie look back instinctively, and her foot caught on a mound of grass. The ground went tumbling over, grass-blades filling her mouth and blocking out the curses dribbling from her lips.

Silhouettes appeared behind the cottage, moving between the trees, holding torches. Hundreds of popping sounds echoed through the clearing, as if the trees were possessed—as if they had come to life and were slowly moving, creeping closer.

Her legs felt like giving way as she wobbled on, but she made it to the edge of the clearing. Hiding behind a tree, she looked back, seeing the figures move closer to the cottage, seeing the torches they held thrown onto her home and its thatched roof catching light instantly.

Birdie turned away and wiped her eyes, held her hands over her ears, trying to block out the distant screams of her aunt. She took a step forward, leaving everything she had ever cared for and loved behind.

The shadows of the forest hugged her in a dark embrace as she fled into the unknown.

Birdie awoke from the nightmare drenched, her fingers digging into something hard.

In her nightmare Bella had been lying on her bed covered in flames and men's faces smiled and jeered at her cries for help. It took Birdie a moment to recall where she was. Another moment to realise it hadn't been a nightmare at all.

It had been all too real.

Pressed up against a tree, sap streaked across her face and hands. A small grey squirrel on a nearby branch looked at her curiously, before fleeing as she began climbing down. The days gone by since fleeing her home were a series of blurred memories. Hunger was a numb sensation in her gut, overshadowed by fear, senses numbed by shock and cold.

The years spent training with Bella had saved her, her body purely moving through instinct. Those winter nights spent avoiding her aunt's detection had sharpened her eyes and ears, kept her alert to shadows not belonging to the forest.

Birdie came to the first marker, a birch tree with a broken branch, followed its direction, then hours later a small pile of rocks built like an arrow. The wind occasionally carried sounds through the trees; sounds not of the forest and that had no place in them. Smells of acrid smoke stung at her nose, cries from far off, and once she'd caught the stench of sweat, but had given its owner a wide berth. Her step was light and gaze watchful as a white deer of the north.

Bella had always told her that when you thought you were safe, that was when the enemy would get you.

The words stung at her heart. She remembered the necklace and checked if it was still there, which it was. Birdie tucked it away as she walked into a clearing and approached the ancient willow tree at its centre.

In her younger days she had spent many days out here climbing the old tree. A squat mossy wall ran up and over a hill beyond it. She sat down by the willow tree, taking her boots off and squeezing the damp from her socks. She grunted as she tore fabric from her soggy pant leg to wrap her blistering feet with.

Boots and socks back on, Birdie stood up and took a long look at the tree, running her fingers over where they'd both carved the letter B. She stopped beside it, felt the worn grooves beneath her fingers, felt the pendant's cold surface pressing against her skin, and with a last lingering glance behind her, she left the tree behind, following the wall up the hill.

The old trail that marked as far as her and Bella had ever gone came to an end far too soon, passing out through a tangle of trees and bush. It crossed a ditch and opened out onto a dirt road. The sign which was supposed to give her directions had been burned, but she needed to go west, or was it east?

"Shit-balls."

Focus.

Birdie shivered as Bella's voice floated through her mind, as if she was still there with her. Checking the sky, Birdie made sure the directions were correct, then placed her foot to the edge of the road, aware that with one more step she would be leaving the safe circle she had spent her entire life in. Her hands shook.

What lay ahead of her? Would she be better off staying at the wrecked cottage, and try to rebuild?

But there was no turning back. Not now.

Not ever.

The path didn't give way beneath her boot, and the road didn't open up and swallow her whole. It also had no fresh tracks, which was always a good sign. Routes around their home were scarcely used as the woods were believed to be haunted. A legend created by Bella's relentless harassing of any traders who used to pass through the area.

But *were* they just stories? Those things last night had to be spirits, demons even.

"Get yourself together, Birdie," she chided. "There's no such thing as spirits or demons, or magic for that matter. It was lies people tell little children to scare them to bed, and you're not a child, so stop filling you mind with absolute..."

Birdie stopped walking. She had smelled something just then, something burning. Smoke from a fire, or somebody cooking in a house, perhaps? Further down the path, she saw a smoke column rising above the trees and decided to leave the path, instead creeping through the trees. Through the gaps, across the clearing, was a smouldering village. Birdie began moving around the clearing, from one tree to the next, being as quiet as possible. There were no signs of life; not even a farm animal called out from the ghostly sight.

At the other side of the village, she crouched in some thick ferns and was about to walk into the clearing to get a closer look, when a hand grabbed her from behind and pulled her back down to the ground. Another hand covered her mouth before she could scream.

"Keep quiet or I'll cut your throat," hissed a voice close to her ear. Birdie looked up at the figure kneeling over her. Two bright blue eyes shone from a woman's face covered in mud. Her hair was braided and caked in mud also. The woman put her finger against Birdie's lips before taking her hand away. "They might still be around," whispered the woman, standing.

"Who?" Birdie sat up slowly, rubbing her neck, also noting that the knife was still very close.

"Who do you think?" the woman jabbed her knife at the village. "Lie down. If I hear you moving..." The woman held up the knife, so Birdie nodded, lying down amongst the thick ferns. The woman disappeared from view, her faint footsteps quickly fading.

Minutes passed. "Come on," Birdie whispered. Drops of light rain fell, increasing to fat beads, dripping into her eyes, sticking her tangled hair to her scalp all the more. More silence, her heartbeat the only companion in the world. It drummed in her ears as the moments stretched out.

The sound of a breaking twig came from behind her. Birdie froze as she felt something tug on her foot and a man's voice growled something unrecognisable. Birdie could only give a pathetic squeak as she felt a hand grab her leg and was dragged out of the ferns.

A man built like a bear had three scars running down over one discoloured eye, yellow teeth revealed as he frowned down at her. The man spoke again in a language she didn't understand. He looked around and smiled as he settled his gaze back on her. He pulled out a jagged, badly forged knife from inside his fur coat and whispered something.

Birdie tried to push herself away from him, snatching at the ferns and grass for something sharp or heavy to use as a weapon, cursing herself for leaving her knife behind in the cottage. He snatched up a short coil of rope from his belt, pulled loose the knot, and tried to grab her leg again. She kicked it away, but the man growled and lurched at her, punching her into the ribs, folding her up like a blanket. He'd the rope slipped over her ankle and tightened in a heartbeat, and she was still trying to suck in air as he pulled her along the forest floor, sliding over rocks, sharp thorns which scratched at her arms and neck.

"No, get off!" Birdie croaked, searching for something to use as a weapon, but all her fingers found were grassy clumps and edges of embedded rocks that wouldn't give way. She managed to slip her arms around the end of a fallen log. He tugged on the rope, making her leg burn with the tension. As she blinked up at him, Birdie couldn't help the fear that rose in her. It bubbled up and clawed its way out of her throat in a whimper.

The man smiled wider.

She kicked her legs at him as he closed the distance between them. "Get the fuck away from me!" she screamed, aiming a kick at his groin, but he blocked it with his leg, returning a kick into her gut, making her gag and curl up once more. The man laughed as he pulled away her arms, putting the knife's tip against her cheek. The world spun then as he pounced on top of her, forcing the air from her lungs like a bellows. He backhanded her into the face with his free hand. Its sting was unnatural, turning the world above her into a spinning chaos of colour. As he pressed the knife's point into the hollow of her collarbone, she could feel blood trickling down the side of her neck. He grabbed her by the hair and went to cut the fabric of her tunic, when a voice spoke from behind him. The man glanced back and stood up.

Air felt like icy shards as it rushed back into her lungs. She tried to push herself up, to get away, but her legs were too weak and she just collapsed onto the log. Using it for support, Birdie crawled away from the man and spat out bloody spit and lumps of dirt. Strange voices were speaking in that piggish language, but she didn't care. All that mattered right now was getting away.

Birdie stopped crawling.

One of the voices was familiar.

Looking back, the woman with the mud on her face smiled, pointing around at the woods, then at Birdie. The man laughed and slid his knife into his belt, rubbing his hands together before glancing back at Birdie and nodding, thumbing his chest. There was an easy expression on his face as he spat into his hand and offered it to the woman. After they released hands, he moved towards Birdie.

Her breath heaved in her chest as they moved closer, the man sliding out his knife once more, lips cracking to reveal rotted teeth. They were both on the same side. She was going to die. He reached out for her with dirt-caked fingernails, jagged blade getting closer, and then there was a swishing sound. His eyes bulged as the sword sliced through the flesh and bone of his neck, ripping tendons like fishing line, and his head went spinning up into the air, landing with a horrible squelching sound, rolling along the forest floor and coming to a rest beside Birdie.

The eyes were still rolling, lips twitching. Streams of blood spurted out from the gaping wound where his head had been, turning everything in its immediate vicinity red, which included Birdie. His decapitated body stabbed at empty air, but thankfully with limp arms which widely missed anything and she jumped back.

The body dropped to its knees. Blood spurted up from the gaping hole once more in a final jet. The woman kicked the body onto the ground, lifted her sword and drove it through the man's back, piercing the heart and stilling the twitches.

Birdie vomited, getting it all down the front of her clothes and her filthy boots.

The woman pulled her blade free and kicked the man's corpse. "Fuckin' pigs," she growled, and then looked down at Birdie. "You OK?"

"You're not with them?" Birdie wiped her mouth with her sleeve, allowing herself a small shiver.

"No, I'm not."

"You're not going to kill me?"

"Maybe, maybe not." The woman spat onto the man's corpse. "Damn animals, surprised they don't bleed shit." The woman leaned down and cleaned her sword on the man's clothes.

"W-Who are you?"

The woman ignored her. "You live 'round here?"

"My house was... was burned, like the village. My aunt... she's..." Birdie couldn't say the words.

The woman nodded. "We need to move. You fall behind, I won't wait. Put these on." The woman tossed her the man's boots and a cloak from his pack, both of which were too big, but mercifully dry. Birdie didn't complain about the smell.

The woman nodded once more and wiped her nose. "Well, I guess you'd best stick with me then, 'til we get to an outpost at least." She walked away into the woods, not looking back. Birdie checked that she was out of view, before kneeling down and taking the dead man's knife. She cleaned it on him, and then spat onto the corpse for good measure, before turning and chasing after the woman.

Chapter 2: Clerics and Schemes

Kassova Kye fingered through the reports on his desk and smoothed back his long, oiled hair with his other hand. He looked back up from the desk, to the man standing on the far side of it. Only the man's eyes were visible, the rest hidden behind a black mask, its bird-like beak pointing down in a curve almost touching its chin. A thick black cloak hid the man's many weapons, which had clinked somewhat noisily as he had entered the room.

Kye hated the Masked Lodge, bunch of bloated up bodyguards, the lot of them.

But then, Kassova Kye hated everyone.

"You were saying, major...?" Kye managed in getting his tone of voice perfect, one-half terminal boredom and the other half icy contempt. The Kye special.

"It's Moore and I said we need more men and powder in the eastern portcullis. You know how explosive the damn stuff is, keeps going off. If we're attacked without it the fire-pipes on the walls won't do a thing to save us. We could also use some more grunts for repairs, but His Supreme and the ministry have ignored any of our requests."

Kye stood up, sweeping around the table and moving closer to the officer, giving him a flash of his metal teeth. "Say that again, would you?"

"We need men. We're undermanned, there's no way—"

The slap echoed off the marble walls, and as the officer stumbled away from being backhanded, he covered his face with a gloved hand. The mask had been pushed askew and revealed heavily scarred flesh beneath.

Kye pointed a finger at the soldier. "You *need* what His Supreme tells you, and that's to hold fast and make do with what you have. Come here again begging for resources and I'll have your body rotting on the eastern ramparts as a reminder to your men. Now get out of my sight!"

The soldier fixed his mask, saluted and moved to exit the room.

"Wait!" called Kye, clicking his fingers, making Vines—who had been silently standing in the corner for the past few minutes, now put an arm against the door. "I have an idea. Yes, Major Moore, I'm feeling generous today, *quite* generous. You have one month to use whatever resources you can gather together. Let's call it a trial run. I'll give you permission to begin taxing the refugees in the eastern valley. Call it... a Life-Levy, if you will. Any who can't or won't pay can join the army or leave, let them fester outside our protection in fear.

"Before one month's time, major, I'll send someone to inspect your progress. Any and all refugees who are drafted will be given basic training and armed, all supervised and supplied by you and your officers."

Moore nodded and saluted once more. Vines opened the door for the man and slammed it shut behind him, making the torches flutter in their brackets. Once back behind his desk, Kye eyed the pile of papers.

Reports, reports, reports. The twelve rings of the underworld are filled with reports, surely.

Scanning through them, they were mostly supply orders, receipts. Though a thin metal vial had been sent from one of his agents, informing him they'd narrowly escaped capture by the Temple's scouts, having been engaged in tracking their movements for weeks just beyond the eastern mountains.

If this agent sends me such a vague and useless report again, I'll castrate him.

Still no word from his other agent, who had probably fled south.

If she ever shows her ginger head around here again, I'll draw-and-quarter the bitch.

A handful of agents he had out there, searching constantly for any sign of Maddox Black and his sister, Bella. The Black Shadow had been a scourge in Mala the past few years, but his occasional bouts of murdering guards or burning buildings had vanished. Kye would find him, even if it was the last thing he'd do, he'd string that b—

A knocking on the door broke Kye's train-of-thought, and he nodded to Vines, who unbolted the door. The turkey-like figure of Quadra-Minister Fleck wobbled in, his too-large official robe trailing behind him like a mummy's quim. He looked in a foul mood—even greyer-skinned and darker-eyed than usual—and the wrinkled skin beneath his chin wobbled as he shook his head.

Kye stood up. "Good evening, sir, to what do I owe the plea—"

"This is no damn time for damn pleasantries." Fleck turned and looked at Vines. "Get out!" Vines shut the door behind him. Fleck paced the room, looking up sporadically and fixing Kye with a cocktail of emotions, mostly bad. "I suppose you've heard, then? One of the eastern outposts has fallen. Those bastards have actually attacked us! The Eclipsi are nothing but savages, and they think they can match us? Attack us, the might of the world!" Fleck collapsed into the chair in front of Kye's desk—without asking—and took out a purple kerchief from inside his cloak and began wiping beneath his chin, which had begun to sweat profusely.

Might of the world, indeed.

"His-Supreme is retaliating?" Kye opened his lower desk drawer, took out the bottle of spirits and poured the bright yellow liquor into a small glass, handing it to Fleck.

The man took it and sipped. "Better, thank you. Yes, of course he is, but he won't be happy with you, Kassova."

"It was unfortunate." Kye nodded, walking around the desk, pacing the space behind Fleck. He knew the man hated it when he did it. "I gave the agent strict instructions. It was their last chance. I was wrong to put so much faith in their abilities. They will be promptly dealt with, have no fear."

Fleck finished his drink. "Worried? Hah, it's not *me* who let Nefaro down. He has *summoned* you."

"What... when?"

"Right this moment, I wanted to come and give you the news, personally. Sergeant!" The door opened, but instead of Vines, an officer strode in, followed by a dozen other members of the Masked Lodge. Fleck smiled. "Come now, Kassova, let's not make this any harder than it needs to be." Fleck shambled out of his seat as the men surrounded Kye, who held up his hands.

Outside in the hall Vines lay unconscious on the floor, his hands and feet trussed up in rope. In the courtyard outside Kye's headquarters, he and Fleck climbed inside a carriage. Four of the masked men sat opposite, two holding small crossbows, trained on Kye. As the carriage began rumbling its way out of the courtyard and along the cobbled road, Kye saw that all traffic on the bridge connecting to the Bone-Portcullis had stopped.

The carriage followed the road away from the bridge, first through the slapped together tenements, where some better off refugees had luckily been allotted beds, to the more maintained parts of the district. Kye thought about the refugees in the Spine valley, below the bridge they had passed, and he was content that he'd soon be at least putting an end to *that* problem.

The valley was an ancient earthwork surrounding the mainland port. The ministry had foolishly sought to put refugees in there. The four bridges—the Spines—the only means of access across and into the port, had let these streams of human refuse across. The Masked Lodge had supervised their transportation into the valley, through the network of ancient mining tunnels. The refugees had been spending the past few weeks and the scaffolding given to them to create thousands of cling-on residences, these now were scattered alongside the cliffs below the Spine like a bad case of crotch rot.

To cleanse the land, restore order, regain power. Nefaro's Mantra drummed through his head, one of many statements of the old man's that Kye held close to his heart. Kye would at least not be failing his master in that respect.

Kye held no doubts that the old man was angry. Kye had been his prodigy, schooled in the Clerics Palace at the early age of seven, then sent to the Palace of War at thirteen, sharpened of both mind and sword by the best at both. But recent events had warped that image Kye had created, had worked hard for, to the point that Nefaro had shoved his champion to the edge of the war against the Alliance, and put him on Gods-damned *clerical* duty, at the fucking east Bone Portcullis...

Kye unclenched his fists and took a deep breath.

It was surely the equivalent of hiring a whore just to re-patch your damned socks.

"What's so funny?" Fleck was frowning at him.

Kye shook his head and stared at the ceiling, wiping off the grin and keeping his face neutral.

The carriage passed through the checkpoints without hindrance, the bonus of having Nefaro's seal of power engraved on the front of your carriage, he supposed. Kye also noted the increase in the Masked Lodge's presence. There had always been a steady supply of the men in masks, but the ministry must've been recruiting more muscle in order to keep the swell of refugees in check.

So much for limited resources...

Once the carriage moved through the civilian quarters and began to descend, the air filled with the salty smell of the sea. Soon Kye heard the cry of gulls above and as the carriage pulled up and they exited, he saw his old nemesis.

The fiend partly responsible for his fall from grace.

Water.

Fleck smiled. "I almost forgot, you don't like water, do you, Kassova? Well, don't worry. You don't have any pirates to fear on this journey, and the Black Shadow is long gone, I'm told."

Kye flashed the old turkey his silver smile as he walked towards the gangway. "I wouldn't fear, Fleck. If we get caught in a storm, I'll strangle you before you drown."

Chapter 3: The Coin Flip

Leek was a coward, or so his siblings had always told him. But Leek knew that deep down inside he had what it took to be brave.

He chewed on his fingernail and spit out a piece, his mother having shaved his hair to stop the spread of lice on the road, so now his nails were bitten down to the quick.

Leek hated himself for being afraid, always afraid, and he was aware of the fact that he wasn't the strongest, or had as much meat on his bones than a starved weasel.

But Leek *knew* he could be courageous.

"Remember Leek, don't show fear," his mother had told him on the way to the gate. She stood beside him now, a dark, worried expression on her face. Not related by blood, but the only family he'd left in the world.

The only reason she'd ever taken him into the family was he showed promise in thievery. Leek had been the youngest of fostered siblings, taken into the fold due to his small body frame which was ideal for window-picking. He'd always been the black sheep and runt of the family rolled into one. His older fosterlings were better at stealing, purse-snatching, and window-tickling, which involved putting his arms into pried open gaps not knowing if he'd get them back out again—some even had the rare gift for entertaining the crowd so the others could get close to work their magic.

Even through the bullying, the teasing, the loneliness, the never-ending travelling from town-to-village, he'd loved them in a way. But then he'd left home for good and helped out in the tavern they passed on one of their many travels, a quaint but lively inn situated in the centre of Willow's Creek. It was years before the White-Spot plague had come and wiped out most of the countryside, turning once bustling communities into ghost towns.

Marlo had been a prodigiously bellied inn-keeper and a great cook, a talent he bestowed upon Leek, but Marlo also had a hunger for old books traded to him for whiskey or fire-water, and had helped Leek learn his letters with these volumes of history and adventure.

But the inn was gone now, burned down by raiders, Marlo slain in the struggle. Leek had returned home to find his siblings filling holes in the ground beside a crumbling church. All that was left of his crooked family and bleak past was his mother, who now jostled him forwards, as they came to the front of the line.

He had to be brave, for her.

"Everyone must flip the coin," the tall man in black robes and mask held out a palm-sized medallion of dark metal engraved with circles. "Take it and don't be holding up the line." Leek glanced around and saw that most of the people in the line were watching him. He took the coin, gasping as cold energy flooded into the flesh of his palm. It swept through nerves and veins, seeming to turn blood to ice.

"You'll never forget your first feel of anatine steel." The man laughed and a few people chuckled. "What's it going to be then? Flip it, and we'll see what happens."

Leek looked at the masked man, then up to the vast gate that rose above them. The Bone Portcullis stood out starkly against the grey sky, a wide moat below reflected the gate and made an impression of two rows of fangs opening wide to swallow him whole.

With all of this weighing on his mind, or in his hand, he flicked the medallion up into the air and watched it spin. Time slowed. Leek watched the light gleaming along its edge as it rose, watched as the twelve circles on both sides glimmered. He waited for it to begin its descent, but it just stayed there, hanging in mid-air, spinning.

The medallion's surface turned a bright blue.

"Look!" the voices called around him, gasping. "He's one of them, Blood of the Twelve!"

"Dirty scum!"

"Step away from the boy, woman," said the man in charge. "He needs to come with us. Don't make it any harder than it needs to be." His mother had been clutching him close as the group of masked men surrounded them, her nails digging into his wrist.

Her eyes filled with tears. "No, please, he's all I have left. I've had him since he was just a youngling. Let me go with him, please?"

"Leave her alone!" Leek shouted, as the men grabbed his mother, struggling to pry them apart. His mother clawed to keep hold of Leek, ripping the skin on his wrist as the men pulled harder.

"Please, don't take him from me, I can help!"

"No, let her come with me, please!" Leek reached out for her. Their fingertips clung together briefly, before she was pulled out of reach and then out of view. Leek was jostled and shoved through the gate.

After struggling for another few moments, one of the masked men finally grew irritated and slapped Leek across the face. "Enough!"

He glanced back, looking for his mother and saw her. She was sitting on the ground with her head in her hands, crying. The masked men were standing around her with drawn weapons.

"I love you! Mother, I love you!' Leek cried out, trying to break free from the men's grip once more. One of the men punched him into the gut, hard, driving any resistance left out of him.

He was dragged away from his mother, hanging limp in their arms.

The bridge curved over a giant ravine where people swarmed, up the walls, building shacks one atop the other. He'd grown silent and placid, so the men had finally let him walk by himself.

Looking down at the small figures below, he could only feel jealous. These must be the lucky refugees, the last to be allowed access into the Spine Ravine before restrictions had been set in place. Behind them, soldiers patrolled the Bone Wall in columns, small as ants from down here. The bridge, no, the Spine was one of four arteries allowing access into the port on the extruding tip of mainland. Leek had heard the stories from men in the inn that any unauthorized ships found in the ministry's waters were sank without question.

Leek rolled these thoughts and memories through his mind again and again for comfort, past lessons instilled to him by Marlo. The four masked men escorting him were poor conversationalists, but at least they weren't hitting him anymore. He could hear the thrum of humanity in the ravine below. There was the faint *thwack*ing of picks, banging hammers, voices piercing through every now and then, which was washed away beneath the crunching wheels of the approaching line of carts, laden with crates, barrels, weapons, these followed by columns of soldiers.

They passed by the last column, where the Spine ended and the path was immediately flanked by high cliffs, shooting up from the ravine behind. Towers had been built into the cliffs, from where archers watched them pass, and the rope bridges inter-joining the towers slightly rocked in the breeze. After what seemed an hour, and about thirty more towers, they came to a palisade wall, where a wide gate was swung open, letting carts through.

After a brief exchange of words and a flash of a scroll they were allowed through the gate, where Leek found scores of men stationed behind the barricade, loitering about, mostly playing cards at tables or sat by campfires. Little heed was paid to him or his escort.

Leek wondered what his brothers and sisters would think if they could see him now. The skinny little wretch of the gang being manhandled by armed men.

As they left the palisade behind, even larger towers had been built above this part of the road, some with strange contraptions visible from here. It looked like a bow, but sideways, and fixed onto hinges and on a swivel, so the soldiers manning them could move them at any angle. They passed through two more barricades, each of a larger size and these built from stone.

Stepping through the gate, Leek felt a wave of dizziness wash over him, as spread out before him was an ocean of humanity. Houses had been built one atop the other, falling away in descending steps that from here looked like a giant's stairwell. Chimneys from these ramshackle houses streamed clouds of black smoke into the air. As they passed along the road citizens gave them a wide berth. Every tree that they passed had been felled, their stubs acting as stunted milestones. Squadrons of masked men could be seen every once in a while bustling their way through the throngs, inspecting carts or searching houses, but security in this mismatched shantytown was heavily outnumbered, and they seemed to be acutely aware of the fact, as Leek's escort kept their hands close to their pommels.

As the sloping ground levelled out and they passed another checkpoint, he found that they had entered into a more developed area—albeit still crowded and houses crammed one atop the other, but the people here seemed more at ease with their squalor. The escorts stopped for a moment at a guardhouse, a squat stone hut with arrow holes pockmarking it, and after feeding and watering themselves and Leek, they ventured back onto the road and continued their journey.

The sun was lowering in the sky as they climbed a hill, Leek's jaw dropped at the sight of unfathomable amounts water in the distance. He had read about the sea, of course, but no amount of reading or imagining could prepare him for the awe it inspired in his heart.

Ships lined the shore, massive warships, merchant ships and small skiffs. It was the latter they ended up boarding after descending through the crowds of seamen and soldiers. Not long after leaving shore he discovered something else that those books had failed to mention.

Seasickness.

Chapter 4: Hall of Faces

Quadra-Minister Fleck's bravery had waned by the time the Hall of Faces loomed above them. They had got swiftly through the throng of civilians that choked the city's thoroughfare, forcing a path along the main road leading to the upper districts. The hall was a pyramid of metal situated at the peak of the city. It gleamed in the sunlight, reflecting the spire rising behind it.

They crossed the wide stone terrace, between stout towers, each crowned with the ministry's red flags. As they climbed the steps the pike-men moved aside, and the metal doors slid silently open. Kye looked up in fascination at the many designs worked onto the doorway. It must have been fifty strides high, covered in artwork, depicting hundreds of gnarled demons and men, all screaming in horror as they disappeared into the shadows.

Kye had scoured the palace's archives when he'd been in-training as a novice, searching for information about the spires' creators. If any records of who they were still remained, they'd been hidden away long ago. Some said an old race of men had built the spires. Some said not men at all, but a more advanced civilization descended from the skies.

"What are you looking at?" Fleck followed Kye's gaze to the roof.

Kye shook his head. The faces on the walls of the inner pyramid were barely discernible from here. No one knew how many there were. Frozen faces stared back from their eternal prisons, both low and high, forgotten pale contrasts to the dark metal that was now their graves.

The Hall of Faces rightly deserved its name and its eerie reputation.

"Isn't it beautiful?" Kye whispered, as they made their way between the metal columns supporting the pyramid. Minuscule veins of blue streaks spiked and writhed on the surface as if alive inside of the dark marble. Tiny yellow dots of light pulsed in sporadic bursts, like raindrops falling and landing against a windowpane. Kye shook his head and wished—not for the first time—he'd been born in that world now long vanished.

Kye was snapped from his thoughts as he noticed figures walking towards them. Two men of the Masked Lodge, escorting a young man bound in chains. He was a skinny thing with big wide eyes staring at his feet.

"Blood of the Twelve," Fleck hissed. "They shouldn't try to harness their powers. Nefaro should string them all up!"

Kye nodded. His stomach churned with disgust for the comment, but Fleck's contempt was strongly shared within the Ministry. Kye himself had harboured similar beliefs, before her that was.

"What are you waiting for?" Fleck beckoned him to follow.

Kye turned away from the group exiting the hall and could see the watching, eager eyes of the ministry's ruling elite sat behind their table. Nefaro was perched highest in the middle, dressed in green robes of silk and a high peaked hat. Kye stopped below the long metal table and bowed.

Ah, the black sheep has returned to the broken family that is the Ministry of Faces. How I have missed you all.

"Step forward," said Nefaro, old voice still filled with a power that made men obey. Kye stepped closer. "As you have all heard, there's been an assault on one of our eastern outposts. We've called you here, Kassova, to inform you that you're being released from your duties at the portcullis. There's greater need for your skillsets elsewhere. Before we move on to further matters, I must ask if you still have agents working in the eastern boundaries."

"I have an agent currently working closely with the Eclipsi and the leaders of the advancing rabble. They've been relaying enemy plans for some time now."

"And *who* is this agent?" Quadra-Minister Powel, sat on Nefaro's right-hand side, didn't try to mask the scorn in his tone.

"With all *respect*," sneered Kye, "my agents' identities must remain anonymous. One has already been compromised."

"The Black heir will be caught eventually, we have no doubts about the matter," said Nefaro, sharing a tired expression with Powel.

Powel sneered down at Kye. He could give a good sneer, could Powel. "How many times can Maddox make a fool of you, Kassova? Leaving you for dead at sea, and then running rings around you in your own city."

Kye flashed Powel his silver smile. "I guess seeing things from behind a desk your entire life gives you a skewed perspective in fighting the enemy. Tell me, aren't you head of security for the city? How is it that the Druids are building a stronghold right under your nose?"

Powel bared his teeth. "Mind your tongue, boy."

"I'm not a boy anymore, old man, and I think you've grown foolish and greedy in your old age. How much coin did it take for the Druids to buy your loyalty?"

Powel stood up, shaking his fist at Kye. "You insolent little shit! I'll have you hung outside my office windows by your fucking balls! I am loyal to Nefaro! To the Ministry! I've served him before you were born!" He turned to Nefaro, pointing a finger at Kye. "You're going to let him speak to one of your commanders like this?"

Kye turned back to the shadows, waving at the figure leaning against the nearest column. The figure walked into the light, pushing back his hood, revealing a pale, smooth face, large beady eyes, skin covered in runes and markings.

"A Druid?" frowned Nefaro. "You bring one of *them* onto sacred ground?"

"Forgive me, Supreme, but this is one of my agents. He's been working amongst the Druids for many years, and he has something you'll want to hear..."

Nefaro looked from Kye to the Druid, then to Powel. "Speak, then."

The Druid stood beside Kye and lifted his hand, pointing a long finger at Powel. "I've seen this man speaking with our leaders. I've seen money exchanged and heard from some of my most trusted friends in our order that Powel will help us seize power. He's been revealing all secrets spoken at this table for years."

Nefaro looked at Powel, his eyes filling with such anger that Kye's smile faltered even though it wasn't aimed at him.

"You betrayed me?" hissed Nefaro.

Powel shook his head. "They're lying!"

Kye took out a scroll from inside his cloak. "His accounts and signatures, Supreme." Kye handed the documents to Nefaro, who scanned through them and slowly nodded. He lifted his head and nodded to the elite guards standing behind the table. "Seize him, bring him to the cells. I'll speak with him later."

"No, they're lying!" shouted Powel. "I never... I've *never*... Bwah-aghah," and he was silenced as the guards gagged him, bound him in iron and led him away.

Nefaro put the proof inside his cloak and looked at Kye. "It still leaves the problem of dealing with these Druids."

Kye bowed. "With your permission, Supreme, I could clear out the spire. I would risk my life it allowed me to return to the ministry's good graces..."

Nefaro thought for a moment, before nodding. "Granted, and we'll speak about this *Life-Levy* afterwards." He scribbled onto parchment and stamped it. Handing it to Kye, he beckoned him closer, the familiar eyes of a friendly tutor smiling. "For whom am I to stop a man bent on filling his own grave?"

Sweat rolled down the side of the inspector's face. He wiped it with a cloth, leaned back in his saddle and waited for Kye to speak. Kye, whose stomach churned from being tossed this way and that after sailing back from Mala's port, fought the rising bile.

"It seems Major Moore has done everything instructed," said Kye, looking out over the edge of the Spine, at the ravine below, teeming with refugees being lined up into ranks. Now dizziness joined his cocktail of sickness and excitement.

"Yes sir, the best of the refugees have been outfitted and armed, any who refused were forcefully removed. The training's been ongoing for some days now. Reports say the conscripted force amount to over fifty thousand."

"Keep an eye on things. Make sure the quality of leadership doesn't slip."

The inspector nodded, saluted, before guiding his horse back across the Spine, away from the eastern Bone Portcullis. Kye spurred his horse along the bridge, passing beneath the ridged supports. Leaving the bridge, he dismounted and tethered the horse at the gatehouse. The tower's door creaked open, awakening the handful of dozing guards inside. They saluted him as he stalked past and started up the stairs. Vines waited for him atop the tower, leaning against the parapet. His eyes were heavily bruised from the scuffle with the guards, but it would take more than a lone squad to break that troll-like skull.

"Sir," Vines greeted.

"Good to see you up and about," smiled Kye. "Look out there, Vines," Kye pointed. "Look out there and tell me what you see?"

Vines shook his head. "Mountains?"

"Beyond the mountains, what lies there?"

"The... border?"

"Exactly, Vines. That's where our enemy is coming from. Over those mountains lies plague and death, but what else?"

Vines pondered the question. "Cold weather?"

"Perceptive as ever, Vines. Yes, it would be cold, but what I see out there is *opportunity*." Kye took the scroll out from inside his cloak. "Look at this. It's an old map, made long ago when the Twelve first ruled. See here? Look how far the territory used to span." His finger passed the thick line of mountains and forest that bordered the Bone Wall on all sides, past the land of Eclipsi, to the once great ancient cities beyond.

"The cities had fallen millennia ago. But I bet my left nut there's still vast wealth hidden there, surely—lost technology, weapons and what-not. This is what will be ours once we exterminate the sages and chase down whatever's left. Once we take care of them, then we explore!" Kye smacked the scroll against Vines' forehead and looked out at the land.

"And the ministry agreed to an expedition? Not like them to set their sights on the mainland, with the Alliance biting at their heels."

"The ministry's filled with old farts who couldn't point out their own mothers, never mind seeing an opportunity when it's right there for the taking. But, yes, I've persuaded Nefaro to give me a chance, at least. We mustn't fail, Vines. Not this time."

Vines nodded.

Kye leaned out over the precipice and smiled.

I will make the people love me and gain their trust. Gain the trust of the ministry.

I will gain my *vengeance.*

Chapter 5: Making Friends

Leek picked up the clothes and stared at them. They were old, covered in patches badly stitched and stains best ignored. After being given the tour of a cramped courtyard and barren food-hall, the fat woman with the hairy chin had taken a razor to his skull, shaving off what little hair was left on his head. The room for the boys had about fifty cots in it, all empty now as they were eating down in the food-hall.

Just then the door opened and two boys walked in, they noticed Leek and walked over.

"I'm Kellick." The taller one with the freckles stuck out his hand. Leek eyed it suspiciously. "Din worry, we all stick together here, like flies trapped in a bucket o' shite. Ain't that right, Paste?" The tall freckled kid, Kellick, didn't wait for his companion to respond. Kellick nodded to the squat man with the frown, who seemed to be around Leek's age but thrice his weight. "He's thick as an ox, but loyal as one too. Ain't that right, Paste?"

"Fuck yerself, Kel." Paste squinted up at Leek. "Where ye from?"

At seeing Leek's apprehension, Kellick smiled. "We're all friends here. Life's cruel enough without us at each other's throat, eh?"

"I'm Leek," he said, shaking both their hands. "Not really from a town in particular, used to travel around a lot. Spent some time working at an inn in Willow's Creek, but it got raided."

"So you're a Mainlander?" Kellick nodded as if it explained some suspicion. "We're both men of the Circle. Ain't that right, Paste?"

Paste frowned deeper, crossing his arms.

Kellick thumbed his chest. "I'm from Tore. Paste here's from the Isle of Bones. Used to be a blacksmith's apprentice, weren't ye Paste? Poor fucker was thrown out on his arse though for sleeping with his master's niece, heh. What, not like it's a secret, is it? I was a beggar, me, not ashamed to say. Family got killed over the years and I was the only one left. So I came here to find a better means of making an un-honest living, and ended up getting snatched by the Maskers. Should've stayed down in Sunnyside, I should've."

"What's it like where you lived?" asked Leek.

Paste shrugged. "Not so bad. Mostly whalers and fishing ships where I'm from. It's a hard life on the bony island, but a fair one... when you're not getting ran out, that is."

"Tore's paradise," smiled Kellick. "But only if ye've got the coin and contacts. No place for someone preying on the sailors and soldiers who fill the Red Bastards coffers."

"Red... Bastard?" Leek couldn't help but smile.

"Yup, rules the city from his throne of tits and ass. Gorges his disciples on rivers of spirits, feasts of exotic food, and as much silver-dust as you could shove up a—"

The door opened at the far end of the room and Chinny, the woman with the bushel of hair on her chin, appeared, silencing

Kellick. "Get down to the food-hall, now." She shut the door behind her.

"Well Leek, my lad, it seems you're about to experience the fine delicacies of this establishment." Kellick led them out of the room, glancing back. "By which I mean, of course, you're about to eat shit."

The metal rod cracked against the surface of the rough wooden table, making Leek jump. A fat, greasy face grinned down at him, black teeth stinking of rot behind a jumble of grizzled hair.

"Are you new, boy? Don't think I've ever beaten you 'fore, 'ave I?"

Leek nodded nonchalantly.

"Early days, yet, yes it is." The guard continued patrolling the room.

A girl sitting beside Leek whispered across to him without looking up from her parchment. "Don't look around, just *write*! Even if you don't know how, do *something*."

Leek picked up the quill, dipped the end in ink and began copying what was written on the wall, *OBEDIANCE.SUBMISSION.REPENTANCE*, just like all the other fifty-or-so girls and boys were doing. Leek and the dozen people around him were the eldest of the group and occupied the back benches in the chamber. With his head tilted sideways, he stole a look at the girl. Her limp dark hair hung over her face, but the shadowed eye glanced up at him.

"I'm Leek, by the way." He smiled.

"Merron." The girl spoke without moving her lips or stopping in her writing. "Some advice. Watch out for Gurth. He's a monster."

"Gurth? That the guard?" Leek glanced up at the fat man now on the other side of the room.

"No," she stifled a giggle. "He doesn't hold a candle to Gurth."

"Why, does he hurt anyone?"

She stiffened at his question and looked away.

Just then the heavy door in the corner opened and a robed man skulked into the room. His face was pale, wrinkled and wretched as he leered about from under the large drooping hood. The eyes beneath it matched the grim and cold room. Leek looked back down at the parchment, heeding Merron's advice, whose hands Leek noticed were shaking holding her quill.

"May the Gods bless His Supreme Nefaro," Gurth's voice was oddly weak, but something about it made Leek think of snakes slithering in a dark basement.

"Obedience, submission, repentance," everyone replied, and Leek managed in joining the last. The Gods knew he had lots of repentance in supply lately.

Gurth stood behind a lectern, giving them all a smile that was more frightful than his leer. "Be thankful for the compassion and mercy of the Ministry of Faces, for the taint of your power is a stain on humanity and your memory shall fall into the cracks of history."

The crowd murmured the three words once more, and Leek was quickly catching on.

Gurth climbed down from the lectern and began prowling the room. Every person around him leaned forwards and dipped their heads, almost touching the paper with their foreheads.

Leek copied the words from the board, praying for the hundredth time that someone would come and save him.

The next morning, after he'd eaten his bowl of slop, Cod-with-a-Rod—what Kellick named the fat guard with the metal rod—told them to line up against the wall. Kellick and Paste stood beside him, Merron at the far end of the wall. She glanced sideways at Leek, giving a small smile which caused a flutter in his chest. She had nice eyes, had Merron, dark green, like the moss that covered the swamps near Willow's Creek.

Gurth entered, muttering something to Chinny. He began pacing in front of them, staring at each of them in turn. "May the Gods bless His Supreme Nefaro," the old man croaked from beneath his hood.

After the usual mantra Gurth nodded to Cod', who carried in a chest from an adjoining room. He began pulling out a long, thick metal chain. Shackles attached at different points were locked first around Merron's wrists and ankles, and then each other person in the line.

When he got to Leek, Gurth eyed him for a moment. "I won't have any trouble with you now, will I boy? You've shown obedience in your lessons, so far."

Leek nodded, staring down at his feet. He could feel the man's eyes boring into him, like ice shards in a storm. Gurth bound Leek's hands and feet—his touch just as cold as his gaze.

Gurth walked down the line, picking up the chain at the front and pulling Merron after him. They filed after her, Cod' tapping each of them to move faster. Passing through a series of corridors and up stone stairs chipped and slimy, they passed through a long hall and came to the entryway. Two burly men in black masks stood guarding the door, a massive slab of iron with a thick metal bar across it. At the sight of the procession, one tapped the other and they began lifting latches, pulling the heavy bulk of metal aside. Gurth paid them no heed as he swept past.

Leek almost smiled at the wash of fresh air on his face, but before he could even look up at the starry sky, he was pulled after the rest, down the flight of stairs and along the street.

"Obey!" shouted Gurth, and they repeated it, walking along the street quickly filling with people. "Obey!" The people laughed and jeered. A small girl sitting in a window watched them pass, eyes wide. The girl's mother lifted a pot, which she emptied out of the window—the piss getting on some unfortunates further up the chain-gang.

"Obey!"

Food was lobbed at them. An old, foul smelling apple hit Leek in the side of the head and splattered sour juice down his neck. Kellick slipped, fell and got dragged across the ground. Paste, too busy in shielding off the barrage of missiles, tugged on Kellick all the more.

Leek managed in getting hold of his arm, hauling him back on his feet.

Kellick, to Leek's surprise, had a wide grin on his face, even as he wiped his bloodied hands on his pants. Kellick smiled at him crookedly. "Having fun yet?"

Chapter 6: Dreams and Nightmares

Darkened woods surrounded Birdie. The cottage was alight in the distance. White swirls drifted out and up from the windows, the ghostly apparitions formed into screaming figures before vanishing. She must've been going in circles this entire time! A bead of sweat rolled down her spine, making it itch. She turned away and ran through the trees, not caring which way she was headed. Jumping a fallen log, her bare foot landed on a sharp rock, the jagged point digging into the skin of her sole. She screamed as she tripped over, landing face first into mud.

Birdie a voice echoed deep within the woods. *Stop running!*

Pushing herself up, the forest began to brighten. "Who's there?"

You have to face your fears!

Birdie stood up. The light behind the trees became brighter and she turned to find every direction illuminated.

She was trapped.

Don't be afraid, fear is only a shadow. You are the light!

"Who are you? Who's there?"

Orange orbs manifested from the light, passing through the trees. Large, dark leering eyes hovered inside of each orb, emitting an oppressive presence. Everywhere she turned they stared back with hungry expressions.

"What do you want from me?" she screamed and balled her fists. The emotion rising inside her now wasn't fear. It wasn't panic. It was anger, red-hot boiling anger.

Your soul. You belong to us and us to you.

Many voices spoke, different from the one before. Unhuman, not even words but thoughts that pierced her mind, laying all her worries and pain to bear.

As the boiling rage welled up within her, angered at their invasion, Birdie screamed, louder and louder, and willed these demons to be torn apart and nothing left behind. Every cell throbbed inside her with the need of it. Every beat of her heart mirrored that searing heat and magnified it tenfold. One orb exploded and the creature inside fled back to the trees. The woods filled with their screams as each of the orbs exploded, sending a glowing trail whirling through the air, making her hair billow.

Birdie watched as the dust gathered together above her, forming into a large bird, wings fluttering, sending the creatures running for their lives. She reached up and the bird began to shrink from the size of a boulder to an apple. Birdie held it in her hands, pressed against her chest, and the warmth emitting from it made her flesh tickle, her mind buzz.

After a moment, she held it out to look at it. Its feathers were black engraved with golden designs, and its two small beady eyes gently glowed with a golden aura.

"Ow!" she gasped as the bird pecked her wrist. She tried to shake it off, but its claws dug into her flesh, holding on tightly to her fingers, and it did it again. "Stop it!" Blood ran down her wrist, streaming from the open gash.

"Wake up!" a voice called through the trees.

"What?"

"Come on, wake up, we have to go!"

She felt dizzy.

The woods began to fade.

Opening her eyes, a dim light showed through the treetops. A fog had gathered during the night, and dew clung to her cloak and hair. Wiping her face with her sleeve, she peered down at her palm. "Where's the bird?"

The woman's shadow stared down at her. "What?"

"The bird, it pecked me."

The woman checked her weapons. "No time for dreams. The real nightmares lie in the world of the living."

Birdie moved her arms and legs to get the blood flowing. "You never asked my name."

"Names are for friends. A burden I don't have time for... You don't talk to people often, do you?"

"What makes you say that?"

"Huh." They left their makeshift camp and began walking through the forest, the woman speaking in hushed tones. "Because there's nothing out here but backwoods villages infested with scum. And the further out you go, the more scum you find, until you can't take two steps without stepping in shit. But I suppose that's all changed now. Not even the scum will be left alive once the Eclipsi get their hands on them. Guess the Temple will be doing us a favour. Until they rip *our* throats out, that is..."

"Temple? The Twilight Temple? Is that who attacked the village?" Birdie had read about them in some of the books in the cottage. A strange cult living in the east, beyond the mountain passes, worshipped the twin moons, Ibis and Sarema. Their leaders called themselves Moon-Sages, and worshipped their Gods from inside an ancient mound of boulders, called the Twilight Temple.

The woman frowned. "Never mind, come on." Around midday they came to a road embedded with smooth stones, making it easier to traverse than the bramble infested forest. Well, relatively smooth, but dry.

Dry was good.

The woman looked at her with a raised brow. "Never seen a paved road before?"

"No."

"Wait 'til you see the cities, fuckin' shit yourself."

"You've been to the twelve cities, then? What's it like?"

"Big. Cities usually are."

"You don't talk to people often, do you?"

The woman glanced back. "We'll see if that smart mouth of yours can fend off the next man who tries to cut your throat."

"I could've beaten him," Birdie lied, checking to make sure the knife was still hidden.

"There's no excuse for failure out here, only the dead favour excuses. The living must learn to accept hard-truths." The woman talked as if reciting a hard-earned lesson.

"Will you teach me? How to survive out here, I mean..."

"I'm no teacher. I get by on my own because I trust myself. If ye want training, then the Sea of Circles is the place to be. Loads of places can teach you how to use that little knife of yours in your belt."

"How did you—" Birdie moved her hand away from the knife.

"Because I'm not blind, girl. If you've a mind on using it, best not stick it into someone who's intending on doing you some good. Don't want to make an enemy out of me, now, do you?" The woman gave her a small smile.

"So, I'm not your enemy?"

"Perhaps, perhaps not. The only thing in this world that won't turn its back on ye is your own reflection when you're facing a mirror."

Birdie shook her head. "You speak in riddles, you know."

The woman stopped and sniffed the air, then moved on after a brief pause. "Perhaps, but the person who reveals all they know, knows nothing themselves."

"Great, leave it to me to get stuck with some insane, tribal philosopher."

"Hmm," the woman looked back, a thoughtful expression crossing her face. "I like that."

In the evening they stopped and shared some of the woman's dried meat. Not long before sundown they stopped by a stream and refilled the water skin. An old, derelict mill downriver still turned, making the water churn and bubble. The adjoining building had collapsed long ago; it's still few standing walls now overgrown with moss and saplings.

It reminded Birdie of her own cottage. Four walls that now are shattered, but once had been a home with warmth, food and family to inhabit them. But soon those still standing walls would crumble, and the forest would reclaim its space. The water would rot away the mill-wheel, until it too was gone, and nothing would remain to say:

Once we existed.

"You see something?" the woman had refilled the water skin and now stood beside her, eyes narrowed as she took in the ruin.

Birdie shook her head and turned away.

"No... nothing."

Chapter 7: False Facades

The spire situated behind the Hall of Faces was a fortified retreat for the Druids, who had been given the upper reaches of it for helping during the downfall of the Twelve and their loyalty since, but the past few years they'd been attempting to undermine the ministry from the shadows, leaving bodies that they were tasked with getting rid of in the streets of Mala for all to see.

A large blackbird had been daubed across part of its exterior years ago with some type of oil. Efforts to erase the Black Shadow's mark had only made it all the plainer to see. Kye ignored it, and instead looked across to the pale-skinned, gaunt Druid stood beside him. "You're sure you have enough supporters? You said they've at least three hundred men in there, along with hired mercenaries from Tore."

The thin man smiled revealing sharp teeth, and eyes cold as steel glanced up at the spire where figures bustled about—more than likely startled by the appearance of a thousand armed soldiers of the Golden Circle army.

"We grow tired of our leaders' squabbling. The Druids need no more power. The Druids wish to return to Trask and further our research."

Kye held out a hand. "Lead the way..."

The Druid walked between the open barricades, where about fifty Druids awaited him. They began turning the levers to open the front of the platform, cranking down on the pulley system that would transport them up onto the lower spire.

"First squadron!" barked Kye, and Vines relayed the order, large frame looking all-the-more imposing outfitted in heavy golden plate-mail, and equipped with enough weapons to supply the revolt of a small country.

The first row of soldiers hurried onto the platform, one hundred men lined up in three rows, arranging shields at three separate heights to create a defensive wall. Half the Druids stood in front, readying various weapons or potent looking vials of liquids, the rest shut the front of the platform, leaving the main lever open, so the men inside could quickly swing it aside.

The chains and ropes began to move, followed by the platform which quickly ascended. Kye watched as it came to a stop, and could faintly hear the sound of missiles colliding against metal. Voices sounded out then, shouting and screaming, as the platform began moving back down. It came to a halt, revealing a dozen men inside, some dead, others clutching bolts in various places. They were carried off, more men moved onto the platform, joined by Kye this time. Vines stood just beside him, large shield in hand.

Kye might've been brave, but he wasn't foolish enough to walk first into whatever those cunning bastards had set up for them.

The platform smoothly rose. Metal armour clinked as men readied themselves, faces all tilted upwards, many eyes filled with fear, voices muttering quiet prayers. And afraid they should be, as the screams coming from above were growing all the louder.

Lights then, bright green flames, yellow ones, a burning body fell and tumbled down towards them, smacking against the metal grate above and sending blood spraying across those below. Vines tried to block the spray with his shield, but Kye had to wipe a few specks away from his cheek.

The platform came to a stop, revealing mangled bodies, melting shields poked with arrows and bolts. Kye followed just behind his men as they slowly stepped over their fallen comrades. They passed golden clad soldiers, a score of Druids, one man still gasping, clutching at an open wound. He gabbled in that raspy language of theirs. Kye opened his throat, before moving on.

Up the first stairs, only wide enough for five men abreast, it spiralled around the outside of the spire. One of their men sat slumped against the outer rail holding in his entrails, some yellow gunk splashed over them, sending smoke wafting as it sizzled into flesh, and the pale man looked wide-eyed as they passed him by without a second glance.

They came to a massive open doorway, which opened out onto the large courtyard. Bodies nearby, but also fighting at the far end, druids lined on top of a wooden barricade, sending down a pain of burning liquid onto the approaching soldiers, who fought to climb both sides of the barricade. Some of their Druid allies climbed the sharpened stakes, unhindered by heavy armour.

Soon parts of the barricade were aflame, soldiers side-stepped around the fire, fighting hand-to-hand against mercenaries. Kye and his men closed the distance. A Druid flung a large gourd which had a fizzing fuse attached to it. The hissing stopped and the gourd exploded, reeking yellow fluid onto the men nearby. Kye could smell death before he heard the screams, but moved on, joining the men climbing the barricade, passing over bodies, pushing behind the men, slowly edging them back to the large wooden studded gate that led inside the spire.

A Druid came screaming through the flames taking Kye by surprise, who just managed to bring up his sword as the Druid swung an axe, catching it and wrenching it from the man's hand. Kye stepped in and drove the butt of his hilt into the man's face, knocking him back into the flames where he belonged. Vines moved past, using a large spear to impale any enemy unfortunate enough to be within poking distance.

His men were soon at the door. Kye turned to see more of his soldiers streaming into the courtyard, carrying battering rams. Arrows flitted down from murder holes in human made battlements, so Kye hid behind his shield like all the others and watched as the men climbed the barricade with the rams.

BANG!

Men pushed in closer as the barricade caught alight more, and men behind them hurried to throw water onto the barricade, trying to douse the wood and hinder the spreading flames.

BANG!

Minutes passed. A score of Druids had climbed the wall and fought their way through one of the many alcoves inhabited by archers and only a handful of them were left as they opened the gate, leaning against the wall, bloodied and haggard.

Kye followed as they rushed onwards, through chambers, into guard rooms, hallways, stairways, all hiding pockets of Druids or mercenaries, trying to avoid traps set about the place. He saw a man climbing an open stairwell walk onto a pressure plate and a wooden spike came rushing out of the wall, impaling him, before hissing back inside of a hidden compartment, tossing the poor bastard over the rail and far below, screaming.

Kye decided to stay at the back of the fighting. That's what foot-soldiers were for, after all.

They left the lower parts of the spire, entering into the sections once inhabited by House Black. Libraries had been set on fire by the Druids, supply rooms also, burning anything that couldn't be carried. They fought a running fight in diminishing numbers into the uppermost section, managing to lock safely away behind a large metal door.

But Kye knew a secret they didn't.

"This way!" he ordered, and led fifty of the freshest looking men and a blood-covered and worriedly smiling Vines along a series of corridors, hallways, stairwells, until coming to a hidden entrance.

Fifty men filed along in a single-line through one of many hidden tunnels, springing out of a wall just a hundred paces from a group of very surprised looking mercenaries guarding the door.

Within ten minutes the last of the remaining force of enemies had been put to the sword. Kye stood on the peak of the spire, cleaning the blood from his sword, looking out over a view of the bustling city of Mala below, with its smoky industrial sector sending up plumes of black clouds into the dying light.

Within an hour Nefaro appeared, looking much fresher and less blood-soaked than Kye.

"Excellent work, Kassova." Nefaro put a hand on Kye's shoulder. "You've done me proud. One could almost forget your past failings. *Almost.*"

Kye nodded. "Thank you, Supreme."

Nefaro turned away as someone entered through the open doorway.

The tall, bald Druid who'd helped them into the spire smiled. "I hope you are satisfied with the outcome?"

"Yes. But I've one request before your men leave."

"Anything within reason," said the Druid.

"Stay in Mala as an emissary between your people and the ministry. Also, I may just have other tasks suitable for a man of your... skillsets."

The Druid bowed and left them alone.

Nefaro stood by the rail, looking down at the city. "I knew giving them this foothold was a mistake. It'd been Powel who'd decided to use it as a type of embassy for them. At least now we can maintain sole control in the city without losing the Druids allegiance."

"Why are you so concerned whether they remain allies?"

"I need their certain... abilities."

"Abilities?"

"I'm old, Kassova, older than you could possibly imagine. They help me sometimes through... Unconventional methods, let's just say."

"You still don't trust me?" Kye turned to look at him.

"I trust you, but I don't think you'd understand."

"You can't keep me in the dark forever. As you've said many times, one day I'll sit at the ministry's table."

Nefaro looked at him. "You wanted to remain in military duties, no?"

"If staying where I prefer involves remaining ignorant of what's going on in our government, then no, I don't." Kye stepped closer to Nefaro. "I deserve to know the truth. What's going on between you and the Druids?"

Nefaro sighed. "Blood."

"Blood?"

Nefaro nodded. "The Blood of the Twelve, to be precise. I need it, or my body will fail. Is failing. All these years I've used the strength of their blood, it's the only thing keeping me alive."

Kye frowned. "So, you... You take a little blood every now and again? Like the witch-doctors in the Sun Islands? Why keep it a secret?"

"My hunger grows as the years pass." Nefaro shrugged. "I've given up making excuses. I know it's wrong. But I guess after all this time I cling onto every day that little bit more desperately. Not to mention how lazy the Druids were becoming in cleaning up after the rituals."

"Wait... You're responsible for the disappearances? In the prisons, and the slums? I've heard the rumours but thought it was just life in the city... But it makes sense, the bodies that the Druids were leaving scattered through the city were yours. Your leftovers... You... You turned against them because they were trying to *expose* you?"

"What? No. Relations failed because they were putting the safety of the ministry at risk! Without me there wouldn't be a ministry, Kassova! Without me the cities around us would become nothing but pits of chaos and cutthroats. I hold this city together. Stadarfell and High Shoals would've turned on us years ago if not for me. I hold the ministry together."

"You're no better than the Druids!" Kye growled, stepping away from Nefaro. "You're just as bad as them and their witches...

No, you're worse! At least they don't pretend to be some holy fucking emperor who shits golden bricks."

"I knew you wouldn't understand, my son—"

"Don't call me that!" shouted Kye, clenching his fists.

Nefaro stepped forwards and grabbed Kye, revealing his façade of being a weak, old man by easily dragging him against the rail, leaning him over it until Kye had to grasp at the edge to try to steady himself.

"You listen to me, Kassova, and listen close," whispered Nefaro, and Kye could only think how unlike his tutor this creature was now to him. "Without me you'd be some mist-loving-fool freezing to death in a damp old tower. I've given you a chance to *rule*. To be something *great*, and all I ask in return is a little loyalty. So you listen when I speak, and when I say do something..." Nefaro tilted Kye back slightly, easing his grip on Kye's collar. "You better run so fast you shoot sparks out of your shit-pipe, boy. Go bring me back the Black Shadow and his little bitch of a sister." Nefaro bared his teeth. "Bring them back to me, *alive*... or by the Gods and the Moons as my witness I'll make every remaining second of your pathetic life nothing but soul-crushing pain..." Nefaro came within inches of Kye's face, eyes filled with darkness deeper than the black sky above.

Kye gave the old man his best silver smile, but with the sweat dripping down his forehead it felt it lacked the desired effect. "You only... had... to ask nicely."

Chapter 8: Repentance

"Get up!" Leek lifted his head from the pillow. Cod' was standing in the doorway, hitting the door with his stick. Leek got out of bed and followed the others down into the food-hall, where they lined up against the wall.

Gurth entered the hall. "Today is a special day," he smiled. "Supreme Nefaro has decreed there shall be daily excursions into the city. Your sins and the sins of your forbearers are to be laid bare for all to see. You shall each thank His Supreme for allowing you to—"

Before Leek knew what he was doing he took a step forward. "Not anymore." He heard the words come out, but it couldn't be him saying it.

Could it?

His body was tense, nerves fluttering in his stomach. He fought the urge to begin munching on a fingernail. The silence in the hall was crushing. He wanted to step back, but why wouldn't his legs work? He felt scared, but he lifted his chin and met Gurth's stare, those hate-filled eyes wide with anger.

"What did you say?" Gurth rushed at Leek, his long nails swiping at Leek's face. But Leek ducked just in time and sprang away, aiming for the exit. Cod' came at him, cutting off the doorway, too large to squeeze past. Leek dodged the rod as it rushed past him, feeling the air close on his cheek, only missing his head by finger lengths. Leek lurched sideways, trying to draw him away from the door, but his foot slipped on something wet and he stumbled for a few steps before hitting the ground.

Before Leek could regain his feet the metal rod bit into his right shoulder and his arms went limp as he hit the floor face-first. The pain sent a wave of fire up his spine and into his jaws and eyes. He couldn't move his arm, so he rolled as he screamed, trying to crawl away, not sure where the door was anymore.

But the rod came rushing down again, smacking into his calf, making him writhe around the floor like a landed fish. He spat blood, gasped in breath and watched in horror as Gurth slowly closed the distance. There was so much pleasure in Gurth's eyes as he grabbed Leek's jaw with one hand and slowly clawed his nails into the side of Leek's face with the other, peeling skin. Leek struggled, but Cod' held him down.

The last image in Leek's mind before he shut his eyes was of Gurth's smile. Leek screamed until the act of crying itself was too much a burden and he fell into unconsciousness.

The first thing he noticed was the burning sensation. His face felt as if it were boiling, bubbling off and onto the floor. But then Leek felt something cool wash against the throbbing, and the burning eased.

"Can you hear me?" asked Merron.

"Gah." Leek's lips cracked, and blood dribbled out.

"Shhh! Quiet now, you need to save your strength."

Leek found a sense of reassurance in her voice. He tried to focus on her face and found that his right eye had swollen shut. "What... what happened?" That's what he said, but his mouth wasn't working properly and his speech was jumbled, so what came out was more like *waugh happwhened*.

"Nothing, don't worry, just a scratch."

"My eye." His eye was more than burning. It felt like it had been replaced with a red-hot coal.

"It'll heal, just breathe."

The vision in Leek's good eye cleared and he went to bite his nails, but then noticed his hands sticking out from a wooden beam. He was in the stockade.

"Huh."

"Hope you're comfy," teased Merron.

Leek smiled. "Ow!" Leek's lip cracked more and blood dripped down his chin, splashing onto the floor.

Merron dabbed it until the bleeding stopped. "Sorry, I'll try not to make you smile again."

"Hah, ah!"

"Here, take a drink, it'll clean the wound." Merron lifted a cup and Leek sipped, choking on the first mouthful, but soon managed in gulping it down. "Why'd you do it, Leek? I warned you. It was—"

"Stupid?" Leek finished the sentence for her. She frowned. "I'm tired, Merron, *tired*. Tired of being treated like an animal... Tired of living in fear."

She looked at him like he was some young child. "Living in fear? We're treated fairly if we obey. The only thing we fear is being found guilty of failing in our repentance. The sooner you accept that and do what they say the easier your life will become."

"No!" Leek shook with anger, but the stockade was solid and didn't even rattle. He was sick of being mistreated.

By fate, for making him an orphan, cast into the outside world alone.

By his foster-family, constantly being tormented and treated like dirt.

By the ministry, accusing him of crimes committed before he'd been even born... for having the wrong kind of blood pumping through his veins.

He wasn't going to put up with it anymore, even if it *killed* him.

Leek looked around at the empty courtyard. "Where's Kellick?"

"He was locked away in the dungeon for trying to help you. Cod' gave him a beating."

Leek could feel his eyes burn with tears. He gritted his teeth and fought them back. After a few moments he looked at Merron. "I'm getting out of here. I don't know how, but I am. Do you want to come with me?"

Merron looked down at her feet. "There's nothing for me outside. The ministry killed my family when they'd captured me. My life is here now."

Leek felt his stomach churn as he pictured his mother outside of the Bone Portcullis, kneeling down, surrounded by armed men.

He forced it away, not letting them bruise him on the inside as much they had his body.

Merron looked down at her feet again. "Sorry, I didn't mean to bring up memories." She trailed off and wiped away her tears.

"You've nothing to be sorry about."

"I'm sorry about your family."

Merron nodded. "I'm sorry about yours, too."

"Merron," Leek said after a moment.

"Yeah?"

"If there is a way out, would you come with me?"

"We'll never get out."

"But if there was, would you come with me?"

"Maybe." She shrugged. "Yeah, sure, why not?"

As the days passed Leek by, the thought of freedom was the only thing that kept him strong. He gave Gurth no reason to punish him further. The wounds would itch to the point of driving him insane, but he never showed his discomfort in front of the man.

At night Leek would whisper with Kellick about their plan to escape.

Well, they had no plan, but they were open to discussion. Mostly they whispered of slitting Gurth's throat while he slept, or roasting Cod' over a spit, or hanging Chinny over a cliff by her bush.

Those talks kept Leek going.

And Merron was coming with them!

It gave him a strange, warm feeling inside. Leek hoped for a window of opportunity, or for some stroke of luck. Was it too much to ask for something to go right, for once?

He'd stood up for himself and those he cared for. He just prayed the Gods would reward his courage.

The door to the room they slept in was always kept locked, the wood too thick to break through. There were no windows or holes to climb through. No floorboards to pry up. Kellick had told him they could try picking the lock, but they didn't have anything they could use to jimmy the mechanism. Leek wasn't the best picking locks, but he'd give it a try if he had the chance. What seemed a lifetime ago, one of Leek's 'brothers' had been the jingle-man of their gang, and Leek spent many nights watching, learning.

They also still had to get past the prison staff outside and a metal door.

What if they did get out of their room, but couldn't get Merron's door open? He couldn't leave her here on her own. At night he would lie awake for hours and imagine the different ways to do it, the different possibilities, each as impossible as the next.

The routine was water-tight, giving no room to organise gathering tools. Meals in the hall were the only time the three of them could plan together. Lessons in Gurth's chamber were always silent, always patrolled. On the parades through the city their hands and feet were bound. At night then they were sealed away once more inside a dark room, behind a thick door of hardwood that might as well have been cast iron.

In other words, they were fucked.

Today was no different, and they lined up against the wall as they waited for Gurth to lock the shackles onto their wrists and legs, then left to begin the usual route through the streets, through the slums, through the shit.

"Freaks!"

"Hang them all!"

"Burn them! Burn them alive, they deserve it!"

Leek dodged missiles of mouldy bread, stones... wait was that a turd?

As they passed beneath an archway of apartments, a group of men leaned out from the windows, holding buckets. Leek heard the jingle of metal as they tossed the buckets' contents down over them, scattering lumps of metal objects onto their heads, foundry shavings and ball-bearings went tumbling everywhere. Screams and shouts sounded around him as Leek ducked and raised his arms, protecting his still tender face as the shower of metal rained. Something sharp dug into his arm and he gasped as he pulled out a long, black nail pitted into the back of his forearm.

Before anyone noticed, he put the nail between his legs as best he could. Cod' grabbed them and made sure they didn't pick anything up from the ground, searching each of them once returning to the prison but thankfully didn't find the nail.

Kellick watched with wide eyes as Leek held it up in the palm of his hand.

Their key to freedom.

As Kellick stared down at the nail, a smile spread across his face. "You little beauty..."

Leek crept to the door, began quietly scratching the inside of the lock, making clicking sounds, but nothing happened. Minutes felt like hours as they stood there, every distant sound making Leek's heart flutter.

"I don't know, Leek," Kellick whispered, looking down at the nail. "I shouldn't take this long, should it?"

Leek's fingertips throbbed from gripping it so tightly, but the mechanism didn't give. Time and time again, he twisted it, turned it, until his wrist burned and his fingers ached. Leek stood back and rubbed his head in frustration. He went back to his cot, deflated, lying down and covering his face.

Something poked at him from beneath the pillow. Reaching beneath it, Leek pulled out a bundle wrapped in parchment.

Got these from Gurth's office – M

There was a coin and small lump of flint wrapped inside.

"Rip up your old tunic," said Leek.

Kellick noticed what he was holding and went to rip up his old clothes, returning after a few minutes. Leek took the bundle of rags and put them onto his cot, then flicked the coin onto the flint for a while before managing to get the dried fabric smoking. Leek rushed over to Kellicks cot to do the same, leaving his friend to nurse the rags until the flames wouldn't die out. As both cots caught light, they stood beside the door.

"Fire!" screamed Leek, until the room was filled with panicking boys. Leek's throat began to tickle as the room filled with smoke. They crouched down beside the door at the sound of keys rattling outside. It flew open violently and knocked a kid onto the floor.

They pushed their way out through the door. Leek heard Gurth shouting for them to stop, but the flames and splintering wood made the boys ignore Gurth's orders. People rushed everywhere, tripping over each other in their haste to get away. Cod' was trying to catch them, hit them, kick them, but missing more often than not. They ran through the hall to the corridor that led to the girl's rooms, but were forced back against the wall as the girls rushed past, Chinny wide-eyed and brandishing a truncheon, but she didn't notice them pressed against the wall.

Merron appeared at the back of the group and they ran into the food-hall together. Gurth stood at the far end, screaming at them to line up and obey. Cod' stumbled over a young girl and his weapon went tumbling, rolling to a stop just in front of the exit. Kellick snatched it up and turned just in time, as Cod' was back on his feet and sprinting at him, fists balled, but the big man was unbalanced. Kellick jumped and with both hands brought the baton down onto fat guard's forehead with a hollow *thump* and the man's legs went limp, collapsing.

Kellick snatched the keys from his belt and they ran out into the courtyard, past the empty stockade. Leek slid the nail out from his belt as they rushed up the stairs, palming it. Entering the entry room, Kellick hid the rod behind his back.

"There's a fire, quick! Gurth needs help!" screamed Leek, pointing back towards the shouting.

The two guards looked at each other, confused. One of them held his arms up, trying to herd the three of them back. Leek tried not to stare at the knife on the guard's belt and waited until he was within reach. He aimed the nail at the guard's eye but missed, harmlessly scraping along the side of the mask, and the guard reached for his knife as he kicked out at Leek. The heavy boot dug into Leek's stomach, folding him over, but before the guard could do any damage with the knife Kellick was there, slamming the rod into the back of the guard's head. Once, twice, the guard was on his knees, then again after he'd fallen. Leek pushed himself up, gasping for air.

Kellick turned as Leek looked around for the remaining guard, went to lift the rod above his head, preparing for the next attack, but as he turned the guard stabbed him through the chest, knife point sticking out the other side, flicking beads of blood into Leek's face.

Leek could only stare in horror as Kellick's legs crumbled, and he toppled to the floor, tearing the knife from the guard's grip. Leek was still gasping for air as he jumped for the knife. The guard reached it first and they struggled, but the guard was too strong and ripped the knife from Leek's grip, smashing the butt into Leek's nose. He fell back, hitting his head against the stone floor, blood gushing from his broken nose. Blurred shapes danced around him, strange sounds that made no sense.

"Come on, Leek!" Merron's voice cried, and Leek's good eye cleared. Merron was struggling for the knife from the ground, scratch marks across her cheeks from the knife. The guard pushed the knife closer to her face. Leek saw the nail nearby and scrambled to it, his blood-slicked fingers closing around it.

"Leek!" Merron screamed as the knife inched closer.

Leek drove the nail into the guard's neck, who screamed as he let go of the knife, pawing at the blood spurting from his neck. Leek stared with a mixture of nausea and dizziness as the man kicked around on the ground, and then stopped moving. The moment felt like a dream, unrealistic.

"Kellick!" Leek turned and crouched over the boy's still body. Kellick's lifeless eyes stared at the ceiling, face ashen.

"There's nothing we can do for him, Leek. We need to go!" Merron pulled Leek away from the body, towards the door. They began lifting the heavy latches, pulling it open as sounds of footsteps appeared in the corridor. Leek's heart beat against his chest. They rushed down the flight of steps, along the cobbled street.

Whizzz

Leek heard it sail through the air behind them.

Thump!

Merron tumbled over onto the cobbles and disappeared. Leek skidded to a stop, ran back and tried to lift her.

But then he saw it...

The tip of a bolt protruded from between her eyes, seeping blood down over her nose and chin. Leek looked up. Gurth was standing at the top of the stairs reloading a crossbow.

"I'm sorry, Merron," he whispered, before fleeing up the cobbled street and ducking into the first dark alley, just as another bolt whizzed past.

Chapter 9: Monsters

As the days passed, Birdie tried her best to get information out of the scout—who she was, why she was out there, but the woman remained tight lipped as they made their way to the outpost. Many times, they'd travel off-road and creep through dense forest. The woman told Birdie to keep the knife in her sleeve, and had her practice how to slip it out in one fluid motion and strike where it would do the most damage. Birdie didn't tell her she'd practised with blades for many years.

After all, where was the sense of giving away that knowledge? She might need to spring a surprise on the woman yet. She didn't know her, didn't know what could happen…

"You go for the knee, you're small," the woman told her one night as they sat by the fire. "Do in their knee and run, that's your best bet. Skinny thing like you wouldn't stand a chance hand-to-hand."

Birdie knew all the pressure points and didn't think her size would make much difference. How to bring someone bigger down had been painstakingly taught to her over countless training sessions with Bella.

Sometimes the woman would leave Birdie alone in a secluded place as she scouted ahead, many times returning scratched and bloodied.

"What is it like, where these people come from?" Birdie asked one night as the woman roasted a hare over a small fire.

"Put no mind to it. You'll be lucky never to set foot in their land."

Days passed to weeks. The land became steeper, the forest barer, making hunting difficult. A heavy rain had begun to fall and they spent the next few days in a miserable, wet existence. Finally, they breasted what seemed the highest hill in existence, when Birdie saw the outpost. A stout fortress situated on a large mound of rock, flanked by high cliffs. Descending the ridge, they approached the entryway.

"We'll sleep well tonight." The woman smiled as they neared the gate. "I was here before, a long time ago. They've good ale. The captain's an old pal of mine. He'll sort us out."

"I never drank ale." Birdie thought of their strict diet of game and river-water and supposed something with actual flavour might not be too bad.

"You've proven yourself not totally incompetent as a travel companion. You'll feast with me tonight in the hall. A cup of ale in your hand and as much boar as ye can stomach."

Birdie's mouth watered.

The outpost had large, white metal bars protecting its gate, the bars pointing inwards at the end. "It's a mimic of the Bone Portcullises, the ministry's four gates of entry to the mainland port," said the woman, noticing Birdie's interest. "The Bone Portcullises are the only way in."

"They're not that big." Birdie remembered Bella and Maddox's stories of the Bone Portcullises and Wall. They'd spoke of giant, cliff-like walls and gates of a bone white metal, giving the ancient defences their names.

"Oh, that's a sorry excuse for an example. Wait 'til ye see the real thing, there's nothing like it in the entire world. It'd take your breath away."

"You've been around the world, then?"

"Well... no, but I've been all over the place. Might tell ye 'bout some of it over a jug of the brown stuff. Let's get inside first, and out of this damned rain." The woman thumped on the gate. "Come on, let us in! Stop fiddling' with your arses!"

There was movement up on the walls, someone leaned over the parapet, took one look at them, and then disappeared. They waited there for a long time, until the sound of bars being lifted and something heavy turning came from deep inside. The pointed bars began to slowly rise, the points disappearing into the wall and the wooden gate opened. A dozen men rushed out and surrounded them, aiming spears at both her and the woman's heads.

A towering man shouldered his way through, hidden beneath a dark cloak. "Who are you?"

"I could ask you the same thing," the woman eyed the man suspiciously. "Isn't it customary for the outpost's captain to greet travellers? Where's the captain of this outpost? Where's Captain Shard?"

The man shrugged his shoulders. "Never heard of him. What are your names?"

The woman reached inside her cloak and pulled out a small metal object. She pulled its lid off and took out a roll of parchment from inside. Birdie saw a little blue circle of wax on one side.

The man swiped the parchment away and inspected it, speaking after reading the scrawling text. "So be it, but I'll have to confiscate your weapons. You'll have no need for them inside."

The woman muttered a curse as she pulled off her bow and quiver, relinquishing it and three knives hidden on her person.

"And the rest?" The tall man asked.

"That's all of it," said the woman.

The man indicated for one of the guards to search them. As the guard searched Birdie, his eyes lingered on the necklace as he pulled it out, but didn't' mention it to the cloaked man. He took her knife.

"Very well, come," the cloaked man turned on his heel and stalked through the gates. After being herded through, the gates closed behind them. Inside men stood in groups, watching from the walls, from little alcoves half hidden in darkness. They followed the man towards a collection of buildings nestled in front of the cliffs.

"Strange..." muttered the woman.

"What?"

"No women, no children. This place was filled with families last time I was here, filled with life. See over there," she nodded at a burnt-out building. "Forge is a vital thing for any outpost, so why's it destroyed?"

They followed the man up the stone stairs, through studded doors and into a cold, dim hall. The hearth was unlit. The long tables empty. Not exactly the warm feast she'd been hoping for.

The guards took their positions around the hall as the man climbed the raised dais and took a seat on a wooden chair. "So stranger, tell me why you've travelled into my land?"

The woman frowned. "*Your* land? Quite generous for the ministry to give land to a lowly captain, never heard the like before."

"Come now, don't play the fool, woman." The man clicked his fingers and a servant entered carrying a jug and silver goblet on a platter. "You know just well whose presence you are in the company of." The man pulled down his hood, revealing long, braided silver. His pale blue eyes were sharp as razors, as striking as lightning. He reached for his goblet and drained it. He feigned a slight bow. "I am Und-ar-Felt, Second Moon-Sage of the Twilight Temple. Now, I'll give you one more chance to tell me who you are and what you're doing in my land?"

The woman spoke, nonplussed. "My niece and I had a farm back east, near the border of Eclipsi, but it was attacked and we barely escaped with our lives. Your men cost us our home."

"I apologise, truly. I understand some of my men can be... heavy handed. I must say, you're well-armed for simple farmers..." Felt smiled.

"Scavenged them." The woman shrugged. "My father always told me dead men don't need possessions."

"A wise man." Felt held out his goblet and the servant refilled it. Felt twirled the liquid. "You don't look like ordinary peasants to my eye, woman. No, you look like a soldier. But whose, I can't decide. You carry the blue seal of passage, either somebody powerful employs you, or you stole it. Which is it?"

"I scavenged it from a dead officer in the forest. Thought it might get us to safety."

Felt's face twitched and he threw the goblet at the woman, splashing dark spirits down her stomach. "You stand under my roof," he hissed, "and lie to my face! Take them to the cells."

"No, we haven't done anything!" Birdie shouted their innocence as they were forced out of the hall.

They turned down into a narrow laneway and came to a squat stone building at a far corner of the outpost. Birdie took a final breath of fresh air as they were pushed out of the daylight and into a dark corridor. They passed down a stone stairwell, the air becoming damp, sickly and metallic. Torches flickered and spat as they passed into another corridor below, where green slime dripped down the cobblestone walls and puddled in places. They passed by rusted doors, groans and moans sounded from behind some, but most were silent. A yellow pool drained out from beneath one door, which Birdie wisely avoided and was pushed by a rough hand.

A jingle of keys as the guard unlocked one of the rusted doors and then the woman disappeared into the cell, her pale face held proud as the door closed. Birdie was shoved into a tiny, musty cell a few doors down, and couldn't help but dig her fingernails into her palm as the door ground shut, leaving her trapped in the darkness.

A rat scurried against her foot. Birdie shouted at it, making it disappear back into its hole and she turned her attention back to the lock, peering through the small hole and listening. Footsteps strode down the corridor, and the light eclipsed from view as the guard passed. Birdie had stopped trying to call out to the woman hours ago. Another shadow passed, making Birdie flinch away from the hole. There'd been no other footsteps, just a shadow, then a muffled grunt, and silence. The lock clicked, door slowly opened and the invading light made her fall back. Light stung at her eyes, and her vision settled on a figure standing in the doorway.

"Quickly now, we must go. Keep this in your hand. Don't hesitate." The guard who'd searched them handed Birdie back her knife. Out in the corridor, she stepped over a dead guard's body and looked towards the woman's cell.

I can't abandon her, not after saving my life.

Stepping as light-footedly as possible, Birdie willed the good fortunes to favour her and not let any guards appear in the doorway. Outside the cell, she looked back at the guard who was now staring at her, motioning for her to follow. But Birdie shook her head and pointed at the door with her knife.

The guard pointed to her cell. "I'm sorry. I could only get your key."

She ignored him and got down on her hands and knees. "It's me," Birdie whispered through the slit under the door.

"Who's there?" the woman's voice was a soft whisper.

"It's me, the smart arse. Someone's helping us escape."

"Who?"

"The guard who searched us, he killed the guard on patrol."

The guard grabbed Birdie by the arm and tried to drag her away, but she shoved him off. "I'm not leaving her!"

Her voice echoed down the corridor, through the lower floors.

The man shook his head. "You can't get her out, it's impossible."

"It's alright, Birdie, go! I'll be fine," the woman slid something under the door.

Birdie reached down and picked it up. The pendant was a bit rusted, well-weathered, but there could be no mistaking the blackbird in the centre. She shook her head, feeling like she was in a dream.

"This is the House Black symbol," she leaned closer to the door." There were footsteps echoing up the stairs now, the guard was frantically pulling at her to follow him. "How'd you know my name?"

"We need to go!" The man pulled at her again.

"Go," shouted the woman. "We'll meet again soon, Gods-willing. I'll explain it then!"

The footsteps were closer.

"What's your name," said Birdie.

"Ariss, now go! I'll be okay, I promise."

The man grabbed and dragged her along the corridor. Glancing back, he flicked his hand and with a flash of metal, a knife hissed out of his sleeve and past her. It thudded into something solid, and turning she saw a guard collapsing through the doorway, clutching the knife in his chest.

Back up the spiral staircase and out they went, through the heavy doors and into the cool night air, abandoning the only friend she'd left in the world. They passed through the maze of lanes and passages, coming to a dead end. The man searched the floor, pulled up a wooden board that had been covered with hay, showing a hole dug into the ground. He pulled off his padded armour so he could fit into the hole and didn't look back as his thin frame slid into the inky black. Birdie shimmied down after him, dropping into the small tunnel.

With no means of light, and no space to hold a torch even if they did have one, Birdie blindly crawled on her hands and knees through the cold dirt, following the man's shuffling and heavy breathing. Walls pressed in on both sides, she could bloody *feel* the damn things closing in. She didn't know how long had passed when she bumped headfirst into a wall, but looking up, relief washed through her as the small gap shone faint light down onto her head.

"Quick, the alarm has been raised," the man hissed, fear heavy in his voice as he helped pull Birdie up into breaking dawn. The grasslands were still dark, but the first rays of light touched the mountain peaks on the distant horizon.

A cold wind bit through her tunic, and she cursed the men in the outpost for taking her heavier clothing and cloak. An alarm bell tolled in the outpost, its walls on the ridge in the distance alight with figures holding torches. The man ran in the opposite direction, Birdie followed, clutching her arms to keep warm, teeth chattering.

They came to a small pool in a hollow and two tethered horses looked up at them disapprovingly. The man pointed to the smaller horse. "Get on!"

"I've never ridden a horse!"

The man looked bewildered, but heaved her onto her horse and shoved her feet into the stirrups. "Just don't let go! Ride to the mountains. Follow the trail to a crossroads. Keep straight and stay on the path until you come to the Bone-Portcullis. It's a short-cut through the mountain passes, so be wary for vagabonds. Talk to no one, you'll have to give them this at the portcullis..." He reached for something inside his cloak, when something *whizzed* through the air between them.

An arrow!

It thudded into the other horse's ribs, making it jerk wildly. He slapped her horse and ran behind her to mount his own. Birdie's horse took off so fast she almost fell from her saddle. After a few minutes she looked back, dark blots moved in the distance, but no sign of the man or his horse appeared to be following her. Birdie set her sights on the mountains ahead.

A sensation came over her. It was that dreaded but all too familiar feeling—like that night escaping the cottage. It was loss.

Losing something that was home in a way, something safe. The woman had been a means of safety for her. But there wasn't safety in the world anymore. Not for her.

Only evil.

Chapter 10: Ambushes and Insubordination

After the first week of marching the army recruits looked a sorry sight. Some of the soldiers lacked weapons, having been traded or gambled away at the various encampments and outposts. To stop this problem getting further out of hand, Kye ordered any soldier found without proper gear equipped would be given twenty lashes.

Any who failed a second time would be hung.

While his methods weren't winning him favour with the recruits, it was effective in hampering any further loss of supplies. He didn't care if they hated him. Kye needed their obedience, not their friendship.

Two weeks on the march and those mountains peaks slowly drew closer. General Markova, proud leader of the Golden Circle army, decided they should skirt the mountain passes, as few of the routes were wide enough for the army and those prone to landslides this time of year. Markova held sway with most of the officers, so when Kye said they should use the passes to their advantage through ambushes and guerrilla tactics, he was laughed out of the command tent. The next day they marched south-west, Kye grumbling vengeances from his saddle, as they stomped across the desert flatland. While they wouldn't be able to replenish water supplies for some time, the few days spent crossing the dry plain could give them a well needed advantage.

Hopefully they'd catch the Eclipsi horde off balance and slaughter them.

On the first night in the flatland Kye entered the officers' tent, bleary eyed from dust. Markova sat beside the fire, browsing the scrolls scattered about on the table and sipping from a goblet threatening to overflow with wine. He frowned beneath his bushy eyebrows. "War Monger, enjoying the journey? Still getting used to life as a real soldier?"

Do I look like I'm enjoying myself, you fat fucking swine? Thought Kye, wiping the dust away from his cloak with a small laugh.

Kye treated the old fool to his silver smile. "I studied in Dogesk, general, hard travel and I are well acquainted."

Markova sat back. "What can I do for you?" The officers scattered about the tent went back to their conversations, ignoring Kye.

"I've received word from one of my agents. It seems that a number of the Eclipsi have reached the passes. If some of the officers had sided with me, I might've laid down traps to catch them in." A nearby captain sneered across a map table at Kye. Kye ignored the captain and reached inside his cloak. "Because of your mistake they're going to learn where we are and catch us from both sides." He threw the scroll onto the general's desk.

"You can't move that many men through high terrain." Markova waved away Kye's statement as he sat forwards, unrolling the scroll and scanning the scrawled message. "We fight on open ground, War Monger. Not back alley shadows and mountain peaks. You'd know that if you'd ever been in a *real* battle." He looked up from the scroll. "This is a joke, right? You think you can take control of the army? You might be given special treatment by the ministry but out here you're just a pile of bones not yet picked clean. We've been the ones keeping the cities safe. I'm not signing this..." he pushed away the scroll.

Kye whipped out his sword and rested the point against the general's throat, right beside the throbbing vein. "I *am* taking command. This will be signed by your name or your blood. Your choice." Markova held up his hand to stop his men, who'd drawn arms the same time as Kye. "I want ten thousand of your best men ready to march into the mountain passes by dawn."

Markova picked up a quill and dipped it in ink. "If you want to go chasing those damn animals around the passes, be my guest. But don't expect any of my men to help you. Take your recruits and freeze up there, for all I care." Markova handed Kye the scroll. "I'll remember this, War Monger. One day, one day soon, you'll find the knife at your own throat."

Kye gave the general one more smile, just because they were starting to warm to each other. "I look forward to it, general."

The sound of snow crunching under boots echoed through the narrow pass. Above the pass large mounds of rock had been loosened, and behind these hundreds of men hid, waiting. Kye crouched behind one of outermost boulders. Hundreds of the enemy cautiously crept through the pass, bows in hand, emboldened by the lack of ambushes so far and the false information Kye had given to one scout party which he'd been forced to sacrifice. The enemy believed this pass was scarcely guarded.

The Eclipsi made their way through the pass, their white furs blending in with the falling snow. Kye gave the signal, and with a single blast of a war-trumpet the soldiers began leveraging their boulders with poles. The valley filled with a grinding echo as the scores of boulders began rolling, tumbling down and into the pass. One man jumped aside, trying to dodge a falling boulder, but only landing in the path of more dislodged rocks. Boulders were rushing down into the pass, squashing, crunching bones and filling the pass with screams of death. And as the enemy fled, even more boulders rolled into the slanted pass.

A score of the enemy reached the mouth of the pass. Kye turned to the flagman beside him. "Release!" The flag was raised and archers perched around the entry let their arrows fly.

After one more volley, the pass was silent.

"Good work," a newly appointed captain nodded as Kye headed back to where the horses were tethered and mounted the beast.

Only a drop in the bucket.

The horse looked back at Kye, baring its teeth. He dug in his spurs and slowly moved along the trail, past sheer drop-offs, swinging rope bridges that groaned under their weight. The mountain passes were a maze of carved pathways on the cliff's edge, criss-crossing tunnels with fifty-foot archways in places. Ancient runes etched into the stone of these archways were almost faded away entirely, their meaning lost through the ages. Supposedly all ore had been mined from these mountains and the ancient race moved their human workers elsewhere.

Kye could almost picture the people who'd spent their lives on these peaks. Hardier men than him, surely, not knowing the kiss of sunshine in summer. Not knowing the smell of grasslands after rain, or making love with the twin moons shining down on naked flesh. Only the haft of a pickaxe in your hand, and the promise of fresh snowfall to cover your world without colour.

Kye gripped the reins tightly in his gauntlet and pushed those thoughts away.

She was gone.

Those days were now as bleak to his mind and empty of colour as these rugged mountains.

Back at base camp, streams of men came and went, as the mountain passes were dotted with makeshift bases, where Kye's minutemen officers could hit the Eclipsi and run before more arrived. Ambushes laid in wait everywhere, from frayed wires on rope bridges, to awaiting landslides which would claim the lives of the enemy.

Kye left his horse tied outside his own tent and went in. A small fire was still burning in the metal grate at the centre of the tent, and Kye smiled as he warmed his red hands.

"It's the small things." He shrugged off his thick, snow laden cloak and padded armour, and was about to pour himself a well-deserved goblet of wine, when a loud cough outside the tent drew his attention. "Yes?"

"A message from Vines, sir."

"What are you waiting for, frostbite?"

The messenger entered, handed him a metal vial, saluted and disappeared. Kye slipped out the parchment inside.

Sir,

General Markova received intel that the enemy army is further north than anticipated. The general has taken command of the army and began marching north to bypass the mountains and meet them head on. Morale of the refugee recruits left behind has begun to wane, as the Golden Circle took most of the supplies. I eagerly await your orders.

Your Loyal Servant,

Vines

Kye threw the scroll into the fire.

Markova, you damn fool. You bloody traitor, I'll see you hung for this, thought Kye.

"Bad news?"

Kye spun around to see a figure standing in the corner of the tent. A hooded fur cloak hid most of the woman's face. Kye saw nothing but scorn in those eyes, a gaze near as sharp as the knife in her hand. But he knew that voice...

"You?"

"Me," she nodded, pulling down her scarf. "You look surprised to see me."

Kye glanced to his dagger on the table. Much too far. She'd have her knife inches deep in his heart before he took his second step. "I thought you were dead, or worse, had betrayed me. After all, I gave you men and passage. All you had to do was find his house and bring them back. After all those missions spent gaining our trust in the ministry, you threw away the one opportunity that would've sealed your place in our ranks."

The woman raised a snow-covered eyebrow. "Oh, really? I'm sorry that it took me so long, but I was busy trying to, you know, not die."

"What happened?"

"The Eclipsi made it to them before us. I only had time to warn them, their scouts were coming through the forest. Only the girl escaped, the sister died in the fire. I tried getting her safely to an outpost, but... it seems this sage, Felt, moves faster than we thought possible."

"The girl's alive, then? And Maddox, where's he?"

"I need safe passage to Mala, and gold. I know the girl's headed that way, and wherever she is, *he* is."

"You're not going to let me down again, are you? You might be one of my best agents, but if you fail again, you'll wish Nefaro had tortured you to death all those years ago."

"I want the blue seal of passage first, signed by you. You give me that, and I'll give you them both, *alive*. Also, I've some other useful information that might just help you out against Felt's army."

"Tell me. If it's good enough, you'll have your seal of passage."

"Ah-ah-ah!" the woman shook a gloved finger. "What kind of girl do you take me for, Kassova?"

The way she said his name gave him shivers along his spine. He smiled and she didn't flinch. "Hmm, still stubborn at least... Wait here while I see to the document and payment, and I'll take *that*." Kye pointed at the knife still in her hand. The woman came closer, spun the knife into the air, catching it at the tip and offering it to him. Kye went to take it, but she pulled it away and flicked it back into her hand, resting the point in the hollow of his neck.

"I have your word, don't I, Kassova? You know I'm not one to mess with... Remember that captain off the coast of High Shoals, hmm?"

Kye cleared his throat, trying not to focus on her scent of sweat. "How could I forget... You can have safe passage, but I'll have to send an escort along. A larger one, of course. I wouldn't want any more... unfortunate events happening to one of my best agents, now, do I?"

The woman nodded, flicked the knife around and stuck it into his belt, resting mere finger lengths away from his groin. The woman walked over to the fire and began to warm herself. Kye adjusted the knife before leaving to get the seal prepared.

So, his agent was still alive? She'd been promised a high place in the ministry's spies and a roomful of treasure to track down Maddox and his family. It had been that or torture in the Hall of Faces after she'd revealed the information to Nefaro and promised to deliver the Black heir. But after a week of contact she'd vanished, along with her escort of six hardened, experienced soldiers, making Kye look a fool in front of Nefaro once again.

He returned to find her still beside the fire. Kye placed the chest on the table and pulled out the parchment. He reached over and picked up the quill, dipped it, and began writing out a seal of passage. Kye lifted it and wagged the parchment. "It's all written up, ready to go, and all it needs is your letter, but first, how about that information."

The woman strolled over and opened the chest, checked the decently sized purse filled with coins and nodded. "Und-ar-Felt has moved his main force to the south and is by now well past these mountains. He left smaller forces to draw you out to the east and north." The woman took the quill and dipped it again, then signed her name.

X.

"Markova," growled Kye, who shook his head and tried to keep his tone level. "He's fallen for it. He took the best fighters north with him."

"The Golden Fool, hmm?" smiled X.

"Indeed... You're sure you want to go by that alias again? Until things are cleared up with the ministry, any officers might be on the lookout for you."

"That's what an escort's for, right? Besides, I'm sure you'll send a message to Nefaro, letting him know you hadn't been betrayed? That his plan for revenge is still in-tact."

"What kind of man do you take me for? My business is my own, as well you know." Kye smiled and went to pour them both a goblet of wine.

"Here's to wine and fire," smiled X.

"And bad aliases... You really should just pick a name."

The woman leaned close, fire writhing in those crystal blue eyes, then looked away, smirking. "Names are for friends, Kassova. I have no time for friends in this world."

Chapter 11: Out of the Frying Pan...

All around was endless grass, grass and more grass. No, wait, there was flies. And grass. By the Gods Birdie was saddle-sore, and tired, and hungry. The prolonged riding had left her stiff-legged and sore in the behind when she would walk. Luckily the man had packed food and water, she'd been only nibbling at the dried meat and biscuit, and the horse needed more water than her. She looked up at the sky, pale blue stretching into the horizon.

By the Gods, let it rain.

Her saviour had also packed warm clothes for when the nights grew chilly. And cold they surely were. At night she would talk to the horse, telling him of days spent in the cottage and the woods. Once she'd seen a dark fleck moving in the distance, but it soon faded.

The land became rockier after the fourth day, the ground grew coarse and the misty air stung at her face like icy pin-pricks. Small pebbles grew to rocks and then to boulders, making her zig zag between outcrops, following the little-used and lesser kept road along steep ridges. Vegetation was scarce, the animal bones scattered along the road spoke how scarce, and she cursed her idle mind for not considering taking grass with her in the pack.

The horse ate what little they found, and it seemed to be just enough to keep it going.

At the moments when she grew weary and considered lighting a fire, the thought of what it might attract made her settle to sleep in the darkness. Nightmares awaited her when sleep finally came. Of Aunt Bella, and the woman, Ariss. There was nothing to do now but press on, no matter how lost she felt. No matter what life threw at her, she would keep going.

She *would* get to Mala and find her uncle Maddox.

She *would* make her aunt proud of her.

She would... She would probably die.

How could a life spent in the woods have prepared someone for this? She didn't know how to survive in mountain ranges. Didn't know which roads to stick to, where the dangerous ones led. Beyond the mountain ranges patrols would be common. Bella might've trained her to fight, but she didn't bloody teach her how to become fucking invisible.

And like this her days went. Filled with self-doubt, panic, then the stubbornness set in and she simply focused on the horizon, ignoring her fears.

Find that inner peace.

That's what Bella would've said, so Birdie ignored those doubts.

They wouldn't put food in her stomach, after all.

As the ground became steeper, with veering drops at times from landslides in places, and rock falls at others, she led the horse by its bridle, calming it where the path grew narrow. Coming to a bridge that spanned a chasm below, she breathed in and imagined the crisp smell of blue pine sap, the sound of the soggy moss squashing underfoot, and birds twittering overhead.

The sounds of the forest filled her mind, and her calmness seemed to spread to the horse, as it quieted its whinnying.

She was just going home. Going back to her Bella and the little cottage. To a warm fire and steaming, spicy trailhead soup.

By the Gods her mouth was watering.

Idling in this daydream, they crossed the bridge unscathed. Looking around at the sheltered pass, the first thoughts of making camp began to form in her mind, but she fought them off and held onto the fleeting images of the trees, of home. She guided the horse further into the pass, and was still playing with these memories, when a voice called out to her. "Don't take anudder step, we gorten ye serrownded!"

Three men appeared on the rocks above. Three appeared behind her and three ahead. Cursing her daydreams, she glanced around but couldn't see a way out. There wouldn't be anyone to help her out of trouble this time. No Bella, no Ariss, no stranger to steal her away into the night.

"Shit-balls..." she muttered.

Keeping her arms at her sides, Birdie made no move for her knife. At the men's orders she raised her hands, feigning surrender, but growled as she jumped onto the horse. Her foot missed the stirrup, but she managed to cling on to the horse's mane. Birdie bounced along, feeling every jarring bump against her sore arse.

An arrow shot past and bounced off a slab of rock, so she kicked her heels into the horse's ribs, managing to slip one foot into a stirrup, driving the heel of her other foot into a bandit's face, sending his head snapping back.

"Get back here ye little bitch!" A voice shouted from behind. One of the men jumped out of the way just in time, but the other stayed where he was, grinning as he swung his axe. He swung low, aiming to maim the horse, but the horse jumped well, knocking him off-balance, breaking bones with a *crunch* as he fell under hoof.

They were past the men, storming through the pass, arrows flitting by.

She was untouchable. She wasn't afraid anymore, fucking bandits. Who did they think they were? She was Birdie Black. She was going to make it. She was—

An arrow thudded into the back of the horse's skull with a hollow *whump*, and the horse stumbled for another few strides, but its legs buckled and Birdie was flung from the saddle, tumbling across sharp stones. Rolling to a stop, she cursed, pushing herself up and on without a backward glance. Thankfully the footsteps chasing her sounded far behind. Her heavy breathing and the crunch of her boots against gravel soon drowned out the chaos. The path veered off to the left and up into the pass, but Birdie left it behind and struck off up a rough path of her own making, and into the mountain, knowing that every step might just be her last.

Like a cloud, her feet glided over uneven surfaces, leaping boulders, bounding across the rocks like a shadow. The adrenaline pumped through her body as she pretended she was simply running through the woods.

It's just another day of training evasion, no danger, just a simple game with Bella.

Her heart thumped against her ribs, feet slapping against rock, breath hissing in her ears. The path stopped rising and narrowed, then came to a sharp turn, which brought her to a series of steps, or more a miniature mountain of rough, square rocks working a way upwards. She wasted no time and jumped the first one, and then the next, climbing a big rock, scraping her wrist bad on a jagged bit sticking out, but there was nothing to be done about it.

Birdie lost track of time as the steps blurred past, not even noticing when she came to the end and finally pulled herself up. Flatland lay far off below in the distance, just visible between the high cliffs flanking both sides of the view. A winding path brought her down towards a maze-like network of passes. Birdie turned back and saw the bandits slowly making their way up after her, but still a way off.

Birdie shouted down at them and gave them the finger, before turning and fleeing towards the passes.

Birdie woke to the sound of footsteps outside the cave.

"She's gotta be 'round here somewhere."

The bandits must have closed the distance as she'd slept. Birdie hadn't been able to keep up the pace and had found a cave where she huddled inside of, just to get an hour sleep and regain her strength.

"That bitch is gonna get it, broke Ergon's leg."

"Boss said to take her back to camp, so no funny business. Not unless you wanna be dropped off a cliff like Sid."

Her pulse raced, heart beating almost loud enough for them to hear.

"See that?"

"What?"

"A cave, there. You think...?"

"Aye, I think she just might." He spoke louder. "Girl, if yer in there, come out now. Won't hurt yer."

The other man stifled a giggle.

"Shuddup, will ye," he hissed quietly. "Come on out girlie, there's naught reason t'be afraid."

The footsteps came closer; Birdie could hear one of them breathing heavily, panting almost. Torchlight flickered on the mouth of the cave. Silently, slowly, Birdie got her knife ready.

If these bastards were going to try and take her, she would make them pay.

A shadow appeared, wobbling from the torchlight. The first man then, in front of the other holding the light. He came into view, creeping past, not noticing the tiny alcove of rock that Birdie had squeezed her small frame into. She let him pass and the other man appeared. The torchlight made her squint, but she took aim, those countless hours of anatomy lessons and killing points taught by Bella rushing through her mind.

Always go for the neck if it's vulnerable, sever one of the main arteries and the fight's finished.

Birdie pounced out and on him like a wildcat. He turned, raising the torch to see what was making that sound, and her knife-arm got pushed askew, making her catch the man in the side of the neck instead of opening up an artery. The blade sliced through useless flesh. Birdie held on to his shoulder with her free arm, clinging to him, bringing the blade back around and aiming blindly for the far side of his neck. He brought his free hand up just in time and it stabbed through the palm, but she'd put all her strength behind it and the man was unbalanced. Her knife pinned his hand against his neck.

He dropped the torch and clutched at the blade as Birdie let go of him, abandoning her knife, but quickly noticing and snatching the long-knife from his belt. The other man faced her with a mace in his hand, but his face showed no sign of threat as he watched his comrade drop to his knees, trying staunch the blood spurting between his fingers.

She'd been lucky.

First rule of defence, Blackbird, always run if you can.

Birdie turned and ran out of the cave. More torches bobbed in the distance, moving closer as the remaining bandit shouted for backup.

"Shit-balls," she hissed, trying to get her bearings of direction as she fled through the dark. The ground was uneven, little light thrown down from the two moons faintly visible behind thick clouds. Birdie felt her way down through the narrow pass, slowly descending the rocks. Ignoring the shouts and gruff voices, Birdie focused on the path ahead, the path to safety, or at least the path away from certain death.

Morning light crept over the passes. Birdie knew that the valley between the twin mountain peaks led east. Following the sunrise, she stumbled on tired legs, held herself with shivering arms tighter, and prayed that the men had given up in their pursuit.

But she knew better.

It was hard to remember how many torches there'd been. Perhaps a dozen, likely twenty. The lack of food and sleep rendered little help to her thinking. What she was running on now was pure and utter instinct, sprinkled with a little desperation, and a cherry called fear. The maze-like passes were a far-cry from her days spent training in the woods, but without it she would have been dead long ago. Scents and landmarks were non-existent in this terrain, sources of food even scarcer. Those large birds that circled overhead did *not* look appealing. More than likely they were eying *her* up for a meal. She didn't like the look of them at all, unless roasting over a crackling fire, that was.

Her stomach rumbled and panged at the thought of hot meat.

"Gods-be-damned, I'm hungry."

A man came trudging into view. He was filthy, covered in dust and dirt, hair wild and dishevelled. Luckily he hadn't spotted her yet, and was facing the opposite direction. Crouching down behind a rock, she peered around it, watching him. The man limped closer, his leg supported with a splint. Birdie ducked down and flattened herself against the rock.

It was the man her horse had landed on.

Great.

She let him come closer, his footsteps just at the far side of the rock. Silently she crept around the other side, praying that she wouldn't make a sound. On the far side, she peeked around the rock, watching the man limp away. Birdie looked up the narrow pass at the way he'd come, the urge to run in that direction almost overpowering. But instinct moved her feet, guided her hands, and she crept after him, keeping her feet away from knocking against any stones. Mere steps away she readied her knife.

You go for the knee, you're small, Ariss' voice drummed through her mind alongside Bella's. *Slit the tendon. Once they're down, they're out.*

The first rule of defence was to run, but if she could take one of them out of the chase, why not?

Birdie took aim and slashed the knife into his good leg, right down to the tendon behind the knee, followed by a quick and well-connected kick into where his bad leg looked worst as he stumbled. He wailed as he hit the floor, but Birdie was already turning, leaving the man to die alone, as he rightly deserved.

She once again set off east, following the rising sun towards the Bone Portcullis.

Towards her future, if she still had one.

By noon Birdie found herself at the end of the mountain passes. She had bumped into one more of the bandits but had managed to lose him awhile back. The path down from the passes was steep and uneven. Thankfully there were dozens of exits from the pass, all hundreds of feet from each other, and none of the bandits were waiting for her outside of the one she came to.

There was little chance that they would leave the passes, just to chase her. The roads bordering the pass were supposedly well patrolled by the Golden Circle.

I really have to stop laying so much faith in hope... My luck will only hold out so long.

But hope was all she had.

Any river or stream she came across had dried up. Trudging along the rocky landscape, following the overgrown trail, it was hard to know whether the thirst, hunger or pain from the long journey drained her energy the most. By midday the sun was unmercifully hot, searing into her eyes, her mind. Every smothering breath felt like it would be her last. Every thumping heartbeat sent black spots fizzing through her vision. Legs and arms were now nothing more but lumps of lead that she had to drag along with her. Picking out a scattering of rock stacks, she made her way along the path, surrounded by cracked dirt that disappeared into the distance. The large birds from the passes had reappeared, circling her once more. A gang of them.

"Shit... balls," her parched throat croaked.

Approaching the rock stack, Birdie's foot clipped an unseen stone, sending her face-first into the dirt. Plumes of dust rose around her as she hit the ground.

By the gods she was tired.

Birdie let her head rest on the rough ground, let her heartbeat even out, and slowly regained some morsel of strength. Flapping sounds grew louder from above as the group of birds landed nearby, sensing their meal was almost served. She eyed them. They eyed her back, the dark bulbous eyes filled with hunger and sharp beaks promising pain. Closer they came, and the bravest of the group ventured a nip at her shoulder. Then the beak nipped into her scalp, sending a trickle of blood down the side of her face.

"Go away..." she whispered.

Birdie's hand snatched out, grabbed the bird under the beak and she slowly started choking its scrawny neck. Or did in her mind, at least. Her body failed to follow the events of her imagination. Even the act of keeping her eyes open seemed a burden too heavy to maintain. They nipped at her, one ripping at her lower leg, another at her arm.

"Go... Go away... Puh... Please." She flapped a hand, barely able to lift her arm, but the bird just scuttled sideways and eyed her closer, aiming for its next shot.

The world grew dim then, blurred at the edges, and the ground spun slowly beneath her.

Was this death?

After everything she'd survived, the thing that would finish her off would be the sun and... birds.

A sound came from somewhere beyond comprehension. Far away, like creaking giant trees on unseen glades which echo throughout the forest. Her mind was cloudy. It grew louder, and she opened her eyes to see the birds flapping away from her, taking wing back to the sky. As the ground began to vibrate along with the grumbling sound, Birdie could hear singing, but couldn't understand the words. The grumbling stopped, footsteps approached. Birdie felt hands grab her, turning her over.

"Drink this," a woman's voice. A kind voice. A flask was put to her lips, warm liquid brushed against her lips, dribbled down her chin, but she couldn't remember how to swallow. "Drink this or die, girl!"

Birdie let the fluids pour into her mouth and down her throat.

It was bliss. Torturous, choking bliss.

The world slowly came into clearer focus. An old woman smiled down at her, face as weathered and cracked as the desert floor she lay on. "Good, do you feel better?" croaked the old woman.

Birdie nodded. "Yes." Her voice was hoarse.

"Quiet now, save your strength." The old woman stoppered the flask, pocketed it and slung Birdie's arm over her shoulder. For an old woman, she carried Birdie's weight with ease, helping her to a horse-drawn carriage. Two pale, stocky horses eyed her with wide eyes as she passed. The doors of the carriage were open, with storage lining one side and the other a pallet and bedroll. Birdie sighed as the woman put her onto the soft bedroll, gave her one final sip of the drink and closed the carriage doors behind her.

With a final sound of a whip crack, followed by horses whinnying, the cart rolled, swaying, and Birdie fell to sleep.

Her mouth was dry, her limbs ached. Birdie knew she wasn't dead, as the Gods hopefully wouldn't be sadistic enough to let spirits feel pain. She cracked open an eye and took in her surroundings. Then the memory of the old woman and the carriage came flooding back.

Wiping her eyes, she noticed that the carriage wasn't swaying. They'd stopped. Standing up, Birdie stretched her limbs and left the carriage, balancing against its side with one hand. The woman was just outside, holding a large jar in one hand and trying to guide a spider inside of it with the other.

"Welcome back to the world of the living, my girl." The woman managed in getting the spider into the jar and shut the lid. She stood up and smiled at Birdie, her face creasing into a web of wrinkles.

Birdie liked the old woman instantly. There was an aura of kindness surrounding her, but that didn't mean she trusted her. If Bella had instilled one thing into Birdie, it was looks can be deceiving. But still, she couldn't stop the smile from breaking on her chapped lips.

"Thanks for helping me back there." Birdie nodded at the jar. "What's that for?"

The woman held it up level to her eye, which must have been at most to Birdie's shoulder. "Spiders make the best medicines, if you know what to feed them and how to whisper the right words."

"You... speak to them?" Birdie couldn't keep the laughter from her voice.

"Yes, but I find they make poor travel companions, as they never speak back." The woman looked past the jar, through the glass, at Birdie and cocked her head sideways. "You though, my girl, are a far more interesting specimen. Those eyes..."

Birdie touched her cheeks self-consciously. Bella had told her she had her mother's eyes. It had been so long since anyone had mentioned it. "Thanks."

"Most welcome. Beauty is a gift from the Gods not to be scorned. I myself would know personally." The woman shambled inside the carriage and stowed away the spider. Once back outside, she raised a brow. "You feel up to riding up front with me? It's been so long since I've had company. I once had a little robot child come along for the ride, beautiful singer he was."

"A... rowboat?"

The woman looked at her and shook her head, as if remembering where she was. "It's nothing, a relic from a distant age, eons past. Forgive an old woman her wandering memories."

The woman shambled up to the front of the carriage and picked up her whip as Birdie took the seat beside her. With a whip crack the horses began to pull the carriage. The land rolled by as the old woman spoke of the world and what she had seen, far and wide, with a distant look in her eyes.

"To the west, beyond the Sun Isles you come to an ancient land. Sand dunes you could fit the entire Sea of Circles into, scattered with enormous pyramids, countless ruins inscribed with strange symbols. Beyond those is a wide and beautiful savannah, where majestic and numerous animals roam that the artists of this land couldn't fathom." Her gaze shifted, pointing the leather whip. "And to the south, through mountains thrice as tall as the ones you passed through, beyond the ministry's land, is empty jungle now. Once there had been millions living there, back when the Old Gods came down from the sky to harvest the soil and bred with a select few to instil a leading sect of humans.

"You see, once upon a time that land had been inhabited and cultivated by distant cousins of the men who built the Sea of Circles." The woman pointed off to the east. "The trade ports of the forgotten civilizations were largely in contact with each other. They had ships that could scale air like water. It was a time of science, a time of greatness." Her eyes sparkled, as she gave the black and dirty abandoned village they were now passing through a sorry, sad shake of her head. "Now is a time of darkness."

"I never took you for a pessimist." Birdie took another clump of the green moss-like substance the woman had been giving her, that wasn't anything like moss once you tasted it, but more like pine nuts, and chewed on it. It sent warm tingling sensations down her throat, into her stomach and through her mind, making her feel relaxed. Her aching limbs were becoming a distant memory.

"Hah! Human words, my girl. I see the world for what it is and what it was and never will be again! You sit there and tell me I look at the world in the wrong light—a pessimist—when you've barely broken out of your own shell. Look at the acorn telling the ancient oak tree which way the sun rises! I'm a pessimist, hah, you try telling me that in another few millennia, after you watch those you love die from war, famine and old age." The woman's hand gripped the whip tight enough to show the tendons sticking out.

"I'm sorry. I never meant to offend."

The old woman nodded. "It's no ache to my heart, my girl, withered thing as it is. I was like you once. So young that you think there's a point to it all, that everything has a purpose... You'll learn."

That night after setting up camp the old woman disappeared inside the carriage, rummaging around in the many pots, jars, chests and other odd items Birdie couldn't put a name to. The entire outside of the carriage alone was covered in shelves, holding small cages with animals; rats, rabbits, lizards, squirrels, others she didn't know. Pots filled with scores of herbs, salves, potions, and the jingling and clatter of the oddments had strangely soothed her during the past few days of travel, almost to a point where her mind and soul didn't ache from the pain of her previous losses.

Almost.

Re-emerging from the chaos inside of the carriage, the woman pointed to the fire. Birdie unclenched her jaw and sat where ordered.

"And just what do you think you're doing with those?" Birdie eyed the curved razor in the woman's hand, and a jar with white foam inside and brush sticking out in the other.

"I'm shaving your head, my girl. You might be lucky enough to avoid the attention of the vicious men that lurk out there, but I find it best not to tempt fate. I am bringing you to the Bone Portcullis, but if you think you're getting past the scum camped around it you are badly mistaken."

"I can take care of myself."

"You're almost a woman-grown. Those bandits from the passes will look like prince-charming compared to some of the scum in the Sea of Circles."

Birdie frowned. "It seems you almost know more than I do about my own life."

The old woman smiled. "Nonsense, my girl. I'm a seer, I know far more. Now hush, tell me a story to pass the time. Tell me, hmm, about how you came to be in the mountain passes?"

"I thought you were a seer? You tell me."

"I prefer to listen. Now, speak..."

After a moment Birdie grunted unhappily, and then as the razor scratched softly against her scalp, she talked...

Chapter 12: Sunnyside Slums

Leek spent that first night after fleeing from Gurth and the prison in a pig sty. On the morning after, as he stood hidden in the shadow of a warehouse, he'd been noticed by a man carting barrels to the lower-sectors of the city, and after a long moment staring into Leek's eyes, had offered him a ride inside one of the empty barrels.

"What you think yous doin'?" the gaunt man fretted as Leek got in. "Ain't no good tryna steals from these folks. Ministry gets awful means when beggars come up in the uppety parts. Yous new in the city?"

"It's that obvious, is it?"

"A bit, lets me give you some advice. Stick to the slums 'til you get youself some coin. Thens you scrubs up a bit, try pays off a Masker to lets ye in the industrial sector. You get youself in there, working a blacksmiths or workshops or some sorts, yous work and keeps y'head down. No one bothers the factory workers. Take my words for it, I used t'live in Sunnyside. And another thing," he pointed at Leek's bloody fingernails. "Yous needs stop doin' that. You show yous scared in Sunnyside folk'll robs your last breath for the extra airs."

They passed the numerous checkpoints unscathed, the man whispering that Maskers weren't too worried about what was coming out of the upper parts, only what was going in. Once stopped and released from the cramped space of the barrel, Leek had to shield his nose from the stench.

"Gets used to it," the carter said, picking up his whip. "Yous goes 'round pullin' faces likes that at the smells and dirts and yous stick out like a sore thumb. Yous don't want that down heres." The carter gave him a sad smile and a final wink, before he cracked the whip and left Leek behind, the cart disappearing down along the hard packed dirt road, through the throngs of people shambling about.

Houses had been built one atop the other, all leaning against the high white walls behind them for extra support. The walls of the city encircled each other spiral-like cake formation, rising one layer after another at a neck-achingly steep angle. Smoke billowed up behind the closest wall, from what must be the industrial sector. The tall spire disappeared into the clouds far, far above, tiny blots of black moved here and there, using pulley systems and carriages that hoisted people up onto the spire platforms. Leek looked away, sickness creeping into his stomach, from the height or from his circumstances, he couldn't say.

Ramshackle stalls sold crudely made weapons, third-hand clothes, mouldy looking breads and cheeses. Even with how distasteful some of the food looked, it still made his mouth water and stomach gurgle. On the sides of taverns and buildings were hand painted suns, giving the dreary architecture an odd quirkiness to it.

Sunnyside Slums, how ironic.

After eating a handful of bread he begged from a passing merchant, Leek began getting to know the branching streets and laneways, avoiding the crowds and blending into the squalor.

After thirty minutes of slowly wandering about, he set off into the depths of the slums, where the houses were stacked even steeper. None of the Maskers patrolled the streets here, a handful of squads had kept order near the thoroughfare, but order here seemed to be solely left to the small gangs of men and boys hanging about on street corners, or sitting on archways over the busy, bustling streets. At one point a thin man with yellow teeth grabbed Leek and searched his pockets, but found nothing and shoved him away.

Coming to a small inn a woman was outside stirring a large pot, and the smell of vegetables and meat made Leek's stomach moan. A line stretched around the corner of the street, and he queued up for a hot meal. He was given a wooden bowl when at the corner of the street. Minutes passed and the line moved, until he was near the front. A group of about ten cudgel wielding men stood guard nearby.

"You again?" snarled the woman with the ladle of stew. The boy in front of Leek flinched away, then held up his empty bowl.

"Please mam, can I have some more?"

"Get out of here, before I skin ye alive! Told ye, ye'll get no more from us!" The woman snatched the bowl and tossed it onto a nearby pile. "Bloody thief."

"But I didn't take two bowls..." The boy shuffled away from the line, deflated. Men avoided his eye, each holding their bowl close as a lover.

He had a flashback then, of his days spent in his family of thieves. How many times had Leek received similar treatment? How many times had he been stepped over, neglected, left to fend for himself and earn his own food?

The boy even had that same helpless, wide eyed stare that Leek used to have.

Leek's bowl was filled with a ladle of greasy looking stew and he was given a heel of bread. Leek followed the boy at a distance, managing brief sips of the scalding stew. The boy stopped outside a tavern, sat on an overturned barrel and looked around. He noticed Leek coming towards him.

"I don't want no trouble," the boy lifted his hands, then pinched his pockets. "Got no coin or food, if that's what you're lookin' for."

"Here." Leek handed him the bowl with half his soup still left inside. "You need it more than me."

The boy flinched away as if Leek had gone to hit him. "No, I don't want it!"

"What? Why?"

"Ain't owin' no debts, is why."

Leek shook his head. "Just eat the bloody soup. You can trade me for information, if it'll make you feel better."

The boy licked his lips as he stared at the steaming bowl. "What sorta 'formation?"

"Dunno... Sunnyside, perhaps? About making coin here?"

"Coin? Hah! I look like I make any coin?"

Leek inched the bowl away from the boy's reaching fingers, and he quickly changed his tone.

"I know where ye can find some folk who know about such things. Thieves and cut-purses, the sort'o folk I avoid." The boy smiled. "But I can tell ye where to find 'em."

Leek stood outside the tavern for half an hour, building up the nerve to enter. The *Foxhole* was alive with activity, the doors on each side of the building constantly opening or closing, as runners came and went. Bull-like men stood guarding each door, checking tattoos or names.

It wasn't until passing cart opened an opportunity, the wheel broke and got stuck, sending a few casks tumbling over the side and hissing as they poured foamy ale across the ground. People standing around the paved crossroads ran, performing magic tricks as they went, pulling beakers and cups from nowhere, ignoring the teamster's efforts with his whip.

The doormen were distracted, laughing and pushing a few urchins out of the way as they swallowed mouthfuls of ale, and Leek slipped in through the nearest doorway unscathed.

People huddled around the rough-hewn tables, playing cards or dice, chatting, some just watching the show, as a few of the tables had been cleared off and turned on their sides, forming a makeshift arena from inside which came the clucking of a chicken. As Leek passed the chicken gave a screech and blood and feathers puffed up into the air. Leek only just glimpsed the tipped ears of a fox. A few men glanced at him but thankfully took little interest. At the bar, Leek balanced on a stool and after a few minutes waved over the innkeeper.

"Ale is it?" asked the fat man with the ruddy expression, his single thick brow wriggling like a caterpillar as he frowned. He wore a thick gold chain that had five or so foxes' tails as pendants.

"No, I'm looking for work. Know where I can find any?"

"Kind of work, lad? Sweeping floors? Got enough help for that."

"The kind that puts coin into an empty purse," smiled Leek. "Preferably not the kind that spills blood. Never liked the look of the stuff personally, especially mine."

The innkeeper looked offended. "What kind of establishment to ye think I'm running here? I run a *respectable* business." He reached up turned a picture of fox den upside down, then gave Leek an almost unperceivable wink as he walked away.

Almost instantly a man took the seat next to Leek. Two flagons of ale were slid onto the counter and the innkeeper gave the man a nod. The man slid one flagon across to Leek.

"So what kind of work precisely are you interested in?"

Leek looked sidelong and got a better look at the man. He had a lazy eye and heavy pockmarks covering his cheeks, and an ancient top hat set at an angle on his head. He stuck his hand out revealing only two fingers on it.

"Name's Parrio Ancheta Savoy, though the brilliant minds of Sunnyside call me Pretty Boy. What's your name, my new found friend?"

Leek took a sip of ale, thinking. He had to make an impression. But how to do it...

"Name's Kellick, but back east they called me Fingers." Leek wiggled his fingers, putting the flagon back down.

"Fingers, what an interesting name. It would've been quite fitting for myself." Pretty Boy wiggled his own two with a crooked smile. "Why'd they call you that, Fingers, if you don't mind me asking?"

"On account of my ability to count to ten." Leek held one hand up, slowly counting, while the other hand quickly, stealthily moved out of his cloak, and inside the man's coat pocket. Empty, and he was already on three, but the hand was already moving on, creeping across the fabric, and inside Pretty Boy's cloak, finding an inside hook holding a money purse, and he teased it.

Five.

Leek slid his hand back out at the same time he pretended to toss something into the air with his counting hand, and tossed the purse over his head and into the waiting hand. Pretty Boy's face twitched, but then he opened his cloak, seeing the purse-hook empty, and a big smile spread across his face. He took the purse and opened it, showing Leek that only coppers had been inside.

A decoy purse.

"Interesting, very interesting," said Pretty Boy, slipping the purse back onto the hook. "Fingers, my good friend." Pretty Boy lifted his mug and knocked it against Leek's. "I think we can do business."

Chapter 13: The Bone Portcullis

The patrol passed by the ruins and headed up the winding hill, toward the distant Bone Portcullis looming on the horizon. Birdie crouched in the shadows, between a pile of rocks and rotted wood, hoping they wouldn't see her.

The old woman with the horse-carriage had dropped her at a crossroads the morning before, telling her to keep straight on. She'd slipped her a green gem necklace and told her to keep it on until she was safe.

What's it for? She'd asked.

It will help fool those who would do you harm. With your shaved head and this, you should be safe. But don't get too close to anyone.

Aren't you going to the Bone Portcullis?

No, my girl, I'm afraid this is where our paths stray. But we will meet again.

She'd left Birdie a pack of dried meats and a skin of water, then the carriage had disappeared down the road. Birdie had felt an urge to call after her, to stay with the carriage and cast her luck to fate, but Bella had told her to seek Maddox, so the carriage stayed rolling, and once again she was alone.

"Got coin? Help an' old soul," the rasping voice of the decrepit old hag begged, hobbling after the last of the patrol.

One soldier broke rank and approached, then looked into her cup. "It'll do." He grabbed the cup and pushed away the old woman, who lost her footing and rolled through dirt, before tumbling down into the ditch. The man emptied the coins into his pocket and threw the cup up into the ruins, shielding his eyes as he watched it rise, staring into the rubble. Birdie cursed and ducked down, pressing against the ground. She could hear him coming closer, footsteps mere strides away.

"Come on, we need to get back before sundown," a gruff voice shouted. Birdie thankfully heard the sound of the man's footsteps fade in the opposite direction.

After the soldiers disappeared over the hill, she crept out onto the road to make sure the way was safe. The old hag called out for help, before tumbling back down into the weeds.

"Shit-balls." Birdie began trampling through the brambles, forcing a path to the old woman. A sorry sight she was, bent and hobbled with scratches covering her face.

"Bless you," the old woman called after her once hauled out of the thorns. Birdie just shook her head without looking back.

Keeping a safe distance from passers-by on the road was easier now, as the charm given to her by the carriage-lady made any travellers simply give her a brief glance before losing interest. She finally came to a scattering of filthy buildings the colour of blood, the lowering sun turning everything scarlet. Her feet were aching and blistered, but she pressed on.

An old man lay face down in the dirt at the side of a building, dead as dead could be. Two men across the road harassed a young woman at a well, until she slapped one in the face and ran, the men pursuing her to the amusement of some drunkards. The woman skirted a corner, the men close on her heels.

Birdie rubbed her shaved head, thanking the cruel gods above for the old woman's foresight.

Turning up another street, two men fell out of a building, growling and punching as passers-by jeered and taunted them on. Birdie avoided the crowd, walking down a narrow, empty lane. The lane branched off two ways, one leading back to a busy street and the other blocked by a high wooden fence, its gate locked with a thick metal chain. She climbed the fence, gaining a few splinters for her troubles, and on the other side of the fence was an old burnt-out building with a small shed hidden in its shade. Checking the shed door, it swung open. Inside was dry, so she shut the door as much as possible, a slight gap letting in a line of fading light.

Closing her eyes, Birdie tried to imagine she was at home in her bed, but the image of Ariss lying in the dark cellar kept pushing its way through. She could almost smell the dungeon stench as she drifted into unsettled sleep.

A loud noise woke her. There were footsteps in the laneway, on the other side of the fence, and rapid panting. Birdie crawled to the door, peering out through the narrow gap. Faint flickering light filtered through the fence's many gaps.

"Get him, there he is!" muffled voices further down the laneway.

"No, please!"

Footsteps, many of them, and more lights appeared in the alleyway, illuminating the shadow of whoever stood on the other side.

"Where are they?"

"Please, I don't know what you're talking about!" the man dropped his torch, fell to his knees and raised his arms, pleading.

"We know you're working with him. What happened to the sister, and the girl? Where are they?"

Birdie's heart was thumping, drumming in her ears.

A tall, stocky figure stepped into the light.

"I don't know where they went, please. Maddox's sister never arrived at the outpost! I lost the girl in the passes. *Please*, I'm t-telling the truth."

"I'm afraid it's too late for that..." the stocky figure backhanded the kneeling man, pulled out a blade, giving a slow metallic hiss. Sounds of muffled cries as more shadows stepped in to hold the man down.

Birdie blocked her ears and shut her eyes just as the man lifted the knife. After a few moments she opened them.

"Look around," the killer said. "He was here for a reason."

Shapes passed along the fence, searching the floor, peering through the thin gaps. One climbed over the fence. Birdie crept into the corner, forcing herself against it and inhaling, willing herself to be as small and inconspicuous as possible. The door opened, pressing right up to her rib cage, but she hadn't hindered it. Moments passed and she willed herself not to breathe.

"Sir, here!" a voice called from the laneway.

"Keep it down, you fool! Kye will have my head if we get caught."

The shed door closed. Silence filled the alley.

"You're sure there's no sign of them? This letter says they were headed for Mala. They both escaped the cottage and fled."

"'Course, you know what the passes are like. They're bones by now."

"Look at the seal, House Black. I knew Maddox wasn't dead. He must be close. The seal's fresh."

"He's a fool then. Nothing left 'round here for 'em but a slow death. Ain't that right, Vines?"

"Not good enough. Kye wants them all, *alive*, and brought to him in secret. *No witnesses.* I need to send a message. You all spread out and check the outposts again. Keep your ears to the ground. Any sign of them, you send word to me, got it? Good, get going." The footsteps faded from the laneway.

Birdie let out a shuddery breath and didn't move until dawn shone through the gap in the door. No one had passed through the alley since the incident. Her legs trembled climbing over the fence. On the other side she found a body sprawled on the floor. She stood there for a moment, staring down at the swollen, pale face of the man who'd freed her from the cell at the outpost.

Reporting the murder could get me into the city, but at what cost? It would more than likely get me killed. Who were those men? And why were they looking for me? Better to keep quiet and get out of here.

But where could she go? Not back to the woods, to her home. There was nothing there for her now. Better to stay the course. If she could get this far, then *perhaps* she could make it to the end, whatever may lie there. She had to put her faith in Bella's hands. She said look for Maddox, so that's what Birdie would keep doing.

The Bone Portcullis looked alive, in a dead kind of way. It was a bizarre criss-crossing network of twisted white metal, with the main support bars curling down like fangs. The road leading up to it was lined with squat towers manned with guards. The road ended at a rampart leading to a bridge that crossed a wide moat.

Once on the bridge, Birdie had to wait behind a line of at least a hundred people trying to get through the portcullis. The ragged cried just the same as the finely dressed as they were turned away by the guards in black masks, featureless except for a pointed nose that slanted downwards, reminding her of a crow's beak. Each person in the line murmured, cursed and shouted as they bustled forwards step by step. Most were turned away. A select few allowed access, having managed in getting their names added to a list the man in charge was checking.

As the line moved, the two men muttering behind her spoke quietly, but Birdie caught most of it.

"Don't be daft, they won't know the difference. Those lads are dead in the valley, skeletons by now."

"Shhh! You'll get us caught, keep it down ye fool."

The men went silent. She could feel their eyes staring at her. Birdie hadn't turned around since entering the line, even when fights broke out nearby and people in front turned to peek.

"Just keep it down a bit, will ye'?" said the other in a lower tone. "An' maybe yer right about it, but just remember not to mention who we really are inside, got it?"

She was near the front, behind only a handful of people now, when a woman pushed her small boy forwards. "Name?" the guard in charge asked. He and another man holding the list sat behind the table, a large group of the black clad men flanking either side of it.

"We're not on the list, but my boy's gifted, I swear it. Show 'em Johnathan, show the man what you can do!"

The boy was only a thin streak of bone holding flesh. Birdie could see from here that he was shaking, but he lifted his hand and opened out his palm flat without hesitation. A flame appeared over his wrist and the crowd gasped.

"Monster!" someone shouted.

The masked man leaned over the table, grabbed his thin wrist and shook it, turned it upside down, and a tin metal rod slid out. A flame flickered from the end where rags had been stuffed in.

"'He's a fake!" someone shouted.

"Hang him!" cried another.

"Yeah, kill the little lying shite!" one of the men behind her added.

The guard grabbed the boy's wrist with both hands and slammed it against the table, bending it back until it snapped. The boy screamed, and another man drove his boot into his leg, snapping the knee the wrong way. The mother had taken a few steps back, pale with shock, but now she jumped at them, trying to pull her son away from the masked men. But the one who'd snapped his wrist stood up and stepped around the table, unsheathing his sword.

"Anyone who tries to fool the Ministry shall be punished," he shouted, with no hint of anger in his tone. He leaned down and stuck the sword's point through the boy's thin stomach like a pin through butter. The mother shrieked, wildly clawing at the man's mask, until another guard punched her into the face, snapping her nose back. She collapsed onto the bridge beside her son, draping her arms around his leg. As the boy stared down with wide eyes at his bloody stomach, limbs sticking out at wrong angles, and his mother's blood smeared face screaming up at him, the guard sheathed his sword and retook his seat.

"Next!" he waved and an over-weight, well-dressed man sauntered to the table, followed by a gaggle of boys.

"Name?" the guard sounded almost bored.

Birdie watched in horror as the men lifted the boy and his mother over the side of the bridge's railing. The boy screamed and begged as they were lifted over it, then the screams faded and stopped with two faint *thumps*.

One of the men behind her chuckled, making Birdie shiver. She thought about turning around and heading back.

Who cared if the cottage was burnt down? She could still fish in the river. Still live off of the land. Still rebuild her home. It was safer than this. It had to be. But the time for turning back was well past. It had been stolen from her as soon as that first torch had touched the thatched roof.

Bella's voice floated through her mind. Something said to her after Birdie had accused Bella of being too harsh, too strict.

One day, Blackbird, you'll see what the world's really like outside this forest. You'll want to run, you'll be afraid, but what I've taught you will get you through. So just put on a brave face and stick one foot in front of the other, and keep doing it.

"Next!"

The fat man and his gaggle of boys were being guided through the portcullis. A man and woman walked up to the table. Birdie cringed, as the woman was pregnant.

"Name?"

The man mumbled his name. The guard scanned the list and looked at the other, shaking his head.

"It must be there. I'm second son of Kris Shaula, head of House Shaula of Dogesk, back from my training in the western kingdoms. I was requested by my elder brother to come to Mala."

"Second son, huh?" The guard asked, looking sidelong at his men. Four men spread out and surrounded the man and the pregnant woman. "All members of the Twelve Lines have relinquished their title and assets to the Ministry of Faces. You'll be transported to the Hall of Faces where your fate will be decided."

"Punishment, but I've done nothing! My brother is working in the upper sector as a jeweller, he said we'd be given safe passage. It's been years since we were home."

"That's for His Supreme to decide. Next!"

The guards grabbed the couple and forced shackles onto their wrists, then marched them through the gate.

Birdie stepped up to the table.

"Name?"

Birdie stepped up to the table, lifted her hand level with his face. Bella and Ariss' silver necklaces dangled from her fist, the circle pendants twirled around between her gaze and his. He took in the blackbird and nodded. "Hall of Faces."

After crossing the bridge and passing through a series of barricades built in a narrow pass for about an hour, they came to a mass of buildings, shoddily built compared to the villages and towns she'd seen on her way here, all stacked one atop the other. The sun moved across the sky slowly as they left the ramshackle houses behind. The buildings improved, as did security. Food stalls, men shouting their wares, people eating, workshops, wagons lugging barrels and cargo back and forth, it was a far-cry from what people only leagues away were living. At the top of a hill the buildings gave way to a port that stretched across the waterline, towers and hulking ships only allowing glimpses of the sea beyond.

She smiled at the sight of it, remembering how many times she'd longed to swim in the sea, or be on one of the many adventures Bella had told her of as a child—sea-raids and distant expeditions to mysterious lands.

Boats were coming in and going out, towering boats that had ant-like people crawling up and down the jungle of ropes. Fishing boats, with stacks of crates and nets piled up on deck. Soldiers were walking about everywhere, inspecting supplies and documents, men went from the ships to the carts, from the carts to the ships, hauling crates and barrels, sacks and animals.

They approached a short, red-faced man inspecting a chart. One of her guards approached him. "Captain, we've been ordered to escort this young boy to the Hall of Faces," her captor presented a roll of parchment to the captain.

"I can't do it, I simply can't. I've too many already—"

"As you can see, we have a permit from His Supreme."

"Look here," the captain pointed at his ship. "We can't keep running you Maskers back and forth. There's too much cargo. General Markova will have my neck if I don't get it moved before the deadline!"

"To deny us is to deny His Supreme."

"Damn Maskers," the captain spat. "Ye'll be the fuckin' death of me. Yeah fine, I s'pose I could find a cabin for ye..." he looked past them, shock spreading across his face, and he stepped back, raising his hands.

Birdie turned, spotting dark shadows in the corner of her vision. Blood sprayed across her face, getting in her eye and mouth, and she dropped to ground, rolling away from the masked men.

Back on her feet, she had a brief moment to take in a dozen more masked men moving in on her escort, which had been cut down to two, the third lying in a puddle of his own blood on the ground.

Birdie turned heel, hearing swords clash, and headed for the safety of cluttered buildings. Footsteps thumped heavily into the ground closely behind her, but Birdie was faster. She reached the entrance of an alley, squeezing by an overturned cart. Chickens clucked and fluttered around the alley, having escaped their bonds, and Birdie quickly made her way through the fowl rabble.

She giggled as she jumped a stack of crates.

"Get out of my way!" a deep voice shouted from behind. "Go around, don't let him get away!"

Halfway down the alley she found it blocked by a backlog of men wheeling barrows. There, in the shadows, was a door hidden between two buildings, and she'd just taken a step towards it, when hands grabbed her from behind. The world went dark as a bag was pulled over her head, muffling her cries for help.

There was just time for one thought before a blunt object hit her in the side of the head, knocking her senseless.

Shit-balls.

Chapter 14: Strangers

Ariss forced a path through the bushes escorted by four of the men, all keeping their hands close to their weapons. So much for privacy. The bastards had never let her out of sight. But she was used to dealing with men like these, military minds with no inkling for guile. Not on her level.

The fools would pay.

The rest of her escort were split into two groups, one scouting the surrounding area and the other setting up camp. They'd taken her weapons before leaving that piss-poor excuse for a command post in the mountain passes. But what they didn't know was Ariss kept her Old Lovers strapped to the inside of her inner thighs, and the men who searched her back at the camp had let her keep on her britches. The twin blades were deadly sharp and thin, easily avoiding previous searches.

Crouching, Ariss put her hands on her waist and stared back at the men watching her. "Draw a fuckin' picture, why don't you?" She gave them her darkest frown, but the men didn't turn away. "Fuck it." She pulled down her britches, slowly, aligning her body so the inner thighs where the blades were strapped remained out of sight. As Ariss done her business, she moved the band around to the back of her leg, making it easier for what came next.

Pulling up her britches while dragging the tips of the blades, wedged between her fingers, she kept her hands behind her back as she sauntered towards the men. The closest backed away.

Fuckers didn't like to get close, did they?

"Hey." She smiled at the man who must have only been a few years out of boyhood. "What's your name?"

"Don't talk to her Jerris." The older man on her left spat on the ground.

"Now, now, we can play nice, can't we?" She edged closer, tilting her head, letting her red locks fall over her shoulder. Slid the hilt of one stiletto into the other hand, free hand reaching up and brushing her hair back, letting her hand slowly trail back along the flesh of her exposed shoulder.

She hated heavy armour. It hindered agility.

Ariss wet her lips, taking a small step closer. "You like what you see, don't you, *boy*?" She leaned forward, and the lad instinctively tilted his head around, listening. The old man growled as he took a step closer to them, moving to separate them.

But it was too late...

Ariss brought the blades out from behind her back as the old man reached for her, palming both, seeing the old man's eyes widen in the corner of her vision. She rolled her hands back, slowly turning the blades out the right way.

The killing way.

Ariss watched the light gleam along that dark metal as she drove the stiletto into the lad's exposed neck. She let go the hilt, knowing he'd keep it safe for her.

Still bringing her left hand up and around, spinning, putting her weight behind it, the tip piercing metal and sinking deep through the old man's chest-plate. The old man's eyes bulged, and he dribbled blood, but footsteps moved behind her now and she had to move. Ariss pulled his blade from its scabbard, backed off in time to make both men falter. They slowly goaded her against the bushes. The blonde man came at her, screaming, blade flashing. Ariss parried his sword, just managed in moving her head to dodge the punch, and stepped in close, hissing as she drove the heel of her palm into his windpipe. He gagged as he dropped his sword, face turning scarlet. Ariss hacked her blade into the back of his neck without looking, eyes locked onto the last man.

"You like to watch, don't you, boy?" She let her sword fall with the dead man. "How was that?" The man turned and ran. Ariss hurried over to one of the bodies, pulled out one of the Old Lovers, took aim... the blade hissed through the air, hitting just wide of the mark, but bringing the fleeing man down, who went tumbling into some weeds.

She pulled the other blade from the man's neck, taking her time.

"Fuh-Fucking traitor." The man watched as she stopped beside him, lying on his side, the stiletto after piercing though just wide of his heart. "Wuh... Why?"

"You like to watch." Ariss shrugged. "I like to live." She brought the blade down, silencing him.

She cleaned the blades. Maddox's gifts. He'd given them to her on passing her training. Their families had been close-knit allies. Her family, a long withering blood-line that held high hopes for Ariss Vanderholm, promising warrior who'd reclaim the glory days once held by Mount Lena.

She laughed at that, looking around at her sad situation. The woman who'd once had the loyalty of thousands of warriors, now brought to pissing in front of brutes like an animal. It was better than being dead, though. Much better. Just ask them.

Ariss headed back towards camp. After five minutes she approached the clearing, nestled against an old farmhouse. They'd gotten a fire going, one soldier turning the rabbit cooking over it, another chopping up vegetables, putting them in a pot of boiling water. One of them was missing, but the fourth lay near the fire, smoking a pipe. He was furthest away, but the only one facing her direction, so he noticed her first approaching the fire and dropped his pipe. Ariss thrust the stiletto at him, but the distance was great and it missed the mark, catching the shoulder instead of his throat. It put him back down though, and that was something.

She ran, taking advantage of their surprise, and grabbed the man chopping vegetables by the hair, forcing his face down into the pot boiling water. The pipe smoker was cursing, trying to pull the blade out of his shoulder, and the man turning the rabbit stood up and pulled out his sword. She let go the man's head as the sword came rushing at her. Ariss backed off, also keeping the man with the stiletto in his shoulder in view, who was up on his knees now.

Ariss just caught the sword as it came at her again. The next attack caught her blade and ripped it from her hand, and she looked around for something else to use. But he gave her no time, coming at her, barely missing, and as she backed off more, tripped on something where it shouldn't have been and tumbled over. Ariss tried to roll out of the way but the bastard drove his boot into her ribs, doubling her up, rolling her over. Ariss spat drool, her eyes stinging with tears, as he kicked her again.

"Fucking... bitch," the man panted, as he kicked her again. "Errin, you alright?"

"I've a blade in me arm, so no. Bitch got it jammed in tight."

"My face! I can't see, Luke. I can't see!"

"Just sit back down. I'll take care of that in a second." Luke pointed a finger at her. "Kye said not to harm you. But I think he can go fuck himself." He went to the boiling pot, used a cloth to pick it up. "I'm gonna make you pay for that little stunt."

The man came closer, smiling as he lifted the boiling pot.

Whoomp!

An arrow slammed into his chest. He fumbled the pot, before dropping it and hitting the ground.

"What in the—" began the man with the blade in his shoulder, but Ariss never heard what he was going to say next, as another arrow came whistling out of the trees, hitting him square in the face and spinning him round.

"What was that?" croaked the blinded soldier. "Luke? Errin?"

Footsteps approached, and Ariss built up the courage to glance over the top of the packs. An old woman came hobbling out of the trees, using a bow as a crutch. She made her way around the pile of packs, stopping just shy of Ariss' reach.

"Are you hurt?" rasped the old woman.

"A bit." Ariss wiped the blood from her lips. "I had the situation under control."

"I might be near-blind, but I can see that's a lie."

Ariss shook her head. "Who *are* you?"

"Just a wanderer, in search for beautiful and exotic merchandise."

"A trader? Hah! You shoot well for a merchant."

"Never said I was a trader, girl, did I? Never said I *sell* any of the things I find." She lifted the bow and slipped an arrow from her sleeve—a small thing two hands length with golden thread wrapped around the shaft. She fitted the arrow, pulled back the string and let fly. It caught the blinded man in the heart.

"That's the last of them, then," smiled the old woman.

"There's four more. Should be getting back soon."

"Then we'd best get moving."

"We?"

"You hardly expect me to leave an injured traveller here, alone and unprotected?"

"Why are you helping me?"

The old woman inhaled deeply and nodded. "This place stinks of death. But not of yours. Your destiny is not to die today, Ariss."

"How..."

"No more questions. Get your things and meet me over beyond that treeline." The woman went to walk away, but then turned back. "And I hope you can tell a good story."

Chapter 15: Bubbling Over

Whoever said it's what's inside that counts never had the misfortune to meet Pretty Boy. An uglier, cold-hearted little-shit there never was. Leek had grown up in poverty, with famine and crime never further than your own shadow. He made a living through thievery with his other siblings—albeit they were unrelated, fostered by a money-grubbing woman who half-starved them so she could drink sherry by the bucketful—but still, it wasn't the worst childhood imaginable. He'd even had cake once.

But Pretty Boy held sway over the children in Sunnyside Slums with an iron purse. Any that weren't already in one of a score of gangs, that is. The thieves Leek had fallen in league with went by the name of *Slaters* as they made the abandoned slate-factory and warehouse their stronghold. Pretty-Boy made all underlings pay tribute, marking out promising victims for his favourable urchins. You could pick out people new to the slums easily, as they didn't blend in with the shit and dirt. The marks ambled in groups, glancing at the food stalls much too eagerly, not baring their teeth at any stranger's approach too fast or hand too near to person.

Leek had quickly grown accustomed to life here, getting reacquainted to the paranoid politics and blatant backstabbing that only being in a gang can provide. Pretty Boy shared power with two other men. Jarratt was a fat, greasy man of middle-age who had a handful of yellow teeth and rheumy eyes, which he leered at everyone with. Wax was a skinny, tall man of a corpse-like complexion and had no eyebrows or hair on his person that Leek could see, when he was unfortunate enough to be in close proximity with the man.

The leaders of the Slaters had foamed from the mouth at the spoils Leek brought back to the safe house, purses containing mixed silver, copper and bronze coins, three silver chains and a flask of fire-water. Leek hadn't anytime to stow away the purses or even slip a few coins for himself, as he'd been out with two younger boys of the gang, whose job was to distract the marks or breach windows. After every lift his take had been closely reported.

His cut had been pathetic. But the leaders had been pleased with his tribute and promised that he wouldn't be burdened with the younger boys of the gang all of the time. He'd be doing this for years before saving enough to get into the industrial sector, and he could only guess what life would be like in there.

On a rare day where he wasn't accompanied, he slipped a copper coin in behind a loose brick he found above a shed in an alleyway, where he would keep his escape fund. He didn't like wandering about the back alleys of the district alone. Many stories told around the fire at night made these dark surroundings ominous to say the least. About strange women who would snatch you out of the street and peel the flesh from your bones. Or rumours of the other gangs who would sneak into the territory and leave your corpse strung up near the safe house, as there were forever squabbles ongoing between them.

The kids also told rumours about the industrial sector and the rest of the city at night around the fire. Many men seemed to fall into the vats of molten metal, or be found with their skin completely burnt off, having been locked into one of the many steam outlets. These made Leek wonder if going to the industrial sector seemed such a good idea.

The older thieves spoke of a man who roamed the shadows, slaying all who crossed his path. The Black Shadow, they called him. Nothing but stories of course, but even the most inflated and senseless stories had to start somewhere, with some morsel of truth to them.

Leek reached the gang stronghold at dusk and entered the warehouse. Inside he dropped the purse on the table. Jarrat curled a feathery eyebrow, swished the few strands of wiry grey hair aside and turned his head sideways, picking up the purse. Dropping it, he nodded.

"Ah, so my ears don't deceive me." He picked it up, sniffed it. "Copper, and such a light load."

Wax emerged from the dark corner with his hands held behind his back. "I had high hopes for you, Kellick."

"It's just one bad day. You can't steal gold from a barrel of shit." Leek leaned down, picked up the purse and slipped the coins out. "If you don't want them...?"

Jarrat's face twitched. "N-No, we'll take them." He held out his crooked fingers, and Leek dropped the coins onto them, tossing the purse onto the table.

Wax walked over, taking three of the coins and slipping them into his pocket. "You won't be getting a cut from such a small take, boy. Best find us a better take tomorrow or not come back at all."

"I know." Leek turned to leave, and Pretty Boy entered through the door, followed by a large shadow of a man. It took Leek a moment to realize why he seemed so familiar.

"Paste?" Leek felt his insides churn with horror. The large lump of a lad from Gurth's prison squinted through the darkness, and then his eyes lit up.

"Leek!"

Pretty Boy looked from one to the other. "I take it you know each other?"

Paste scratched his head, his eyes widening. "He, ah, yeah we came to Mala together, right Leek?"

Leek winced.

"Leek?" Pretty Boy closed the door behind Paste, leaning against it. "I thought your name was Kellick?"

Paste looked down at his feet and blushed.

Leek nodded. "Just a nickname. One that I'm not much fond of."

Paste smiled and shrugged his wide shoulders. "Sorry."

"Since you both seem to know each other so well, Fingers can show you around in the morning. Can't you, Fingers? Or Leek, or whatever the fuck your name is?"

Leek smirked. "Either's fine, once you pay me my cut." Pretty Boy laughed at that. "And sure, I can do with the challenge."

"Here," Wax slid Pretty Boy his cut of the three copper coins across the table. "Your new prodigy only brought us three coppers each."

"This won't do, Kellick. Bring us more tomorrow." Pretty Boy had lost his charming tone of voice. "I have high hopes for you. Don't let me down."

"Yeah, yeah, Wax already told me. Can I go now?" Leek left the room and went down to the basement, where the cots were. A few members of the gang were sat around the fire, sharing a flask of what he presumed was fire-water. Leek nodded to them as he entered and sat by the fire, accepting the flask of watered-down spirits. The one with the squint was talking.

"I'm gonna get into the industrial sector tonight. Heard they got iron ingots crated up in Farrah's warehouse. Be a nice chunk of change if we got one o' those crates back."

The fat one with the missing front tooth pointed the chicken leg he'd been chewing on at the squinter. "You best not even think of thieving at night, Ainsley, or ol' Black Shadow will get ye. Not hear about the Maskers strung up on the wall? That bastard's an artist!"

The squinter laughed and looked at Leek. "Don't mind him, there's no such thing. The Black Shadow is only a story to scare cutpurses from going into the upper sectors. I wouldn't be surprised if the ministry made him up."

The younger boy at the fireside sat up eagerly. "I saw him!"

The fat one scoffed. "You saw the Black Shadow? Bollocks."

"I did a few months ago. It was down by the docks. Four Maskers got their throats slit in an alleyway. Crowd blocked up the alley so much I couldn't get in t'ave a look. But I saw someone up on the roof, black as a storm cloud at night. It watched the crowd for a moment, still as a dead root in winter it was. I could feel the cold off 'im from down in the street." The boy shuddered.

"You're full of shite, Allen."

The boy crossed his heart slapped a palm against his forehead. "Swear it on me life."

Leek nodded his thanks as he passed back the flask and nodded to Paste, who was still stood in the doorway. "This here's Paste, he's one of us." The lads nodded to Paste.

"It's unlike the bosses to bring two new fellas into the gang so soon."

Leek smiled. "Well, if you boys weren't so shit at stealing maybe they wouldn't have to?" Leek left them laughing by the fire as he showed Paste to the cots, a six-tiered scattering of bunkbeds. The one in the corner where Leek slept was empty, and they sat down on the bottom bunk. Leek looked at Paste. "So, what happened? How'd you get here?"

"Escaped, most of the prisoners did. Gurth caught a few of us, but most got out. I made it for a while with a few of the others, but they got caught yesterday. More than likely back at the prison by now. I met Pretty Boy in the industrial sector's sewers and he offered me a place to stay."

"You know about Kellick?"

"Yeah. Sad, I liked Kellick."

"Me too."

"What about that girl you were always talking to? Marrow?"

Leek paused as he remembered that night. It was still painful. "Merron. Gurth murdered her."

"Bastard."

"There we can agree." Leek stood up. "Get some sleep. Tomorrow, we need to find some serious coin. Or else we're back out on the street. On our own."

"They wouldn't do that, would they?"

"We're on our own now. But we can trust each other, can't we?"

Paste nodded. "Of course."

The next day Leek woke early and had two bowls of porridge for him and Paste readied by the time the big lad got himself out of bed. Paste gratefully accepted the bowl from Leek and they ate as another of the gang got a fire going.

"So, what's the plan?" muttered Paste.

"Not much. Head to the upper gate and hide about. Hopefully we'll catch some fool leaving the city with a dangling purse. Merchants are often guarded but you never know. And there's always the docks, which are slim-pickings usually but we might get lucky and find a drunken sailor."

"If I could get into the industrial sector, I could find work in a blacksmith?" Paste finished his food first and set the bowl down on a table. "I used to be apprenticed."

Leek shrugged. "Maybe later, but for now we need to make the leaders of the gang happy. Ten silver coins should set us straight with them over the next couple days."

Paste blew out his cheeks. "Be a hard find in Sunnyside, that."

Leek stood. "Well, we won't find it down here. Come on, we'd best get going."

They left the gang stronghold and weaved through the narrow laneways, making their way towards the upper gate. This time of the morning there were always drunken stragglers lingering around, and these they avoided with a wide berth. After about twenty minutes they came to the thoroughfare and watched the foot-traffic from the shadows. Leek got comfortable sitting on an empty barrel and began cleaning his fingernails with a jagged scrap of iron while waiting for a mark.

He hadn't been chewing on them recently. The job of being a thief wasn't exactly what he wanted to be doing, but it took his mind off larger worries. Like how was going to get him and Paste out of there. He couldn't abandon Paste, even if an opportunity to escape arose. He hadn't liked him at the start, back in Gurth's prison, but after everything that happened since, Paste seemed like his only friend.

How sad was that?

But then, Leek had always been loyal. Even after all of the torment and bullying he'd experienced from his foster-siblings, he'd never dreamed of running away or betraying them to a town-watch—even though he'd spent many a night in a cell for his stubbornness. He'd taken his mother back at the blink of an eye when he'd found her in their home, alone after burying the last of her fosterlings, all dead from the plague.

"Deep thoughts?" said Paste, looking at him from a dark doorway.

"Just thinking of how fucked we are if we don't bring back some coin tonight."

"We could always ask Gurth nicely to let us back in."

"Heh, that would be something. It'd almost be worth the beating to just see his face."

After an hour of no promising marks, Leek took a copper coin out from his stocking and tossed it over to Paste. "Fancy getting us some food while we're waiting? I'll keep watch."

Paste nodded. "Anything particular?"

"Something hot and sweet."

Paste left the alleyway and the minutes stretched by as Leek watched more people flood in and out of the gate. All of the money-making and anything worth stealing was over that wall.

Trying to find money in this shithole was like trying to fish for gold nuggets in an old boot. An old, smelly, mould-ridden boot that could snap down on your wrist and swallow you whole.

Leek froze as he noticed a figure sweep out of the gate. Wax strode quickly in and out of view and Leek scrambled up, peeking around the corner of the alley. He saw the skeletal man walking along the thoroughfare, his tattered robe trailing behind him. A boy was walking beside him, hands bound and head tilted forwards. Leek left the alleyway and followed, keeping to the edge of the road in case Wax looked back and he had to dive out of view.

He didn't know why he was following him, except for the fact that he'd never seen the man outside of the gang hideout, or not hidden half in shadow. Saying that the man gave him the creeps was like saying the far north could give you frostbite.

Wax seemed to be in deep thought as he paid little to no heed of his surroundings or the boy walking alongside him. It showed how little of the street-life the man had ever endured, as any two-bit urchin knew to take your eye off your surroundings was to invite a cut throat and a slashed purse.

They left the thoroughfare at the crossroads near the city gate, crowds filled the path, and Leek only just managed in keeping the tall man's bald head in view as they headed down towards the docks and Sunnyside. Outside a fortified building, a carriage rumbled out of an archway between the safe house and a tavern next to it. The driver was a Masker, his eyes quickly scanning the street and settling on Wax. Leek crept along the edge of the road, mostly concealed behind a stack of flour bags. He watched as another masked guard hopped down off of the back of the carriage and knocked on its door. Its window slid open halfway and an old man's face appeared.

Leek recognised it, but from where he couldn't remember. The old man smiled and looked from the boy to Wax and nodded, then held out a large purse, which Wax quickly took and slipped it beneath his cloak. Wax pushed the boy forwards as the old man opened the carriage door, and then forced him in.

The carriage door closed, window shut and Wax turned and walked away. Leek slipped into a side street beside the bakery, letting Wax pass. As Leek looked around the corner, he saw the carriage rattling down towards the docks, the guard sat on the back seat now holding a loaded crossbow.

Leek's fists clenched as he looked back and watched Wax strolling along the street, as if he hadn't a care in the world, and hadn't just sold a person into gods knows what kind of torture. But Leek would find out what was going on. He would put a stop to what Wax was doing, even if he had to...

Had to...

Could he do it?

He shook with anger, but there was still that doubt inside of him. He'd never been a killer. But innocent lives were at stake. The lives of young children that he could protect. And he wanted to help, didn't he? Wanted to make a difference.

How many times had he wished someone had protected him when he was younger?

And now there was something he could do.

Now there was someone to bring to justice...

Chapter 16: Out of Body Experiences and Truly Frightening Events

The metal shackles chafed her skin. Breathing through the canvas was a task on its own, having dampened and now clung to her mouth. Birdie had no idea how long she'd been here, or where *here* was for that matter. More than likely the inside of a cell, due to the stench. There was a flickering light visible through the canvas, a torch perhaps. The questions flooded through her mind, again and again.

Who'd taken her?

What did they want?

What were they going to do to her?

How truly fucked was she?

That second last question kept popping up with answers she couldn't help but worry over. She couldn't understand it. Her shaved hair had passed her off for a boy, and the charm had made anyone fall for the ploy. Or had she been naive? Why had she trusted the old woman after all? She'd been a stranger. Had she really believed it'd been some sort of magic charm that would protect her? The men that night had known a *girl* had escaped from the outpost. Birdie hadn't thought that showing the chain would've got her in trouble so quick, at least not until reaching one of the islands, and perhaps being whisked away by her uncle before danger could claw its way around her.

Who am I fooling? They know it's me. I should have known better than to come here. I'm just a fool...

There was the sound of a door opening and then footsteps.

"This is the boy who had the necklace?"

Boy?

A smidge of relief welled in her chest and she fought it down. Now was no time for hope.

"Yes, master. We kept an eye out for a woman or girl bearing the Black crest, but we thought best to capture 'im."

"And my instructions were followed exactly as given?"

"Yes, master. Only one was left alive. All ties t'be traced back to the Masked Lodge."

"You did well."

"Thank you, master."

Footsteps approached, shadows moving in front of the torch.

"How thin you are, boy." A man's voice, deep and coarse. The cord was loosened and the bag pulled off. Birdie looked up into the dark face. One side was visible, covered in scars, the other hidden behind long, thick black hair. One pale green eye watched her, the other also hidden. "If you answer my questions truthfully, you'll have as much food as you can stomach. No harm will come to you if you are honest, I promise."

Her surroundings smelled worse now that the bag was off, dank, slimy and putrid. Water dripped down from the ceiling, covering most of the stone walls, scratch marks covered the stones, marks of past inhabitants.

"Look at me, boy." The man snapped his fingers. Birdie looked back at the scarred man, who'd knelt and was peering into her eyes. "I have no desire to hurt you, but I need to know how you came by these." He reached into his cloak and pulled out Bella and Ariss' necklaces. "Did you steal them? Tell me the truth. I'll know if you're lying."

Birdie shook her head. She tried to fight the fear, tried to remember some shred of advice from Bella, but the days spent in the safety of familiar woods seemed long, long ago. So Birdie forced down the fear as best she could and stared at the necklace, mind racing, clawing for some story to tell. But no great idea formed, just the same word over and over inside of her mind.

Shit-balls...

The scarred man shook his head, stood up and paced the tiny cell, avoiding the brown slime in the corner. "Right, I gave you a chance. Let's get it started then." He turned and watched as the dwarf shuffled towards her. "What's your name, boy?" the scarred man asked, but Birdie just stared back, her lips moving uselessly like a landed fish. No words came to mind.

What if she told him the truth and he cut her throat anyway?

The small man rushed in, much quicker than anticipated, and slapped her across the face. Birdie had little to no energy and was flung to the ground, the smell of damp and mouldy straw thick in her nose.

"I know you didn't kill him," growled the scarred man. "But you need to tell me how you came into possession of these necklaces? Was it on the road? Did you steal it, from a woman perhaps? Or a girl?"

"Please, they'll kill me!" Birdie touched her lip and saw it was burst, speckling drops of blood onto the straw.

The dwarf picked her up by the collar, shaking her, and Birdie felt the necklace given to her by the travelling woman snap.

"It was given to me by my aunt," she cried.

"Liar!" the scarred man slammed his fist against the wall.

"It's true! My aunt Bella gave it to me! Before she died, she told me to come here and find my uncle, Maddox Black. That's it, that's why I have it!"

The dwarf raised his fist, to punch her.

"Wait!" The scarred man grabbed the other and pushed him aside. He knelt down and lifted her chin, turning it this way and that. "Get me the torch!" The small man pulled it from its bracket and brought it over. "Birdie?" asked the scarred man, bringing the torch closer to her face. He touched the snapped necklace and frowned. "Enchanted..."

"Who are you?" Birdie mumbled, the feeling still coming back into her mouth.

"Get those chains off of her, now!" Once the shackles were opened the scarred man helped Birdie to her feet. "Leave us!"

"Yes, master." The door closed behind him.

"I thought you were dead." The man shook his head. "You've changed so much. And the charm was strong... Where did you get it?"

"Who are you?" Birdie had never laid eyes on this man before.

The man reached up, feeling his scarred face. "It's me, Birdie. Maddox. I know I look different from when we last met, many years ago." He pulled up his left sleeve, brandishing a tattoo on his wrist of a blackbird. "See?"

A buzzing sound filled her head then. She stood, swayed on weak legs and looked at him closely. "Uncle?" she heard herself say, before collapsing into his arms.

Birdie stood in the abyss, surrounded by an endless rift of nothingness. Time passed her by, and she tried to focus on her surroundings. There were footsteps, somewhere far away. Black rifts turned to grey swirls as they rushed by at speed, flying through the air. The wind blew through her wings.

Hold on. I don't have...

Looking behind her, there were two great black wings fluttering through the grey swirling rifts—she could fly, she could actually fly!

She flew past a towering torch, almost burning her wings. Maddox swept by her, striding into a room and laid Birdie onto a bed.

No!

Flying closer, she couldn't believe she was staring at herself.

Uncle?

Birdie called out to him. He stopped, glancing around the room momentarily, but then shook his head and picked up a small blue vial from the desk.

How thin and sickly looking I've gotten, no wonder I passed for a boy!

Maddox popped the lid of the vial open, pouring some into her mouth. He picked up a wet cloth and dampened her forehead. "Birdie, can you hear me?" His voice boomed through the room. "If only your mother could see you now, she would be proud. You've grown into a strong young-woman, Blackbird." He put his hand to her forehead. "I'm proud of you, too. No matter what happens, know that I am." Pulling the blanket up over her, he kissed her forehead. "Sleep well now. I've business to take care of."

Standing up, he put on a black mask and left the room. Birdie soared out after him before he locked the door. He gave a group of men instructions to wait by the door and not let anyone in.

"Yes, master," they spoke in unison. Maddox strode through dark, narrow passages, finally coming to a door. A masked man pulled open the locks and Maddox stepped out into the night. He took a left, turning down a narrow laneway, and then another, constantly avoiding detection and the light. Most of the houses were dark and streets empty, except for the odd patrolman.

Birdie had begun to feel dizzy. Her vision kept blurring and shaking. It felt like she was on a wave of water, constantly rolling this way and that. She followed Maddox through the maze-like streets and lanes, and just over there was the Bone-Portcullis, towering above the landscape, walls and buildings alike. Maddox stopped at the entrance to an alleyway. Two guards were at the far end, warming themselves beside a fire pit. They laughed and joked as Maddox crept up the lane, pressed against the wall. A door opened midway. He paused as a guard emerged from the doorway and stumbled past.

What is Maddox doing?

Maddox crept after the guard until they got around the corner, where he took out a knife. He grabbed the guard and held the knife to his neck, his other hand over the guard's mouth.

"D- Donth," the guard mumbled through Maddox's fingers.

"Shhh," Maddox whispered, as he took his hand away from the guard's mouth and held his left forearm in front of his face. A yellow glow appeared from Maddox's arm, where the blackbird tattoo was. The man's eyes widened and his body went slack.

"Where are the guards?" said Maddox.

"There are four in that 'ouse there I just come out of, master. Two are in the gate'ouse and three patrolling the wall. Twelve in the barracks, but they won't be expectin' to go on duty for hours yet, so will be off-guard."

"Anything I should know?"

"All 'eavily set, master. Pressure plates in the barracks by the door and the upper floor. The men in the 'ouse are drunk. 'Alf the men in the Barracks are off duty, could be asleep or in the mess room. Gate'ouse guards are alert though, armed to the teef."

Maddox slid his eyes up and looked right at where Birdie was hovering, making her draw back between two dark buildings.

"How many of them witnessed the person with the Black necklace?"

"Who? The boy, master? Only one's in dare actually seen 'im was Burke, Ashram and Tim. But they told us all well enough what 'e looked like. We's gonna 'ead down to the docks soon to see where the escort's 'as gone."

"Good, now, here's what I need you to do..."

Inside the barracks Maddox avoided the pressure plate, sending the guard he'd brainwashed to take care of any men upstairs in the sleeping quarters. Maddox crept through the armoury. Both daggers tightly gripped in his hands like old lovers as he kicked open the door. Inside the mess room three men sat around the hearth at one end, four were sharing a pipe around a table in the centre. The two men reading documents on a table seemed to be officers. They were closest, and big bastards.

All eyes were on Maddox, who smiled and spun his daggers. "Death beckons."

"What's the meaning of this? Who are—" the larger officer's questions were silenced as the dagger thudded into the man's forehead, making him fall back out of his chair, both legs flailing wildly. The other officer dumbly looked down at the corpse, fingers twitching over the documents, but Maddox was already on top of the table now and drove his boot into the man's jaw, sending him sprawling onto the floor.

Jumping down, Maddox pulled the dagger out of the officer's skull and took stance, watching as the soldiers readied their weapons to hand, but one fool by the fire had left his axe resting against the wall, and was sidling closer. Maddox rushed at him, kicking the axe as the man grabbed for it, blocking the man's punch with his wrist, catching the arm under his, driving the dagger through his heart with one quick thrust, before shouldering him aside, eager for the next man who rushed into the fray.

Two men came at him, not one. These bastards liked to play dirty, but old Maddox could oblige. He ducked the lunge to his head, side-stepped, feeling the air whisk by his scalp, shouldered the bastard into the other, making them shuffle together and topple against the wall. Two quick jabs with the old lovers, one into a lung, and the other into the side of a neck.

They slid against the wall, clasping their wounds. But Maddox was already turning.

He could hear the footsteps, could *feel* the intent of attack before he even saw it, could smell the fear in the room turn to anger as they inched in, cornering him. Maddox turned just in time to knock the sword away, which caught him in the shoulder, slicing through flesh. He reeled back, taking the man's weight as he grabbed out, and using it against him, tossing him into the fire headfirst. The flames were large, engulfing the man, filling Maddox's nose with the stench of burning hair.

Maddox was down for only a moment, but now crouched, slowing the men's attack just in time. Three men now stood before him, spaced out to take the best advantage they could.

"Get'im Derren!" the smallest squeaked.

"You fuckin' get'im!" the tallest shouted back.

"It's the Black Shadow..." the smallest looked sidelong at the other two. "Has t'be."

The stockiest of the three gripped his sword tighter. "I'll bloody carve you a new fu—"

His head was lobbed through the air as the sword sliced through his neck. The guard Maddox had claimed brought his weapon back up, ready to attack the next man, his face and arms covered in blood. With the two others now distracted, Maddox moved in, quickly finishing the first, and between them they had the last man down in a heartbeat.

After, he slapped the claimed guard on the shoulder. "Good work. Now, let's get the rest."

The old man clutched the door knob with his bloodied hand. Everything was blurred and he couldn't remember why he'd gone outside. Maybe to throw up, because he still felt pissed.

He stumbled through the door, closing out the morning cold behind him.

How had it got bright so fast?

The smell of smoke and stale ale greeted him inside, and the aroma drew fresh, horrific images of dead guards on the wall, the barracks strewn with bodies and burning.

Master had told him they were nearly finished. Down the smoky hall he passed, towards the laughter. Four men sat at the table. They glanced up from their cards as he entered, nudging each other.

"The old man no'able for it no more, eh?" one taunted him, making the rest laugh.

"Does old Harold need a walking stick?" roared another, and they clutched their bellies, tears streaming in their eyes. Then they noticed the blood covering him. The blood of their comrades.

Harold.

It was not his name anymore. These men once fought beside him, saved his life many times. But they were nothing now, nothing but enemies of the Master.

He picked up two handfuls of ash from the heap in front of the fire. He turned towards the men, who eyed each other with eyebrows raised, then broke into another fit of laughter.

"Compliments of Maddox Black," he hissed, and threw the ash into the further men's' faces. He pulled his sword free, slicing open the guard on his right's throat with one fluid movement.

The two blinded men jumped up, grunting as they blindly fumbled for their weapons.

The old man elbowed the man on his left into the nose, following through with the sword's pommel into the forehead, making him stumble back, trying to dodge the sword. It curved down, biting into his skull and tearing through until it hit the jawbone. The blade was wrenched from the old man's grip as the man fell. At the same moment, the man with his throat cut reached out for the old man, before dropping to his knees and hitting the table, spilling coins and cards everywhere.

Two of the red-eyed men now squinted at him as they unsheathed their weapons.

"What the bloody shit, Harold!" the one on the left shouted.

The other lifted his sword, about to make a charge. "I always knew you were a traitorous—" his curse was choked off from a black sharp point piercing out through each man's throat. They looked down in horror, dropping their weapons to the floor and clawing at the stream of blood spurting from the now gaping holes. Master's face came into focus as he pushed the two men's bodies to the ground.

"You've done well, but I can't leave any witnesses," said Master, before sticking his knife into the old man's chest.

The old man fell to the floor, smiling.

Chapter 17: Escape

"Down there, are you kidding me?" Birdie said to Maddox, looking down at the gaping hole in the middle of the floor of Maddox's office. That morning she'd awoken in Maddox's bed feeling refreshed. Maddox told her she'd slept for an entire day. After eating, Maddox got their things which he'd packed earlier.

He nodded at the hole. "We need to leave without being seen."

Birdie leaned over the hole and peered down. Wooden sticks had been beaten into the dirt, making a makeshift ladder which disappeared into blackness. Putting her foot on the first wrung, she tested her weight.

"It's safe. If it holds me, it will hold you." Maddox tied a rope onto one of the packs.

"When did you build it?"

"There's no time to explain. We need to get moving, please."

Birdie sighed and began climbing down the narrow tunnel. The smell of wet mud filled her nose as she clung onto the sticks. Maddox waited until she'd gotten to the bottom and lowered two packs with the rope, and then followed her down. The hatch was shut behind him, throwing the tunnel into total darkness. At the bottom, Maddox shuffled about noisily, emitting an odd curse, but then sparks appeared in front of her. As steel grinded on flint, the sparks caught alight to a torch he was holding. "Good, you take this pack and I'll get the heavy one. How do you feel?"

"I'm a bit dizzy and sore in places I'd not thought possible."

"Ah, that would be the elixir. You'll feel better once you get moving." Maddox shouldered the larger pack and began down the tunnel at a brisk pace.

"Moving where?" Birdie slung on her pack and ran after him.

"To the Sea of Circles, namely Mala, our ancestral home. You remember the stories?"

"Of course, majestic white spire, rich markets filled with beautiful, exotic people, as many stars in the night sky as sand on a beach. It's all a bunch of horse-shit if it's anything like what I've seen so far!"

He frowned back at her, face more shadow than not. "Inside of the cities it isn't so bad."

"But you made it sound so perfect! Were they all just lies? Stories for a little girl to wonder at?"

"Things have changed since then, Blackbird. Outside the world has always been random, unpredictable, and now I fear that poison has leaked into our land. Mala is on the brink of collapse. The Twelve were a necessary evil, you understand? The twelve ruling families each held power over one of the islands. There's always been betrayal, feuds with other family lines, but men like my father, *your* grandfather, held these cities together for hundreds of years. Perhaps it was out of fear and persecution, blackmail and downright assassination that our families held power, but the citizens had never been in danger from the Temple. We treated them fairly. The ministry is to blame for the mess we're in."

"Ministry?"

"The Ministry of Faces. Nefaro was responsible for the deaths of our family. He bullied his way to power, eliminating any threatening power holders in the city, mostly the Clerics who were stripped of all official status, and were made into underlings. They were once the political muscle of the Twelve Lines. Their job was to keep order in the Sea of Circles, and to oversee the army, but what they really did was undermine our family."

"And they control the cities?"

"They like to think they do. The ministry turned on the Twelve. There's only a few of us left alive, that I know of, but most still alive have relinquished their titles and forfeited their namesake."

Maddox stopped and rounded on Birdie, the two of them were now stood quite close in the narrow tunnel. "Understand that I never wanted any part of this. I never wanted what my father offered me. I had hopes of leaving this life and never coming back. But when they turned on our family, I had no choice but to rally against them and do what I had to."

"But how did you survive the attack, and Bella?"

"Now there's a good question. How *did* we survive?" Maddox turned and strode on. "I guess you should know all of it, but the truth of the matter is that I don't know exactly how we survived."

"What?"

"What I mean is I don't know *all* of it. I got a letter on the night the ministry stormed our spire, warning us of their intent. Most of the passages were already being blockaded, and in this letter it told us of a secret passage that would bypass the Maskers."

"Maskers?"

"The Masked Lodge. Nothing but vicious dogs who think they're more than they are. They're more mercenaries than soldiers. They're an over-bloated order of bandits created by Nefaro."

"And you fled that night, when the fighting began you left the city?" The air was oppressive, stale, and the quick pace was making the questions hard to voice. She panted along, stubborn as ever, curiosity getting the better of her.

Maddox stopped then and looked at her, his eyes seemed glassy, but the light in the tunnel was too poor to be sure. "That night something happened... Your mother had been pregnant with you. My father had been ashamed of it, a high-born pregnant out of wedlock. It was a stain on his inflated honour. As if he had any. He would keep her hidden away, you see, so no one could know and wonder who your father was. That's another mystery."

He put a hand on her shoulder.

"Your mother had only given birth days before the night the Maskers stormed the spire. She was struck by a wayward bolt and with her last breath she told me to save you. Well, I did. I got you out of the spire safely and we managed to slip out of the city. It was too risky to cross open land, so the stronghold was out of the question. We hid away in a cart and got passage through the port.

"Why didn't you ever come back to us? You left us alone."

"I had dealings in the other cities. And then the Eclipsi invaded, and the land grew too unpredictable to try to find you.

No, it was safer to wait and have the ability to secret you both away if you did happen to arrive at one of the Bone Portcullises. Don't think I didn't act, I sent word to my agents. I had dozens watching the outposts, waiting." They walked on, the tunnel seemed to be dipping downwards, the walls became narrower.

"Was one of them the guard in the eastern outpost? Who freed me?"

"Yes, he had blood in him that was akin to the Eclipsi. He'd been working with them for some time. After receiving the scroll from him, I knew that you were alive. I received one last scroll stating you'd set off through the passes, headed to the eastern Bone Portcullis and that he was trying to catch up."

They came to a round metal door covered in moss. Maddox grunted as he pulled open the thick iron latches and pushed it outward. "Been awhile since it's been used." They walked out into the sunlight beyond. Maddox shut the door behind them, and Birdie glanced at the stone wall they'd just come through.

She couldn't see any sign of a door. It was just a rock wall.

Maddox simply smiled at her.

The daylight seemed strange and invasive after the darkness of the tunnel. They stood on a beach with a fast-flowing river streaming past, spraying up over rapids and sharp rocks, winding down a slope and disappearing behind cliffs beyond. Birdie squinted up at the steep cliffs towering around them, jagged rock faces were lined with pillars and corroded columns, crumbling statues lay covered in moss. Seagulls soared through the mist that was falling from a waterfall further upriver.

"We're near the sea," shouted Maddox over the noise. "We just need to go downriver until we get out of these cliffs. At least we'll be hidden for now from prying eyes."

Birdie frowned, looking around the beach for a boat or raft but saw nothing except for some thorny brambles, and she was sure they didn't float too well. She pointed at the river. "And how do you expect we get down that? Look at those rocks! We'll have our heads caved in!"

"First lesson, Blackbird, always have a plan," and with that Maddox strode off towards the far end of the beach. She followed him, shaking her head as he began clawing the sand over his shoulder.

"What are you, some kind of pirate looking for his buried treasure?"

"Actually, now that you mention it, I was a pirate. Done some smuggling too, out of the Sun-Islands. It wasn't nearly as fun as you'd think, or as sunny."

"Liar, I wouldn't' believe you if you told me that the world was flat."

Maddox stood up, pulled down his collar and showed her a big white scar in the shape of a 'P' on his chest. He gave her a wink. "Some of my stories have some truth to them." He went back to digging, looking like some oversized mole throwing sand over his shoulder, until he hit something solid. "It's still here. Give me a hand get it out, would you?"

Birdie walked around him and gawped as she saw that there was wood sticking out from the ground. "What is it?"

"What do you mean, 'what'? What do you think it is? It's a damned boat, girl! Are you daft?"

Birdie helped him dig and scratch out the sand, until lying there on the embankment was a wooden boat with two oars. "How long has it been here? Would it still float?"

"Been here some years. Still looks in good shape though, eh? It's Dogwood from the Wildlands. Stuff never rots. Tough as old boots." Maddox gave it a kick for good measure.

It's not big, but it bloody beats swimming.

As the boat was pushed into the water, Maddox held it steady and ushered her to climb aboard. Maddox climbed on after her and sat on the other end, smiling as he picked up the oar. Birdie frowned at her oar as if it would bite her, but picked it up at Maddox's goading and they began floating downriver.

Maddox instructed her in what to do, roaring at her to stop her fiddling after she nearly ran them into a sharp rock. Water sprayed up over the sides and into her face. The cliffs rushed by, making her duck and dodge overhanging branches. As they bobbed up and down over the rapids and tilted around bends, Maddox guided the vessel safely through it all. Far above was an arched bridge where faint shouts were slightly audible over the tumultuous roar of water. Birdie thought she even saw a face looking out over the side of it, watching them float by.

They travelled in relative silence, besides the orders and curses escaping from Maddox, until the cliffs became further apart and the river slowed. Birdie was about to ask where they were when they turned a corner and the Bone Wall appeared, they were at the gate. It was just opening and a lone ship passed through. Maddox hurried them and they just made it through.

Once on the other side water opened out over the horizon. Birdie stood up and stared out at the sloping waves that rose and fell, crashing onto each other in a trance-inducing rhythm, nothing but every shade of blue and white for as far as the eye could see.

"Yeah, it sure is." Maddox slowed the boat. They both stared out over the sea in awe.

"I could never have imagined this much water. How far does it go?"

"The Sea of Circles stretches past the twelve islands, out towards the Sun Isles beyond, and to distant lands beyond, to the Western Kingdoms. But this little boat couldn't make it that far."

"You mean we're not safe?"

"As far as Mala, yes. But beyond that, no, we'd need a bigger ship. It would be dangerous, though, with a bigger ship, as any unpermitted boats in these waters would be destroyed without hesitation. If only you could see the size of the waves out in open sea, Blackbird. Why, there were nights I spent sitting sideways in my hammock, tossed this way and that over waves as big as those cliffs!"

"I feel a little dizzy. It's not like being in the woods at all."

"You'll grow your sea legs soon enough. You're my niece, after all. So, you miss the woods?" They picked up their oars and set to guiding the boat out to sea.

Birdie nodded. "I didn't realize how small of a world I'd been living in. I thought the woods would just be there forever. I used to dream of coming to Mala and seeing you, but not like how it happened."

"The world is a dangerous place, Blackbird. When you lose your home and all you've known, it clips your wings. I used to want to sail the seas and discover new lands. I got my wish, hah! But with blood on my hands and the weight of our family's vengeance on my shoulders."

Birdie tried to listen to him as he told her about places he'd been, but she was still dreaming of home. "What I'd give for a bowl of trailhead soup and Bella to be sitting with me beside the fire," she muttered.

Maddox seemed to be in his own world. He talked without looking at her, gazing out over the sea. "I'd never given it a second thought, to be honest, when I was doing it. Sailed for the biggest cutthroats and wanted to be just like them. Still that young fool I was, the same lad who batted away his father's wishes and instead preferred the sword instead of the book."

Birdie turned back to the cliffs. "I wonder if the cottage is still standing. It's probably just a pile of ashes by now, blown away in the wind. No trace of her left... the years we spent laughing and crying together, gone in an instant."

"My father was a hard man, but I couldn't see that he had the best intentions for us. That amount of power and responsibility scared me. I just wanted to travel. Money and women is what sounded good to me. I wanted to explore the world and he would hear none of it. 'You are just like your mother,' he would say. 'She was just as strong-headed and stubborn as you are!' Hah! That would always make me cringe, but what I'd give just to hear it one last time."

Birdie snapped out of her daydream and listened as Maddox spoke of his mother—Birdie's grandmother. Bella had never spoken of that part of her life.

Maddox wiped back his hair. "I guess that's why he was so hard on all of us. He had that extra weight on his shoulders after our mother died."

"How did she die?"

Maddox looked startled, as if he'd forgotten she was there. He cleared his throat and leaned forwards, hunching over the oar against the wind.

"Please, Bella only mentioned them once, and not much at that."

They rowed for a while in silence. Maddox had a frown set on his face, as if he regretted having said so much. Birdie had almost given up hope that he would speak.

"A fire," he muttered, so low she almost didn't hear it. "Not accidental, someone tried to burn us out, hid barrels of firewater and oil in the upper spire. There was a lot of hatred for the Twelve at that time. Father became distant, always holed up in his study. I'd been inquiring into passage to the Sun-Isles, was going to try my hand at exploring. What a fool, huh? Anyway, before I could escape, something happened. Your mother had begun to show her first signs of pregnancy."

Maddox had a big grin on his face, as Birdie had grabbed hold of the seat as a wave almost tossed her overboard.

"That gave me a reason to stay," he continued. "Your mother asked me to be there to watch over you because she'd little faith in our father at the time, and with good reason. I'd decided to secret you both out of the city once she'd given birth. The lands outside the Bone-Portcullises are no easy traveling for a woman with child. I'd never dreamed the clerics would turn on us so savagely. And as you know, when we tried to escape that night, they fatally wounded your mother. Her dying wish was to get you away from there. I got you out of the city and far away. And the rest you know." He cleared his throat. "Right, enough of that, you'll have me blubbering like a little girl before we get to where we're going. We need to pick up the pace."

They rowed in silence. Birdie ploughed the oar into the water, keeping pace and feeling the burn in her arms and shoulders. The land became paler as it shrunk away, until it grew smaller and further on the horizon, and all that remained of the world was the sea and the sky. Her back ached and the skin on her hands became red and swollen as she gripped onto the rough handle. The salt water stung into her wounds, but she stayed quiet, blessing her good fortune and thanking whatever gods that had answered her prayers for letting Maddox find her.

She was safe at long last, headed somewhere that might offer some reasonable means of safety. There would be no more running. Bella had been right. Even after all the things Birdie had seen on the road here, she knew that Bella had saved her life that night by sending her away.

Birdie looked at Maddox, who was expertly ploughing the oar through water while hunched over in a furry ball, looking like a giant beaver. She couldn't imagine the loss he'd experienced, the loss of his parents and all of his kin. Birdie hadn't known them before they died, so the loss was a simple emptiness. But for him...

All they had left in the world was each other.

Maddox must have sensed her looking, as he glanced over and caught her staring at him, and must have thought she was staring at his scars, because he reached up and felt them. "I suppose you were wondering of how I became so dashingly handsome?"

"No, I wasn't!"

"It's okay, not a long story. Just keep rowing. I was doing some work down south, just past the iron mines in Villach. It's just some little village near the southern boundary, full of inbreeds. But there was a greedy little goblin of a chief by the name of Marot. He'd hired a bunch of no-good bandits to clear out a neighbouring clan."

"I wasn't looking at your scars, uncle, honestly!"

"Oh, right then."

"But I'd like to hear about your story."

"Sure. Where was I?"

"Something about a greedy inbred?"

"Oh right, Marot, yes. He hired a bunch of savages for some bloody work."

"And you killed them?"

"No, Blackbird, I was in charge of the no good, bloodthirsty savages. Marot needed his trade routes to stay moving to the Twilight Temple, but his ore had all but dried up. Only recently had the rumour spread that some fool had found iron ore while digging out a foundation for a blacksmiths forge in a neighbouring clan's territory. Well, word got around, too much for their own good, because that greedy little mutt Marot began drooling from the mouth."

"What's the Twilight Temple like?"

"Only ever been around that land once, but it gave me enough shivers to last a lifetime. Bunch of cannibals and wild animals that live out there, no rules they understand except for a firm fist and a sharp sword. Don't ever go out that way, Blackbird."

She nodded. Maddox fixed her with a long stare to back up his point. Eventually he looked away and carried on with the story.

"Anyway, where was I? Oh yes, the village. Villach was on a neighbouring territory ruled by a weaker chief. Marot decided to wipe out the entire clan. We burned it all, slaughtered all. Then they mined all the iron and little Marot rolled in the gold. We had our share and were happy for a time.

"The best thing I ever did, Blackbird, was sending you away when I did. I've seen so many families torn apart, some by my own hands. It would make you wonder what the gods think of their creations, because the world outside of the Sea of Circles isn't any good."

He turned towards her. "You have to understand that I was filled with so much hatred back then. I couldn't get near the ministry. I wanted to tear down the Hall of Faces with my bare hands and bury them under it. I'd only ever gotten into the middle sectors. So instead, I turned my anger on anyone I could find. I'm not going to sit here and pretend to be a good man. I did some evil deeds back in my day. But I've tried to make some good out of it. Told Marot to go fuck himself, and my crew did this to me as a parting gift." He pointed to his face. "Before I fled from Marot's territory, once I'd healed a bit, I mean, I put as many of the bastards to the sword as I could. I'm sure many folks down there would still like to see me strung up."

Birdie leaned over and put her hand on his. "It doesn't matter uncle. You have the rest of your life to make up for what you did. You saved me from who knows what, and I'm forever grateful for that."

Maddox nodded and set his jaw. "Come on, we've been lagging. This trip will take us some time."

Birdie looked at her chaffed hands with worried eyes, but stayed silent. The boat felt like a tiny leaf in a great pond as it rose and fell through the waves. Birdie fixed her eye on the horizon as she rowed. She daydreamed about home and the smell of the woods.

Chapter 18: Into the Fire

Leaning over the bridge, Leek and Paste tried to blend in with the crowd of beggars and invalids surrounding them. It wasn't difficult, as they looked just as ragged as the next pauper. The guard-patrol stalked past and gave them no interest. They'd both rubbed soot over their faces, and their ragged cloaks stunk.

Paste looked back at Leek. "So, we don't leave the gang?"

"No, best keep our heads down. Show our faces every few days and try to hand over a few coins. We need to be able to get close to Wax."

Paste nodded, looking a bit glum. "Means we stay stealing."

"I've a stash of coins hidden nearby. I'll use it to drip feed the leaders for a while. Give us some time to come up with a plan."

"Easy." Paste cracked his knuckles. "We smash his fuckin' head in with a hammer." Paste thumped the side of the bridge with his fist. "Bam, it's easy!"

"When and where? What do we do with the body? Where do we go afterwards?" Leek shook his head. "It's not as easy as just taking him out. We need to be smart. No one can ever find the body."

"Burn him?"

"Where? Every inch of the city's too crowded. We try burn a body someone will smell or see it as soon as we spark a wick. No, we need to do better than that."

Paste shook his head. "Can't think of nothin' else."

Leek snapped his fingers. "Go down to the docks. Ask around about a boat, big enough for two or three people. Do it quietly, don't give anyone your name."

"I'm not thick."

Leek smiled. "I know that, but just do it."

"And you?"

Leek clapped the big guy on the shoulder. "I'm going to look around and see if I can get us into the industrial sector. If we can get in there after taking care of Wax, we'll be out of the gang's reach."

Paste nodded. "Sounds like a plan."

"Meet me around the *Foxhole* in about two hours."

They parted ways and Leek headed back towards the main thoroughfare, falling into the slow stream of foot-traffic and making his way up to the industrial sector's gate. At a side-street he left the crowd and after walking past a few shops turned into an alleyway. At its end he climbed onto a shed and found the loose brick on the wall. Pulling it out, Leek took the purse of coins from inside and hid it inside his cloak.

Back at the thoroughfare, he wandered about the area surrounding the industrial sector's wall. It had a score or more of warehouses. These were largely empty, and the guard-houses scattered throughout the area were scarcely manned. Leek searched through the area, slowly working up a plan in his mind, but seeing no opportunity to suit it.

Most of the two hours had passed and he'd circled the area three times, when he came to one of the warehouses, this with a handful of Maskers standing guard outside. The large door of the warehouse was pulled ajar and a cart waited in front of it. Shouting came from inside the warehouse, but guards gave it little heed. Two of the Maskers eyed Leek closely as he walked by, and he stopped at the corner, watching as three men appeared from the door and one of them gave the cart a kick.

"Robbery is what it is. I'm goin' down to the docks, where ye get decent coin for a day's work."

The complaining man stopped and turned around as a tall, stocky man followed them out. He had a long braid of red-hair, with burn marks covering his arms. He lifted a hand and held a purse in the palm of it. "You leave now and ye get nothin'."

"I don't care!" the man growled. "Four days we've been slaving for ye, with feck all to show for it. Keep the coin and shove it." The three men stormed off, leaving the man alone. He pocketed the purse and sighed as he looked at the guards.

"I don't s'pose any of you will help me get this order loaded?"

The five guards ignored him.

"Fuck." He kicked the cart, wiping his face, and then looked around.

Instead of shrinking into the shadows, Leek stepped forwards and let the man see him. He waved at Leek. "Fancy makin' honest coin, lad?"

"Sure," said Leek. "How much?"

"Two coppers a day, with food and ale as a bonus."

Leek walked over and leaned against the cart. "That purse looked a lot heavier than two coppers."

The man scowled. "Then ye may get your eyes checked. Two coppers, take it or leave it."

"Ten."

The man's eyes widened. "Hear this?" He spoke to the guards, who were ignoring the both of them. "I thought ye were here to stop me gettin' robbed?" He looked back at Leek. "Five, 'cos ye've got a bit of spine, lad." He held out his spade-sized hand.

Leek grabbed it. "Done. Five for the both of us."

"Ye little... Both of ye?" The man looked around. "There's only you."

"I've a friend, and he could carry twice as much as I could."

"I need this ore shifted now," growled the man. "You can't work now, ye can piss off."

"Twenty minutes, and I'll be back with help."

"Ten minutes, and not a second more. Yer not back and I'll shut the warehouse and find help in the industrial sector."

The man let go Leek's hand and Leek forced himself not to rub it, as the man's grip was vice-like. He turned and ran, but after a few steps the man called after him.

"What's yer name?"

Leek stopped and turned back. "Kellick."

"I'm Haakon. Be quick now, Leek, not waitin' for long."

Leek ran back through the street, along the thoroughfare and down the side-street to the *Foxhole*. Paste was sat on a barrel outside and watched as Leek came to a gasping stop.

"What's wrong, you in trouble?" Paste frowned back up the street as he hopped off the barrel and loosened his neck.

Leek shook his head. "W-huh... Work." Leek took in a deep breath. "Got... Got work, loading a cart. Will get us... Get us into the industrial sector."

"Yeah? Not bad. But we'll be watched. How we s'posed to slip off when we're bein' watched."

Leek waved the question away. "We'll worry... about that later. Build trust first. Haakon's giving us a pittance for labour... but... uhuh... we show him we're good help then we might find some way to exploit him."

Paste shrugged. "Better than nothin'."

"You get the boat sorted?"

"Ten coppers. Bastard wouldn't hear of loaning his boat for just one night. Said it's for a week or not at all."

"It'll be worth it if we stop any more children going missing."

Paste agreed.

"Come on," Leek said. "We need to get going. He won't wait around for long."

It took the best part of three hours getting the cart loaded with crates of ore. Haakon had picked up the first with ease, and Leek foolishly tried to carry one and had gotten a bruised foot for the trouble. But together he and Paste managed in getting their share of the cargo loaded onto the cart, and by the time the warehouse had been emptied and Haakon was shutting the door, they were both in a sweat. Haakon sat up front and reached under his seat, then tossed a skin to Paste. "Drink."

Paste took a long swallow and then passed it to Leek, who felt dizzy as the water trickled down his throat.

"You've a strong back there, lad. What's yer name?" Haakon asked Paste.

"You can call me Oxen, I suppose, since it's what I feel like."

"Aye, a good name for ye. Come on then, we'd best get these to the smelter."

Paste had a flash of excitement in the eyes. He looked at Haakon. "You're a blacksmith?"

"Aye. Where else does a bloody shipment of iron-ore belong?"

Paste looked at the man's scarred arms. "You're a smith? I knew it."

"'Course, now come on, ye've only earned half yer pay so far."

Leek and Paste sat up front beside Haakon and the guards escorted the cart along the thoroughfare and through the gate. Leek could sense Paste's excitement as the gate opened and the sight of the industrial sector greeted them, not to mention the smell. The thoroughfare was the same as before, with two wide separate roads leading in and out of the city. But here small cranes had been fitted every hundred strides or so, and after asking what these were for, Haakon told them it was to lift broken carts of spilled goods, as some cargo being loaded onto the back of the carts could weigh the same as a house.

The houses in this sector weren't any better than the last, but were at least made from a treated wood that wouldn't burn, Haakon told them. These houses were mostly blackened by the steady stream of black smoke that clung to the sector, and the vast vista of the city above them kept disappearing behind thick clouds of smog. Tall smokestacks of the smelting houses and factories wafted the worst of the smoke away from the people, but a steady supply drifted back down over the city, ensuring that a sight of blue sky from this sector was a rare-occurrence.

The incessant banging of hammers echoed through the streets like city bells. In this sector there were no vendors, no merchants—and more importantly—no gangs. The thoroughfare and network of streets and alleyways were constantly patrolled by the Masked Lodge. The guard houses here were four times larger than the ones in the previous sector. Gibbets hung outside the guard houses. Haakon told them that the people inside were thieves, caught trying to smuggle ingots or weapons out of the smiths or foundries. Some of these were eventually sent to the smelting houses, where the unfortunate workers didn't last long. Many were forced into the labour for past crimes, or others simply liked the high-risk pay.

Finally, the cart pulled into a street and stopped outside a warehouse. Adjoining it a foundry sat idle, its chimney not spurting smoke like others they'd seen. Paste had an odd expression on his face as Haakon opened the warehouse door and then drove the cart inside. Sentiment, perhaps? Longing?

They shifted the cargo off of the cart quicker than they'd loaded, Leek struggling to keep up with Paste's eager pace. Haakon laughed at Paste's determination as they finished and he showed them into the forge. Paste walked around, touching the various tools and equipment. The blacksmith took out three mugs and a small cask, pouring each of them ale to the brim and sliding their two mugs towards them. "Sit, you both deserve a drink."

Leek downed half his before Paste had even lifted his mug. He smiled at the smith. "Thanks, it's good ale."

"I know a man from the next sector who brews the stuff. Have an arrangement of sorts." He looked at Paste. "So, you like it?"

"Like it? I don't want to leave." Paste took a sip of his ale.

"You ever work in a smith's before?" asked Haakon.

Paste lifted the sleeves of his tunic and showed them both burn marks dotted around the skin. "Not many marks, as I didn't make many mistakes. I was the best apprentice my master ever had."

Haakon clapped his hands. "I knew it! Knew ye had the look about ye." He looked at Leek. "You?"

Leek shook his head. "Not my kind of work. I used to cook in a tavern." Haakon's eyebrows went up.

"Well, the gods are good!" The blacksmith held up a finger. "I needed someone to help out in my forge, and the gods provided." He held up a second finger. "I needed someone to cook, and the gods provided. You two could do worse than help out 'round here. Better than starving down in Sunnyside, so it is."

"I'd have to agree with you there," said Leek, finishing off the ale. "You really offering us a place? Why? You don't know us."

"I know what life's like in the shit and the dirt, lads. I crawled through that mess, worked my way out and never looked back." Haakon refilled Leek's mug, then Paste's as he finished his drink. "Let's just say I know the gods' will when it shows itself. I'm from Lubbock, y'see? We're awful superstitious folk out that way, but it's in me blood, and I can't turn a blind eye to it. So, the offer's on the table, if ye will."

Leek and Paste looked at each other. "We've some business to finish first, in Sunnyside. But we'd be glad to work here afterwards," said Leek. Paste nodded.

"Well, then it's done, and once ye finish whatever needs doin' ye'll have a place here." Haakon lifted his mug and they sealed the deal.

Leek had an idea. He sat up. "Would you trade our pay for goods?"

Haakon frowned. "Listen, I'll not ignore the will o' the Gods, but ye're fucked if you're takin' any of me tools."

Leek reached inside his cloak and withdrew a purse, then tossed it onto the table. "Silver coins, ten of them. And also our payment for today. That should cover the cost, and then some."

Haakon picked up the purse and opened it, checking the coins inside. The blacksmith looked at Leek. "What will ye be needin'?"

Chapter 19: Hidden Passages

Birdie wiped away the spittle and sat back after vomiting for the second time that morning. The rolling waves unsettled her stomach. She looked up at the island as they approached. Maddox had been right about it being out of place. The wall rose straight out of the sea, as perfectly smooth and steep as a cleaver's blade, stretching along the horizon on both sides. Behind the wall she could faintly make out the white spire and the upper parts of the city in the distance, but they were mostly hidden behind a mist that had arose the past couple of hours.

Last night Birdie had torn fabric from an old tunic in her pack and wrapped it around her blistering palms. She cursed boats, and oars. Especially oars. The wall was just ahead, not fifty strides.

"We're nearly there, keep going," said Maddox.

Birdie gripped the oar and rowed, her gaze fixed ahead, not letting him see her discomfort. "And where are we going, if we're not going to the port? I don't suppose this is some kind of magic boat that passes through solid walls?"

"Straight ahead does it!"

Birdie looked at the wall and back at Maddox. "You're joking, right?"

"I don't joke about sailing. Straight ahead, easy does it." He pointed at a part of the wall that looked exactly like the rest of it. "We're aiming for that part of the wall."

"But there's no way in, we'll crash and drown!"

"There's always risk when sailing."

"Don't joke about it, there's no way in."

"Have faith, Blackbird."

Bile bubbled in her guts with every painful heave of the grating oar. The waves rocked them roughly. Maddox reached down and flipped a wooden board open, revealing a brown lever inside, which he turned and it clicked loudly. The boat—now within crashing distance—spun around in a sickening lurch, almost capsizing them.

The wall was less than five strides away.

Birdie leaned forwards and puked for the third time that day. As she wiped away the spittle and focused on Maddox's stupid, grinning face, he laughed at her reaction. She couldn't hold the anger back. "Are you trying to kill us?"

Maddox leaned out, feeling the wall. "Don't take it personally. My father did it to me. Call it a tradition. Now, where... is... I was almost sure... ah, here it is!" Maddox shouldered his pack and cut a length of rope, then tied one end to the boat. He reached up and began tying it in a knot, anchoring the boat to the wall. "Get your pack on."

Birdie did. Maddox began tying the rope around her, under one leg, over her shoulder, then the other leg. He tied a knot, looped the rope in his hand and began doing the same to himself. Without looking back, he began pulling himself up, swinging slightly as he used sheer upper strength to hold his weight, then used his legs, finding unseen footholds to scale the wall.

"Follow me. Just keep reaching up with your hands and you'll feel the gaps. Don't worry about falling. We all do the first time."

"How encouraging. Who exactly are *we*?"

"Our family."

Birdie reached up and blindly felt around, and there it was. A slight gap was hidden from below, but downward grooves allowed for easy gripping, allowing her to slide her fingers into the wall. "We can't do this the whole way up, can we?"

"It gets easier. There are footholds out to the sides."

And there was.

Birdie followed Maddox, who patiently waited when she struggled to find a foothold. They were virtually impossible to see until you were above them. Up they climbed, the wind whipping at her cloak. Up, her chafing hands screaming in agony. Up, as the clouds thickened and the sea slowly began to disappear into thickening fog. And still they climbed.

A slight rain began to fall. She cursed the rain, and this wall. She even cursed Maddox silently, though she took it back after saying it. The moments dragged on. Her comfort zone was taken, smashed, burned and trampled. Her spine was drenched in sweat, arms and legs burning with pain.

Gods-be-damned, I hate this fucking wall.

Birdie had never minded heights, but when she would have to look down to ensure where the footholds were, the sea visible through fog was dauntingly far below. She looked away and tried to focus on Maddox. A strong gust of wind pulled at her and Birdie struggled to hold on. As the wind grew stronger, the clouds darkened. Seeing the swirling storm clouds, Maddox began to climb faster. Waves crashed against the wall, making it vibrate and moan as if alive. Birdie pressed against the wall to regain some morsel of strength, and flinched away when sounds came from within.

There are voices inside of the wall!

"Maddox?"

"Yes?"

"The wall, there's voices!"

"I know, spectacular, isn't it?" he laughed as looked down at her. "It's the same with the spire. Mind you, I can never make out what the damn things are saying."

"What exactly *is* it?"

"How should I know?" He gave her a sly grin. "I don't speak wall."

She shook her head. Imagining that people, or spirits at least, might be trapped in there somehow gave her goose bumps, and she didn't lean up against the wall again, no matter how much she wanted to.

"We're about halfway!" shouted Maddox, when an even stronger gust of wind took her by surprise.

She lost grip of the wall and fell, the world tumbled around in dizzying angles. The rope snapped taught, crushing the air from her lungs and jolting her like a kick from a horse. She would've vomited if there'd been anything in her stomach.

"Grab onto the ledge!" Maddox screamed.

Her eyes swam with tears and she tried to scream but all that escaped was a bubbly gasp.

"You need to turn around and find a hold to take the weight off your lungs. I can't do it from here! Push against the wall and grab onto a ledge to begin pulling yourself around! Quickly, before you lose consciousness!"

Birdie blindly searched along the wall, her fingertips grazed a handhold, but another strong gust blew her away, making her spin. After the wind died down Birdie again blindly searched for a handhold. Her fingertips threatened to snap as they found a hold and took on her weight, turning herself the right way around, letting her manage to suck in a lungful of air. It cleared her mind and more importantly vision, letting her easily look and find a foothold. As she pushed herself up with one leg she clung to the wall and let the dizziness pass, soaking up the precious air.

Maddox tugged on the rope. "Come on, it's going to get worse. We need to keep moving." Birdie cursed him as they climbed higher, and this time she didn't take it back. But Maddox had been right, of course, about the weather getting worse. The clouds above were black by the time she finally pulled herself over the edge at the top, and the deep grumbles of thunder growled their warnings. She told herself not to look back over the edge, but she couldn't help it.

Tall spiked waves broke against the wall with violent intent, looking for a crack or crevice to exploit but finding none. Birdie could only guess at the height they'd climbed. Five hundred men could easily stand one atop the other and still not reach the top. Maddox tapped her on the back and she glanced around and he was pointing away from the sea. She stood up and turned towards where he was pointing.

The city was surrounded by an enormous moat and vast, unkempt landscape. Grasslands here, forest there and mountains in the distance. But Mala itself rose above the landscape like a cake of stone and metal, layer upon layer of civilization, with a metallic pyramid like the dizzying cherry on top.

It was the Hall of Faces, she knew from the books she'd read, and the spire rose behind it, piercing through the clouds. Walls surrounded different sections of the city, thickening out as they descended.

"Look all you want, but we won't be going into Mala, not yet." Maddox pointed to the mountains in the distance. "*That's* where we're going."

"What's so important in the mountains?"

"Home, Blackbird. That's home."

They sat and rested for a while, then began their descent. Birdie descended first, much to her disapproval. Maddox was impressed when they reached the ground, as Birdie hadn't slipped. It'd been far easier as the gaps were now visible. At the bottom of the wall the ground was rocky and uneven. They made their way across rough, wild terrain, through thick vegetation that scratched at her face and arms. Beautifully coloured birds flapped by overhead. Massive support arches branched off from the island's surrounding wall, and in some places there were houses built onto the arches, quaint ramshackle huts, but only a handful of these had smoke trailing from the chimneys, the rest looked abandoned.

"How in the world did they get up there?"

"Pulleys bring you up so far in a carriage, just like the spire. The Arches are virtually empty these days, though."

They travelled without saying much, by evening leaving behind the tangled foliage for open grassland. Her arms and back still ached from the rowing and climbing, but it felt good to be on dry land. They stopped at a stream and freshened up. Birdie watched the silver flash of fish dart past and thought about her days spent fishing near the cottage. In another life. She soaked her hands and feet in the cool water, easing the throbbing pain.

"This land used to be tilled for industrial farming." Maddox was digging into the ground beside the nearby bridge. He'd cleared away a few bushes clogging up beneath it with his sword and now pulled up a long taper, wiping the dirt from its surface. "But that was centuries ago, back when the land was still cultivated by the ancients. They used humans to work the land and transport it. Used us to mine, chop trees, labour in the shipyards. It sounds like a bad deal, but there was no hunger, no famine, no disease, and no war." Maddox sighed.

"What happened to them?" Birdie picked a blade of grass and rolled it between her fingers, smelling the fresh scent.

Maddox shrugged. "No one knows. They left the Twelve in charge and vanished."

After eating some of Maddox's rations of dried meat and the roots he'd dug up, they crossed the bridge, and they followed it until they came to a paved square. Crumbling columns and statues bordered it, mostly choked with weeds and moss. Six roads led in different directions from the square, the largest towards the city. Birdie reached down and felt the stones worked into the ground and smiled a secret smile, thinking of her first time feeling paved road beneath her feet.

She wondered where Ariss was now, and hoped she'd found some way to escape the outpost.

They took one of the roads that veered away from the city, spanning across rolling hills, toward the mountain range. "Aren't you worried about being caught?" Birdie swatted away the flies trailing after them.

"Caught? I've been tormenting the powerful men of Mala whenever I could free myself of the major's responsibilities. Albeit it's been some time since I was here, but I know this island better than most."

"Why?"

"I wanted to keep the city on edge. Stir up as much trouble as I could and hope that the cracks in Nefaro's foundation began to show."

"Huh?"

"I paid contacts in the city to spread rumours. Killed a few of the officers in the Masked Lodge and left their bodies in the open for all to see. I spread the truth about Nefaro and his dark secrets."

"Secrets?"

"About murdering the leading family of the city by selling them out to the Twilight Temple? Or how about his web of blackmail, coercion and assassination his been knitting together these past sixteen years? And if that's not reason enough to want the old bastard dead, how about the hundreds of children who going missing every year?"

"No!" she gasped.

"He's been killing them for their blood since he took power."

"Their blood? Why?"

Maddox looked at her. "The children he takes aren't just normal children. They're relatives of the Twelve, children to those spared during the purge. Nefaro want's that power himself. Many have already disappeared, including some of their older relatives. It's in our blood, you see. He's tried to catch me, but I know Mala better than most."

"Then why run? Why leave the city behind if you could've stayed safe here?"

"It was filled with spies, both Nefaro's and his allies among the Twelve. We once had alliances, but even some of them rolled over for Nefaro, being promised more power. Fools thought they could handle the old man even if he tried to betray them.

"Don't underestimate him, Blackbird, ever. He's taken apart the houses of power piece by piece."

"What about the other cities? Does Nefaro control them? The books we had were outdated. Bella often read them to me, and I was fascinated with the stories, but I knew deep down she was worried about how things might be back in the Sea of Circles. Worried about what had happened to you."

"I wish I could have gone and got you both. There wasn't a day that went by that I didn't think of you and Bella."

"I know."

Silence passed for a few minutes.

"There's Breccia," began Maddox. "They call themselves a free city-state, but it's a viper's nest of thieves and pirates, ruled by the Hangman. Then there's Trask, a nice holiday destination, if you're type of holiday involves being enslaved by some witch or having your skin flayed off and bones sold by the cannibal gangs of Druids that govern it. They deal in slaves, don't ever go near Trask.

"There was an uprising in Stadarfell, the prison island, a few years back. But after Nefaro's lackeys had the revolt put down and impaled the revolt's leaders on the city gates it broke their resolve, and they haven't put a foot out of place since. Might be worth reaching out, but I haven't had the chance."

"Then there's Tore, City of Dreams. A harem where men of the sea while away their money and lives, many never seen again. It's ruled by the Red Bastard, also known as Lord Scarlett. The Isle of Bones is mostly a whaling island, though they do some navy work for Nefaro when the need arises. They're closely linked with Seandra, practically sister islands, and many of their inhabitants are closely related. What other cities... Ah yes, Dogesk, home to the Palace of War, where War Mongers are trained. Mount Lena, the Fortress." Maddox paused and cleared his throat. "Less said about that the better."

"Why?"

"It's not important. Ah, there's High Shoals, centre of culture and art. Ki Helm, island of mist and warrior monks. Finally, King City, ruled by the Powder King, who has fallen into insanity from silver dust."

Birdie's head ached with trying to picture the different cities. She rubbed her eyes and changed the subject. "How long is it until we get to where we're going?"

"A few days, give or take. Two if we keep a brisk pace. Shouldn't run into any problems out here. Not many people travel this far into the exterior, and any that *do* don't ask questions, if you catch my drift."

Maddox was right. They didn't see anyone, not even a footprint. By the second evening they came to the mountains, traveling up into one of many narrow passes, where they fought through more and more thorny bushes. At the end of the pass a small, decrepit looking wooden cottage leaned against the cliff.

Its roof sagged and door hung ajar, showing dirty, rough floorboards.

"Here we are." Maddox smiled.

"You can't be serious?"

"What? No, not that old thing." Maddox walked over to a stone arch. It looked like it'd been sculpted out of the mountain rock long ago, as the surface was smooth. "It's this, the portal." He stood beneath the arch and pulled up his sleeve, and then with a dagger sliced into the blackbird on his wrist.

"What are you doing?"

Maddox put his arm inside of a hollow in the archway. Birdie was about to speak, when an icy wind rushed through the pass. Clouds above the mountain were beginning to shift, being pulled and pushed apart, and the ground beneath her feet began to hum and grumble and rattle like a pot on the boil. The clouds encircled the mountain and the streams of vapour spiralled down and around, resembling a coiling serpent. It crept over the rock above the pass, then down further, covering the archway. As the vapour passed over the rock's surface, blue lights flashed deep inside the stone, sparkling and intensifying. The air between the arch and the wall glowed, solidifying into a wall of blue light.

"Give me your hand!" Maddox shouted.

She reached out and grabbed his hand, and they were sucked into the light. Birdie felt like her skin was bubbling from inside, and her eyes watered from the air rushing past. She struggled to keep grip of Maddox's hand, as streams of colour and sparkling light rushed past them at speed. Her lungs burned, crying for air, but she was afraid to breathe. Her nails dug into the flesh of Maddox's hand as the ground suddenly lurched beneath her feet, and Birdie found herself face down in dirt, still clinging onto his hand.

"You alright?" asked Maddox, crouching beside her.

"Peachy," she croaked.

"It gets easier." He helped her to her feet.

"It's fine, honestly, but I'm never doing that again."

Maddox smirked. "Your mother said the very same thing."

Birdie wiped the dirt from her clothes and looked around at the high cliffs surrounding them. They were still in the same mountain range, at least it looked the same. A path led up to an arching bridge spanning a chasm below. Short columns flanked the path, topped with dark orbs which emitted a faint blue light.

"We'd best get going. It'll get dark soon. This pass can be dangerous to walk at night."

Birdie thought the bridge was of the same material that the walls surrounding the island were made of, though she didn't put her ear to it to make sure. They crossed the bridge and followed a path carved into the side of the mountain. The path worked its way along the gulley below, a waist height metallic barrier lending little sense of safety to her stomach. Small, narrow bridges crossed back over the chasm, delving into the rock, or leading upwards. The barrier ended and the path was now fully enclosed by rock on both sides, as the path curved in towards the mountain. Torches flickered to life at their approach, but then extinguished after they'd passed.

After some ten minutes the path emerged back into daylight and they found themselves at a bridge. It led over a drop that would give vertigo to a mountain goat, and the bridge spanning it was only wide enough for five men abreast. They crossed the bridge and stopped outside a metal gate. High walls bordered the gate on both sides. It wasn't a plain straight metal bar type portcullis. Instead, the metal was like the Bone Portcullis, but worked in vine-like patterns that twisted and curled around one another, the gaps not large enough to fit your hand through. But it was what was beyond the gate that took Birdie's breath away.

The castle was short and stout, its roof shaped like a pyramid. Towers surrounded the castle, each topped with a dome of glass windows that sparkled in the light of the dipping sun. The entire stronghold clung to the side of the mountain like fungi to a tree, the mountain peak rising above it, capped in snow.

"It's beautiful," said Birdie.

Maddox put his hand on her shoulder and smiled. "Welcome home, Blackbird."

Chapter 20: Bullseye

Sir, still no sign of the girl or the woman. What are your further commands? I am eagerly awaiting your instructions. - Vines

Kye threw the parchment into the fire and gazed out across the heavily trodden landscape. The days had blurred past since he'd left the mountain passes. Resources were dwindling, and he hoped that the army would arrive soon. If the enemy army happened upon them now, they wouldn't' stand a chance.

Road wearied his men plodded on with no complaints. The enemy was slowly headed to the southern or western Bone-Portcullis, and Kye had sent scouts out, desperately trying to keep some kind of awareness to their location. With any luck their leader, this Felt, had underestimated the Bone Wall defences. It could all work out. If only that fool Markova hadn't taken most of the army in the wrong direction.

Kye wanted to be the one who defeated the Eclipsi and brought safety to the people. To march home victorious, parading through Mala showered by their love. To be a name for every citizen in the Sea of Circles to know and cheer for. And to do that, he had to take command.

The last thing he wanted was Markova taking all the glory and being named the hero of the Sea of Circles.

He stood up and walked back to the new steed he'd requested, his old one sizzling over the fire pit outside his tent. He mounted up and rode back towards camp, his thoughts turning to X. She'd promised him to send word after reaching the mainland port. The squad of soldiers watching her every move would keep her in line, left with strict instructions to slit her throat at the first sign of betrayal. But he'd expected a message from the squad leader by now.

X.

She was a mystery. Intriguing, dangerous. He'd tried to sway her to his bed for years but she'd never succumbed. The best agent he had, most definitely. But if she vanished again he'd stick her in a gibbet.

Inside his tent Kye pondered over the map table, following the network of main roads and minor, wondering where exactly the enemy would attack. Not to the east gate, surely, they'd know the Golden Circle army were skirting the mountains to the north and passing that way.

Kye didn't like the lack of contact between him and his agents. His streams of information had all but dried up. Not one message from the handful of sleepers he'd placed in the Eclipsi ranks. *Not one.* Someone inside of the ministry must be working against him. But who?

Even though the Quadra-Ministers hated him, he never imagined they'd leak information to the enemy just to undermine him.

"Sir, a raven just arrived," a voice called from outside.

"Enter!" Kye watched the soldier as he entered holding a metal vial in his hand. "It's about time." Kye took it and popped out the scroll. The soldier bowed and exited the tent.

The scroll hadn't been from one of his agents as he'd hoped. It was from a contact in Mala. One of the eastern Bone-Portcullis barracks had been burnt to the ground. The citizens were agitated, as Maddox Black was believed to be the culprit. Graffiti of a blackbird was found in an adjoining alleyway of the burnt-out barracks.

Not what he needed with so much anger and fear already festering within the populace, but manageable, surely.

The scroll also read that a sentry for the eastern portcullis had found bodies just outside a small deserted village. A necklace had been found wrapped around each man's throat, bearing the emblem of House Black.

Kye threw the scroll into the flames.

It seemed that X had chosen to side with the enemy.

It would be her undoing.

"When did he arrive?"

"Just moments ago, sir." The soldier bowed.

Kye pushed the soldier out of his way and looked for Vines in the arriving streams of cavalry. He found Vines about to leave camp. "Make sure you get them moving quickly. We need to make it to the hills south of the wall before dark and begin raising defences." Vines nodded.

Kye had been dreaming of this moment for days now, ever since Markova defied him and left him dangling up in the mountain passes like some prize turkey. He waited outside his tent and watched the general's approach. Riding a white war-horse at the front of group of officers, General Markova was the picture of martial perfection. Kye waited until they neared the command tent and lifted his hand. The row of men crouched behind the overturned tables stood up, lifting their crossbows and shouldering them. The general didn't notice what was happening until it was too late.

"Fire!" Kye brought his hand down.

The bolts whistled through the air. The general and his officers at the front pulled on their reins, trying to evade the shower of missiles, but their fate was sealed long ago.

Markova's eyes bulged as a bolt caught him in the eye and he was tossed back from his saddle. His boot got caught in the stirrup and his corpse dragged behind his horse, limp arms trailing. Other officers fell to the ground, dead or writhing.

"Reload!" Kye shouted, but the men were already sliding on fresh bolts. They aimed and waited.

The remaining officers watched in stricken horror as their leader was bounced and twisted along the muddy ground behind his valiant steed.

Kye fixed them with his silver smile. "Does anybody else want to question my authority?"

They left the officers' bodies beside the road for the passing army to see. Kye immediately stripped the remaining officers of their rank and sent them to fight in the front line of the army. He'd been tempted to string them up on a tree that he passed, but why waste the manpower? They'd die in the battle just the same as a noose, surely.

At noon he stopped to drink at a stream and watched the army pass. Their numbers now were some forty-five thousand. Some had died in the passes, but not nearly as much as from the heat of the desert and the long march north. Kye knew that the bulk of the army were untested recruits and had never fought in battle. But he had to make it work.

He couldn't fail.

It was three days of hard marching and little sleep before they came to the crossroads, and another six days marching to the hills south of the nearest Bone Portcullis. His scouts had done well and had skirted the enemy to the north. The Eclipsi were just picking through the last of the empty towns, hoarding what plunder had been abandoned.

The enemy's numbers were roughly estimated to be between sixty to eighty thousand. At a glance the scouts thought them lightly armed, more a rabble of wild tribes than a functioning army. Six to seven days to raise defences and ready his men. But who knew when they'd be spotted? If they were caught on open ground like they were now, tired and unprepared, it would be a bloodbath.

As they arrived at the southern hills, Kye could breathe a sigh of relief. He ordered a command tent to be set up on the top of each hill and they'd use signal flags to relay orders during battle. He sent a rider north to get supplies from the portcullis commander, whatever they could spare. Ten thousand of the refugee force were sent west, where they would harvest trees and another supporting five thousand men would cargo the logs back, using an assortment of means, as there were only so many carts. Rollers, horses, and teams of men would work night and day getting the logs back as fast as possible, while the remaining refugee force dug ditches, sharpened logs, placed palisade, and done the hundred other necessary duties in raising fortifications.

The new order of officers handpicked in the mountain passes were growing into their roles. He spent hours debating the best defence strategy for making the best of higher ground and what way to layout the army. In the evenings after the army would eat and rest for a short-period, he would drill them, using the signal flags and trumpeters to organise retreats, flanking manoeuvres. He pitched columns against columns in mock battles to see who held the strongest shield wall, and finally had a rough idea of which should go where.

By the fifth day he was exhausted, and let his second-in-command officer take some of his duties for the morning. He surveyed the area and was quite content with the progress for such little time. His elite force, the Golden Circle, hadn't needed as much drilling and they'd been set instead to sharpening weapons and checking equipment in their free time. The ditches had been dug and palisade set in layers around the hillsides, allowing him to place archers here, or replacements there.

He would switch the ranks at the front every few hours, using the retreat and switch tactic taught to him at the Palace of War. The palisades would siphon the enemy into his maze of sharpened logs where two forces on each side would charge, overpowering the enemy and forcing them back while cutting off a number of them. While this wouldn't work every time, the fact the fresh soldiers would easily overcome tired could easily be the determining factor for victory.

Kye would deploy the Golden Circle into groups of five hundred. These groups of the elite soldiers were placed in pivotal places, where they could halt routes, reinforce the weaker columns and such.

His main army by now were somewhat used to the mock battles and would know what to do when the time came. All that was left now was to wait and pray.

As he well knew, hope and courage are the only crutches a soldier can rely on.

He mustn't fail.

Nefaro depended on him.

The fate of Nefaro's empire hung in the balance.

Chapter 21: To the Depths

Night came sudden as a shutting coffin.

Wax appeared in the street, sauntering through the industrial sector's gate and along the thoroughfare. He once again was accompanied by a child whose hands were bound. Leek followed them from the dark rooftops, having to clamber down when having no more means of scaling onto the next building.

Now back on ground, he tried avoiding the patches of light emitting from the blue orbs on top of high columns. These lit up a large space surrounding them, but were few and far between and only situated on the outer rim of the thoroughfare, so weren't hard to skirt. Leek shadowed Wax easily, as he'd spent many nights with his fosterlings sneaking through dark alleyways of the towns they used to roam, bringing back plunder to their foster-mother. He'd always tried to copy the better sneaks in the family, and though he didn't live up to their skill, he at least could avoid detection.

Wax seemed to be headed in the same direction as last time, which was good, because his plan depended on it.

Coming to the crossroad, Wax took a right turn and followed the road towards the docks and the slums. Leek had to keep his wits about him, staying hidden in doorways as groups passed by. He waited as the familiar carriage clattered out of the archway between the warehouse and the adjoining building. The window slid open but it was far too dark tonight to see anyone inside. The twin moons were hidden behind thick clouds, and the streets which were gloomy during the day from the crowded tenements and overshadowing plumes of smog from the industrial sector were now inky black.

That suited him fine.

Leek heard voices but could only make Wax saying one thing before the window shut.

"Yes, Supreme, of course."

And then it clicked. He remembered the old man's face from the carriage. It had been the same man who had spoken to him in the Hall of Faces.

Nefaro. The man who ruled the city. It was him inside the carriage!

The ground rumbled as the carriage rolled by and Wax strolled past the mouth of the alleyway where Leek had crouched behind some crates. Wax walked by, robe trailing after him. Leek sneaked around the corner and after the man, until they came to the mouth of the next alleyway and Leek took a deep breath, making his voice as deep as he possible.

"You!" he growled, squaring his shoulders and trying to look bigger. "Don't move!"

Wax stopped, reached inside his cloak and slowly turned to face Leek. The man's cold eyes met Leek's. Serpent's eyes.

"Do you have any idea who I am?" his sharp teeth were revealed as his lips curled back into a grin. Wax slipped a curved knife from inside his robe and pointed the sharpened end at Leek. "Turn around and run. I'll give you five seconds. One..."

Leek didn't know what was taking Paste. He should've been here by now.

"Two."

"Just—just wait a minute!" Leek forgot to deepen his voice and it made Wax frown.

"Do I know you?"

Leek shook his head, balling his fists. He'd have to attack or run.

Where was Paste? He should've been here.

"I do know you..." Wax lifted his knife and his smile spread wider.

A noise from the alleyway, and Wax turned just in time for the maul to come down hard on his forehead. Paste hadn't put his full weight into it, but the force was enough and Wax's legs gave out beneath him. The man collapsed, the knife tumbling out of his grip. Leek picked it up as Paste went back into the alleyway and returned dragging a large wooden box.

"What took you?" hissed Leek.

"It's dark as a whore's breeches in those back alleys. The damn box got caught on something."

"Never mind. Help me with the body before someone sees us!"

Together they got Wax into the box and dragged it into the alleyway. Leek searched Wax and found the large purse hidden inside his cloak. Leek hid the purse beneath his own cloak as Paste locked the clasps on the box. They carried opposite ends, Leek grasping the iron handle bar and quickly breaking a sweat from the weight of the box.

Not to mention the fear of what would happen if somebody decided to inspect their cargo.

Paste had the heavier end of the box and didn't complain as they made their way through Sunnyside, having to switch back-and-forth between streets and alleyways to avoid loitering drunks or the like.

By the time they reached the docks Leek's arms and back burnt with pain. They'd had to stop several times, and Leek's forehead was covered with sweat. He was no good at manual labour. Picking pockets or the like was a breeze compared to this back-breaking torture.

Paste guided them to one of the further jetties, and a good thing too as it looked as two military ships were docked at the opposite end. The soldiers in golden armour hadn't paid the two street rats any interest as they'd passed.

Leek let out a sigh of relief when they'd set the box down inside their small boat and pushed off. The hardest part of their task had been accomplished. Now was the time for answers.

The shouting was muffled. They had lashed the box to the boat so Wax couldn't shake it, and the lingering fog hanging over the bay helped to hide their boat as they paddled further out. Ships of War prowled the waters surrounding the bay, but were easy to see from the scores of lights illuminating their deck and were quite a way off. The sea towers that circled the bay were even further out, and wouldn't cause them any trouble.

When they were far out enough, they took in the oars and Leek slid open the slat on the front of the box. Wax pressed his face up against the mesh, or Leek presumed so as he could hear the gasping man sucking in air. Paste slammed his fist against the gap.

"Who are you?" Wax asked.

Paste gave the box a hard slap. "We're asking the fuckin' questions!" The man fell silent.

"You're both dead. You've no idea who—"

"One more word and you go for a swim!" growled Leek. Wax quieted down.

"Why were you selling children to Nefaro?" Leek asked.

"Selling? No, not selling. I'm just the middle-man. Gurth sells the children out of the prison and I meet him to exchange goods."

"Don't lie to us!" shouted Leek, slamming his fist against the surface of the box. "One more lie and you go for a dip!"

"Fine! Nefaro needs me..."

"For?" asked Paste.

"To cleanse the blood. He drinks their blood."

"He does what?" Paste frowned at Leek.

"He needs their strength. I don't harm them, it's just Nefaro! Please, you have to believe me. It's between Nefaro and Gurth!"

"Let's throw this piece of shit into the water, Leek."

Wax stopped laughing. "Leek? I-I do know you. Gurth mentioned your name before... but that's not it. I know your voice."

"That's good, because it's the last thing you'll ever hear." Leek nodded to Paste. "Grab your end." They unlashed the box from the boat.

"Wait! You asked, I answered!"

Leek pulled his side back. "Tell me why Nefaro needs their blood?"

Wax pressed his face against the mesh, and Leek could just make out the light in his eyes.

"Our High Supreme isn't what he seems, boy. He's shepherded the people and made himself a slaughterhouse that runs by itself. He hungers for the power which once ruled, but can't grasp it, only it's shadow. And it haunts him, that blood that he cannot taste. That hunger that he cannot sate." Wax giggled.

"And you know this? How?" Paste looked pale and was holding his stomach.

"Because my people know the dark secrets of the city, and we serve a purpose. We do what needs to be done."

"What people?" Leek stood closer. "Who?"

Wax screamed then, a soul curdling shriek that made Leek stumble back, and Paste steadied Leek just in time to stop him falling overboard. Paste grabbed the slat on the wooden box and slammed it shut, muffling Wax's screams somewhat.

He turned back to Leek and wiped sweat from his brow. "That fucker isn't human."

Leek shook his head. "He's human. But he's not alive. Not in the way we are. Come on, grab your end. Let's put this piece of shit where he belongs."

And they did.

Wax's muffled screams sank deep into the depths of the bay of Mala.

Morning greeted them through the breaking clouds as they arrived at the warehouse beside the industrial sector's wall. Haakon was only arriving when they turned the corner and if the man suspected what they'd done with the box and chain, he made no mention of it. They silently set to loading the cargo and soon were rolling along into the industrial sector.

The forges and smelters never stopped in their work, but the streets of the sector were only beginning to wake. The lucky inhabitants who avoided the gangs and danger of the lower sector worked either night or day shifts, and the taverns were always crowded no matter the time.

In one of these taverns they soon found themselves after unloading their cargo. Haakon was happy they'd kept their word in returning and wanted to treat them. The three of them sat in a corner and huddled over their flagons of ale.

Haakon stared down into his drink. "Whatever happened last night's 'tween ye both, none o' my business. I just don't want the Maskers knocking down me door, is all. Do you both swear I won't have no trouble if I take ye on?"

Paste shook his head. "There's no trouble. We're done with Sunnyside. Isn't that right, L—Kellick?"

Haakon frowned at the slip up.

Leek looked from the blacksmith to Paste. "I'm done with Mala.," he said. "All of it. I'm done with the crowds and the stink and the shit. I want out." Leek pointed a finger at Paste. "But you should stay here, stay with Haakon. This is what you wanted, to work in a blacksmith."

"I'm not leaving you on your own!" Paste pointed at Leek and then himself. "We stick together."

"I'll just give ye both a minute." Haakon stood up and went to the privy.

"Paste, I know you mean well, but your place is here. You know it, I know it. You have an opportunity here. You can do what you always wanted. You're not gonna find that chance where I'm headed."

"And where's that?"

"That's the thing. I don't know. But away from here. Away from the noise and the crowds."

Paste looked down at his drink and clenched his hands. "Leek..."

"I've grown fond of you too, *Oxen*." He laughed and leaned forwards, clapping the big guy on the shoulder. "But it's for the best. I can look out for myself no matter where I end up. Don't worry about me."

Paste shook his head. "You're sure?"

"Sure as I've ever been." Leek touched his cloak, where Wax's purse was hidden beneath. "We've to split the take from the other thing though, first."

Paste held up a hand. "Look, I know you'll be fine no matter where you end up, but it's dangerous out there. The Eclipsi have invaded, I heard. And the plagues still kicking about. You'll need all the coin you can get your hands on. Passage to the mainland isn't cheap, I heard."

"I'm not going to the mainland." Leek finished his drink. "Tomorrow, I'm finding myself a ship bound for the Sun Isles." Leek smiled. "I'm going to somewhere sunny, that's not Sunnyside."

They woke that morning fairly head sore, and Haakon wasn't happy Leek was leaving but understood why. He gave Leek a plain but strong knife, nothing flashy that'd draw attention, and a sheathe to put it in, dried meat and his wages, along with a few extra coins. Leek and Paste slapped shoulders once more outside. After all, it wouldn't do to be seen hugging in this area. Just because there weren't gangs didn't mean you could look weak. Leek gave Paste one final nod and walked away without looking back.

He left the industrial sector, knowing full well that he couldn't get back in if he changed his mind without Haakon there. As the gate shut behind him, Leek felt relief and sadness well up like a ball of weight inside of him. Relief that he had enough coin to leave Mala, and that Paste was safe. Sadness that he was once again on his own.

Leek put one foot in front of the other and made his way for the docks.

"Are ye serious?" The man with the fishy smell laughed as he frowned at the coins held out in Leek's hand. He'd been arguing with a merchant just before, and by the way the crew regarded him, Leek guessed he was in charge. "Is that all you got?" the man said, so Leek added another silver.

"I can help out, on the ship." Leek glanced up at the ship about to make way.

The man looked at the coins once more, then at Leek. "Right, but if you get sick, your off. I don't have time to be mopping up some landlubber's lunch, got it?"

Leek nodded.

The man snatched the coins from Leek's hand and walked up the gangplank.

Leek slowly made his way along the board, eyeing the lapping green water pushing weeds onto the rocks below. He made it safely to the other side and jumped down onto the ship's deck. A burly sailor pulled the gangplank back on board and shouted instructions at the men, who tugged on ropes, then pulled down the massive, patched sails which billowed in the wind. Watching the ship begin to pull away from the dock, Leek leaned against the wooden railing.

He didn't know where he would end up precisely, but anywhere had to be better than here.

As the ship drew away from dock and slowly waded through the bay, a large, grey-bearded man with one-eye appeared from below deck. Leek froze as the man's icy gaze fell on him.

The man strode over to Leek. "And who the bloody hell are you?"

Leek frowned. "Kellick, sir. Here to work for passage."

"Call me captain, boy, and my bloody arse you are. What are you doing on my ship?"

"Your ship?" Leek pointed at the man he'd paid, who was now standing on the upper deck and looking at some charts, but glanced up and smiled. "He said this was his ship, paid him to come aboard."

The one-eyed man looked up to where Leek was pointing. "Damn it, Tarrant! How many times do I have to tell you to stop bringing strays onto my ship? One more time," he said, grabbing Leek by the scruff of the neck. "One more time and I'll find a new navigator, and you'll be off like this fool!"

Leek was thrown overboard and the water came rushing towards him. The cold water sucked him down, he kicked, but the damn knife and cloak were weighing him down. He tore at the straps, let the knife sink, then ripped the cloak off, snatching the purse from inside. Leek surfaced, awkwardly managed to pull off his boots with one hand to swim better and as he kicked water, he watched the faces leering down at him from above deck.

The laughing taunts slowly sailed further and further away into the distance.

Leek swam back to shore and hid the purse in his britches. Sailors laughed as he walked by, dripping wet, but he paid them little heed. He hid himself in an alleyway to gather his thoughts. Leek shivered with the cold as he slid the purse from his britches and opened the leather strap with trembling fingers, dimly remembering he'd checked it while blindingly drunk the night before, but unsure what was inside.

Warmth emitted from inside the purse, or seemed to, as about twenty gold coins twinkled inside beside a handful of green gems. Leek picked one gem up and twirled it around. This would get him back into the industrial sector. He could plan another way out of the city and resupply from Haakon's merchandise, or arrange passage on a ship that wouldn't cast him off like fishbait.

Then he remembered Haakon would be loading cargo right about now.

Leek pocketed the gem, shut the purse and hid it again in his waistband. He tried not to look in a hurry, and it was late-morning by the time he arrived at the warehouse. The familiar cart was outside, with four Maskers standing guard nearby. They watched him approach but made no move to stop him. As Leek approached unfamiliar voices were coming from inside the warehouse. An old man Leek had never seen before walked out of the open doorway, followed by three muscular men. They looked at Leek and the grins quickly faded.

"What you want, boy? Your kind should be down in Sunnyside. Best leave before the Maskers set on ye."

"Where's Haakon?" Leek asked.

"Not working the cart no more. Got his cargo of ore, didn't he?" The old man gave the three men a nod and they went back into the warehouse. "What's the matter?"

"I need to get inside the industrial sector."

"Hah! Good luck with that. Ye need a worker's writ, and something tells me ye not got it. Now go on, get on 'fore I set 'em on ye." He nodded to the Maskers, who were watching Leek closely now. He turned and left the area, and found himself back outside the *Foxhole*. Leek sneaked to his old hiding place, and before putting the purse behind the loose brick, Leek took out a few gold coins and one gem. He didn't know how he was getting inside the next sector but he wasn't walking around with a purse full of trouble.

Leek entered the tavern and paid for a room for the night, a hot meal and a bath, after stealthily sliding the coin to the fat barman. With a pocket full of silver, he sat beside the fire sipping a mug of ale inside one of the many private galleries and tried to figure out how he could get back to Paste. After the tavern had somewhat emptied, Leek called the innkeeper aside and asked him did he know of any way a person might find themselves inside the industrial sector.

The man frowned and shook his head, foxtails swinging. "No, there's certainly not!" He looked back at Leek as he walked to the bar, shaking his head again.

Leek walked over to the bar and slid his hand onto the surface. He moved his hand aside, letting the man see a green gem that caught the firelight and sparkled.

The man swallowed. "I could lose my license." He licked his lips.

Leek slid a gold coin beside the gem.

"The Maskers could hang me..."

Leek placed a gold coin on the other side of the gem and slid them closer to the man. "You'll get another two when you get me into the industrial sector." The barman looked around at the empty tavern and nodded, snatching them from the counter.

"I know a way. But it's dangerous. Get some sleep and I'll wake you before dawn."

Before dawn Leek went to the alleyway with the loose brick in it and got his purse. He went back to the tavern where the innkeeper was waiting for him with a satchel of food. He also supplied Leek with an old, thick cloak and knee-high leather boots.

"You'll need them," he told Leek at seeing his questioning look.

The innkeeper brought him out the back of the tavern and locked the door. They made their way through the familiar maze of alleyways and lanes. He came to a squat hut made of solid oak that was nestled between tenements at the end of a long alleyway. The man checked they were alone, before pulling out a key on a chain from beneath his shirt. He unlocked the door of the hut, and they entered.

Inside was dark. The man lit a torch and Leek then noticed that built into the floor was a grate of thick iron bars. The man took out another key on the same chain and unlocked the grate, letting Leek go down first. At the bottom a roughly carved tunnel brought them to the sewers, and Leek avoided the mess by using the raised curbs to either side. The air was dank and icy, and Leek wrapped himself tight in the cloak. They travelled for a few minutes in silence, until they came to where the sewer opened up to several different tunnels. The man walked over to the nearest wall and pointed.

"Stay here until you've this map memorized. I take no responsibility for your life from here on. I leave you the torch and my blessings, and the best of luck t'ye, young sir." After Leek slipped him the last two coins the barman walked back the way they'd came.

Leek spent an hour memorizing the map to the best of his ability, having to light another torch from inside the pack, and when he was confident he knew the way, Leek followed the correct tunnel and hoped the gods were smiling on him.

The last torch died, leaving him in darkness. He must have made a wrong turn somewhere, and now he was blindly following the wall along the tunnel to who knew where. At one point he heard a distant voice and had turned around and ran. Since then, he'd heard nothing but the trickling sewer, and his legs burned from the constant ascending and descending of the tunnels.

Leek was reciting a recipe for sour cakes when his hand came to a metal rung in the wall. His heart jumped and he had to double check what he'd found.

A ladder!

He climbed, coming to a round metal grate above him and blindly felt around and found a latch. Turning and pushing the latch, he squinted as light flooded into the sewer. Leek climbed out, shielding his eyes as he tried to figure out where he was.

Leaving the grate open, he walked down to the mouth of the alleyway and looked both ways. Children played on the street to his right, but to this left he could make out an open expanse beyond the distant houses. Leek realized where he was. It was the market sector, one of two sectors where those proved loyal to the ministry could enjoy a normal life.

He'd travelled much further than the industrial sector, but there wasn't a chance he was going back down through those sewers again, so he went back and shut the grate, but making sure to leave it accessible, then found a place to hide his purse.

There was a bright side to his blunder. The market sector was densely populated, and as all thieves know the world over, a crowd is the best place to hide.

By the following morning he'd stolen clothes off a washing line, and seeing as the crowds grew large enough to drown in, had chanced stealing food, slowly growing braver, working his way through the throng and liberating people of their hard-earned coin.

Leek hesitated, the woman was distracted looking at the jeweller's stall, and her satchel was within arm's reach and bloody well asking for the taking. His fingers slipped in as a large cart with crates rolled by, and by the time it rolled past, he'd already disappeared down a side alley.

With little to no competition in the market sector, only having to avoid the Maskers, Leek had already built up a collection of sixteen silver coins, twenty-three copper, and enough food to see him out for a few days if things went awry. Inside a dark courtyard he pulled open the clasps and pocketed the handful of copper coins. Discarding the purse, Leek turned into an adjoining alley, and froze mid-step. A Masker blocked the end of the alley, bludgeon held tightly in fist. Leek turned back, but more Maskers filed down the alleyway towards him.

"Fuck," he muttered.

The one in front pointed at him with his bludgeon. "We've been watching you, boy. Can't pick pockets with broken fingers, can ye? Let's see how much coin ye've got, then."

Leek turned heel and ducked past the guard who tried to grab him. He skidded in the dirt as he turned the corner, the Maskers' heavy footsteps following close behind. The twists and turns of dirty lanes and dark courtyards passed by in a blur, and Leek more jumped than ran across the small bridge spanning the narrow, fast-flowing river.

A moment of madness and he didn't think further, just dived in, drowning out the shouts of his pursuers and being dragged along by the current. He fought it, kicking his legs and emerged moments later, followed by a loud splash from behind. Peeking back, two Maskers had jumped in after him. Leek swam sideways, kicking with all his might and finally reaching and pulling himself up onto a ledge. With a brief, deep suck of air, he stood up and ran into an adjoining alleyway, pushing over a man carrying sacks of flour on his shoulders. White dust puffed up around him, and he left the cursing man and laundry women to their angry cries, delving deep into the warren of lanes between the steep buildings.

Leek could see Maskers flashing past the end of the laneways to either side. He knew the market square wasn't far, and well crowded this time of day.

A good place to slip a hound hot on your trail.

At a junction of alleyways, a Masker came running around the corner, snatching out at Leek and making him flinch. Mercifully his cloak ripped from his shoulders, throwing the Masker off-balance and the guard tumbled over. Leek ran on, towards the market square, its loud din growing all the louder. He left the alleyways and winded through a wide street filled with people coming to and from the market, jumping stacks of firewood, crates of fish, vaulting over a crouching old woman inspecting fabrics.

"Sorry!" he tossed over his shoulder as she let out a scream of shock.

Leek fled into the busy market square, packed with buyers and sellers, bumping into a juggler and making him tumble to the ground, sending burning torches flying up into the air. The onlookers cried as the torches rained down on them, but Leek was already pressing on through the crowd. The hounds bayed close behind.

Chapter 22: Moonlit Room

"Ah, that tastes delicious." Maddox leaned back in his chair, goblet in hand.

Birdie smelled the wine's sour scent in her goblet and pushed it away. "I want answers. Why does our family have a castle hidden in the mountain, and how did we pass through that thing, the portal?"

For days now after going through the portal she'd explored the castle. Maddox told her stories about when he'd run through the halls with her mother and aunt, how the place would be so lively, filled with all their kin. Any time she'd tried to get some idea of their plans for the future—or even better—revenge, he would frown and change the subject.

"You can't keep avoiding my questions. How did you pass through stone? Are you some kind of wizard? Is that why you're able to do magic?" She was only half serious.

Maddox choked on his wine and spluttered it down the front of his shirt, then quickly wiped the dribbling liquid from his chin. He indicated to his stomach and then his face. "Do I look like a skinny little old man with a great big beard to you?"

"But it was magic, wasn't it?"

"What do you know about magic?"

"I know what I saw." She took a bite out of one of the rolls. "And another thing that's been bugging me. Why didn't you just hideaway here, in the castle? You've food, water. You could've stayed here with me and Bella."

"What you saw at the portal was just a simple illusion, nothing more. Sometimes the best place to hide something that you don't want to be found is right in front of the people you don't want finding it!" Maddox winked at her as if he had imparted some valuable chunk of wisdom. "As for staying here, it was out of the question. These strongholds weren't safe, not back then, as many of the Twelve swapped sides. Some had access to secret passages to each other's strongholds, you see. Alliances were always switching back-and-forth, even in times of peace. For all I know this place was swarming with enemies after our escape. Any who might know the way now are dead. It took me years to hunt them down, but I got them eventually."

"So you can't do magic, but you can walk through stone? Is that what you're telling me?"

Maddox frowned, as if he wanted to say something, and then thought better of it. "There's much you don't know, Blackbird."

"Then tell me. I came this far and survived, haven't I?"

Maddox smiled. "You have your mother's eyes. Do you know that? Her frown too."

"Don't change the subject!"

"She had ones just like yours, silver with yellow flecks, just like our mother had before her." Maddox sat up and pulled up his sleeve. "Fine, you have her stubbornness, so I know you won't let up. I'll show you something. Watch..."

He glanced around the room, eyes falling on a loaf of bread on the table, which a small mouse was nibbling on. Maddox lifted up his wrist and the bird tattoo began to glow, casting the table's surface and its contents into a slight yellow hue. It became brighter and brighter, until the space above it thickened and yellow particles formed into a sphere, which then formed into a golden bird. It hovered in the air for a moment, and then sped off along the table, hurtling toward the mouse, knocking bowls and tankards in its haste. Instantly the mouse fled, jumping off the table, but too late. The bird dived onto the mouse, disappearing from view behind a chest.

Birdie looked at Maddox, who was watching her intently. He flicked his hand out and rested it on the table. Birdie gasped as the mouse reappeared and ran down the table, then jumped onto the palm of Maddox's hand. Maddox smiled as she reached out and stroked its fur.

"It's great, isn't it?" Maddox smiled.

"That's incredible."

Maddox let the mouse jump down and the bird returned to its normal black colour. He lifted his hand and showed it to Birdie. The blood had drained beneath the flesh and was only now returning.

"Even small tasks performed with magic have a cost. But the more you grow and train the less it will affect you, and the smaller chance it can be fatal. But never treat magic lightly, Blackbird. It could cost you your life."

Maddox's snores rippled through the hall, his hand still clutched the goblet, albeit its contents spilled onto the table. Birdie lit a candle and made her way to the door and out into the long corridor, past the tall arched windows letting the moonlight fall onto the carpeted floor. Turning the corner, she passed by dozens of doorways, and at the end of the hall, Birdie climbed down one of many twisting stairways.

Her feet passed over the worn steps, faded from use of long vanished feet—a ghost of the castle's history. Outside of the castle, Birdie crossed the narrow bridge that spanned the vast dark chasm below. Bridges connected the twelve outer towers to the central castle and shorter bridges connected the towers. Maddox had told her that the ancient race who'd built the cities had always used the symbols of twelve and circles, so when their family's ancestors built this stronghold, they had copied the pattern.

Up here the night sky held millions of twinkling stars. Twin pale moons dominated the scene, hanging over the spire and the sleeping city of Mala. Birdie supposed it wasn't such a bad place to stay until they were ready to enter the city. Thousands of small, dark buildings and twinkling orange lights nestled below the spire, like a forest floor beneath an ancient tree, and the scene made her hungry to go and explore.

That very city was the place where her mother had been born. Her mother walked those very streets. Had known its alleys and laneways, sights and scents. Birdie could almost feel her presence.

This is where she was meant to be.

The cottage and the woods would always hold a dear place in her heart, but this was her home now.

Birdie entered the dark tower, up the spiral stairway. Corridors passed by, identical to the adjoining towers. The tower became narrower as she climbed, until at the top she came to a large, beautifully gilded door with an engraved blackbird at its centre. As she passed through the doorway, hundreds of windows illuminated the room. She passed along the smooth tiles that felt cool to the bare skin of her feet. Tall twisting pillars of white marble supported the transparent, domed ceiling, all engraved with sculpted animals and vines.

At the centre of the room was a huge bed, real withered vines clung to its four-posts, drooping down as if bowing to her arrival. Birdie ran her fingers along the soft silken fabrics of the bed and decided she'd found her room. She crouched down and placed the candle on the floor beside a large wooden chest at the foot of the bed. Wiping away a thick sheet of dust, Birdie saw that on its lid was also an engraved bird. She popped open the chest and pushed back the lid.

The first thing that caught her eye was a beautiful silver hairbrush. Its handle was made from some twisted, white type of metal and pearls were embedded into the butt and ran up along both sides. Birdie put it down and picked up an old portrait that was partially hidden beneath some scrolls of parchment. Lifting the portrait her heart fluttered, as she found herself staring into her own face—if a somewhat slightly aged version of it. Birdie realized she was looking at her mother for the very first time in her entire life.

Black curls fell down over petite shoulders, past a silver necklace that looked very much like the one she was now wearing. Carrying the painting over to a tall mirror on the far side of the room, Birdie's skin appeared ghostly blue in its reflection. At arm's reach she looked from one image to the other. The likeness was extraordinary. In both the yellow flecks seemed to glow over the silver bands of both their eyes. Her mother looked quite happy in the painting, a slight smirk touched her lips, as if she were about to laugh.

"She was a beautiful woman, your mother," Maddox's voice drawled from behind. Birdie turned, noticing her uncle's dark frame stood by the doorway.

"You were asleep. I thought I'd get accustomed to my new home. Sorry."

"Don't apologize. Anne also had a curious nature. I knew you wouldn't be able to stay away. I meant to clean it up a bit." Maddox walked across the room and stopped beside her. He looked down at the painting and reached inside his coat. "I was going to give you this after you got settled in, but seeing as you've your mother's ways, you'd probably discovered it beforehand." Maddox handed her a black leather-bound book. "I haven't been able to finish it. Haven't even looked at the bloody thing in years, best it goes to you. You can read, can't you?"

Birdie gave him a scolding look, but smiled as she took the book and rifled through it. Birdie looked at Maddox. "It's her diary!"

"I know. I'd hidden it here after returning to Mala. I felt bad leaving it behind. A part of me thought it should've stayed with you, at the cottage. But the idea of coming back here and giving it to you one day personally, well, it gave me hope. Sounds selfish, I guess." He shrugged.

Birdie put a hand on Maddox's shoulder. "Thank you."

He shrugged and rubbed his eye. "Damn wine must've gotten in my eye."

They laughed. Maddox took her hand and kissed it. "Now," said Maddox, giving her a wink. "Get some sleep, and tomorrow we'll see how things fare in the city."

After waking and washing, Birdie ate a breakfast of honey and bread, smoked fish and mint water. Maddox left the hall and returned dressed as an old man. Birdie had to look twice at his wrinkled face, greyed hair and bent back. He hobbled his way from the castle, making her laugh until tears streamed from her eyes.

The mountain pass outside was hidden in mist, making her wrap the thick cloak tightly round her. A shrill cry pierced the air. Looking up Birdie saw an eagle dip down through the fog, hunting a smaller bird. They dived below the bridge Birdie and Maddox were crossing and disappeared from view.

Once at the portal Maddox activated the stone with his blood and the blue emulsion formed in the empty archway.

"Keep hold of my hand!" shouted Maddox. "The second time's harder than the first."

"What do you mean?" she shouted back, but he took her by the hand and pulled them into the portal. Her skin felt as if a wave of ice rippled through it, before the crushing pressure eased and she was flung to the ground. Maddox still held her hand, and helped her regain her feet.

"Thanks," she muttered, wiping herself down.

The air around them swirled and formed with air currents in various colours. Maddox led them through the tunnel-like patch of space that seemed almost normal, except for white spheres that floated in the air like dandelion seeds. "What are they?" She reached out a hand to touch one, when Maddox pulled it back.

"Best not touch anything. We wouldn't want to upset them."

"*Them?*"

Maddox nodded. "Spirits of the dead. Wouldn't like being poked for no good reason now, would you?"

Birdie was unsure if he was messing with her or not, but had no more time to think about it as the air was beginning to thicken around them. Maddox had to hold on tighter to her hand.

"Don't let go!" he shouted, and she felt that familiar sense of ice tingle across her flesh once more.

One second she was squinting through flashing strobes of light, gritting her teeth at the pressure pulling her in a dozen different directions, and the next she was face down in dust, spitting out her breakfast between choking sobs. Maddox knelt down beside her and offered her a kerchief once she'd regained control of her stomach.

"Thanks," she said, wiping her mouth.

"Told you it'd be worse, but you get used to it."

"I can't wait."

But she could.

They camped that night in a scattering of bare trees. Birdie fell to sleep staring up at the flickering lights of the city and the spire. As clouds drifted around it, the spire now resembled a church tower nestled among a ramshackle village.

By dusk the following day Birdie and Maddox approached the gates to the city. Her uncle's demeanour as they came into view of the line of guards was comical, as he used the crutch heavily, his arm shaking. Maddox handed a guard papers from inside his coat, and after a few moments they were walking through a side-gate.

"Stay close. Things will be safer once we get to the middle sector of the city, but if we stay on the thoroughfare, we'll be fine." Maddox offered Birdie his arm and she took it. A small wall in the centre divided the flow of traffic, with most moving further into the city, each direction having two lanes for cart and foot-traffic. Tall trees of unknown species were planted every fifty steps or so, their pointed fronds gently blowing in the breeze. From this section of the city Birdie could make out more walls higher up, with a vista of rooftops visible between these, and the upper section of the spire looming above it all.

Birdie noted the dilapidated state of the leaning houses away to the sides of the thoroughfare, all leaning just as precariously as the city did above them. Many of the corner houses on her left side hung signs with a roughly painted sun outside their door.

"Sunnyside," muttered Maddox as he followed her gaze.

"Huh?"

"Sunnyside slums, this is the division between it and the lower sector. It's a melting pot of Mala's unfortunates."

Her foot clipped something, part of a broken crate and she stumbled, but Maddox caught her. "Best keep your eyes on the ground, Blackbird, until you get used to looking up and walking, that is." Maddox smiled and she nodded.

After walking along the thoroughfare for some thirty minutes or so they came to a gate and Maddox showed the guards his papers once more. They passed through unhindered and the next sector of the city was somewhat of an improvement. This, Maddox told her, was the industrial sector. A steady stream of the masked guards patrolled this sector, and when Birdie asked Maddox why they hadn't seen as many in the sector before he nodded.

"The ministry like to use the city's gangs to control the rabble in the lower sector. Most of the people in these districts or the upper parts wouldn't dream of breaking any laws, as they'd be tossed down into the slums so fast it'd make their heads spin. But the ministry still like to show the public who's in charge. More than likely we'll see their bludgeons being used before we leave."

The guards travelled in squads of four, and would often turn and sprint off into one of the side-streets, chasing some unseen perpetrator.

"Are the other cities like this?" Birdie asked as they stopped at a tavern in the next district and refreshed themselves with two mugs of ale.

"Haven't been to all of them, but the closer ones are pretty much the same. They're all terrified of Nefaro and his network of spies. Some officials fought back, but since the twelve ruling families were killed the night of the purge, it's been a losing battle. He got rid of those foolish enough to voice their disdain for his methods."

"Are there any left? Of the Twelve, I mean."

"Well, not really. A few might still be hiding in the furthest cities. But most of our family's allies are long dead." Maddox edged closer, glancing around and lowering his voice even further. "You have to remember, the twelve ruling families distrusted each other, changing loyalties, aiding in the assassination of the higher members of the other families. It was a cutthroat society, with my father one of the blood thirstiest. Morin was one of Nefaro's main targets in the purge. That's why he's so fixated on having my head decorating his hall. I'm a thorn in his gullet. And I quiet like my head."

A few civilians came into the quiet tavern and Maddox eyed them as he sipped his ale. He sniffed the cup. "It's a far cry from the vintage wine back at the castle." He pushed the mug away. "Onwards we go!"

"Where?"

"I could show you the market district, if you'd like? I've some business in the industrial sector to take care of, but it can wait."

"I can go to the market district and you can follow me? The thoroughfare seems pretty safe."

Maddox cocked an eyebrow. "Won't make me regret it, will you? Won't start any fires, revolutions, pick any pockets or join the mercenaries?"

Birdie smirked. "I'm not you."

"No, I guess you're not. Well then, I suppose you'll be alright. If you can handle yourself in the passes, the market sector should be a breeze. I won't be long anyhow. Just make sure you stick to the thoroughfare."

Birdie crossed her heart and held up a hand.

Once the guards at the next gate checked her papers Maddox gave her and allowed her through, she couldn't stifle the bubble of excitement building in her gut. Birdie soaked it all in, smelling the aromas of fresh bread, grain, hearing the cries of the vendors shouting their wares.

Birdie slipped a copper from her purse and bought an apple, biting into the fresh fruit as she followed the growing stream of civilians heading further into the market district. The houses suddenly gave way to a large plateau filled with stalls, small crowds bustling from one to the other, some lounging near a stage where people stood atop performing. Passing the stalls filled with clothes, fabrics, jewellery, art and other merchandise, Birdie sat on a cushioned seat near the back of the audience and listened to the man and woman who were performing a play about two ill-fated lovers.

She finished her apple and tossed the core towards a handful of birds that were pecking at any scraps discarded by the crowd. The performers bowed to the applause as the play ended and Birdie clapped along with them. People dressed in costumes rushed about the crowd, carrying jugs to refill drinks. Birdie stood up and shook her head as a small boy dressed as an owl offered her wine and walked away. The number of stalls further along increased. It seemed that the merchants would fold up their stalls and move to where the crowd was thickest, a type of movable market.

Birdie followed the thoroughfare through the throng, where she found more entertainers, magicians and jugglers, mock fighting. The crowd here was hard-pressed, only giving the entertainers the space they needed. The stalls sold sweetmeats and cakes, hands stuck out and offered coins, whipped away once they were traded with and holding food. Birdie stared up in awe at the semi-circle of high columns that seemed to enclose this part of the square, each shooting crystalline jets of water into the air. Houses were visible beyond these, indicating the end of the market sector.

Birdie was already being pressed in by the crowd, when someone came jostling into her, knocking her over. She felt the air being forced from her lungs as the person landed atop her, and she pushed back, trying to slide them off. It was a young man with short spiky red hair sticking out in every direction. He stared down at her with wide blue eyes.

"You're... crushing... me." Birdie couldn't get a good grip, otherwise she would've pulled that red hair, hard.

He grimaced as he pushed himself up. "Sorry, didn't see you there." He wiped his hands on his shirt before offering her his hand.

"It's fine." Birdie took his hand and wiped herself down once back on her feet. The young man nodded and disappeared into the crowd. Birdie was about to make her way back to the performing platform, when she noticed that her purse was missing.

"Shit-balls!" she shouted, realizing he'd robbed her. Birdie turned and shouldered her way after him, his red hair just visible through the bustling crowd.

There wasn't a chance she was letting *that* go.

Birdie managed in keeping the man in her vision as she shouldered her way through the throng. They left the crowd and entered the street flanked by large stone houses, which were surrounded by ten-foot stone walls. She noticed a group of four Maskers patrolling ahead, and the thief slipped into a side-street. Birdie had to run to catch up, but he had vanished.

Running down the deserted street, the few stone benches sat empty. She passed two stone houses and came to a tall stone building with loud grinding noises coming from inside. White clouds of dust streamed from its many windows. She trusted her gut instinct and walked around the side of the building, catching a glimpse of red hair for a second, and then it was gone. At the side of the building was a large pipe letting a stream of water out of the building. The thief was inside the pipe, having sidled through a gap in the bars, and was just opening a familiar looking purse.

Birdie crept through the gap. "I'll give you one chance to hand that back." Birdie clenched her fists and the knuckles cracked loudly.

The lad jumped, but kept hold of the purse and looked up at her. "Who... Oh." He stood up and held the purse out. "You after this?"

Birdie held out her hand. "Now."

"Why? You don't need it. I bet you've loads of purses at home, filled with daddy's silver." The boy slipped her purse inside his cloak. "Just leave, I don't want to fight a girl."

Birdie smiled as she shook her shoulders and neck. "Oh, it won't be much of a fight." She took position and balanced herself on the balls of her feet. The narrow space might work to her advantage, because he was a head's height taller and had a longer reach. "Come on then, let's get this over with."

The lad looked taken-aback. "I could have a knife."

"And I could care. Make a move or give me my purse." She edged into the narrow space, making the lad back up.

"Now wait just a minute!" He held up his hands. "How about half? I'll give you half back, just so I don't have to hurt you?"

Birdie ignored him. She focused her strength and tensed her shoulder, aiming.

"Fine!" the lad shouted. "What's wrong with you? Chasing thieves... must be gone in the head." He tossed the purse onto the floor. "Now, take it and leave me alone."

Birdie picked up the purse. "This is just the start. You made me chase you, and then there's the fact that I want to kick your ass. What are you willing to pay to avoid that, hmm?"

"Leave it out. You've your purse. The rest of my gang will be here any minute now. Don't want to be around when they get back."

Birdie gave the lad a long, assessing look. His cheekbones were prominent, hair tangled and filthy, eyes dark and sunken. "You're alone."

The lad smirked. "No I'm not. Paste, grab her!" He'd said the latter to someone behind her, and Birdie spun, ready to ward off a blow, but the red-haired lad had been lying and took his chance to barge into her, knocking her off-balance. She hit the ground but used the momentum and swung round with a kick. But he was fast, and her kick met only air.

Birdie cursed and chased him back into the street. His legs were much longer and by the time they'd remerged into the street he'd gotten a dozen strides ahead. Birdie reached inside her cloak, grabbed her purse and stopped running. She took aim, hoping her knife throwing skills might come in handy here.

The purse missed his head by inches and landed in front of him, making him skid to a halt and snatch it up. "Thanks!" he gave her a thumbs up before turning back around. He was about to run back towards the thoroughfare when four Maskers turned the corner. They froze as they took in the scene. Birdie was tempted to shout *thief* but no matter what the man had done, she knew the punishment would be too severe. The man backed away as the four guards came down the street towards them and spread out, using the flanking high stone walls to their advantage.

Birdie considered running but the thief seemed frozen in place. The four men were only paces away now, edging closer, when a call came from the end of the street. They turned, seeing an old man hobbling down towards them.

"There you are!" Maddox cried. "I've been looking all over for you!"

Birdie had to stifle a cry of relief as Maddox gave the guards a wide smile and nodded as he shambled past them, making the two in the centre lift their cudgels.

"And what do you think you're playing at, old man?" One of the guards held up a hand to stop Maddox. "Turn back around and fuck off."

Maddox looked at Birdie. "Granddaughter, be a dear and bring an old man his purse." Birdie took the purse out of the thief's hand and walked over, handing it to Maddox, who opened it and looked inside, rooting through the coins noisily, then nodded and handed one coin to the guard who'd spoken. "Here, a simple reward for keeping our city safe. Have a drink on an old man, eh?"

The guard snatched the purse from Maddox's hand, and nodded as he looked inside. He pointed his cudgel at the thief. "What about him? Doesn't look like he's from 'round here. He with you?"

Maddox looked at the thief for a moment, and then nodded. "A sorry sight, but he's my grandson." Maddox tapped the side of his head. "Not all there. Prefers the company of pigs to his own family, but we love him nonetheless."

The guard pocketed the purse and nodded. "You have our thanks, old man. We'd be glad to wet our beaks on your coin." He looked at his men. "Come on, we've time for a quick one."

The Maskers left the street and Maddox was staring at the thief. After a minute he broke the silence. "And what just happened here?"

Birdie considered telling him about the stolen purse, but then he'd more than likely hurt him. "He helped chase down a thief. It got snatched in the market. He was bringing it back to me when the Maskers showed up."

Maddox frowned, looking from one to the other. "Fine, don't tell me the truth. What's your name, boy?"

"Kellick."

"One more lie and I'll call those guards back. Your name?"

"Leek."

"Well Leek, you're coming with us. Grab your stuff."

Leek looked down at his clothes. "I've got them."

Chapter 23: Into the Fray

The ancients who inhabited the Sea of Circles manipulated the elements at will to make the world in their own image. They lay with mankind, and all who corrupted their souls with these beings were therefore known as having 'Blood of the Twelve'. Those infected with their powers began to turn on the weaker race of man, using them for labour, mining and ore production. The beings slowly vanished into the shadowy corners of the world, leaving their human bloodline to govern the people. As the entire known world fell into an Age of Darkness, plagued by the Twelve, the Order of Clerics secretly began undermining their masters, and the Ministry of Faces was born...

Kye grunted as he leaned back and rubbed his tired eyes. The words swam on the parchment. Nights spent reading for hours in this oil-lamp's weak light made his vision blurry. The study hall had been deathly quiet all night. It was a far-cry to the Palace of War, where'd he'd spent most of the past ten years training, but he didn't disapprove of the rest.

Only he and a handful of clerics were crouched by their lamplights. Kye heard the rustle and touched the parchment in his breast pocket.

I wonder what she's doing now. Lillith, where are you?

Kye forced away the whispers that repeatedly intruded upon his studies. Weeks had passed with no response. She didn't love him—it was obvious—but the whispers remained cruel and unyielding.

The entire room filled with deafening alarm bells, startling him. The clerics all came to life and tiredly stumbled out of the hall, down into the gathering crowds in the main courtyard. Confused men conferred and muttered to each other in suspicious conferences as Kye passed. Huddles of men were gathered beside the raised platform in the centre of the courtyard, eying the empty lectern warily. Kye shouldered his way closer to the high platform, and found a thick ring of masked men surrounding the platform. Each man was heavily armed and the crowd awaited their leader well out of arms reach. Robed men filed in from the gate. The leading members of the palace flanked the Head of State, Cleric Nefaro, who climbed the stairs of the platform and stood on the speaking block alone. Nefaro held out his hands to silence the already still crowd. He cleared his throat.

"The Twelve... have fallen!"

Silence. Kye fought the churning anxiety building in his chest, the tide of despair that was threatening to drown him.

"From tonight, I declare that the Twelve are defunct. There has been an attempted coup, and drastic action is required!" he shouted, quieting down the building whispers. "From this night on, a new order shall rule the Sea of Circles. The Ministry of Faces will rule for the people in this time of turmoil. The men you see standing before me are the new head of security, superior to the army. The Masked Lodge are the sole military power within Mala from henceforth, they are my inner shield.

The remaining members of the Twelve have bowed to our wisdom, or fallen to our wrath."

The crowd held its breath. This was treason of the highest order. Clerics often whispered about their unhappiness with the Twelve, but never in public. Kye's only thoughts were for her, and of that sweet smile that he might never see again.

"Lillith..." he looked up at the spire, where figures roamed like ants, torches bobbing like yellow stars, and his heart filled with dread.

Kye awoke from the nightmare drenched in sweat. He searched the tent's dark corners, feeling a presence inside of the tent, good or bad he couldn't decide. As he crept out of bed and tried to calm his mind, he tossed kindling onto the embers in the fire-pit, letting the warm glow push away the threads of dreams.

"Lillith," he whispered. Her name felt good on his lips, like cool water to parched lips. That ball of hatred that was always boiling in his stomach was gone. He felt empty inside, and it terrified him. He could almost picture her face in the flames. But the image of her face faded, and the comforting ball of thorns retook its place at his core. Kye could almost hear their screams, still clawing at his mind after so many years. Those massacred in the Spire.

An image floated through his mind's eye. Flames spreading inside the spire. Of the swishing streams of light as burning bodies hurtled towards oblivion. Kye had been there. He'd seen the slaughter first hand. How those screams still haunted him...

Kye stood up and listened.

The screams weren't in his mind.

He rushed out of his tent. Men were running down the hill. Below the hills and palisades, where the first ranks of infantry had been positioned, hundreds of tents were ablaze. Screams wafted up the hillside with the stench of blood and fear. He could hear the pleas for mercy and the cries of death.

The battle had begun.

He ran back into the tent and pulled on his gear arranged in the war chest, hardened leather with thin scales of anatine steel. Kye buckled his long-knife onto his belt, and—for the first time since leaving Mala, pulled open the long, black wooden box. Blessing himself with the Prayer of War, he pulled open the box and lifted out the Shield of Faith and Bloodblade. Its gleaming surface of midnight red anatine steel glowered in the firelight. At his touch, veins pulsed along the blade like serpents of the underworld—his own blood worked into the ancient metal by the Brothers of Mist now activated at his touch. The feel of the cool metal as he pressed it against his lips filled him with reassurance, and the comforting Trance of Battle embraced him.

"Gods of War, guide my blade. Gods of Death, steady my shield."

Outside, he mounted his war-horse and sped off after the tide of men already pouring down the hill. Officers were screaming to form rank. Faces blurred past, terrified, pale, wide-eyed faces. Both hillsides were alive with activity. The attack seemed to be mainly focused on this hill's rear.

Kye made his way through the throng, jumped down and threw the reins to a nearby soldier. The palisades made a wall on both sides of the line of defending soldiers. Beyond these, in the outer camp, men screamed as they were put to the sword.

The Eclipsi had overwhelmed the defences, but were now being pushed back as they collided against shield walls everywhere. Kye ordered a column of elite soldiers stationed nearby by to gather in support behind the line. He strode past the columns, giving the odd order or word of encouragement. He came to where the palisades branched out on both sides, making a T shape. Waiting on both sides were spearmen, archers and a column of Golden Circle soldiers behind these.

He made his way back to the front, where the vast number of Eclipsi had begun to inch their way forwards, two men streaming in for every one that fell. All the while keeping watch on the adjoining hill. But so far the only signal flags were for the officers. No part of both hills defences had given way.

Trumpets responded around the hills, blasting into life and then being lost beneath the drum of battle, relaying orders. Kye looked at his trumpeter and nodded.

Hearing the trumpet, slowly the men fell back, keeping their line up as best they could. Minutes passed which felt like hours. Kye watched as the enemy beat relentlessly against their shields. He moved with the columns behind the front line as they rushed back to the junction, and Kye nodded again to the trumpeter. The front line gave way and the men retreated, fighting a running battle.

The waiting columns opened up to let the fleeing men through, but closed as the enemy came near. They flooded into the junction, hundreds of them, then slowed to a jog, but were pushed from behind by their allies. The spearmen had already lowered their weapons and now moved in, creating a pincer. Archers flooded the enemy rushing in from behind with arrows. The enemy at the front turned and tried to retreat but were trampled underfoot as they fell. Spears closed in on both sides, the column of soldiers clashed against the oncoming tide, holding steady.

It was pure slaughter.

The spears decimated their numbers, the archers deflated the charge, and as they eventually stopped pressing and fled, the Golden Circle rushed in to route their number, hacking down hundreds before they'd fled through the outer palisade.

Kye praised his men and mounted his horse, guiding it back to the hill and followed the wide trench which connected both command posts. From the high ground he could see the line held on both hills, with most still engaged in battle.

Kye tethered his horse outside the command tent.

Vines greeted him at the map table. "Sir, we're surrounded."

"Nothing slips past you, Vines, eh? You'll be a general one day, surely." Vines grinned.

"They're threatening to break the opposite hill's rear defences." Vines pointed at the location on the map. "We stationed a large number of the refugee force there."

"They're holding. The enemy were pushed back."

Vines frowned darkly out at the mass of men just visible beyond the outer defences. "I thought they were still supposed to be more than a day's march away?"

"As did I."

They both stared off over the sea of battle. The Eclipsi surrounded them on all sides. Metal instruments of war glittered as they were raised and the clang of blade on blade was near deafening.

"Any word from the ministry? Any reinforcements?"

Kye shook his head. "No. We make do with what we have. You stay at this command post. If the worst should happen, if I get killed or we're routed, you're to take command. The officers have their orders." Kye clasped Vines' hand. "Just make sure you make them pay for every inch of ground."

"I'll make them bleed. Until the ground runs with rivers of red."

"Good man. I'll make a fucking War Monger out of you yet, Vines."

They let go hands and parted ways, both men fixed on the deadly task at hand.

Chapter 24: Chance and Fate

They made their way through the market sector, Leek being held tightly by the arm by the old man. The girl followed close behind, or so Leek saw when he could sneak a look in at her.

"Keep your eyes on the road, boy," growled the old man.

Leek considered telling him to shove his crutch somewhere dark and uncomfortable, but as the grip tightened on his arm, Leek decided to remain quiet. They made their way through the series of gates without much hindrance, towards the lower section of the city. Leek would've slipped the old man if he'd been alone and hadn't a vice-like grip on his arm, but the thought of being chased by the girl again made him think twice. She had steel in her, that one.

Passing through the industrial sector, Leek wondered what Paste was doing now. Could one of those hammering sounds be his friend at work? And how was the man getting through the gates so easily, when he knew the hardship and cost it took to make it from one zone to the next. Were these people dangerous? Might they cut his throat once somewhere secluded?

He battled his doubts and knew that if the man had wanted, he could've let the Maskers take care of him. At least his stash of coin was safe. He'd be back someday, visiting Paste, and could get it then.

The lamps atop the columns on the main thoroughfare were coming to life. Large bright orbs of blue light emitting a blue wash on the surrounding buildings as the sky darkened.

"Where are you taking me?" Leek asked as they were out of earshot of any other foot traffic. He heard the panic in his voice and fought the urge to nibble on a fingernail. Now really wasn't the time.

The man looked at him. "Does it matter?"

"Who are you?"

"None of your concern, boy. Let's just say we're your only chance of escaping this city." The old man was quite nimble for his age, pulling him through the streets and side alleys at a brisk pace, avoiding Maskers or officials in places. Leek's back was slick with sweat and his legs began to ache.

The girl was quiet and followed closely behind, always watchful. Finally, they approached the entrance gate, where hundreds of soldiers below and above the gate bustled in their duties, hoisting crates atop the wall with metal cranes. Squadrons of archers patrolled the walkway, or watched from the high towers. Teams of builders swarmed scaffolding, making repairs to the towers above.

"Be quiet, boy. Let me do the talking." The old man let go of Leek's arm and made his way up the road to join the line of people waiting to pass through the gates.

"Name?" the soldier asked the old man once they reached the front.

"Farron Alstone the Second, high-merchant of High Shoals. I just came in this way not too long ago. Not remember me, boy?"

"Better mind who you call boy, old man, or I'll give you a real reason to limp on that crutch."

"Ah, fighting! It's a young man's game. Let an old man be on his way, I have a long journey ahead of me." The old man made to pass by the soldier.

"Wait, who's he?" the soldier pointed at Leek.

"My grandson. A sorry story. His mother died, and I came to bring him home. Not all there, you understand. Takes after his father that way. They even mislaid his papers, can you believe? I had terrible trouble getting permission from the ministry..." the old man reached inside his coat and took out a large purse. "But they led me to understand this would clear things up." The soldier's eyes widened as the purse was opened. Leek just had time to spot the golden gleam of coins before the purse was hidden away inside the man's cloak.

The soldier nodded. "Very well, be on your way. Let them through!"

Leek stayed silent as they made their way through the side-gate and down the descending road, away from the city. Leek could almost cry. They travelled in silence, and as the day passed into evening they came to a crossroads. Stopping for a rest, the old man reached up to his face, and to Leek's astonishment, pulled his long grey beard and thick, ragged hair from his head, before stuffing them away inside his cloak.

"Damn things itch like mad. I can never get used to them." He took the water-skin from the girl, drank, and then offered it to Leek. Leek hesitated, but then took it and risked a sip.

"You'd best come with us to the castle." The girl smiled and the man frowned.

"Getting the poor wretch out of the city is one thing, Blackbird, but bringing a stranger to the stronghold? No chance."

The girl shook her head. "Don't mind him. He forgets what it's like to be on your own and without help." She gave the man a meaningful look. "I could be a pile of bones in a ditch somewhere right now. You really going to leave him out here to fend for himself?"

"I don't know. What did you say your name was?"

"Leek."

The man frowned. "Your mother a bloody vegetable? What kind of name is Leek?"

The girl held out her hand. "I'm Birdie, and this is my uncle. You can come with us. We've spare food and clothes."

"You're too kind." Leek shook her hand.

The uncle sighed but seemed to give in to Birdie's decision. "You spend time in Sunnyside, Leek?"

Leek nodded. "Too much, I'm afraid."

The man took a moment, looking into Leek's eyes. "If you survived that rat-den, then you might just be of some use." The man held out a hand. "Alright, you can come with us. I'm Maddox, by the way."

Leek nodded again as he shook Maddox's hand. "Heh, don't suppose your second name's Black?" At Maddox and his niece's exchanged look, Leek laughed. "It's a joke. You know? The Black Shadow?"

Maddox's grip tightened as he leaned in close, his black hair spilling over to hide half his face, and it made Leek want to step back. "Jokes aren't funny when they're true, boy."

It was after nightfall the following day when they arrived in a narrow valley hidden in the mountain, coming to a decrepit hut tucked beneath the shadow of the cliffs. Maddox cut himself and stuck an arm into a hollow in the stone, and the next thing he knew the whole valley had been thrown into a bright blue light. He didn't have time to ask any questions as he was pulled after Birdie, and stumbled through the barrier of blue pulsing light. The world moved around him in bright circles. His stomach churned as if at the edge of a cliff. And just as quick the light faded. Leek found himself on the ground, puking. Maddox chuckled as he leaned against the cliff.

"You'll get used to it."

After Leek regained some composure, they passed up the steep, narrow trail and crossed over a high, arched bridge that loomed over a sheer drop, making Leek hold onto the railing as they coaxed him across. Once across, they walked through a tunnel. Torches flashed to life by themselves, making Leek cringe away at first. Leaving the tunnel, the high peaks of the mountain were a majestic backdrop to the towers and castle just over a final bridge.

Maddox placed his hand on the gate's polished surface. A deep vibrating rattle came from below their feet and the gate slowly lifted up, disappearing into the wall above. As soon as he'd crossed over the gate's threshold, the gate plummeted back down and sank into the ground, making Leek almost soil his pants.

"Forgot to mention that," Maddox chuckled, sweeping across the courtyard and up between columns of dark marble pillars, their surfaces covered with blue streaks of light that pulsed and crackled.

"I've seen something like these before, in the Hall of Faces." Leek reached out and ran a finger across the column's surface. It was icy cool to the touch.

Maddox pushed open the heavy double doors. Inside the entrance hall, spiral staircases in the corners led up to upper levels. Marble stairs at the far side of the room rose in three different directions, left, right and centre. Maddox led them up the centre one.

"The ancients who built the Hall of Faces were builders of incomprehensible skill." Maddox chatted without looking back as they came to a high-ceilinged corridor. Its walls were decorated with large, colourful canvases depicting landscapes. Plinths made from the same material as the pillars held busts and other mysterious objects. One item had strange multi-coloured tubes covering it that fizzed and rattled as bubbles passed through them.

"Now you have the Twilight Temple threatening to invade, wanting to tear it all down for their twisted beliefs." Maddox led them up a wide flight of stairs and Leek saw that each step had a bird worked into its centre. Passing through networks of corridors and great chambers filled with beautiful furniture, artwork and an army of books, Leek's legs began to burn by the time they filed down a wide corridor and turned into a large hall with a long table taking up most of the space. Maddox sat down at the head of the table. Leek eyed the table's contents and felt his mouth water. There was so much food. Cheeses and fruits, dried meats and smoked fish, nuts and breads. Birdie sat down at the seat beside Maddox and tossed Leek an apple.

"Help yourself." Birdie grabbed a chunk of dried meat and began chewing on it.

Leek took the seat opposite Birdie and began with piling meat and cheese on a chunk of flat bread.

Maddox poured wine and watched Leek closely. After some time, he pointed at Leek. "So how did you get those beauty marks on your face?" Leek glanced from Birdie to Maddox. "Your scars are scratch marks, I'd guess?" Maddox took out a cloth and small vial, doused the cloth, and began rubbing his face, revealing burn marks across one side. "I've a few marks of love myself."

Leek swallowed his food. "I was taken from the Hall of Faces to a prison ran by a crooked minister named Gurth. He gave me these for not being the good little whipping boy."

"You were at a blood vault, then? And escaped. You're proving yourself quite the resourceful young man. You would've been sent there, Blackbird, if I hadn't gotten you away in time."

"Blood vault?" asked Leek.

"I've no solid evidence, but Nefaro's keeping relatives of the Twelve in secret locations. Drip feeding his need."

"I... I heard something of the sort. From a man named Wax. He used to run a gang in Sunnyside."

"Wax... I've heard of him. He was Druid, but Nefaro decided to keep him close-by. So he's still alive?"

"No. Me and a friend... took care of it."

"Impressive."

"I don't think it did much good. They'll still be killing them."

"Perhaps, but you did what you could. That counts for something, at least in my book. Nefaro is virtually untouchable.

The upper district is inaccessible, and heavily guarded by the Masked Lodge."

"What about the tunnels?" Leek sat up. "An innkeeper showed me an entrance, it brought me to the market sector."

"No good. I know the tunnels like the back of my hand. They only go the middle districts. But not to worry. Soon things will change. And in the meantime, I get to make the Masked Lodge's lives a living nightmare." Maddox grin widened.

"I've had a special place for them in my heart since a squadron of Maskers gave me this." Maddox pulled down his collar and showed Leek a white jagged scar on his chest in the shape of a P. "Caught me off the coast of the Sun-Isles trying to smuggle firewater." He glanced at Birdie and winked at her. "But I managed to pick the lock of the brig." Maddox grabbed the jug of wine and refilled his goblet, laughing at some unknown memory.

Birdie rolled her eyes. "Uncle was a pirate." Birdie smirked. "Or so he says, but I think he's filled with more shit than a fat man's privy."

"Mind your tongue, Blackbird. Being blood only gets you so much slack. So, Leek, how *did* you escape the prison? Where were you before being locked away?"

A lump rose up in Leek's throat at the painful memories. He told them about how the White-Spot plague had taken his siblings. How after arriving at the Bone-Portcullis and thinking he was safe, the Maskers separated him from his foster-mother after flipping the coin, and sent him to the Hall of Faces. About the prison and how he'd been marched around with the other prisoners through the city like a bunch of freaks. Then he told them about the plan to escape, and the fire he started and the scuffle to get free.

It all spilled out, like a torrential river that wouldn't stop. Leek talked about how his friends, Kellick and Merron, had been murdered just on the cusp of freedom. How Merron had been shot down like a dog. His fists clenched at the thought of the old man, Gurth. His sneering face burned through Leek's memory like a hot forge of hatred.

The room was silent after he finished the tale of how he thieved a meagre living in the slums for a time, and what followed between that and meeting them. Maddox had an altogether different look in his eye than when he had first met Leek, he was staring off into the darkening corners of the hall and shaking his head. Birdie had pulled her chair around to where Leek was sitting and nodded every so often.

Birdie broke the silence as Maddox began lighting a fire in the hearth. "Well, you don't have to worry about anything anymore, Leek. We're safe here, right uncle?"

"That's right," Maddox said from the fireplace.

Leek smiled despite himself. "I just wish the dreams would stop, you know? I try not to think about it, but when I sleep I can't help seeing their faces."

Birdie placed a hand on his shoulder. "No time for dreams now, the real nightmares lie in the world of the living."

Maddox's head snapped around. "What?"

Birdie repeated it. "It was when we were traveling to the eastern outpost. The woman who helped me said it a few times. I guess it stuck with me. I told you about her, didn't I?"

Maddox shook his head, and Birdie looked confused.

"Her name was—"

"Ariss," Maddox finished for her, turning back to the flames. "She's alive..."

Chapter 25: Nightmares, Awake and Dreamt

Kassova Kye was in the land of the dead.

He stood beside his men, and together they watched the sunrise. The water ran red with their blood, flowing past. The current choked with bloated bodies. The hills and the mountains dripped scarlet with their sacrifice. They called to him, pointing to the city in the distance. Mala and the spire were aglow in a fiery red haze. Towering plumes of black smoke wafted from the countless windows. Hundreds of burning bodies fell, hurtling to oblivion.

A woman emerged from the water. Her golden robes drained the colour from the land, until all that surrounded Kye was darkness. Feminine sunshine eyes watched his as her silken hands came within touching distance. Her soft, icy touch made him shiver.

"Lillith?" he whispered, as her warm fingers glided along his cheek.

Yes, my love. You look in pain, let me help. She ripped fabric from her golden cloak and began dabbing it over his cuts.

"Am I dead?"

No. You have not entered the water of death yet, and wont for some time. You are still needed in the world of the living. Rest now and let me heal you.

"How am I needed, tell me?"

Our child still lives and needs you.

"Our child?"

A shadow crept over the land. The spire had vanished. Mala was an empty shell of a city, the beautiful white walls blackened and decayed. He looked around, searching for Lillith.

But he was alone.

Endless battle can drain the strength and will of even the most seasoned warriors, and upon awakening Kye felt like his soul had deserted his body. His muscles cramped and back ached, but looking down he found that most of his cuts were gone, now nothing but thin white marks.

A healer during the night... surely?

But Kye didn't believe it. He'd seen her, and could almost still smell her scent. Still feel the warmth of her fingers on his cheek.

Putting on his armour, Kye shook off the dream and belted his sword before exiting the tent. The Eclipsi hadn't begun their next attack and the hills were unnaturally quiet. Mist crept along the grassland surrounding them, but the rising sun would soon take care of that. The men had piled and burned as many of their dead as possible, but stacked the enemy beyond the outer defences and left them to rot. Carrion birds choked the sky like midnight snowfall.

Kye found Vines in the command post surrounded by officers, surveying scrolls laid out on the table. Vines looked up and saluted. "Sir, rested well I hope?"

"Well enough. Have the numbers come back?"

Vines grimaced.

"Tell me, what's the damage?"

"We've lost more than half, sir. Perhaps thirty-five thousand." He added quickly, "but almost three quarters of the Golden Circle remains."

"That's something. Any word back from the ministry?"

Vines shook his head. "Seems we're on our own."

"I didn't expect much help, but I didn't think Nefaro would abandon us to our fate. I guess he's busy putting down the alliance."

"I could send a rider, sir? To the portcullis, I mean," offered a captain. "My brother-in-law's an officer there."

"Send him a rider. There's no harm in casting our net wide. Our messages might've been lost or captured by the enemy."

The captain saluted and left the tent.

Kye moved aside the scrolls and pulled across the map. "Food and water are running low, and it's coming to a point where we've to pick what columns to reinforce. Any ideas?" He asked the latter to the officers.

Lieutenant Varrant—a man of early twenties who was still getting used to his recent promotion—scratched his beard and looked at the map, puffing his cheeks. "They've adjusted to our tactics, sir. The next time the enemy attack they'll be ready for us. They've already broken through the opposite hill twice and were barely pushed back."

Major Tierce was more experienced and had the scars to prove it. He pointed at the map. "Concentrate forces. Have the Golden Circle form an inner circle. Arm the archers with spears, as we're running low on spearmen. Form phalanxes here and here..."

And so it went for the next hour, planning their defences. Kye sent the officers on their way with orders and sat outside the command tent, eating his breakfast of stale bread and water. He watched the mist thicken and creep closer. Watched as the sun rose and didn't thin the fog. Watched as the men grew anxious and listened to the murmurs about ill omens.

The opposite hill was abandoned. The army watched, silent, as the fog crept to within bowshot. Weapons dripped with moisture onto blood-stained grass. Armour scraped against sword as men nervously shifted feet. Spear knocked against shield as men's arms fought to hold steady.

Something was coming in the mist.

They could feel it.

Kye stood and watched the fog swirl closer. He gave a signal to the flagman nearby, who then raised the banner, letting officers know to prepare for attack. Trumpeters echoed commands. A hiss of thousands of swords being drawn sent a shiver down Kye's spine.

The Eclipsi appeared from the fog and came screaming towards the front line, and the line of shields met the attack and held steady, only wobbling in places. Kye watched as spearmen thrust points over the shields, of shield walls breaking open and being sealed shut. The fog crept uphill, turning the scene of chaos to murky shadows. Kye's field of vision was soon cut to only the men in front of him, and he pushed his way through the soldiers, trying to keep the front line within view.

Something drew him closer, and he ignored the warnings of an officer to stay near the command post. He could feel that danger approaching through the fog. He came to where the palisade was only wide enough for fifty men to stand abreast and grabbed the trumpeter, dragging him along. He at least could keep in contact with the closest officers should the worst happen. They passed through one more of the palisade funnels before coming to where the fighting was ongoing. The dense fog muffled the sounds but as they got closer, Kye could make out some of the screams of the fallen. He turned to the trumpeter.

"Stay here!"

The trumpeter's face was pale and eyes wide, but he nodded.

Kye drew his sword and spoke the Prayer of War, then slapped the man's shoulder. "May the gods give us strength!"

And may they indeed, for what he sensed held great power.

He pushed his way through the ranks of men. Most hadn't readied their weapons, and he shouted at them to draw steel as he pushed past three ranks of columns before coming to the shield wall. The column here was at least ten men thick and Kye could make out the spears of the enemy over the shields. The enemies' spears were much shorter, but the enemy had arrows and these clanged against armour and occasionally brought down a soldier.

Kye slipped his shield off of his back with his free hand and held it above his head.

It was getting closer.

His sense of time was muddled in the fog and din of battle. It could've been minutes or hours before he heard that snarl above the carnage. A monster appeared above the shield wall. It stood at least ten feet tall, clutching an enormous double-edged great-axe. Its arms and torso covered in mail, golden and silver beads shone in its dreadlocked hair, which was as bright as quicksilver.

The men before the monster held their ground, but to no avail. The axe bit into the wall of shields and sent men reeling. Men poured in through the gap and hacked at the stunned soldiers with hatchets. As the giant stepped through the gap he swung his weapon again, taking down three more to his right. The display of unnatural strength made the soldiers falter, slowly backing away.

Kye gripped his sword tight and made his way to the giant. "Fill the gap! Don't let them in!" But while some men regained their will and fought back against the enemy now streaming in through the widening gap, their number was too great and were soon overpowered. The monster all-the-while swung his axe, ignoring a sword-thrust through his calf. The soldier tried to pull his sword back out to only have his head smashed in by the butt of the giant's axe.

Men were falling back. Kye stood alone before the giant, its gaze fixed on his. The monster pointed a clawed finger at him and bellowed. Kye swished his sword, trying to figure out how best to bring the beast down.

There was only one thing he could do, now surrounded by the enemy. He sliced the Bloodblade through the skin of his wrist, invoking the Blood Surge—a desperate act for a War Monger.

The beast roared, flecks of blood flinging from its mouth, and the deep base of its shriek vibrated Kye's teeth in his skull.

Up the axe went as the monster came running, and he just had time to dive as the axe bit into the ground.

It moved fast for its size.

Circling the space made by the watching Eclipsi, Kye ducked beneath the sweep of the axe by a mere hand-length, whipping his sword down onto the beast's hamstring. It bellowed in agony as the steel cut through to bone, then came stumbling after him, trailing dark blood. The beast caught Kye's sword on the haft of its axe, locked it beneath the beard and spun him round, into the edge of the crowd. An Eclipsi pushed him, knocking him off-balance and he tumbled face first into the dirt. The giant's axe bit into a man's skull, spurting blood over the men behind him.

Kye quickly regained his feet and only just avoided the axe as it whistled around at him. The circle grew wider, and monster laughed as it made Kye dive and dodge, unaffected by the cuts it suffered. Kye managed to get the beast off-balance and rushed in, focusing his power on the tip of his blade, concentrating the Blood Surge along the metal which gleamed and heated to a red glow, and Kye drove it through the monster's heart.

But it caught on something before piercing through flesh, and with a sharp crack the end of his blade shattered apart. His hands lost grip on the hilt as an enormous surge of energy erupted from inside the metal and he was hurled back across the circle. He bounced off a shield and hit the ground, but kept his eyes locked onto the beast as it fell to its knees. It looked down at the wide hole now in the chainmail covering its chest and touched a necklace pendant hanging there, which was blackened and smouldering.

The beast let out a deafening moan and large lumps began to form over its skin. Kye watched in horror as red beams of light shone from its eyes and the beast began to shrink, or fold in on itself, filling the circle with the sickly sounds of popping bones, before finally taking the form of a man.

The man let the axe that was now too heavy fall from his grip. His hands instead trembled as he slid the necklace over his head and let it drop to the ground. The man looked up at Kye, tears brimming in his eyes. "You broke the moon-stone."

Kye regained his feet and picked up his sword, which still had half a blade. He pointed the jagged end at the man, and glanced around at the circle of Eclipsi, who stared at the pendant with wide eyes and horrified expressions. Then one of them let a morbid shriek, and the rest followed. They turned and fled back down the hillside, into the fog, their shrieks becoming lost in the murk.

Kye looked back down at the man.

The man touched the pendant. "You've broken the moon-stone. How? A sage's moonstone is unbreakable." He shook his head. "You've damned us all."

Kye put the blade against the man's throat. "You're a sage?"

"You see clearly for a dead man, War Monger. I'm Und-ar Felt, Second-Sage of the Twilight Temple. I beg you. Kill me if you are merciful."

"You'll have your wish, sage, but not by my hand. Your fate lies in the Hall of Faces."

Chapter 26: Cat's Out of the Bag

Birdie turned the page in her mother's diary, trying once again to find some clue as to who her father might be.

Things in Mala are becoming almost too hostile to bear. I hear father in his study when he speaks with the family council. He is terrified that he left it too late, that the Clerics have been undermining them from the shadows for longer than expected. The Malian citizens are torn between hating and loving the Twelve. Last month three servants didn't return from visiting the lower sectors. I fear it is too late for us all...

Birdie shook her head, closing the diary. She had read the damn thing three times now and still found no mention of her father. She pushed the diary under her pillow as a knock sounded on the door.

"Birdie?" Leek called. "You in there?"

"Come in."

Leek entered and shut the heavy door behind him. He walked towards the bed, but then something caught his eye and he turned direction, moving to and touching the portrait hanging on the wall. "Woah," said Leek, touching its surface. "You look so real."

Birdie stood up and walked over to him. "It's my mother."

"You're very alike."

"It's the only painting I could find of her so far."

"It's pretty good. I only ever saw cheap prints on market day, but this, she seems almost alive. What... happened to her?"

"She died. It's only me and Maddox left. The ministry murdered the rest."

"I used to read the books Marlo kept at the inn whenever I had free time. In those texts it said the Twilight Temple were responsible for the purges."

Birdie nodded. "Lies spewed by Nefaro. He controls what people believe now."

They turned, hearing footsteps on the stairs. Maddox appeared at the doorway. "Meet me in the main hall. I need to talk about something with the both of you."

Once back at the hall in the castle, Maddox sat at the usual head of the table. On the table in front of him were four large packs. Birdie sat on his right-hand side, Leek on his left.

"Leek," Maddox gave him a brief smile. "I don't know why, but my niece has taken a fondness to you. At first I thought your presence might be a burden, but perhaps you can assist her in her training while I'm away. It's not hard.

"While you're here, you are ensured safety and will be given some basic training, to assist in the protection of our home. For these services I am also paying you beforehand with a favour." Maddox nodded to one of the sacks. "Open it."

Leek looked from Maddox to Birdie and finally let his gaze settle on the sack. He reached out and began pulling open the drawstring. Opening it, Leek glanced inside and gasped. He dropped it back onto the table. Birdie flinched as it hit the solid wood with a sickening squelching sound, and the contents rolled out across the table, staining a red trail on the polished surface behind it.

"Gurth..." Leek stared down with wide eyes.

A decapitated head stared glassily at the ceiling—the expression frozen in a silent scream of horror. Birdie put her hand to her nose, blocking the metallic scent of blood, and looked away as a fly landed on one of the eyeballs.

"This is not only a gift, but a promise." Maddox pointed a finger at Leek. "It's a promise that the same fate awaits anyone who would do my family harm, or harm to those who aid them. Understand?"

Leek nodded.

Maddox stood up. "I've to go into the city. Before I go, I'll show you both how to use the Spinning Room."

Birdie grabbed Maddox by his wrist as he made to turn away. "What about Ariss? You never explained how you knew her. You're going to try and help her, right?"

Maddox hesitated. His lips moved but he said nothing.

"She helped me, saved my life. If you could find a way to get her out of that outpost, or at least find out if she's still alive?"

"I'll try, Blackbird. But Ariss is well capable of protecting herself. She's probably well clear of the outpost by now."

"You didn't say how you knew her?"

"It's a long story." Maddox tried to walk away but Birdie held his wrist.

"I deserve to know the truth."

Maddox turned back. "You can have the short version." Birdie let go of his arm. "Ariss is of House Vanderholm, once ruling family of Mount Lena. A first-born daughter and royal pain in her father's arse. He couldn't wait to marry her off and my father, Morin, wanted to join our houses together. He wanted to use the Fortress as a refuge in-case of an emergency. He agreed to the match.

"I didn't want more responsibilities or to be tied down with some dolt who I'd never met and probably had a wandering eye, so I began arranging transport out of the Sea of Circles. But then your mother got pregnant and begged me to stay, which I couldn't refuse. So I stayed, and as the wedding drew nearer Ariss and I finally met.

"I was surprised, as she was beautiful, and had a sharp mind. But a few weeks before we were to be wed Nefaro made his move for power. She survived the purge and fled her home like us. I hadn't known she was alive until I received a message from an agent one day at the cottage. I left you and Bella to find her, but arriving at the town she'd been hiding-out in far to the south-west, I found it burnt to the ground. An official in a nearby outpost told me it had been pirates from the Sun Isles. But I knew the sea surrounding Mala was too well patrolled for a pirate ship to slip through this far south. I knew my best bet to find her would be in Stadarfell, the prison island.

"Using contacts in High Shoals I made a false identity, putting the coin I'd stored in a bank on the island to use. I found Ariss in Stadarfell, working in the mines and offered to buy her freedom, but to no avail. So that night I killed a few of the guards on duty, broke her free and we escaped on a merchant ship bound for the Isle of Bones."

"Why didn't you both just come back to us? To the cottage?" Birdie asked.

"Not possible," said Maddox. "Nefaro had begun seizing power in the nearby islands. He brought in strict policies, high taxations and executed any who stood against him. We lost contact with most our allies and had no way back onto the mainland. We both decided the best thing to do was undermine Nefaro from our position. We combined what wealth we had left and bought a ship, then slowly built friendships in Breccia. King City also reached out, and an alliance was made in secret."

Leek's eyes widened. "You met the Powder King?"

Maddox nodded. "Ubba's not as insane as they say he is. He despises Nefaro but he won't make a move until the people of the other cities turn against their master. Ubba might be considered a madman, but he's no fool.

"Breccia took some time before they began to trust us. The Hangman demanded that we help out in a series of raids on neighbouring islands before he decided we could be trusted." Maddox pulled down his tunic, showing the scar of the letter P. "It was on one of the raids that I got branded.

"Ariss and I spent years building alliances with those who hate Nefaro. We have the Hangman and his fleet of pirate ships, a dozen tribes of the Sun Isles, and Ubba the Powder King. But we're still outmatched. Nefaro's navy is as strong as ever, and all of the more powerful cities still pay Nefaro tribute and pledge allegiance to the ministry."

"You can't leave it there!" cried Leek. "Tell us more about Ubba. Is it true he forces pitched battles between his subjects?"

"Another time, Leek, I promise. For now, I need to show you both the Spinning Room and then I really must be on my way."

The Spinning Room was a room filled with rotating beams covered with padded leather, swinging chains, and snapping metal loops that you had to time just right to slip through. Maddox had Leek spin a large wheel connected to a series of pulleys, and then briefly showed her how to move through the obstacle course. It was a far-cry from the climbing of trees and swimming lengths she'd had to do with Bella, but Birdie didn't hesitate when Maddox indicated for her to attempt it.

What he hadn't told her was there were hidden pressure plates in the ground, and stepping on these would make the rhythm of the entire course change, or the metal chains to momentarily extend in length. At the end of the course she was covered in sweat and a handful of marks that would soon bruise.

"Leek, you can stop now!" Maddox called, and the room slowly fell silent. He looked at Birdie. "It's pretty simplistic, and only the beginning of what I'll teach you, but it's something to do while I'm gone."

"Will you be gone long?" asked Birdie.

"I'm not sure. Just keep training until I return." Maddox looked at each of them for a moment, before giving a brief smile, then turned and left.

Birdie slipped the diary out from under her pillow and flicked through the pages. She'd read the entire thing again, but found nothing new. The writing in it spoke of her mother's daily life, both court and personal. It told of the problems in her life, the growing distance between her mother and father. About the stress of life in the spire, and having to deal with scores of cousins and relatives—like a bustling anthill.

Birdie couldn't help but feel a pang of sadness for the life she could've lived had things worked out differently.

She flipped through the pages once more, expecting her eyes to fall on some hint to her father's identity. But there was nothing.

Why wouldn't she leave me a hint? Why had she ignored to leave any trace of who my father really is?

'Why couldn't you just be here?' Birdie muttered as she tossed the diary onto the end of the bed and rubbed her temples, feeling a headache coming on. The diary bounced off the edge and fell off the bed.

"Damn it." She leaned over the edge and picked it up. But the cover had partly slid off, revealing a thin slip of a compartment underneath. It seemed to be sealed shut, but she began digging and clawing at it with her nails. After a few minutes it cracked open, and inside were two things. One was a very old and dried petal of what she believed was the lilly plant. The other was a small note written on a scrap of parchment. It had one sentence scrawled across it.

For my one, my love, my Lillith.

Chapter 27: Strange Company We Keep

After retrieving a special box within the castle stronghold's hidden chamber, Maddox left through the portal and entered Mala under disguise of the old merchant once more.

Once inside he found Mala was alight with a nervous energy. The Masked Lodge were gathering in large groups at every gate and guardhouse, with little to none on patrol. The streets of the market sector were unusually quiet, market stalls stood empty, shops and tavern doors were shut and windows dark. As night passed into dawn, Maddox found himself headed back down to the industrial sector. Hidden away in a shadowy corner of a crowded tavern, Maddox met an off-duty soldier and got him blindingly drunk.

The soldier said he was part of a cavalry unit and had been sent to bring a message to an officer at the portcullis. But the garrison there had been instructed to give no aid to the army south of the portcullis. The rider had then decided to get passage to Mala instead of returning to a battleground and more than likely his own grave.

The drunken soldier smiled widely as Maddox once again refilled his tankard to the brim. "Thank'ee kindly, shur. Where wash I? Oh yesh! More than sheventy thoushand men marched out thoshe damned gatesh, and how many had come back, huh? Shit-to-none, thatsh how many! I hated marshin' with that War Monger. Bone Wallsh could'a held thosh Ecslipshi. Curshed everything under the open shhky, sho I did when that Kye shed we musht fight. But now, now I feel blesshhed, cosh my corpshe would be rottin' in shome ditch or field jusht like mosht the resht of 'em if I hadn't been shent back here."

"And you saw this War Monger with your own eyes? Kassova Kye?" Maddox whispered, refilling the man's tankard with ale. The man nodded.

Kassova Kye had been there the night his family was slaughtered. Kye was Nefaro's little lapdog, and if he could kill him, then it would be some shred of revenge. Kye hadn't ordered the death of his family, of course, but he was known to have been one of the blood thirstiest fighters as he fought his way through the spire.

"What about this sage? Did you see him?"

The soldier's glassy eyes narrowed as he focused on the dark patch beneath the hood that was Maddox's face. "Well that's jushht a tale, ain't it? I heard the mansh a monsther, I sware. Eyesh that would freeshe yer bonesh. Eyesh that could peer into your shoul. *Hic!* I thought I'd... I thought I'd be a hero, bringing back that messhage, but I wash glad I didn't have to tell Kye I failed. Jusht yeshterday I wash given ordersh to be in the military shector atch noon, but I'm gettin' outta here ash shoon ash I can find ashhlip... A shhhliip... A ship. *Hic!*"

Maddox filled the man's tankard once more to the brim. "Would you care to sell your uniform and papers? I could find you some means of transport to wherever you want to go?"

The soldier's eyes narrowed. "For wash?"

Maddox pushed the tankard towards the man and gave him one of his most innocent smiles. "I always wanted to serve in the army, but failed the physical. I suppose being a cavalryman might suit my body's limits better. I'd give you a good price?"

The solider gave the room a sideways glance, making sure they were out of earshot. He looked back at Maddox. "Perhapsh. But people will know yer not me." The soldier looked closer at the dark patch beneath Maddox's hood. "Though I can't shay if we look alike or not."

"You let me worry about that. All I need is your uniform and your papers. Agreed?"

"How mush?" The soldier's eyebrow curled.

Maddox leaned closer. "Thirty... gold... coins."

The soldier licked his lips. "Forty would be bettcher."

"Thirty five." Maddox held out his hand. The soldier shook it. "Meet me outside in the alley in ten minutes, I'll have the coin. Do you have the uniform and papers nearby? What about your horse?"

The soldier nodded. "Won't takesh me a minute to get 'em. Eh, butch I shold the horshe."

"Then call it thirty and we've still a deal. You go first."

Maddox had considered just cutting the man's throat and dumping him in a basement somewhere, but if the body was found and recognised then using the man's identity would be impossible. No, it was better to pay the man and leave no risk for disaster. Maddox recovered two of four coin purses stashed nearby, and then returned to the tavern's alleyway. The soldier had the uniform and papers in a large satchel and they exchanged items, then parted ways.

Maddox found an old building where he could change into the uniform. He took out a roll of powders he used to colour his fake hair. He dyed it the same colour as the soldier's, then cut it to the same length. While it wasn't perfect, the disguise and papers should get him close to the sage and the War Monger.

When under the disguise of the major, he'd never had just cause for being in the city, mostly having to go unseen. He hadn't been able to use the alias for access into the upper sectors. Using the cavalryman's papers would get him into the military sector though. Also, the city seemed distracted. News of Kye's victory might just work in his favour.

Maddox's thoughts turned to Kassova Kye as he made his way towards the market district. He'd heard quite a bit about the War Monger over the years. The Ministry of Faces boasted Kye as their elite fighter. He was their greatest champion, but had fallen from grace after Maddox evaded capture in a sea battle.

Kye's father had been a member of the Order of Mist. After his father died, the Order had kept the boy close to hand. But Nefaro threatened to invade the island after hearing of the boy's promising abilities, so the Order had given him up.

Maddox entered through the gate to the market sector.

Ki Helm. The Island of Mist. He'd never visited but would love to see it. The spire on the island had been blasted in half by some unknown force. The Order of Mist used the ruin as their seat of power. It was also where they trained novices, but their number was few these days due to Nefaro's restrictions.

Nefaro had supposedly known Kye's father well, but had slighted the order's wishes by entering the boy into the Clerics Palace at a young age, then the Palace of War once he'd turned ten. Nefaro hadn't sent Kye back when he was of an age to become a novice as promised, but the Order held their tongue, knowing their anger would only doom themselves.

Once he entered the market square Maddox found an empty stall. Taking out a bag of fire dust, he hid it beneath an empty crate and placed a long fuse inside a hole in the bag, leaving a finger-length sticking out beneath the crate so he could light it when ready.

After about thirty minutes the plateau began to fill with merchants. One tried to take the stall Maddox leaned against but thought better of it after noting Maddox's uniform. Civilians wandered past the stalls, tasting wares. One nearby woman spoke of a boat just arrived in the port. The War Monger had docked with his prisoner not long ago.

After about an hour citizens lined around the thoroughfare, leaving the stalls neglected, eager to catch a glimpse of Kye and this sage. They pressed in tight, and the air filled with cries and applause and cheering as soldiers appeared waving banners. Maddox waited until they were midway through the square before he lit the fuse and hurried away.

Lost in the crowd, the ground vibrated as the fuse caught light to the powder, and the procession halted as the crowd began to scream and push away from the explosion. Maddox timed it perfectly, slipping into the procession as soldiers pushed their way to the stall. No one had been seriously injured except for a few burn marks, and after seeing there was no further threat, the procession returned to parading along the thoroughfare.

Maddox slowly made his way through the ranks of men. Near the front, he was rewarded with a glimpse of a tall man in dark steel armour riding a large black warhorse. When the man waved to the crowd and turned his head, Maddox recognised him immediately.

Kassova Kye glanced around at the crowd and smiled, pushing back his black hair, the sunlight catching on a mouthful of silver teeth.

"The Sword of Mala!" someone screamed, to which the crowd answered with applause and cheering. Confetti covered Maddox's shoulders and hair as he followed the stream of men through the crowd and along the thoroughfare. As they entered the military zone and through the next gate, the sun sparkled off the metal pyramid that was the Hall of Faces. Maddox pushed his way closer to the front, earning himself hard jostles for his trouble from irritated soldiers. He came within sight of the prisoner. The sage walked just in front of Kye, and was tall, with braided silver hair that ran past his knees.

The citizens of the military district were in awe of the sage. The families of officers and officials, well dressed and wealthy, could only point and shake their heads in wonder at this strange man. For their saviour though they tossed flowers from windows overhead, and waved flags emblazoned with a white sword on red fabric.

The Hall of Faces sat at the far side of a wide square, bordered by white pillars of marble. The city's crimson colours billowed atop metal poles high above each pillar. From behind barriers atop the pillars, Maddox spied archers.

The square was packed with onlookers and Kye dismounted, then led the procession up the steps, still waving as the doors to the hall slid open. It had been many years since Maddox set foot in the cold, cavernous interior of the hall, and he hadn't missed it in the least.

After crossing the hall, Kye stopped in front of the raised platform, where Nefaro and the Quadra-Ministers watched silently.

Maddox felt the weight of his sword on his belt. He felt the weight of his daggers beneath his cloak. With a thrust of his Old Lovers, the heads of both serpents would be severed, here and now.

The temptation was almost overwhelming.

For most of the past two decades he'd dreamed of nothing more than to see Nefaro dead. It was the thought of Birdie that kept his hands empty. Maddox couldn't bring himself to leave her alone in this world. He owed it to her to stay silent. To stay alive.

Nefaro didn't change his blank expression as Felt spat on the ground, but watched with sharp, piercing eyes as the easterner spoke.

"I am Und-ar-Felt, Second Sage of the Twilight Temple, Scourge of the East, Bringer of Chaos and Crusher of the Golden-Circle, and I—"

"And a terrible bore for a so-called terror," croaked Nefaro. "We know your titles, sage. Want another one? Prisoner to the ministry and soon to be corpse hanging over our city walls. How do you like those?"

Felt went to speak, but Nefaro cut him off.

"Quiet!" Nefaro pointed to Kye, waving him to step closer. The War Monger stepped up onto the platform and bowed his head as Nefaro whispered into his ear. After a few long, silent minutes, Nefaro clapped Kye on the shoulder and the War Monger bowed his head once more before stepping down from the platform.

"Listen, old fool," growled Felt. "Your time has passed. The Temple has grown weary of your old-fashioned ways. It's time for you to step aside. You've no place in this world of ours. The twin moons wish you to—"

"Kye, if this fool speaks once more without permission, cut his throat."

"Yes Supreme." Kye slid his sword from its scabbard and rested the jagged end against the sage's throat. Maddox could only look in wonder at the scorched, broken blade of anatine steel.

Maddox could see the muscles working in Felt's arms and neck as the he fought to remain silent.

Nefaro let a smile show on his lips as he stood up and spread out his hands, giving the large crowd pouring its way inside the hall a sweep of his gaze. "Good citizens of Mala, soldiers of the Circle, sons and daughters of the ministry! Long has been the day since the scourge of the Eclipsi threatened our borders! Long has been the night our people shivered in fear, cowering behind walls. But no more!" The crowd cheered, but then fell silent as Nefaro waved them down. "Our most valued son, our champion among champions, Kassova Kye, has led your brothers, your fathers, your sons and husbands to victory!"

Nefaro let the crowd cheer until they fell silent. "But our time of peace has come at great cost. Many have fallen beneath the tide of the enemy, but their sacrifice will not be in vain! They have been the breakwaters against the storm! They have given their lives so we may ready ourselves for the next era."

Nefaro shook his fist. "And an era of strength it *will* be! Too long has the Eclipsi infested the land..."

The crowd remained silent.

Nefaro lifted his hands, as if embracing the crowd. "Hear me now, both gods and mankind. I promise we shall march out against them, and we will drive them *back* into the jungles. *Back* into the shadows and the caves where they rightly belong. On my life I will give you an Age of Prosperity. Before my time in this world ends, I will leave behind a civilization that could match the power of the ancients!"

The crowd cheered, shouting Nefaro's name now alongside Kye's. After four or five minutes the cheering eased and silence once again filled the hall.

Felt began to laugh— a deep, echoing laugh that travelled far in the vast space inside the hall. "The damage is already done!" cried Felt. "I've finished what I came here to do, old fool. The White-Spot will consume your city!"

Felt slammed his shackled fists into the ground, sending silver jagged lines shooting across the ground's surface and encircling the group. A thunderous vibrating jolt of power blasted the soldiers around him from their feet, and made Maddox's legs shake.

Kye stumbled away, dazed and unsteady. Felt reached up into his tangled hair and pulled out a tiny black vial, which he threw up into the air. It exploded and green powder fanned out into wisps of vapour and began circling around them, making the ground crack and pull apart. Maddox was moving, hand inside his cloak, ready to activate the box.

But then the ground pulled away beneath him and beyond the green swirls of vapour all he could see was black abyss.

And then—in a brief moment—the green swirls dissipated into thin air, and Maddox could only gaze around in numb shock at the change in scenery. They now stood on an elevated platform. Four arches of jagged stone connected above it, and the platform sat above a lake of shallow pale water bordered by barren hills.

But it was the path ahead of them that drew his attention.

Just beyond the platform lay a cobbled bridge that spanned over the lake. Maddox felt his stomach lurch as he came to the realization of where he was, a place he swore never to see again.

The Twilight Temple...

Chapter 28: Marked

Birdie entered her room covered in fresh bruises. The Spinning Room was quickly becoming one of her least favourite places in the stronghold. Leek had left a basin of water near the bed, and after freshening up she dressed in clean clothes and went to look out at the landscape. A light flickered in the castle, where Leek was most likely pondering over another book. He'd been scouring the libraries in his free time. When she wasn't fishing, Birdie explored the tunnels in the cliffs. She was beginning to believe they were simply made to confuse any trespassers, and didn't actually lead to anything.

Her attention peaked when she noticed that the light wasn't coming from one of the many windows, but emitting from the front door of the castle, which had been left ajar.

Had she forgotten to close it?

Once down the stairs and across the bridge, she could see a sphere of light hovering inside the entrance-hall. It drifted up the central stairway, disappearing from view. Birdie ran up the steps three at a time, skidded around the corner and just managed to catch a glimpse of it before it disappeared at the end of the corridor. Hallways dipped in shadow passed by as Birdie steadily followed the orb through the castle, through twisting turns and down steep, dank smelling staircases, she kept it in view but didn't dare get any closer.

Even when she and Leek had explored the castle and the outer towers, they'd never delved this deep. Through a large door she saw a library filled with statues and skeletons and all sorts of oddments. The orb was motionless, hovering in front of a bookcase. She ran her fingers over a globe that occupied the centre of the room.

Her eyes swept over the rows upon rows of large bulky tomes strewn with cobwebs. The orb began to vibrate, and a heavy clicking sound came from behind the bookcase. As the wooden frame lifted and swung silently outwards, the golden orb passed through the now open space in the wall. She followed it through the dark, cramped tunnel, passing corners and down a series of narrow marble stairways. The air got cooler, making her breath come out in pale streams. At the end of a stairway, the orb passed by torches that flickered to life, blue flames spitting from inky blackness, lighting up a long bridge which curved over a dark void. Pools far below reflected the outline of the bridge. She crossed the bridge and passed between tall marble columns that crackled with blue sparks

The path ended at a tall metal set of doors engraved with an enormous blackbird. The door clicked, bird rotated fully around, before sliding open inwards. Inside was a large high-ceilinged chamber and its walls were adorned with ebony banners of House Black. There was artwork—so much artwork, depicting tall and proud figures of what must be her ancestors, battle scenes and unknown landscapes. Stuffed heads of unknown beasts from ancient hunts watched her, their beaded eyes reflecting light from the torches that were still coming to life around the chamber. Her fingers touched the cool, dust-laden weapons laid out on beautifully carved and finished stands.

She paused at a portrait of a gaunt man whose cool green eyes reminded her of Maddox. His hands were resting on two daggers set to each side of his belt, armour adorned with the House Black emblem on the chest and upper arm. Birdie wiped cobwebs away from a metal plate beneath it, revealing *'Morin Black'* etched onto its surface.

So this was her grandfather. Once the most powerful and feared man in the Sea of Circles and leader of the most powerful family of the Twelve.

Birdie followed the orb towards the centre of the chamber, where tables were set about in a circle, covered with scrolls, books and funny looking different little things in jars. On one table was an assortment of powders in pots and liquids in vials. Warily passing them, she followed the golden orb as it passed through the large, thick red curtains that covered a section of wall. Birdie pulled down on the drawstring and they slid apart, revealing an alcove. There were dozens of priceless looking antiques inside, gold encrusted sculptures, a beautifully-coloured large egg that was covered with gems, metallic tablets, each uniquely and intricately designed.

Her eyes settled on a small dark marble pillar which seemed to be the centrepiece. Sat on a platform above the rest, it held a small golden box atop it. Birdie stepped onto the platform, reached out and slowly lifted the lid.

Inside was dark and hard to see, until the orb began to gently glow, and it began flashing, getting louder and the light intensifying. She reached in and picked up the tiny golden orb which now lit up the alcove, illuminating her palm to an intense bright white hue. She poked the ball with her finger, and the ball began moving, unfurling out into a small blackbird, flapping tiny wings silently.

"What are you?" she whispered.

The blackbird pointed its beak at her, its two emulsion-like eyes shone from grey to brown to gold. Then suddenly it dug its beak into the centre of her palm, ripping at the flesh.

"Ah!" she shook her hand but it clung on, and before she could swipe it off, the bird began to burrow, making the skin of her palm bulge up like a monstrous wart. Birdie gasped and scratched at her palm, but the bulge flattened out and the white light beneath the flesh turned to a yellow glow, and then slowly faded.

It was twenty minutes before she stepped foot out of that chamber and made her way back up to the castle. She wanted to tell Leek what had happened, but a part of her worried that he would laugh and think she was jesting.

"Leek?" Birdie called as she entered the great-hall. Leek was sat in his usual seat nearest the fire, but had it pulled around and facing the flames. As she walked around the chair to tell him, she noticed his hands weren't cradling a book. Instead they were...

Oh Gods, no!

His hands were bound behind his back, and a cloth gagged his mouth. He stared up at her with wide, frightened eyes.

Birdie jumped as the door to the great-hall shut with a bang. She turned, facing a figure leaning against the door. In its hand a crossbow steadily centred its bolt on Birdie's chest.

"Ariss?" Birdie couldn't believe her eyes.

The red-haired woman smirked. "Hello Blackbird. Long-time, no-see..."

Chapter 29: The Twilight Temple

Maddox kept quiet, frozen in place like the other soldiers. He could feel the dust that Felt had thrown around him working its way inside his mind, numbing his senses. But he fought to keep control, and was thankful when the sage motioned for the soldiers to follow.

The bridge crossed the lake and weaved between ancient looking stone structures. The ruins were being slowly reclaimed by the marshland. Remnants of the great man-made cities of ancient time, now mostly crumbling, covered in moss or vines. Huts built on stilts had been made from woven vines and layered moss. Women and children stared out from the dark doorways. The elders sat in groups on bridges between the huts, weaving vines or harvesting animal carcasses.

The ground sloped gently upwards, out of marshland. Wooden posts the height of five men had been inscribed with runes. Bone talismans hung there rattled as they blew in the wind, some noticeably human. Maddox noticed the low, vibrating sound of drumming coming from deep inside the temple. The temple was a mound of boulders hundreds of feet high, laid out in a circle, with the centre hollow. Every boulder had been moulded together with some type of mortar. Men in furs greeted the sage at the entranceway, and after searching and taking all of their weapons, a score of the Eclipsi escorted the soldiers into the temple.

Maddox had to force himself not to react as they found and took his Old Lovers away. Luckily the box was hidden away in a concealed pouch of his cloak, well-padded so no one would feel it.

They passed through a high archway and entered a dark junction, through one of a dozen tunnels. The drumming grew deeper and louder. Men inside the tunnels chiselled designs into the boulders, which glowed with a sickly yellow hue. The designs pulsed in a rhythm in-sync with the beating drums. A cold sweat covered Maddox's body, and looking around he saw the soldiers' faces dripping with sweat, eyes dilated.

Passing through the tunnel, they came out onto a platform that encircled the temple. Four bridges connected this outer platform to a large fire in the centre of the temple. Shadows thinly outlined against the fire appeared to be... dancing. Below them, descending wide steps had been carved out of rock, and people sat around campfires in small groups.

They began their way over the nearest bridge and stopped midway across. Felt turned back and pointed to the ground. "Disrobe. You shall be given the honour of feeding the flames, but only your flesh."

The soldiers seemed to be in a trance as they began to follow Felt's orders, and Maddox panicked. He tried to turn back, but one of the Eclipsi pushed him and he stumbled back, grabbing for a handhold but only managing in pulling whatever it was down with him.

Over he went and the steps below came rushing up at him. He tried to roll with the impact, to limit the damage, but the ground almost shattered his spine as he hit the ground. Maddox rolled on the floor in agony and after a few moments of groaning in self-pity, he had the presence of mind to check and was glad to see his legs still worked.

He stood up, or more crouched, and slowly checked the rest of his limbs. Satisfied that the extent of the damage would be a few cringe-worthy bruises, Maddox glanced around, and realized with horror that the handhold he'd brought down with him had been a large and mean-looking bastard who was presently staggering towards him.

As the Eclipsi came closer, he barked something in his language as he wiped dust from his fur-cloak, cracking his neck from side-to-side. He stared at Maddox with his one good eye, the other scarred and sealed shut, but when Maddox didn't reply, the one- eyed man decided to move closer, clenching his hands into fists and shaking them.

One-Eye lunged at Maddox, who ducked and rolled just in time to avoid the ham sized fist. Noise came from around the campfires and above on the bridge.

Laughter. The bastards are laughing at me.

There could be no mistakes made. He had to defend himself, but not kill this fool.

Maddox dived, avoiding the other fist as it came whistling down towards his head, and managed snatching up a rock as he rolled back onto his feet. One-Eye saw the rock, looked around him, and then shouted out to the group sitting at a campfire nearby. With a flash of metal, a figure tossed something up to One-Eye, and the man picked up and waved a scythe in his hand. Maddox glanced down at his the now-less-appealing rock.

One-Eye came rushing at him. Air *whish*ed by his head as Maddox ducked past the arcing blade, coming up in a twisting swing behind One-Eye, who was still in motion from the attack, growling. The rock came smashing down into the side of One-Eye's head, and his legs gave out under him like rotted wood. One-Eye hit the floor, legs twitching.

The people at the nearby campfire began to scream at him, and about ten men came running up the steps, axes and spears in hand. Maddox picked up the scythe, turned and fled, coming to and grabbing one of the many rope ladders tied onto the side of the bridge.

He'd just pulled himself over the side of the bridge when a sword came rushing down at him. Maddox leaned back and let it hit the bridge instead, grabbing a handful of the screaming man's hair, Maddox threw him off the bridge.

Eclipsi were running towards him, more streaming onto the outer platform. Maddox turned and ran along the bridge, towards the central fire pit. Bare-chested drummers in animal skull masks beat large drums with man-sized sticks. Naked men and women danced around the fire, bodies slick with sweat, coming dangerously close to the edge of the raised walkway and threatening to fall down into the flames. They were mercifully unarmed and uninterested in the chaos going on around them, as they bowed, jumped and shrieked at the flames.

Maddox ducked beneath one of many slanted pillars of rock jutting up from the ground, touching the fire and burning bright red at their ends. Maddox ran to first exit, but found the bridge also filling with enemies.

Tall stone seats had been carved from boulders, placed high enough to view the rituals taking place around the fire, but they were too far to be of any use in escaping. Two of the four seats were occupied by old men swaying in trances, eyes closed, arms raised above their heads as they chanted in unison with the fire-dancers.

Footsteps could be heard over the chanting, and Maddox saw shadows appear on the slanted pillars. They were coming at him from every direction.

He was trapped.

Men flooded in around him, grunting, growling with hungry, wild expressions. Maddox spun the scythe deftly through the air, taunting them to come closer. The first two men lunged at him. An elongated dagger flashed through the air. He ducked it and bit the scythe into the man's wrist. Still spinning, he caught the next man's axe and deflected it, pushed the man away and drove the blade down into the back of his skull. The man gurgled, dropped his axe and fell off the walkway, down into the fire. Maddox kicked the kneeling one-handed man over the side of the platform, to follow his friend.

More were closing in, slower, more cautious. Maddox crouched and grabbed the dagger on the ground, prying the hand away from it quickly, and dived aside as a great-axe swung by a red-haired bear of a man bit into the floor where he'd just been.

"Stop!" someone screamed, followed by more commands but in the eastern tongue. Felt jostled his way through the crowd, his eyes burning with anger as they fell on Maddox. "You too, spy! This temple is sacred and you will spill no more blood."

Maddox pointed his weapons at the men surrounding him. "They started it."

"Put down your weapons and tell me who sent you, and I might let you leave with your life." Felt shouted something in their language and the men backed away a few steps.

Maddox kept his weapons raised. "I've no intentions of surrendering. You and your bastard horde helped murder my family. Your fate was decided when you stepped foot inside the spire."

"Spire?" Felt frowned. "Which one, in Mala? Hah!"

"What's funny?" growled Maddox.

Felt shook his head. "I was betrayed, fool. Nefaro betrayed us, his people."

"The people of Mala, you mean?"

"I wouldn't piss on your city if it was on fire. Nefaro was once our leader. He hid us and smuggled us into the spire, told us he had fooled the army into working against House Black. But as soon as we put Morin and the rest of his family to the sword Nefaro turned on us too. I barely made it out with my life."

"The way he tells it you found a way into the city by yourselves." Maddox shook his head. "It doesn't make sense."

"Nefaro is a sage, you blind fool. He was our leader, the First Moon-Sage... I must kill him before I can ascend. That bastard swore to infiltrate the city and open the doors for us, to turn every city into a new temple. But he has grown corrupt by power and wants the Sea of Circles and its riches for himself. He has forsaken the ways of the twin moons." Felt pointed a finger at Maddox. "So, who do you serve, if not Nefaro?"

"My father." Maddox gritted his teeth. "You confess to killing him?"

"I didn't kill him, fool-spy. I destroyed him. I made him squeal like a little pig. I drank his blood and sacrificed his soul

for the twin moons. The same I shall do to you. But not here!"
Felt clapped his hands together.

Maddox dropped his weapons, as if he was complying. "I
have something for you..." He stuck his hand inside his cloak,
ripped open the hidden pouch and snatched out the box stowed
away inside. Maddox opened the lid and placed his wrist over the
box.

Instantly his skin began to burn.

Forgive me father if I fail.

In a heartbeat, the blackbird on his wrist turned red, smoke
wafted out of the box and yellow steaks of light shot around
Maddox, who then threw the box down into the large fire pit.
The memory of what his father told him came burning through
his mind.

*If we ever lose this castle—if something should happen that
we are found out and overrun by enemies, I want you to activate
this box like I taught you. I want you to sacrifice yourself for your
bloodline.*

"You fool!" screamed Felt, as the ground grumbled beneath
them. The world seemed to slow, the surrounding men moved
as if wading through water. Energy flooded from the box. The
walkway began cracking, shards splintering and shooting in
every direction. Large sections nearby collapsed and men were
tossed into open air. Felt's face drained of colour.

And that's when Maddox saw him.

His father, hovering in the air above him—a thick orb of
light swirling around the ethereal figure that could only be
Morin, his long nose and arching brow easily recognizable. The
figure drew closer, within touching distance, and his father
smiled down at him.

You have grown strong, Maddox. But bravery is not what I need from you now.

His voice was a whispery hiss and his lips did not move, but there could be no mistaking the voice.

I need you to live. Go back to the castle. Live. I need you to live.

An energy that was cold and otherworldly, invasive and horrid rushed through him, seeming to splinter pins of molten metal through every bone in his body. He found himself gazing in on the situation around him from outside of his body. There he was standing on the raised platform which was collapsing piece-by-piece, men trying to keep their balance but being cast down into the fire.

Don't be afraid his father's voice spoke, soft and distant.

Around them the air thickened, orange wisps spun out from Maddox's wrist, the blood in his veins aglow like streams of molten fire. His body was rigid, bent back and arms akimbo. The light twirling through the air kept him floating like a feather in the wind as the platform beneath his feet gave way. Beams of white light erupted from Maddox's wrist, and within moments they were surrounded by a transparent golden-like sphere, which shuddered as if alive. It spread out wide wings that swept them up through the top of the temple and out into empty air.

Und-ar Felt's pale face slowly disappeared into the darkness, hidden by the collapsing stones and engorging flames. The wings fanned up and down, the ground shrunk away below them and into the distance. The only thing Maddox could think of as he fell into unconsciousness's sweet embrace, was that he must have mercifully died and was reunited with his father, at long last.

Chapter 30: Lost

"But... how?" said Birdie. Ariss lowered her crossbow and motioned for Birdie to sit down.

Ariss took the seat opposite her, resting the crossbow on the table. "How what?"

"How'd you get here, through the portal? How'd you escape the outpost?"

"Oh, that!" Ariss waved away the question as if the answer were obvious. "Easy, the sage, Felt, released me. I tried trackin' ye but got ambushed by bandits in the—"

"Why would he release you?" Birdie's guard went up, and her fingers involuntarily twitched, but she stopped her eyes flicking to the knife on the table beside her.

"Gods, I don't know! He said he'd no use for me and being at the outpost was only creatin' unrest between his men. So I was set free, without food or weapons mind you, to wander 'til I died. Barely escaped the mountain passes with me life."

Birdie didn't believe a word of it. "That was nice of him."

Ariss shrugged. "I didn't wait 'round to ask for an explanation. Didn't think I'd ever see the outside o' that outpost ever again."

"But here you are..."

"Aye, here I am."

"And how did you get through the portal? Maddox said only one of our bloodline could open it."

"Didn't use the portal in the pass, did I? There's more than one way to choke a donkey, and other ways into this castle."

Birdie lifted her chin. "You always this fond of keeping secrets?"

"Humph. You've grown a bit since I last saw you. Lording it up in a castle suits you more than shitting your britches in a forest." Ariss picked up a jug and poured herself some wine. She picked up the goblet and sipped. "So, where's Maddox hiding? Unlike him to leave a jug of wine neglected."

"He's somewhere below the castle. Should be back soon."

"You're a shite liar, you know that?"

"Guess that makes two of us."

They watched each other for a long moment. Ariss broke the tension by smiling. "Still a smart-arse, hah! Got your uncle's sense of humour at least, if not his looks."

"That a compliment?" Birdie eased slightly.

Ariss sniffed her wine. "Take it whatever way you like."

Birdie nodded to behind her, where Leek was still tied up. "I'm going to untie him now."

"I won't stop ye."

"I won't get a bolt in the back as soon as I turn around?" Birdie curled her eyebrow, only one-tenth jesting.

Ariss picked up the bolt and tossed it away, then unstrung the crossbow. "Happy?"

"Thrilled." Birdie took out the cloth gagging Leek, and then unfastened the bonds around his hands.

"Thanks," said Leek, rubbing his wrists. "I thought I was finished."

"I wouldn't harm a handsome young man like you," smiled Ariss, as Leek took the seat beside Birdie. But remained standing beside her seat, resting her hands on the table, the knife still within reach.

"You need to begin telling the truth," said Birdie.

"Like?" Ariss refilled her goblet.

"Like how you really got in here, and why Felt let you go. And what you want with Maddox."

Leek leaned forward. "And why you knocked me out and tied me up before even asking me any questions."

"When I see a stranger in my betrothed's home, I don't give 'em a chance to defend themselves."

Leek frowned. "You... and Maddox?" His face lit up as he fought to keep a grin off his face.

"Something funny, boy?" Ariss put the goblet down and clenched her fist.

Leek shook his head, holding up his hands. "Not at all! I just... didn't think of him as the settling down type."

Ariss' face darkened. "And what would a scrawny little runt like you know 'bout it?"

"Scrawny runt?" said Leek, offended. "What happened to 'handsome young-man'?"

"He went head fucking first out that window!" growled Ariss, pointing to the double windows at the end of the hall. "Same will happen to you, if you don't keep that mouth shut."

"Shut it, the both of you." Birdie looked at Ariss. "Maddox told me about your history, and you've saved my life before, so you're welcome here. This is Leek. He's helping us out around the castle." Birdie looked at him. "Leek, this is Ariss. The woman who helped me after my home was burned down."

"Birdie told me all about it. Fortunate you just happened to be at that *precise* village." Leek's eyes narrowed.

Birdie nodded. "He has a good point. How *did* you happen to be at that village? I haven't considered it until now, but if you knew Maddox it was hardly an accident that you were so close to where I was living."

"Sure, I wasn't just scouting like I'd told you. I was looking for the cottage. Maddox told me about it and said if I ever needed a safe place to stay the cottage was always there. I used the information to get passage through the mainland and got rid of my escort. Not long after I came across you. Lucky thing for you, eh?"

"I don't trust her," whispered Leek from behind his hand. "Her story stinks worse than a week-old bucket of shit."

"And *she* has ears as sharp as an owl's, boy." Ariss tilted her head. "But I'll agree with you about the aroma. The road's been hard, and I couldn't find a way into Mala. Looked for that secret way up the wall Maddox told me about, but it's like tryna find one pebble on a beach of the bastards."

Birdie sat down. "So how *did* you get in here?"

"My family's stronghold's is near Mount Lena. We've a secret entrance, also. Took me a few days but I got there." Ariss sat forwards. "There's a link, see? A way between this castle and my family's stronghold, but we can't use it often. Y'never know who could be watchin.'"

"Show me," said Birdie, and after Ariss finished her wine, she motioned for them to follow her.

They left the great-hall, Ariss leading them down through the castle and along a familiar route. But when they came to the room where the hidden entrance to the chamber was, Ariss passed the bookcase by. Instead she brought them through a small door in the corner of the chamber, which led down a spiral staircase and into a dry vault where more books were stored in chests. Birdie had briefly explored the room—Leek more so—and he'd told her it was records on court, family history, and other official documentation. But Ariss ignored the chests and walked by them, coming to the back of the vault. She told them to turn around, which they did, and before Birdie could sneak a peek, there was a loud vibrating groan, and when they turned back, part of the wall was sliding aside.

Down a short stone stairway, they entered a round room. Four columns surrounded a square platform.

"This is it." Ariss pointed to the platform. "There's a certain way to activate the link, but you'll have to wait for Maddox to show you how."

Leek touched one of the columns. "It's the same material."

"What?" said Ariss.

"In the Hall of Faces, there are columns there like these." Leek stood back and shivered.

Birdie watched him for a moment, before looking back at Ariss. "What's it like, your stronghold?"

Ariss smirked. "You'll have to wait and see for yourself."

Birdie folded her arms. "I really am beginning to see why you've no friends, Ariss."

The woman laughed, her statue-like mask of seriousness breaking apart. Ariss opened her mouth to return a jest, but the ceiling shook as something far above them made a loud crashing noise. Ariss turned and ran through the open door, and Birdie ran after her. By the time they'd gotten back up to ground-level, the shaking had stopped, but Ariss seemed to be locked onto the location it had originated. They ran up the corridor and past the great-hall, up the spiral staircase that led to—

And Birdie's breath caught in her chest as she realized where Ariss was leading them. They climbed the stairs, and there, lying on the floor of the room she'd never been allowed into before, was Maddox. He was unconscious, hair fluttering in the breeze coming in from the large doors that stood ajar. Ariss crouched down over him and checked he was breathing. She looked back at Birdie and nodded.

"He's alive." Her expression darkened as she lifted his wrist, and Birdie gasped.

Maddox's wrist had turned black. Not just the skin. His hand looked rotted, as if belonging to a decade-old corpse. The flesh sagged from the bone, and there were no nails left on his fingers.

"What happened?" gasped Leek.

Ariss shook her head. "The fool almost died, that's what happened."

"Can you help him?" Birdie rushed over to Maddox and her heart skittered in her chest as she took in the sorry sight. His face was snow white. Deep, dark shadows surrounded his eyes, and for a horrific moment Birdie thought she was looking down into the face of her plague-stricken aunt.

"Get me the sheets from the bed!" Ariss ordered, and Leek rushed to get them. Ariss pointed. "Your belt!" And Leek quickly took it off. Ariss wrapped the belt around the uppermost part of his arm and tightened it as much as possible.

"What're you going to do?" asked Birdie, but Ariss ignored her. Instead, she unsheathed her sword and stood up.

"Stand back!" And after they gave her some room, Ariss cut Maddox's cloak off, then cut through the laces of his leather armour. The sword quickly cut through the fabric of the tunic below. Once Maddox was bare-chested, Birdie could see the extent of the damage. His torso was covered in bruises, veins extending from the blackened arm looked swollen and were turning discoloured.

Ariss lifted her sword over her head and took aim. "Gods forgive me..." She brought the blade down onto the left arm just below the shoulder-joint.

Maddox didn't even twitch.

The limb fell away as black fluid spurted out of the open wound. Ariss let it, until the blood began to colour naturally. She took the bedsheets and began staunching the wound, getting Birdie to apply pressure.

Ariss now looked as pale as Maddox, and as she wiped away the blood from her hands Birdie saw there were tears in her eyes. "Damn fool!" hissed Ariss. Her fists clenched and she looked as if she were about to punch the unconscious man. Instead, she lightly touched his remaining arm. Ariss looked up at Birdie. "He's lost it. It's gone."

Birdie didn't understand.

Ariss looked down at the dismembered limb. "His mark, the blackbird. It was on his arm. The arm he lost." Ariss looked back up. "It held all his power. And now... It's gone."

Chapter 31: The Sword of Mala

The island stretched across the open landscape, the sea visible beyond the Bone Wall. Shapes moved in the city below, through the market square, along the many city walls. Kye waited for Nefaro to speak, but the old man remained silent.

He'd summoned Kye that morning and it had taken the best part of two hours making his way up to the top of the spire. The barricades and bodies had been cleared away and workers were steadily rebuilding it to suit Nefaro's needs, turning it into a fortress, with more checkpoints and traps being set up than there was in the city.

Nefaro stayed facing the city and spoke in a low tone. "I've been debating whether Felt's escape was your fault or not. Twice now you've let the chance to prove yourself slip through your fingers. Maddox, and now the sage..."

Kye wanted to tell Nefaro it wasn't his fault. That no one had imagined Felt could escape so easily. That there had been hundreds of armed men surrounding Felt, but still he'd escaped. Instead Kye remained silent, knowing any excuse would be in vain. He bowed his head. "I'm truly sorry, Supreme."

Nefaro turned around and reached out, lifting his chin, looking deep into Kye's eyes. The slap stung as Nefaro lashed out with his hand, slamming it against the side of Kye's head.

Kye didn't flinch. "How many times will you disappoint me, Kassova? Was I wrong taking you in? Was I wrong keeping my word to your father? Perhaps you'd be better off returning to the Order. Perhaps *they* can turn you into the warrior that I've failed to mould."

"My place is here, Supreme." Kye met Nefaro's gaze briefly, before looking back down.

"Then earn your place, boy! Rid the city of these... these parasites!" Nefaro walked over and leaned against the parapet, looking out across the city. "Do you know people are beginning to believe he's still alive? They've all seen the mark of the blackbird. For years I've managed to stop the rumours from spreading. I managed to turn them against him, against the Twelve, but now whispers creep in from the other islands. Our power is being threatened. Maddox is building allies, growing in strength. The Alliance has become more than a small revolt. I have it on good authority that King City has sided with the rebels."

"They're still too few in number, sir. Even if King City stands beside them, they wouldn't stand a chance."

"But barricaded behind their defences they are *safe*. They can bide their time and wait for me to die or the foundations I've built to crack. You know just as well as I how difficult it is to infiltrate Breccia's ranks. We've no idea what they're planning, or how large their numbers have swollen."

Kye nodded. He'd lost a dozen spies in Breccia before deciding the pirate force couldn't be infiltrated. They executed anyone on the island found with documentation. The Hangman ran the island like clockwork, having gang-leaders and pirate-captains run hourly check-ins with their crews. Any who weren't accountable were locked away in one of the island's many dungeons for a year with no questions asked. If you failed a second time, you'd be hung from one of a thousand gallows built onto the island's spire. The Hangman's Tower was decorated with many of the ministry's good men.

Kye looked across the cityscape and sea beyond the Bone Wall, towards the direction of Breccia, thousands of leagues away to the north. "What would you have me do, sir?"

"Go to Dogesk and take control of the Palace of War. The ministers in Seandra have seized fifty warships to aid in our excursion to Ki Helm. Take your War Mongers and confront them."

"Ki Helm?" asked Kye. "Why?"

"The Order of Mist have sat idle too long. There can be no neutrality in the times to come. If they turn away the hand of peace..." Nefaro nodded to a servant lingering at a door, who then approached carrying a glass sphere filled with a bright yellow fluid. "Then I want you to burn them to the ground, with this."

Nefaro took the sphere and held it up. "Skyfire... We have enough to destroy their sacred tower. Once it's gone, the order will cease to exist."

Kye had spent his first years of childhood on Ki Helm. Blurred faces drifted through his mind. Forgotten friends, hazy memories now more dream than reality.

Could he really put people he'd once thought of as allies to the sword?

Whatever conflicts that warred inside of him, Kye kept his face placid. "I'm ready to serve, Supreme."

Nefaro turned away. "Good, you leave in two days. It will give you enough time to enjoy the celebrations. After all, the people see you as their hero. Don't embarrass me."

Kye's face was the definition of nobility. His eyes stared out over the market, towards the sea, frozen in a searching, thoughtful gaze. His long hair billowed out behind him, caught in a breeze that wasn't there. His weak jaw had been squared, lips pulled back, revealing a dazzling smile of twinkling gems for teeth.

"It's definitely an improvement on the real Kassova Kye," laughed Vines.

Kye grinned. "A terrible truth when cold marble holds more warmth than the real man." Vines had finally made his way back from the mainland after finishing some business with some of Kye's agents to the south.

Standing up on the raised dais, the real Kassova Kye waved back at the cheering crowd. Nefaro watched without expression from a viewing box nearby, surrounded by armed guards and reinforced glass. The old man didn't look happy as Kye basked in the glory. But really, how often do you get to be a hero?

Something he'd always dreamed of. Something that had driven him in his training. And now here he was. Hero of the people. Sword of Mala.

"Is that jealousy I detect in your voice?" Kye looked sidelong at Vines. The big man didn't smile or wave at the crowd, but stood towering beside Kye like a living statue, arms folded, shrouded in a cloud of restrained violence. "I do recall somebody being made honorary captain of the Masked Lodge?"

Vines shrugged. "Damn waste of time. Nefaro has enough lackeys in the city. I'd rather be out there, doing some real fighting, instead of sitting around with my thumb up my ass."

Kye turned to the other side of the crowd and gave them a show, flourishing his sword through the air. He tossed it into the air and caught it behind his back, then flashed it around and held the point to Vines' heart. "I need someone here in the city. I need to know what's going on when I'm gone. Just keep your ear to the ground and thumbs in your pockets."

"As you say, sir."

Kye circled the platform once more, smiling and waving.

The Sword of Mala, that's what they called to him. They screamed it from the choked streets, from the packed balconies. Banners cluttered the city skyline, peasants swarmed the rooftops, all waving red flags emblazoned with a white sword. He'd got everything he'd ever wanted—the love of the people and fame. His name was known across the Sea of Circles and instilled fear in every pirate's heart. And tomorrow he would set out for Dogesk, where he would storm the Palace of War and take control from the men who had once tried to break him.

Years he'd spent among the War Mongers, training in what was closer to torture than education. Rigorous fights, tests that had claimed the lives of many, where your mind would be strained just as much as your body.

But he'd survived.

Kye had survived the scorn and the hatred showered upon him by his peers. He'd risen above the torment and grew stronger from the beatings from the other novices. He'd hardened to be one of the most-skilled War Mongers to ever have been blooded.

Tomorrow he would set the balance right and prove to Nefaro he could be a leader.

Tomorrow he would secure the foundation that was beginning to crumble. He'd stamp out all discontent and secure the ministry's grip in the Sea of Circles.

He would make the Order swear allegiance or crush them beneath his boots.

Tomorrow, he wouldn't just be the Sword of Mala, but the sword that pierced the world.

Chapter 32: A Sick Man's Ailments

Morin Black was two men. First was the strong, stoic leader of his family. He was a sombre, reserved man with a courtly face of marble—always blank, always watchful. Morin held a viper's nest of secrets inside his mind, this they all knew. He held secrets about the other powerful families of the Circle, about every official, high-classed merchant and crooked officer in the army. He weaved his web of spies, blackmail, threats and violence like an enchanted loom, the latter of these acts always executed in shadow.

But Morin had another side to him. It was one that only those inside his close-knit circle ever saw. Morin was a teacher, patient and thorough, showing his sons and daughters how to read charts, debated with them on history, politics, war and life in general. He taught them how to bind a wound, how to break a fever, how to mend your heart—or at least shield it.

Times like these, with Maddox, Morin, Bella and Ann alone in the forest, were Maddox's favourite moments. His little brother Mikal was too young to be allowed come on their trips to the mainland, where Morin would show them how to read the terrain, how to survive with little to no resources.

They sat around the campfire now, listening to Morin speak of the old mining shafts still being explored on Stadarfell, and of the monstrous creatures that the ships on the Isle of Bones brought back from their hunts out in deep sea. He spoke of the mist-shrouded island of Ki Helm, where the Order of Mist meditated in their Blasted Tower and worshipped the stars. About the feuds constantly arising between Dogesk and Mount Lena, the two cities claiming the honour of breeding the best soldiers.

Ann fell asleep to the stories, although she'd looked so tired all day no one could blame her. Something seemed to be draining her strength. Morin laid a blanket over her and continued with his tales, and by the time he'd finished detailing the intricate workings of the tribes in the Sun Isles, Maddox was the only one left awake listening to his father. Morin motioned to follow him away from the fire, and after getting out of earshot, Morin sat on a stump and offered Maddox a wineskin.

After handing it back, Maddox inhaled a deep breath and looked up at the stars. Only one of the twin moons was fully visible, the other partly obscured behind cloud.

"One day those moons will bring us great trouble, son," said Morin, following Maddox's gaze. "The Twilight Temple is building in strength."

"The moon-worshippers?" asked Maddox, imagining them as nothing but a wild people who lived in mud huts.

Morin nodded. "They sound harmless, but their numbers are swelling. Every tribe from the jungles beyond the lands of Eclipsi are bending to their sages will, worshipping their twin sister moon-gods, Ibis and Sareem. Then there's this new political power, Nefaro. He's new to the game, and not the youngest, but his mind's sharp. Some say he had the officials in High Shoals eating out the palm of his hand in under a year."

"Mala's different though, right? He won't find allies here."

"Perhaps not, but my heart tells me to be wary."

Maddox had noticed the escalating paranoia in his father's lectures these past weeks, the shadows building around his eyes.

"The Sea of Circles has always been held together by the frailest of bonds," said Morin. "You know as well as I how difficult this game we play can be. You know how quick the Twelve change allegiances, how the smaller powers play these feuds to their advantage. I've held our family in a position of power for decades now, but I won't be around forever." Morin leaned forwards and placed a hand on Maddox's shoulder. "Just know that whatever lies in the months ahead of us, whatever may meet us at the end of this road, that I'm proud of you. I *believe* in you."

Morin's face looked pale, almost marble-like. Maddox looked back up at the sky, seeing the twin moons now visible, but both burning in a bright red hue. Maddox gasped and looked back at Morin to show him, but his father had vanished, and instead of looking into his father's face, he was staring into the cold, calculating eyes of Nefaro. The old man gripped his hand, sharp nails digging into flesh.

"Maddox," hissed Nefaro. "Why won't you die?"

"What?" Maddox looked around, but the forest was gone.

Instead they stood on a battlefield, bodies covered the land around them. Blood ran in streams and carrion birds filled the sky. Maddox tried to pull his hand free, but looking down, he saw the flesh pierced by Nefaro's nails was turning black, spreading up his wrist. He could feel it spreading through his arm, through his veins, aiming for his wildly beating heart.

"Why don't you just die, boy?" Nefaro hissed. "Just die already!"

Maddox sat up and inhaled deeply, chest shuddering, heart thumping beneath his ribs. His body was covered in sweat, eyes quickly adjusting to the darkness surrounding him. As they settled in the inky black, he expected Nefaro to show himself from one of the room's pitch-black corners, but he was alone.

It took him a few minutes to recognise his room in the castle stronghold. Maddox shook his head, then his hands, still able to feel the old man's nails piercing the back of his hand.

By the gods his arm itched something fierce. But he couldn't move it.

"Ah!" He reached over with his left arm and searched for where his hand should be, his wrist, but all he found was a stump, bound in bandages. Maddox held his head in his hand and waited to wake up, but the minutes passed by, and the horror crept in that this was real.

This was very real.

He slid out of bed and tried to stand, but his legs gave out beneath him and he collapsed, grunting from the pain.

The door opened and light spilled in. Maddox looked up to see an unfamiliar face lit by a candle. A young man with a shock of red hair looked down at him. He turned and fled through the doorway. "He's awake!"

And wasn't that the sorry truth?

Ariss pushed Birdie out of the way as she ran up the staircase two steps at a time. Leek was inside the room, helping Maddox up. Maddox sat back against the pillows and looked up at Ariss, his pained expression easing. She sat next to him and checked his pulse, his temperature.

"Leek." Ariss pointed to the jug, and Leek poured out a cup and handed it to her. Drink this." Ariss put the cup to Maddox's mouth, but after the first mouthful, Maddox spat it back out.

"By the gods! What is that? Piss?"

Ariss put the cup back to his mouth. "This potion helped break your fever, fool. Drink!" Maddox looked at her for a moment, before opening his mouth and grimacing as he swallowed it down. "Be thankful your niece here was shown how to make it by your sister." Ariss nodded over to Birdie, who was still standing near the doorway.

"Blackbird," croaked Maddox. "Do you like torturing your relatives?"

Ariss pinched his leg. "Only when they've been foolish enough to deserve it! What were you thinking?"

"Revenge," coughed Maddox, looking down at his bandaged stump. "Although I think I drew the short straw. The very, very short straw."

"This is no time for jokes!" Ariss handed Leek the empty cup. "Tell me everything that happened right now or I'll have Birdie make up a fresh batch but without sweeteners."

Maddox held up a hand. "No, please. I'm in enough pain." He looked at Leek. "Don't suppose a cup of wine is out of the question? For a sick man's ailments."

Ariss pinched Maddox again. "Answer me! Then we might see to your ailments."

Maddox sighed and began telling them about how he impersonated a soldier, and how he slipped in among Felt's escort. About how he'd been transported to the Twilight Temple, where he'd used the special box to bring down the temple.

"So it's not a total loss, I guess," smiled Maddox, gently scratching at the stump of his arm.

Ariss looked at Leek. "Would you fetch this fool a cup of wine?"

"Of course." Leek left the room.

Birdie looked at Ariss, then to Maddox. "I'll go help him." Birdie followed Leek out of the room, shutting the door behind her.

Ariss looked at Maddox. "I could kill you right now, you know that? If you hadn't come so close to death already, I'd be sorely considering it. What were you *thinking*?"

Maddox shrugged. "I got my revenge. Some of it, at least. Waited long enough, haven't I?"

"How many times have you told me about your father's lessons?"

"Not now, Ariss."

"I thought your father taught you to value patience? What do you think he'd say if he could see what your rashness cost you?" She nodded to his arm that wasn't there.

Maddox rubbed his eyes. "No point crying about it now, is there? What's done is done."

"How're you going to fight Nefaro now, with no powers? Hmm?" Ariss didn't wait for an answer. "You've fucked things right up, Maddox. We were getting somewhere, and we needed you."

Maddox gave her a small smile. "I haven't gone anywhere." He put his hand on the back of hers. "I can still do what's needed."

They sat in silence until there was a knock on the door. "You guys decent in there?" called Leek.

"Come in!" answered Maddox.

Leek set four cups down and poured wine into each. He handed one to Ariss, then Maddox, and lastly Birdie. The young man wore a sheepish grin as he lifted his cup. "I'm not family, and sure as shit not your lover, but it's good to see you back alive."

"Here-here," smiled Birdie as she knocked her cup against Leek's.

Maddox frowned at Leek, then at Birdie. Ariss reached over and lifted his cup to his mouth. "Just drink it, you old fool."

"Old fool? Just who dhoo eww—" but the last of his sentence was cut off as she tipped his cup back and he had to drink.

"We've a lot to talk about tomorrow," said Ariss.

"Indeed," coughed Maddox, after swallowing down his wine.

They spoke briefly about Birdie's training, and Leek finding some helpful information in the libraries scattered about the castle. And soon their cups were emptied and Ariss was alone with Maddox. The potion was beginning to take effect, and he sighed in a sleepy, content way as he lay back on the bed and she lifted the sheets over him.

"Goodnight, you bloody fool." He smiled as she kissed him on the lips.

"I'm a cripple now, miss. And you better... treat me..." and with that, the potion overpowered his rebuke, and Maddox fell to sleep.

Chapter 33: Sell-outs and Skyfire

Dogesk appeared on the horizon against a backdrop of blood.

The rising sun turned sky and sea alike into a canvas of a thousand colours. Kye watched from the bow as they entered through the gate, past the nearest crescent island, where villas dotted the hilltop like marble conch shells covering a sandy beach. The tiered villas surrounded a wide square at the island's centre. Kye couldn't see them from this distance, but he knew Dogesk's elite army would be drilling in both of the outer island's squares, being spectated by most of the officials and their families. He'd picked the day especially for that reason, when the central, smaller island would be only half-garrisoned.

The Palace of War was a high-domed building surrounded by tall columns, situated on the summit of the central island. The dome had been built around the island's spire, which rose fifty feet above it. The nearby watchtower signalled for their ship to dock, and once his feet thumped down on the jetty, Kye allowed himself a small smile.

Who knew all those years ago, when as a frightened boy climbing the path to those gates, that he'd one-day return to take control?

Kye led his column of men, the most elite of the Golden Circle army, from the dock to the gate, where the guards grudgingly allowed them entry. They passed through the columns at the front of the building, entering into a large courtyard, where the palace's three masters were waiting.

"Lord Kye, it's been too long." Lord Sothic spoke in a tone that implied he was as welcome here as the White-Spot plague. Sothic stood a good head's height taller than Kye, flanked by his two lackeys—the oddly shaped pair of wrinkly balls this prick called his second and third in command. Lords Barrow and Curr were polar opposites in as much temperament as appearance, Barrow being a tall wrinkly ball and Curr a small, fat ball.

"Lord Sothic." Kye gave the three of them a flash of his silvery smile, catching Curr's eye and holding it.

"What brings the *Sword of Mala* to Dogesk after all these many years?" Barrow's nasally voice dripped with scorn.

"I have a writ of power signed by the Supreme." Kye took out the scroll from inside his cloak and held it out for Sothic to see. He wasn't bent on playing around and trading insults. Kye had learned long ago to strike first and final.

Sothic tried to grab it from his hand but Kye pulled it out of reach. "Ah-ah!" Sothic leaned in and read the writing after Kye unrolled it, the man's dark frown growing all the darker.

"This isn't possible... The War Mongers control the palace!" Sothic looked at Kye and bared his teeth. "Probably begged Nefaro for years to sign that fucking writ, hmm? Asked daddy to pay back us mean men for all those nasty bruises... I told him you were too soft, too fucking—"

Kye's fist smashed into Sothic's nose like a hammer on an anvil, his steel gauntlet making the bone crunch approvingly loud. The man stumbled back, shook his head and wiped the blood away.

Barrow's hand was on the hilt of his sword, Curr's was already out of the scabbard. Barrow took a step closer. "Your writ might give you power here, Kassova, but harm another War Monger and you'll find that paper shoved tightly up your arse."

Kye slid the writ beneath his cloak. "The Palace of War is now under my domain. Captain!" The officer and a dozen armed men approached and surrounded the three War Mongers. "You are being escorted to Stadarfell, where you will serve—"

"The fuck we are!" growled Curr, jowls shuddering. "You might be a sell-out, boy, but the shit I'm bending over for that old fool!"

"—your sentence of twelve years," continued Kye.

"What's the charges?" asked Barrow.

"For failing in the training of the Supremes' most valued warriors." Kye took out the writ and checked it once more. "And, ah, yes, more treachery, some negligence, brewing discontent... and also for being a sack of worthless shit." Kye smiled. "But I added that bit in personally."

"I'll cut you bloody—" began Curr, lifting his sword. Kye gave a flick of his wrist and the soldiers moved in, seizing Curr and disarming him. They bound the three masters in shackles.

"Escort Curr to the cells. I'll deal with him personally." Kye gave the man another smile and Curr's face drained of colour. "Bring the others on board. They'll right their grievances through hard-labour."

The officials were stowed away in the ship's brig. Kye went to speak with the remaining War Mongers, who were silent and understandably grudging towards him, but once they followed his orders and boarded the ship he couldn't care less.

After they began readying to set sail, Kye went below ground to the cells. Curr had been tied to the chair and was gagged. Kye took out the gag. "We don't need that now, do we?"

"What do you want? Why aren't I sailing to Stadarfell with the others?"

"Oh, I was given permission to personally decide your punishment." Kye walked over to the table, where a rolled-up leather satchel waited for him. Kye unrolled it, revealing a collection of sharp dental tools.

Kye picked up one and faced Curr. "I never thanked you for giving me these." Kye smiled and tapped the pliers against his metal teeth. "Though I must say, your method was much more... heavy-handed."

"I didn't mean to snap... I just—"

"Shhh! Save your breath," soothed Kye softly. He took a step closer and grabbed Curr's hair, pulling back his head. "You're going to need it."

As his ship pulled away from the dock and back out to open sea, Kye changed his clothes inside his cabin and told a servant to burn the blood-stained robe. He went above deck and inspected the one hundred War Mongers waiting for him.

He relished at their expressions of shock when they noticed the fifty warships waiting just on the horizon.

Mount Lena had supplied the men, Seandra the warships. Fifty of the newest and fastest ships ever made, each filled with battle-hardened soldiers from the Fortress.

The Order of Mist was doomed.

Ki Helm is notoriously eerie, with its ruin of a spire enshrouded with mist. Each warship was fitted with a catapult at its bow, and each of these was readied and filled with Skyfire. The armada encircled Ki Helm before Kye sent a lone boat with a message to the Order, giving them one chance to swear their allegiance to Nefaro. But the boat soon returned, its crew pale-faced as they told Kye what they'd found.

"What?" repeated Kye.

"The gate's open, Lord Kye. Should we send in a ship to scout it out?"

Kye nodded. One of the warships broke rank after the signal flag was raised and sailed into the mist, soon vanishing among the murk. From here only the upper part of the Blasted Tower was visible. Just as the boat had done, the ship returned, sending a boat to relay their findings.

"The island's empty, Lord Kye," said the soldier. "We sent a scout party into the Blasted Tower but it's been abandoned."

Kye nodded. "They've made their choice quite clear. Burn it down!"

The fuses were lit and fifty warships flung burning missiles flaming up through the mist, mostly hitting the Blasted Tower. The liquid caught light instantly. Kye had held some doubts, but soon it was obvious that whatever the Skyfire consisted of could melt the spire's material. One-by-one Kye watched as the missiles struck, and the revered home to the Order of Mist was burnt to the ground. He turned to the captain.

"Send word to the Supreme, let him know the Order have chosen to side with the Alliance."

The captain saluted and went to deliver the message.

Kye turned his attention away from the burning tower, towards his next destination. Breccia, City of Thieves and Pirates, ruled by the infamous Hangman.

But the Hangman's rope was fraying...

Brother Orlot watched as the fire took hold of the Blasted Tower and fought the pain tearing through his heart. Most his life he'd spent in that tower. His fingers dug into the dark wood of the ship's hull and he let it go, touching his chain's pendant.

No matter what that tyrant Nefaro done, his brothers would always hold a piece of their home close to their hearts.

"Brother Orlot?" asked Brother Finn. "What do we do now?"

Orlot turned and faced his brothers. The last of the Order of Mist consisted of forty men, five of which were too old to fight. "We need to find this Black Shadow. As much as we don't agree with the Twelve and their ways, we need allies. Set a course for Breccia. The Hangman will be able to arrange a meeting."

Their ship dropped sail and pulled away from the orange mist, its camouflaged hull and canvas lost in the vast water. Orlot gripped the pendant tighter and broke one of the Order's vows.

He swore vengeance in anger. He swore it on his sacred piece of the Blasted Tower that he would see Nefaro dead for what he'd done, no matter the cost.

Chapter 34: All Aboard

Maddox looked like a walking corpse. There could be no arguing the fact. The weeks since he'd lost his arm had drained him, and looking at him now Birdie couldn't help but think the loss had been more than a limb. He relied on copious amounts of wine to numb the pain and it was clouding his judgement. Ariss fought with him about arranging their next move, angry that they were wasting time, but Maddox just kept saying they needed to wait and choose the right moment.

As the days blurred past, Birdie's training intensified under Ariss' supervision. The woman wasn't as good with a sword as her uncle had been, but she didn't hold back. Birdie had the bruises to prove it. Leek sometimes watched, but he'd become more isolated, dedicating most his free time to the libraries. He'd been given basic training by Ariss, and had proved virtually helpless at most forms of combat, although he was showing some promise with the crossbow.

In his spare time Maddox had begun teaching Leek basic alchemical recipes, sleeping and restorative draughts mostly. Birdie was too tired from training to even pay attention to their conversations at night in the hall. The four of them had fallen into a steady routine, slowly growing accustomed to each other.

Ariss left for a few days to see to some business in the city and had just returned. Birdie could tell by her smirk that she had some big news. Maddox watched her for a moment before sighing and spreading open his palm. "What is it?"

"Our friend in Breccia sent word. The Powder King and the Hangman are meeting and want you to attend."

Maddox frowned. "They know better than to try slip past the Seandra navy."

"That's the thing. Most the navy's been called away, some business in Dogesk. The way's open for us."

Maddox idly scratched at his wound. "I don't know how they'll take my change in circumstances."

Ariss waved it away. "They didn't agree to fight alongside you only if you've all your limbs."

Maddox glanced at Leek and then Birdie. "It's not just that... Ever since losing my arm I've... I've had trouble calling my power."

"We know that," said Ariss, crouching in front of him and taking his hand. "It doesn't change anything."

Maddox lifted his hand and aimed it at a fly that was buzzing around the room. "I used to be able to control squads of full-sized men. Made them fight against life-long friends without flinching. Now I can't even make a fly stop flapping its wings."

"What happens to them now?" asked Birdie.

Ariss frowned. "There were reports of bodies being found in various places around the city."

Maddox nodded. "Once the link is severed, their bodies fail."

"That's unfortunate, but..." Ariss pointed her finger to the side of her head. "You've still got this. You can still control people's minds. You just have to change the method."

"Always the philosopher," laughed Birdie.

"Someone's gotta be the brains of the group." Ariss stood up and offered Maddox her hand. "And it's about time you stopped feeling sorry for yourself. Start working that anger towards something useful."

Maddox nodded, reached out and took her hand. He wobbled unsteadily for a moment, but inhaled a deep breath and regained his composure. He turned to look at Birdie, the flame of his old self in those eyes once more.

"Pack your bags, Blackbird. We're paying a visit to the Hangman's Tower."

"Do I really have to come?" Leek groaned for the hundredth time.

"Yes," answered Maddox, for the hundredth-and-first.

"But what good can *I* do? I pick pockets and tickle window latches... I can even do a decent stew. But fighting in a war is well out of my comfort zone."

"Doesn't matter if you're uncomfortable. There's more to it than fighting. Those potions I've been showing you, for example, can help. And we might be in need of a decent stew."

Leek pulled a face. "Hah-hah-hah, *very* funny. But seriously, we could get killed."

"Yes," said Maddox.

"I mean, dead. No more. Ceased to exist."

Ariss walked past smiling. "Yes."

"I mean... What's wrong with you? You've enough food and water here to last out Nefaro... Just stay!"

Maddox finished lashing the rope and faced Leek. Maddox's hand clenched into a fist as he spoke. "Look, Leek. You're with *us* now, and that means you help when and where I tell you. I might just have one hand, but by the gods above if you complain or ask me one more question, I'll strangle the—"

"Everything alright?" called Birdie from below deck, and her head popped up over the hatch, smiling.

Maddox's face changed and he smiled back, grabbing Leek and slipping his arm around Leek's neck in a friendly embrace.

A bit tight, though.

"Just debating over a potion's recipe. Isn't that right, Leek?" Birdie looked at Leek and her eyes narrowed.

Leek smiled as best he could. "Yup."

Birdie went below deck to help Ariss who was just securing the last of the crates in the hull. For a small ship—or more fittingly a large boat, it had managed to stow away most of their supplies. Weapons and armour, food and water, Maddox's disguises and a small lockbox that she guessed held the documents of his many fictional personalities.

The sea had been a thing of wonder most her life, a dangerous and mysterious place. Standing here now, enclosed by the security of friendship, she couldn't help but feel that the ship would become as much a home to her as the cottage in the woods.

She frowned.

Well, as much as the cottage until it got burned down, that was. But now they weren't just hiding. Not just waiting for something bad to happen. They were setting plans in motion, and actually doing something instead of training and preparing. It felt good.

With the supplies stowed away they went on deck and Maddox once again drilled her and Leek about what to do and where to do it. Leek was confused to discover that the poop deck wasn't a privy.

As they turned the capstan and Maddox took hold of the helm, freeing Ariss to climb the mast. Once the anchor was raised, Birdie joined Leek at the bow, watching the Bone Wall and the spire grow further and further away.

"You sure about not being seen?" asked Leek.

"Maddox is right. The hull is designed the same way the Order of Mist design their ships. Their crafts have never been captured in a thousand years. I think we'll be safe."

Leek wiped back the mess of red spiky hair, damp from the light rain and shook his head. "Still don't see how I'd be any help in their plans."

"Better out here helping them than hiding away in a castle." Birdie blew on her hands for warmth and rubbed them together. The weather was getting colder. Ariss said that the first frosts weren't far away, sweeping in from the north-east, and they'd be lucky to avoid them.

"You forget what it's like?" asked Leek, looking at her sideways. "The sheer panic, having to constantly watch your back, afraid to sleep at night even though you feel like you'd sleep for a year? Because I haven't..."

Birdie hadn't forgotten.

Not the burning cottage, or the dark woods. Not the damp dungeon or arid mountains. The bandits and soldiers, one just as fear-inspiring as the other, weeks spent afraid that any stranger met on the path might be an enemy in disguise.

"No, I haven't forgotten. But we can't let it stop us. Maddox needs us. They both do."

"I know." Leek winced. "It's just after surviving my family's apprenticeship of crime, the road to the Bone Portcullis, the prison and then the slums... It feels like I'm tempting the fates by asking to survive another shit-heap of a disaster."

She nudged him with her elbow. "Don't worry, I'll protect you."

"Tell me... why... did I..." coughed Leek, before spitting up more bile. "Get on... this boat again?"

Maddox laughed from the helm. "Breathe that fresh air in, Leek! It'll put hairs on your chest."

"I'd settle for my stomach not trying to climb up my throat right about now." Leek wiped his mouth and pushed away from the side of the ship, as staring into those churning waves wasn't helping. Birdie was up in the crow's nest with Ariss.

Well, as much a crow's nest as a branch is a mighty oak tree.

Maddox waved Leek over. "We're making good time."

"Yeah, it's great." Leek didn't try to make the lie sound convincing.

"You'll get used to it. Want to steer?"

Leek shook his head. "I can barely control my stomach right now. I think I'll take a miss."

"If you're going to be a part of my crew you need to know how to steer a ship. What if we're boarded and you have to take control of the helm? If you can't fight you must contribute in other ways."

Leek frowned at Maddox. "I thought this ship couldn't be caught? A thousand years, and all that."

"Well... Yes, in a way. But if another ship somehow comes crashing into us, I dare say they'll notice. Don't you?"

"I'll give steering a try tomorrow."

"Can't keep hiding below deck with a book, boy. Take the helm and *feel* it. Feel the waves beneath your boots. Feel the blood pumping through your veins, and the wind coursing through your hair." Maddox smiled widely, not noticing Leek as he flinched at another jolting wave. "There's nothing better than being on the open water. Out here a man is free to do what he wants. To be who he wants." Maddox let go the helm and pushed Leek towards it. "Out here you can forget your past. You can reinvent yourself."

Leek grabbed the helm in both hands and turned it with all his might. The sleek wooden handles vibrated through his bones and up his arms, waves crashing into the bow of the ship and spraying up into his face.

He was utterly terrified, but had never had so much fun.

After a few minutes his queasiness was subsiding, and he found himself enjoying the thrill of the ship's motion, moving with the waves instead of letting it make him dizzy.

"That's it, my boy!" Maddox shouted, placing his hand on Leek's shoulder and grinning through the spray. "You're a fucking natural!"

Birdie heard Maddox shouting and looked down, seeing him holding Leek's shoulder as Leek held the helm. "By the gods," she muttered. "He'll kill us all."

Ariss looked down and smiled. "Ah, nothing to worry about. Maddox could guide this ship through a swallow's arse. He'll not let the boy crash." Ariss pointed back towards the direction of Stadarfell. "Once again. Why are the ministry mining on Stadarfell?"

"The iron deposits. Because the ancients mined the mountains, the mainland has precious little resources. You'd have to go into the Eclipsi's land to find new minerals. Do you think Leek should be steering? I mean, he couldn't even steer the boat properly coming onto the ship."

"It'll be fine, now concentrate on the lesson. Why?"

"For weapons."

"And...?"

"To work any enemies or trouble-makers to death, or send power hungry officials to their doom, where they'll mysteriously take a dive head-first down a mineshaft."

"Good, but you forgot about the ancient network of collapsed tunnels. And the Powder King, why didn't he help his family during the purge of the Twelve?"

"Because he was too busy trading their weight in silver dust."

"Which is...?" Ariss cocked a brow.

"Controlled by Nefaro, along with any other contraband supplied to the allied cities."

"Better. Now, a bit of underhand knowledge. Why did the Hangman allow the Powder King to join his Alliance? Why would he trust a man sworn to serve Nefaro?"

Birdie thought for a few moments but couldn't recall anything. "I don't know."

"Not such a smart arse now, are you?"

The days passed with Birdie going over lessons with Ariss, Maddox showing Leek how to work the ship, Ariss fighting with Maddox over sneaking on board a cask of wine, and Ariss fighting with Maddox over drinking said cask of wine...

And finally the island of Breccia appeared on the horizon. The island's Bone Wall was just for decoration, as its two gates had been destroyed in ancient times. The island was divided into two terrains, one side being low-lying and covered in trenches and rotting palisades.

The island steeply rose, with narrow pathways littered with debris. Some of the cliffs had been blown up to make a moat, and a rope bridge crossed over to a small, squat metal gate flanked by stone walls. Beyond this was the Hangman's Tower, a stout spire outfitted with a plethora of battlements. As their ship sailed through the nearest gap in the Bone Wall, Birdie began to make out the swinging shapes decorating the tower.

Hundreds of skeletons hung from the Hangman's Tower—Nefaro's spies, agents belonging to the Druids, who occasionally tried to cross the lower part of the island and breach the gate.

As they got ready to disembark, Maddox donned his leather armour for the first time since losing his arm. Ariss had removed the extra sleeve for him, but he still wore both Old Lovers, replacements which he'd found in the secret chamber.

Now in her own armour, she couldn't help but laugh at Leek, who'd tried to wax down his spikes but just looked like a greasy hedgehog. He wore a brown leather outfit which Maddox had given him, with a long dagger at the belt and a dark brown cloak.

"What?" he caught her smirking and she looked away.

The wind on the steeper part of the island was strong and the rope-bridge swung back-and-forth as they crossed. The drop below must've been at least a hundred paces, and in the space made between the cliffs Birdie saw ships anchored. Figures watched from guard towers above them, giving no greeting or warning. They waited in front of the gate for an age before there was movement above, and a dark-skinned woman appeared, frowning down at them.

"The Black Shadow returns!" her voice was strongly accented. She spread her arms wide. "Open the gate!"

A deep grinding came from within, and the squat gates slowly opened. The woman greeted them inside, after passing through a series of black iron portcullises first, where dozens of off-duty archers watched idly. The dark-skinned woman approached Maddox smiling, clasping his arm and making no sign of noticing his missing limb.

"It's been too long, Maddox! We thought you were dead."

"I would have been, if it wasn't for these three. Axilla, this is Birdie, my niece." Maddox let go of her arm and motioned to Birdie.

Axilla bowed her head. "It is good to know another of the Black Shadow's kin still lives. You are most welcome here."

Birdie bowed her head and smiled in return.

"And this is Leek, a friend of my niece's and a servant to House Black." Maddox pointed to Leek.

"Most welcome." Axilla bowed once more. Then her eyes moved to Ariss. "This one I know too well."

Ariss clasped arms with Axilla and laughed. "Still not over it? I didn't mean to burn it down, did I?"

"Let the past stay where it is, hmm? It is good to see you." Axilla turned and led them through a tall archway carved from stone, where torches flickered from brackets in their hundreds.

Ariss stayed behind Maddox and Axilla, who were chatting, and spoke in a hushed tone. "Flames for their lost brothers in arms. Every flame here is kept lighting for their fallen comrades."

They passed through the archway and up stone steps, where the Hangman's Tower loomed above. It must have been less than half the size of the spire in Mala, but the many windows had been extended into battlements, from where archers stood guard. Walkways skirted the outside of the spire, and from these the many hanging skeletons swayed in the breeze.

Glancing at Leek, Birdie thought he looked as ill-at-ease at the tower's decorations as she felt.

At the top of the stairs spearmen lined both sides of the entryway, and as they pushed open the doors for Axilla, noise and warmth spilled out. Long tables filled a large hall packed to the rafters. Men and women of every creed and race sat laughing, eating, drinking, playing dice or cards, arm-wrestling, knife-throwing. Birdie smiled as she saw a tall, lean man pin a coin to a board with his dagger and could almost hear Bella's voice in her mind telling her not to aim, but to feel where the blade was going to hit.

Children sat on the rafters above, singing, watching the revelry, swinging from ropes. Some of the older ones sipping from cups. It was chaos, and it made her grin like an idiot.

A few of the nearest tables had noticed the new arrivals and were quieting down, staring at Maddox. The silence spread like a fog, wiping the room of the revelry and bustling activity moments before. The entire room watched them, wide-eyed and open-mouthed as they crossed the room and passed through a door guarded by more armed men.

"Well that was a warm welcome," muttered Leek as the door shut behind them.

Axilla shook her head. "It's not like that. They remember the promises made to the Alliance. With the arrival of the Powder King and now the Black Shadow, they know the time has come."

"What time?" Birdie asked.

Axilla tilted her head. "Their time, of course."

The room they entered was small, and as the door shut the floor shuddered beneath them.

"Up we go," said Maddox, as the walls began to slide below, and the ground moved upwards. The roof slowly crawled closer, and near the top they jolted to a halt. Axilla pressed in a series of hidden pressure plates in the wall, making a large picture frame slide open, revealing a large alcove behind it. Axilla unlocked a thick metal door and they entered into a dark chamber.

She shut the door behind them and locked it, leading them up one of three stairways, along a narrow hallway and to a door. The light spilled out into the hallway as the door was pulled open, making Birdie shield her eyes as she followed them inside.

Axilla followed them in and shut the door behind her. The bright room overlooked Breccia, and the churning sea beyond. Two figures sat at the long table, watching them.

"Hello Maddox," said the Hangman, his pale green eyes the only visible feature behind a golden mask. He shifted in his seat, a throne-like chair of dark polished wood, and motioned for them to come closer. "It's been too long, my old friend."

Axilla stood just behind the Hangman. Maddox gave him a bow and sat in the seat he was waving towards. They both watched each other silently for a few moments, before the Hangman looked away, those pale green eyes lost as sun caught on the golden mask. Ubba sat on the Hangman's other side, those dark shadows surrounding the Powder King's eyes having deepened since he'd last saw him. Ubba leaned forwards and took a long sniff from a pile of silver dust on the table.

"Must you?" said the Hangman.

"Ubba likes to do business sharp witted." Ubba wiped his nose and sat back in his chair, holding out a hand, inviting Maddox to try some.

"Forgive my colleague and his rogue ways." Hangman turned and faced Birdie. "I heard rumours another of your bloodline survived. I'm sure Nefaro's frothing at the bit knowing there's more than just one of you now."

"This is Birdie," said Maddox. "My niece."

Birdie stepped forwards and held out her hand, and the Hangman looked taken aback, as his eyes widened briefly and his fingers twitched.

"I take it she doesn't know about my condition?" said the Hangman, taking Birdie's hand in his gauntlet and shaking it. "Not many are so forthcoming."

"Ubba fucking hates leprosy," growled the Powder King.

The Hangman let go of Birdie's hand. "Don't worry, dear. My outfit stops the infection from spreading to anyone else." He picked up a glass of clear liquid and placed the straw into a hole in the mouth of the mask.

"Is it painful?" she asked. His eyes switched back to her, narrowing. "I know a potion that can stifle the pain, if you'd like?"

The Hangman placed the glass back onto the table and looked at Maddox. "Not just her mother's eyes, but kindness too."

Maddox touched his missing limb with his hand. "She has many fine traits. The traits of a leader. Her potion won't do you any harm."

"I might just take you up on your offer, Ms. Black, but for now there are more pressing matters than my own mortal discomforts." He looked back at Maddox. "My people look to me for guidance, for strength. Even as my body fails me, I must show them I'm still strong enough to lead them."

"Ubba says these bastards wouldn't last a year without you..." growled the Powder King, glancing at him sideways. The Hangman placed his hand on the Powder King's, giving him a look that quieted him.

"You may have heard Nefaro has loosened his hound. The Sword of Mala is on the hunt. Kassova Kye has taken command in Dogesk and has the War Mongers behind him. My sources say they left Dogesk to join up with a Seandra navy fifty warships strong."

"Damn it," growled Maddox. "My estimates were less than *half* that number."

"As were ours. Also, the ships aren't carrying simple soldiers of the Golden Circle, who are still resting from their encounter with the Eclipsi. No, they've conscripted elite warriors from Mount Lena, leaving the Fortress virtually empty." The Hangman looked at Ariss. "Now would be as good a time as ever to lay claim to old titles."

"Those traitors can go choke on a whale's cock for all I care." Ariss lifted her chin. "I owe as much allegiance to Mount Lena as you do to High Shoals."

"Fair point, Lady Vanderholm, but the men of the Fortress aren't as slippery as those on High Shoals. They're old fashioned. I'd wager they still harbour loyalties to the Twelve deep inside. Just look at the few of them who tried to revolt not long ago."

"The generals have no loyalty. If I show up they'll just—"

The Hangman waved it away. "Let's not dwell on the past and our many misfortunes. As of now, with the tribes of the Sun-Isles and King City behind us we still stand a good chance of winning." The Hangman looked at Maddox's missing limb for the first time since he entered. "Though a battle without our champion might undermine morale..."

"I can still fight," said Maddox. "I'm still able to hold a blade."

"I've no doubts about your ability to fight, Maddox. But now I need a general more than a champion. You've shown us your loyalty. Your valour. Ubba has the men but lacks experience to lead them into battle. Don't give me that look, you know as well as I it takes more than power to win a war."

"Ubba agrees." The Powder King looked away, sulking, taking another sniff of silver dust."

"How many men do we have?" asked Ariss.

"The tribes are promising about fifteen ships, small but swift. Three hundred souls to a ship is four and a half thousand. As you well know the Sun tribes are fierce warriors but don't use armour, and any chance of them actually leading a charge is unlikely. My followers amount to ten thousand, and Ubba has just under twenty thousand armed soldiers ready to fight, but lacks the ships to get them quickly to any one location in time. We need to take control of a location where we can keep them close at hand."

The three men sitting turned and looked at Ariss, who was frowning right back at them. "I already told ye I'm not goin' back there"

"We could use the Fortress as a garrison," said Maddox. "The defending force would be in the hundreds."

"Ubba thinks you forget how hard it is to breach those walls." Ubba rubbed his eyes. "You think Breccia is difficult to attack? The Fortress walls have *never* been breached in a thousand years!"

Maddox looked at Ariss, his eyes curling up into a smile. "Oh, but we know a way. A *secret* way. Don't we, Ariss?"

Ariss shook her head as she finally gave in. "Shit."

Once formalities and the sharing of news was out of the way the Hangman brought in a man of about forty, ghostly pale and completely smooth skinned. A chain hanging around his neck held a large stone pendant, and Leek leaned in to confirm Birdie's suspicions.

"A brother of the Order of Mist," whispered Leek, and she nodded her agreement.

"Allow me to introduce Brother Orlot of the Order of Mist." The Hangman waved his hand and a seat was made available for him at the table.

Brother Orlot gave a brief nod but remained standing. "Thank you for seeing me, and also for sheltering my brothers. But what I have to say won't take but a moment." Brother Orlot cleared his throat. "A few days ago, Kassova Kye led an army against us, threatening to destroy our order if we didn't bend to Nefaro's will. The Order has always avoided the politics of the Twelve, but now our sacred temple is lost we must change with the times. We will join your fight, as long as you promise to make them *pay* for what they've done."

The Hangman looked at Maddox, and then at Ubba, both nodded. "We accept your offer and welcome you and your brothers to the alliance. Rest now and regain your strength. We might just have a mission for men with your... skillsets."

Chapter 35: Tore, City of Dreams

"What do you mean, 'fight'?" Lord Scarlett asked again, powdered face creased in false confusion. "We are known for our passionate ways, our soulful music, Kassova... not our fighting prowess!" The man—if you could call the degenerate that—was almost naked, only a thin shawl draped around his torso and legs shielded Kye from an unpleasant view. Scarlett was sprawled on a pile of cushions and holding a pipe that's fumes made Kye's head spin in the few minutes he'd been in the room. The Red Bastard's palace was situated on the hill above the sprawling harem of Tore. Everything in his palace was red—the walls, lights, servants' clothing and masks, even the naked people sprawled about were daubed with red oils and paints.

Kye ignored them. "His Supreme has ordered all ally cities aid him in this campaign. You are to provide coin to help fund it or half the number on that scroll in able bodied men ready to fight."

"Twenty-five *thousand* men? Hah! I don't have a standing army, Kassova. I couldn't even spare a thousand. Now if we were to be, say, planning a dashing rescue of some maiden in a high tower... Now that I could assist with!" Scarlett took a long pull from his pipe, tilting back his head as a girl poured wine into his mouth from a golden jug.

"You will assist when and where the Supreme commands!" Kye couldn't keep the anger from his voice.

"*Supreme*!" squealed Scarlett. "What's that old fuck supreme of, eh? Except a table filled with old fools. You're a long way from home, Kassova. A long way from the docks and your men. You'd best remember that."

"Are you threatening me?"

"Very perceptive, isn't he?" Scarlett spoke to the dozens of naked figures sprawled around the room, and they laughed. "Why so stern, Kassova? Take a seat and drink some wine, relax! You Unholy Trinity boys are so... dreary!"

A woman stood up from the many cushions filling the room and walked over to Kye, brushing up against him and lightly kissing his ear.

"There are more pressing matters than of the flesh, Lord Scarlett. Is this your answer? You deny the Supreme?" Kye pushed the woman away, making her make a rude hand signal and hiss at him.

Scarlett tilted back his head and shouted. "This is Tore, Kassova! City of Dreams. We play by our own rules!" He laughed as Kye bowed stiffly.

"I'll relay your answer to the Supreme. The Gods have mercy on you and your people." Kye turned and stormed out of the room, escorted by a score of Lord Scarlett's armed men.

"We'll miss you!" Scarlett called as the doors shut behind him, followed by more laughter.

This was the first time Kye had the misfortune of having to enter Tore. Its white-washed buildings were red-tinged by lights proclaiming the large whore-houses that made up at least three-quarters of the island's economy. Sailors and citizens from other islands choked the streets, and a more unwary visitor might think it a place of paradise. But Kye knew about its dark underside. Black markets sold human body parts to the Druids and witches on Trask. After all, with the amount of prey and the size of the whore-houses, men were swallowed up by the night and never seen again.

His escort got him back to the docks and he boarded his ship. Kye was proud of his trained men, not one had tried to sneak off-board and into the city. Passing through the city's Bone Wall gate, Kye watched as a dark ship sailed past them, and the ship's captain gave a brief nod as they glided past.

Nefaro might not burn the city down like Ki Helm, but the old man had his ways.

Tore bustled beneath the night sky, a thousand voices spilling across the bay.

Now Tore would be known not just as the City of Dreams, but the City of Dreams and Syphilis...

Trask was the last city on his way to Breccia. The home to the Druids and their witch mistresses was a desolate scattering of rock, towers clinging to the outer rim, fires visible from their roofs. Rope bridges connected the towers, with their spire glowing emerald at the centre. The Druids used their knowledge of the arcane to dye the exterior of the spire, and as Kye was escorted inside the air filled with exotic smells, thick vapours. Witches huddled in groups, whispering, bartering with bones, others helped Druids as they fiddled with their beloved rituals and devices, and a hundred atrocities greeted Kye's eyes before he'd even reached the stairs.

By the gods, was that a wolf's head being attached to a man's body? Where did they get the wolf?

At the top of the spire the leader of these animals greeted him, inhumanly tall and lean, face sunken and eyes pure white.

In other circumstances Kye would've been impressed, but by now he was sick of all these political visits. He wanted Breccia, and was in a hurry to finish this business.

"A War Monger has never desecrated this island before by their presence," the man's voice was empty, grinding. "You stink of dirty blood. Speak and be gone."

"Orders from Supreme," droned Kye, taking out the scroll and showing it to the man, then realizing that he probably couldn't read it. "You're to provide all possible support in the breaching of Breccia. The gods know you've been trying long enough..." Kye trailed off as the old man had begun laughing.

"Something funny?" Kye asked, annoyed.

"Breccia needs no invasion, War Monger. The City of Thieves is almost empty. The Hangman has taken his ships and fled, leaving only a skeleton crew to man the walls. It seems you're too late, War Monger."

Chapter 36: The Fortress

The Hangman's ship was enormous, three times the size of the next largest vessel in his fleet. Black sails rippled above as they set sail, ships pulling out of the cliffs below Breccia's fortress in their dozens. The pirate crews expertly navigated the waters surrounding the island, managing to pass through both gates in two single-file lines and moving into formation outside. The handful of warships sailed at the front and back, with the smaller ships in the centre. The following day even more ships were sighted on the eastern horizon, and the Sun Isles tribes joined their ranks. Their sleek hulls sailed high in the water at odd angles but cut through the rolling waves at a speed twice as fast as their own, large curved sails set at every angle.

As one of the Sun Isles ships got closer, Birdie borrowed a spyglass and took a closer look. The dark-skinned crew sat silent on the deck, faces and arms painted in white runes, and the drummers on the front of the ship were the only movement on board.

The fleet made good time sailing for Mount Lena, skirting Seandra as much as possible. The Hangman prowled the deck, making sure everything was in order. The Powder King was in the warship sailing beside them, his flag hanging proud above the mast, bright red with a black crown above a black skull.

Mount Lena was known as the Fortress, and as dawn lit the sky and the sea's monotony was broken by a shadow on the horizon, Birdie soon understood why. Mount Lena rose from the water as one enormous column of stone, the fortress more carved out of the rock than built atop it. A spire rose above it, windows dark and empty.

They waited until nightfall to begin their mission.

"Are you ready?" Maddox asked them, and Ariss nodded.

Leek waved at her, face a thin veneer of worry. "Good luck in there..."

"We'll be fine," Birdie smiled, not letting the worry show on her face. "Ariss could do this blindfolded."

Leek edged closer, lowering his voice. "Then let her do it on her own."

"I can't. This is something I've to do, to show Maddox I'm ready." Birdie turned away and followed Ariss into the boat. A crew of six men rowed them towards the gate, approaching out of view, behind three ships lined up beside each other. Another boat approached the gate and distracted the guards as Birdie and Ariss dived off of the boat and swam towards the Bone Wall. Ariss kept touching the wall in places until finally finding the first handhold.

"You ready?" asked Ariss.

"Can't be any worse than Mala."

Ariss smiled before pulling herself up and taking hold of the next hole, and the next, finally finding a foothold. Birdie followed her up, teeth gritted as she used sheer strength to pull herself onto the second handhold, ignoring the faint vibration coming from inside the wall. Climbing got easier once using the footholds and the height of the wall wasn't half as tall as Mala.

Once at the top, she wiped her hands on her legs and checked her daggers were still on her belt before sliding across the top of the wall and down the other side.

Mount Lena was only a hundred paces away from the wall. A wide platform connected the wall to the fortress, and luckily the patrol was looking out at the ships at the gate. Birdie followed Ariss down into the water, and they swam to the fortress where Ariss dived below the surface, searching for something beneath the water.

"Take a deep breath," said Ariss, after she next surfaced, which Birdie did. "Now hold it..." and after a couple of minutes later Birdie let it out, panting.

"What's that for?"

Ariss had been holding her breath also and let it out. "Helps hold your breath for longer. Now we go under." She took out a short piece of rope from a pocket and tied one end to her wrist. "Tie this 'round your wrist so ye don't get lost. You OK?" To which Birdie nodded. "You'll be fine, just don't let go of the rope. Ready?"

Birdie tied her end of the rope around her wrist and took in one last breath, before following Ariss down into the water. They dived until the light faded, and the rope tugged Birdie in through a gap in the stone, which became wider after pulling herself through. The tunnel worked its way upwards, taking a few turns.

Her eyes began to fill with white lights zig-zagging through the darkness, when the tunnel brightened and Birdie could make out Ariss' swimming figure just ahead of her. The tunnel brightened even more, and they surfaced into a small cavern where a globe hung from the ceiling. Birdie sucked in air as she climbed up onto a ledge beside Ariss.

Once they'd gotten their breath back, Ariss led them into the corner of the cavern, where a tunnel veered up and around, finally coming to a slab of stone which Ariss was able to push forwards and slide it across. They entered another tunnel just as narrow, and Ariss pushed the hidden entrance closed, leaving the gap that was there moments before now a solid wall. Ariss leaned in close and whispered, "keep quiet, many of these passages run along hallways."

Birdie nodded and followed her along the tunnel, turned left, then right. Muffled footsteps could be heard on the other side of the wall, before coming to a dead end. Ariss listened with her ear against the wall for a few moments before looking at Birdie and nodding. She pushed the wall forwards and it slid across, revealing a dark hallway with a faintly burning torch in a bracket further along. Ariss shut the entrance behind them and led Birdie to the right, peeking around the corner, and holding up a hand to wait.

Footsteps approached, and Ariss disappeared from view. Birdie heard the beginnings of a curse, which was quickly muffled, followed by a loud thump, which was then followed by an even louder thump. Birdie turned the corner to see Ariss pulling an unconscious guard by the legs.

"Grab his arms!" she hissed, and they quickly carried the man back to the hidden entrance, where they hid him inside after bonding his wrists, legs and gagging him. Ariss had donned the guard's jacket and helm, before shutting the entrance. They continued up the hallway, coming to the platform they'd passed upon climbing the wall. "Wait here, if anyone sees you, run and jump back into the sea..."

"What are you—" but Ariss was already running along the platform, then briskly pacing along the Bone Wall, towards the gate. She watched as Ariss disappeared inside the gatehouse and shut the door behind her.

The minutes dragged by and Birdie was almost about to follow her into the guardhouse, when the gate let out a loud grating sound and began to open, making the water churn below. A handful of guards rushed towards the gatehouse on the other side, just as Ariss reappeared and barred the door shut behind her with the spear. She drew her sword as a guard came running along the wall to Birdie's right.

Ariss caught the man's spear thrust and knocked it away, shouldering him off the wall and down into the sea, before tossing his spear after him. More guards were appearing on the platforms, a dozen on top of the guardhouse, pointing and shouting at Ariss. She tossed the guard's jacket and helm down into the water as she reached Birdie, laughing.

"What's so funny?" asked Birdie.

"The fools recognised me but couldn't place me. Hah! Thought my name was Sheen and one of the guards even thought I was his distant cousin. I locked the bastards out and knocked out the two left on gate duty."

Guards were nearing their platform from the other side. "We'd best not expect them to keep bein' foolish though. Let's get movin'." Birdie just had time to see the Hangman's ship pulling through the open gate before following Ariss back inside.

They pulled open the secret entrance just as footsteps echoed through the hallway, and the stone wall closed behind them.

Ariss smiled at her through the dark gloom of the tunnel and cracked her knuckles. "Easy as choking a chicken."

The ships entered the narrow port of Mount Lena, quickly overpowering the guards on the platforms by sheer numbers. Once the defenders saw who was leading the assault, Ariss Vanderholm, a living member of their once ruling family, they decided that it wasn't defeat but were laying down their arms to begin a process of diplomacy.

They now sat in the spire above the Fortress, Ariss at the head of a long marble table, flanked by Maddox on her right-hand side, the Hangman on her left. The Powder King paced along the large windows behind the Hangman. Birdie sat beside Maddox, Leek on her other side.

The two officers standing at the end of the table waited for Ariss to speak. Birdie noticed that Ariss had lost her aura of mischievousness and good-natured aggressiveness. Now she sat in a throne that looked built for her, with a face as cold and hard as the marble table, and eyes filled with as much strength and depth than the churning sea outside.

"So what do I do with the two of you?" Ariss' voice was ice, echoing off the walls. "What did my father do with traitors?"

The silence in the room stretched out for a minute.

Ariss jumped forwards and smashed her fist against the table. "He never had to deal with fucking traitors! You both sold him out like a prize pig for the slaughter!"

"It was Blasius, my lady, he was behind it!" The smaller, fatter officer inched away from the man standing beside him.

"Bullshit, Casso! You were the one who first spoke to Nefaro's diplomat." The big man thumped a fist against his chest. "I served your father for twelve years, my lady, always loyal to a fault! I had no choice but to bend the knee when Nefaro defeated us. This little shit was behind it. He's was in control of the Fortress, before you arrived."

"I never went behind your father's back, my lady. I was always—"

They fell silent as Ariss gave a wave of her hand and a soldier nearby tossed a knife onto the floor, landing right in front of the two officers. "Let the gods decide the truth."

The little man, Casso, dived for the knife and just managed to get a grip of the hilt when the big man, Blasius, kicked him into the ribs, sending him rolling. Casso curled into a ball as the big man kicked him again, trying to knock the blade from his hands which were protecting his head, but only managed in sending the prone man sliding around on the floor and shrieking.

Blasius kicked him again, then reached down and grabbed Casso's hands, prying the knife away. The small man whimpered and spat blood, then glanced up, pushing himself along the floor and away from Blasius.

"How long I'd dreamed of slitting your fat throat, you little cock-sucking—"

There was a blur before Birdie's eyes, followed by the sound of a crossbow letting fly. The bolt caught Blasius in the back and he grunted, then looked down and coughed. Turning, he looked up from the bolt sticking out from his chest. Ariss nodded and five soldiers surrounded Blasius with drawn swords.

"You... fuchenn... bweetch." The big man spat blood, dropped to his knees and let the knife tumble from his hand. The five men moved in and brought down their swords. Metal flashed, and Blasius let out a final choke, before the blood of a traitor pooled across the floor.

Casso was still getting hold of himself, but now stood up and stared at the corpse of his former comrade with wide eyes. "How-How did you know?"

"I didn't." Ariss gave one more nod and the soldiers surrounded Casso.

"But he was the traitor! He was Nefaro's lackey!" Casso cringed as the five soldiers lifted their swords. "Have mercy, please!"

"Fuck your mercy," growled Ariss, and Birdie saw she didn't even blink as the blades were brought down, and Casso fell beside Blasius. The Hangman smiled behind his golden mask.

And the Fortress was taken.

Chapter 37: I know you...

Kye watched as the last of the Druids rushed inside the gate, now hanging on its hinges and smouldering. Only one barrel of Skyfire had been used to put a hole in the gate which had kept enemies at bay for a thousand years, from Eclipsi to Sun Isles tribes, and more recently enemies of the Hangman.

"Let's go!" he ordered, and the column of men in front of him beat their spears into the dirt before beginning to march up the path to the gate. Screams were coming from inside, along with flashes of different coloured lights. Fighting had begun up on the wall, a couple of burning bodies fell screaming, quickly quieted on the jagged cliffs below. The Druids were a foul enemy to have, their weapons unforgiving, and the hundred men they'd provided had been eager to be the first through the gate.

Bodies lay strewn inside, a few of the Druids but mostly burnt remains of the enemy. Fighting was still ongoing on the walls and he sent two score of spearmen to put them to an end. A Druid running ahead of his comrades got shot by a bolt, making him stumble as he ran up the stone steps, but still managed in throwing a glass sphere filled with Skyfire up into one of the lower wooden battlements, which caught light instantly.

"Storm the spire!" shouted Kye, waving them on, and the spearmen climbed the steps behind their shields, rogue bolts finding weak spots and opening quickly closed gaps. "Bowmen!" the archers following closely behind the spearmen, trying to even the odds of the enemy's defensive advantage. "Get those fucking barrels moving!"

The latter was shouted at the next group of Druids carrying a barrel of Skyfire. They wore thick leather sleeves and masks, with pouches over their mouths and noses filled with only the gods knew what. The dozen men hauled the barrel up the steps, guarded by soldiers carrying shields. Men on the walls above were pointing and screaming, archers dotting the large shields like pincushions. One Druid got hit and fell, but the rest kept going, placing the barrel just in front of the gate.

The fuse was lit and the men rushed away as fast as they could, a few getting hit by arrows. The men around him flinched as the Skyfire took light, flashing as bright as the sun. The fluid inside exploded and covered the gate, melting it until it cracked and gave way, collapsing.

"Next barrel!" he screamed, ears still ringing, and the next group of Druids rushed past. As they neared the portcullises inside the gate, the men on the walls above abandoned their posts and ran inside the spire. The portcullises stood no chance and after the next barrel exploded they soon melted away.

Men poured inside of the Hangman's Tower, Kye following them in, but staying well back out of danger. Bodies lay scattered about the hall, burning, melted, catching light to the tables they'd landed on. Soldiers stifled the flames as the battle moved through the connecting corridors and rooms.

Within an hour Breccia had gone from an impenetrable stronghold of the notorious Hangman, to a broken shell of an old world. Kye gave the officers praise and left the men to pillage anything they could find.

Nefaro would be pleased.

"I suppose I should be pleased..." muttered Nefaro, sitting behind the long table. His face was pale and drawn looking, and for once, Kye noticed he more slouched in his throne than sat, letting it hold him up. The Hall of Faces was eerily silent, only Kye himself had been allowed entry. "But I can't help but wonder why you haven't finished this matter yet. The Black heir still lives, and there's rumour another of his bloodline survives. Every day they draw breath is another crack in our foundation. Another piece of my soul which withers away. The Twelve are still revered in some parts of the world, Kassova. And now the Alliance has taken hold of Mount Lena, I fear more will flock to their cause.

"You still have a long road ahead of you, before you secure your place by my side. Bring me Maddox and his niece, Kassova. Do this for me."

Kye bowed. "It will be done, Supreme. I swear it on my life."

"Empty promises." Nefaro looked around at the hall. "How the world has fallen from once greatness. How the might of heroes has crumbled." He fixed his tired eyes on Kye. "But we must make do with the tools we are given. Go to Mount Lena, Kassova. Infiltrate their defences and bring me back what I ask." He climbed down from his seat and moved around the table. Kye helped him off the dais and Nefaro put a hand on his shoulder. "Be the son I never had, Kassova. Become my true heir and show me my life's work hasn't been in vain."

Kye bowed once more. "On my life... *father*... I'll bring them to you, no matter the cost. I'll put an end to this Alliance even if it kills me."

"See that you do." Nefaro lifted his chin so they were staring into each other's eyes, and Kye saw a glint of that old razor-sharp mind. The old man slapped him across his face, harder than ever before, sending him stumbling back a step. "Because if you fail me once more, Kassova, it will..."

The streets of Mala were quiet, emptied by the heavy rain washing away at the grime and soot choked roofs. A far-cry from the previous hero's farewell he'd received. Kye was beginning to realize how short people's memory-spans actually were.

His small procession of guards drew only the odd glance from a citizen in a doorway.

It seemed favour for the Sword of Mala had dulled.

Kye now had thirty ships under his command, given a handful of old warships that were surplus to patrolling duties in the Sea of Circles. With the troops and supplies refreshed, they made way and the lack of wind made their voyage a crawling monotony. By the seventh day they reached Mount Lena, pirate ships separated but in a defensive formation. Kye ordered a lone ship to approach, flying a white flag of truce. An hour later he was on a boat and entering into the Fortress, accompanied by a small guard of a dozen elite soldiers.

Once through the docks and inside the Fortress, a dark-skinned woman with a heavy accent greeted him. "I am Axilla. I shall escort you to the planning room."

Kye followed her up a series of stairs and through heavily guarded doors, into a room filled with a long marble table. About fifty men and women sat around it, a few even familiar faces. One in particular drew his eye. The Powder King smiled as Kye stared at him, even gave a slight wink before he sniffed heavily from the white powder piled in front of him.

"The famous War Monger Kassova Kye, Right-Hand of the Unholy Trinity, Loyal Hound to Nefaro, Sword of Mala. You've gained quite the reputation and gathering of titles." The Hangman sat at the head of the table, golden mask revealing two green eyes as sharp as anatine steel.

"As do you, Heir to High Shoals, Hangman of Breccia, Leper and Traitor..." Kye allowed the satisfaction as Ubba growled and went to stand up, until the Hangman grabbed his arm and pulled him back down. "I always knew there was something odd about you, Ubba. I knew you had a fondness for boys and powder, but rotting flesh? That's unusual, even for you..."

The Powder King snatched out a long knife and stood up. "I'll cut off your balls and shove them up your mother's shrivelled—"

"Enough!" shouted the Hangman.

Kye gave them all a flash of his silvery smile, scanning the crowd once more and noticing another familiar face.

"Well-well, if it isn't the Black Shadow." Kye gave a mock bow towards Maddox. The man didn't reply, but the hatred in his eyes would have unsettled lesser men. "You look good. Lost weight?" Kye moved his left arm around and smiled as he stared at the missing limb.

A red-haired boy sitting beside Maddox sat back from view, revealing a young woman between him and Maddox.

Kye felt his stomach churn, like molten metal swirling through his body, flooding through his veins. "I-I know you..."

It was her, those eyes. He could never forget those eyes...

Lillith looked at Kye, then at Maddox, who whispered something in her ear. Maddox looked back at Kye. "This is Anne's daughter. You remember Anne? My sister who was killed after you and your ministry stormed our home?"

Kye felt the pieces click into place in his mind. There was no mistaking those eyes and that face, she could only be Lillith's daughter. She was the image of her, like a mirror.

So, Lillith had been pregnant?

Had she given me a false name?

It would explain everything. Her avoidance of him, followed by her total disappearance...

She hadn't hated him, and was probably locked away by her over-bearing father, Morin...

"Gentlemen, we have more pressing matters to discuss right now than the past," said the Hangman.

"Precisely," said Kye, struggling to pull himself together, feeling like his head was floating away from his body. The ground seemed to rolling beneath his feet.

Was that his... *daughter*?

"More pressing matters." Kye nodded. "His Supreme offers a pardon to any members of the Alliance who lay down arms and swear an oath to serve the ministry. Any who don't comply will be shown no mercy.

"You have until dawn tomorrow to decide. Raise a white flag over the spire if you accept the Supremes' gracious offer." Kye gave the girl one final glance, her eyes fixated on his, making that ball of emptiness at his core shift and loosen like a nest of eels. "And may the Gods have mercy on your souls if you refuse..." He turned and left the room.

He had a daughter.

A daughter that tomorrow he might turn to a charred corpse.

The gods had a cruel sense of humour. But he would think of something, surely.

He had to.

"Didn't you see how he looked at you? You're sure you've never seen that man before?" Maddox asked her, hovering over Birdie as she sharpened her daggers. Birdie shook her head, not comfortable with the crazed expression on her uncle's face.

"Maddox, you're not making any sense." Ariss put her hand on Maddox's shoulder, pulling him away from her. "How would Birdie have ever met him before?"

"My father suspected it was someone close to the ministry." Maddox walked away and sat at the table in Ariss' old living quarters. "A blind man could read Kye's expression."

"What is it?" asked Leek, entering through the doorway with a book in his hand.

"Maddox thinks that man, Kassova Kye, might be my father," said Birdie. "Personally I don't see how it makes any difference if he is."

Maddox turned around, looking at her. "We can use it! It's a chink in his armour. If he knows you're here he'll try to avoid attacking the Fortress until he can come up with a plan to capture you."

"Why would he even care?" Birdie put the dagger down. "Just because he and my mother once had a thing doesn't mean he'll hinder Nefaro's plans to save some girl that might be his daughter or mightn't."

"She makes a good point," said Ariss, kneeling down in front of Maddox. "You're only clutching at straws. We need to act fast and act now. If we wait until morning, we lose our element of surprise."

Maddox looked down at his arm, then around at the room. "We've lost too much already. Risking you or Birdie's life once more when there's a smarter alternative is foolish. I don't want to but I'm pulling rank on this. I'll speak with the Hangman and see what he thinks." Maddox stood up and ignored the dark glare Ariss was giving him. He left the room, shutting the door behind him without a backward glance.

"Well, I guess His Highness has spoken," growled Ariss, storming from the room, leaving a bewildered looking Leek staring from one door to the other.

"I don't know why," said Leek, gnawing at a fingernail, something Birdie had been noticing him doing more often since leaving Mala. "But I've got a *bad* feeling about this."

Maddox left the room without looking back, not wanting them to see the doubt in his eyes. He had to act fast if he was going to take advantage of Kye's hesitation. If it could save the life of his niece, Maddox owed it to Anne to do all he could.

The Hangman and Ubba were alone in the planning room, sitting close beside one another, talking in hushed tones over a bottle of spirits. They waved for Maddox to join them.

"There's a plan brewing behind those eyes," said the Hangman. "Something to do with the War Monger's confusion, I don't doubt?"

Maddox nodded. He filled them in about how his sister had been with child and who he thought the father was, and how it could be played to their advantage. Morin had kept it secret, letting no one outside their small circle know.

"Excellent," said the Hangman. "Let's just hope the noose doesn't snap..."

Chapter 38: Battle of Mount Lena

Pulling the shiny, oiled hair back, Maddox tied it into a ponytail, then helped strap on Birdie's armour and daggers. "I'm proud of you for doing this. I know you don't have to, but it means a great deal to me."

With a final nod they left the spire and descended through the Fortress. People rushed about in preparation for battle, ignoring them as Maddox led them to the docks. They watched as Birdie's figure made its way through the sailors and across the gangplank, onto the lone ship that would leave through the gate.

Maddox had sent a message to Kye the previous night, informing him that they would trade Birdie for his oath to sail away. Kye had agreed to these terms, and it had pained Maddox to even think of betraying his niece. But he knew he had to keep her safe, by any means necessary.

He watched as the ship raised anchor and made its way through the gate.

Now all he could do was pray.

Kassova Kye was not a sentimental man, anyone could tell you that. He'd scorned his birth right to join the Order of Mist, pissed on the men at the Palace of War who'd made him one of the most feared warriors in the world. He'd joined the battle in the spire of Mala, when Nefaro seized power, slaughtering his lover's family to try to save her.

He wasn't sentimental. So why was he going behind his master's commands just so he could save a girl he'd never even spoken to before?

Did it really matter if she was his daughter?

Since seeing her he'd felt a part of him inside awaken. A shadowed land caught in twilight since Lillith's death now for the first time glimpsing light on the horizon. So when a messenger had offered him a way of saving her, of saving Birdie, at the cost of backing down and sailing away, he'd jumped at the chance.

Birdie.

After all, once he had her aboard, there was nothing stopping him from raining Skyfire down on the Fortress... She would forgive him, in time. At least she would be safe.

Kye watched as a lone ship sailed through the gate. The hull was high-sailing, long and sleek, and even against the wind it swiftly moved across the waves.

"Isn't that..." He turned to the nearby captain. "Your spyglass, quickly!"

Taking the instrument, he glimpsed through the eyehole, watching the ship's sails being let out further.

"My lord, I believe it's a vessel of the Sun Isles. Shall we engage?"

"No!" shouted Kye. "Cut it off! Send a signal to capture it, but *do not engage*!" The captain bowed and went to relay the message to a ship further down the line. Ships further along were breaking formation and moving to block where the tribesmen's ship was headed.

Kye looked once more through the spyglass, and he could almost swear he could make out Birdie's figure steering at the helm. "Make way, let down full sail!" the captain was bellowing, and while it took them a few minutes to begin moving, and the small ship was already cutting past them and veering side to side, Kye knew they would trap the ship by encircling it.

She wouldn't get away...

The ships were lined up, more moving about, cutting off the flanks. Kye gripped the rail as his ship slowly increased its pace, watched as their target closed the distance with the first blockade. He inhaled deeply as it rushed towards a tiny gap in the formation, too small to fit through, but as it collided into the other ships' hulls the speed of the vessel and its oddly-shaped bow forced it up out of the water, rattling between both ships like a carriage on a badly cobbled road. It grinded its way through the gap, splashing down on the other side, leaving deep score marks in the hulls it had scraped over.

Kye let out his breath. "Get us around them, now!"

The ships on the far side were closing around the target, a few even managing in hitting the small ship's sails with chain shot, taking down the centre mast. The target ship slowed, but still outpaced any of theirs. As it reached the next line of ships its front mast fell, only just managing to breach through between the two ships, limping through the gap and slowly bobbing away. Kye's ship circled around, quickly cutting off the path of the target ship. Its masts lay broken on the deck, a sailor was caught under one, screaming. The dozen sailors still remaining tried to cut the ropes to free him.

Bowmen lined Kye's deck and as they neared the target its crew gave up any idea of fighting, dropping their axes and daggers.

And a skeleton crew it was, surely.

They were lined up at the bow as Kye climbed aboard and made his way to the helm.

Birdie stood at the stern, staring back at the Fortress. Kye walked over and grabbed her shoulders, turning her around to face him. Instead of Birdie, though, Kye now stared into the face of a young man with red eyebrows and a nervous expression.

Kye snarled as he snatched off the wig, revealing red, spiky hair. He grabbed him by the collar and shook him. "Who are you? Where's Birdie?"

"I'm Leek," he squeaked, chewing on a fingernail. "And I'm really sort about all of this. Please don't kill me."

"My Lord!" shouted the captain, making Kye turn and look at where he was pointing. Ships had slipped through the gate while they were chasing this impersonator's ship. More were appearing on the horizon to the east. Sun Isles ships, and a lot of them.

"Load the Skyfire!" he screamed, pushing Leek towards a soldier. "Get him to the brig." Kye climbed back aboard and noticed the captain's expression had grown pale. "What now?" asked Kye, and after the captain mumbled something incoherently, Kye had him repeat it.

"Empties," said the captain. "The Skyfire barrels have been swapped with empties."

"Load the barrels!" screamed Birdie, swinging the helm around as they veered through the gate, following close behind the ship Maddox and Ariss were on. The Hangman's warship stormed through the waves just in front of them, more ships following in their haste.

It had taken all night between sneaking aboard the nearest ships and swapping the barrels of the Skyfire for empty ones, but the brothers of the Order of Mist had been an invaluable help. The Hangman had kept their camouflaged ship nearby, and once beckoned and instructed, they'd crept aboard the enemy ships as silent and unseen as ghosts, silencing guards on watch duty.

Her first barrel was loaded just as the Hangman's ship closed the distance enough to let its own fly, and their barrel hit one of the enemy ships in the middle of the formation. The ship quickly erupted into flames. Men atop masts flung themselves into the water, the rigging snapped and wood splintered. Maddox's ship was next to send a barrel soaring, just catching the nearest ship at its bow. The enemy ships pulled away from their burning comrades, circling around to attack the oncoming enemy head on.

Now lacking their barrels of Skyfire, the enemy ships settled for simple rocks, which hit the Hangman's ship at its bow, smashing more than boards by the screams floating across the water.

"Fire!" she screamed and after the signal was given, the catapult at the bow of the ship let loose, barrel soaring up into the air, deck vibrating beneath her feet enough to rattle her teeth. The ship's engineer was solely in charge of aiming—a task she was grateful not to be responsible for. They only had six barrels to a ship, namely hers, the Hangman's, Maddox's, Ubba's, and the two other remaining warships. The rest would try to close the distance and board while the bigger ships were engaged.

Her barrel hit the middle mast of the closest oncoming ship, the fiery liquid catching flame to canvas and raining down on the unlucky crew.

"Load again!" she screamed. She held no pity for them. Their fate was of their own making.

The next barrel hit, the third missed, gaining the engineer dark frowns from the ship's officers. Any missed barrels meant more enemies for them to fight. More friends and family lost to the cause. There was no time for a fourth barrel, as the Hangman's ship was already under attack from boarders, Maddox readying to repel a ship mere seconds away and more enemy ships rushing to join the fight.

"Crews get into fighting positions!" screamed the captain beside her, yelling at his officers, quickly forming the chaos below into something resembling a crew of ready fighters. "Bowmen ready!" he screamed, and the line of men crouched behind the rail. They stood as the enemy ship came within distance. "Loose!"

The bolts flitted into the air, lost in the sky, a barely audible shower of thuds as they landed among the enemy deck.

"Again!"

The bowmen released one more volley before the enemy ship was alongside them, casting grappling hooks which clawed into the wooden rail and caught tight. As were her crew swinging their own instruments, men swinging from the mast as they boarded, bowmen shooting any fair game within sight. They screamed in anger and pain below the helm, one crewman helping out on the catapult behind her gave a choking cough as a bolt caught him in the neck, sending him tumbling down into the water. Birdie ducked as another bolt came flying towards her, its shooter quickly taken down by the group of bowmen assigned to keep her safe.

The two ships closed distance, both crews pulling the hulls closer, until boarding planks were slid across and the bravest of both ships stormed into the fray, some falling from bolts finding their mark, others managing to get across and making room. Men spilled across both sides like a river of madness, faces buzzed among the press, snarling and red-faced. Blood splashed up through the air like sea spray. Swords flashed in the gleaming sunlight and crossbows thrummed one after another. Birdie just had the presence of mind to notice the catapult had just been loaded.

She didn't even bother keeping an eye on its progress as it was flung up into the air. "Load again!" she shouted, but the crew in charge of the catapult were already at it, and she felt as useful in this situation as a third armpit.

By the Gods, what was Maddox thinking putting her in charge of a ship?

She scanned the crowd below, noticing the stream of enemies coming aboard was increasing. "Get the catapult aimed at their ship!"

The captain paled. "Madness! We'll get caught in the fire!"

"Just do it!" and she grabbed an officer and pulling him close. "Take the helm!" She waved for her depleted guard of bowmen—now five instead of eight—to follow her down onto the deck.

Bodies pressed in, heads bobbing in and out of view. A hand hit her across the side of the head—no an elbow, thrown back by one of her crew as he threw a hatchet at a solider crossing the boards, which glanced of his armour harmlessly.

Bodies lay on the deck, wood slippery and scarlet. Birdie already had her daggers out and didn't remember unsheathing them. A tall man in front of her with dreadlocks took a sword thrust through the chest and fell to his knees, revealing a young, pale faced man trying to pull the sword free. Birdie got pushed from behind and stumbled, just managing to keep her feet. The pale faced solider growled as he locked eyes with her, and Birdie watched as her hands instinctively worked for her, old habits coming into play quicker than her mind was working.

Her right hand brought the dagger up towards his face, making him cringe away and close his eyes, lifting his hand to block the thrust, but too slow. The dagger took him in the throat and he grabbed her wrist after letting go of his sword, pulling both of them down. She landed atop him, getting a spurt of blood straight into her face before she had time to roll off. The man clasped at the dagger, only making the blood flow all the more.

Birdie gasped as she wiped the blood off, and couldn't help but stare into the man's eyes. He stopped struggling then, and his eyes lost their focus.

Birdie felt sick. She stumbled away from the body, trying to wipe the blood from her hands in vain. A bolt bounced off the mast nearby and just avoided her face on the rebound. A soldier came at her swinging a mace. She stepped back, almost tripping on a body, but steadied herself as the man brought down his weapon. Somehow she managed to get her dagger in front of it, holding it between both hands, arms trembling from the weight behind it. The man ripped the mace away, snatching the dagger from her grip, the sharp points of the mace cutting into back of her hands. He growled as he smashed his elbow into her face, catching her nose.

The bone didn't break but blood spurted down her leather armour, and through the fog of pain she grabbed out, taking hold of the mace's hilt, screaming as she kneed the bastard into the groin, making him double over and let go his weapon.

Her eyes filled with tears as she stumbled back a step, head buzzing like a wasps' nest, but Birdie just managed in taking advantage of the man's pain before he could pull himself together, driving the mace down into his face and leaving it there.

She snatched up her knife from the deck nearby and stumbled away from the noise, letting the world come back into focus. Someone—one of her bowmen she guessed—handed her a cloth which she held against her nose.

"Bet you really hate your uncle right about now?" a familiar voice with a heavy accent.

Birdie looked back as the face came into focus, recognising the dark-skinned woman who'd greeted them in Breccia. Axilla, the Hangman's right-hand woman.

"Just a bit," she croaked, tilting back her head. "Why didn't Bella ever mention the pain?"

"Hmm?" said Axilla, pulling Birdie down with her behind some barrels.

"Nothing." Birdie looked around, seeing her crew had managed to repel their boarders, and the ropes were being cut. Then Birdie noticed the flames on the enemy's ship, realizing how close they were to catching light to their own sails. Their ship pulled away with only minor damage to the rigging.

Axilla once again took charge of Birdie's throbbing nose, spreading minty smelling ointment all over her face, bringing tears to her eyes once more. The battle was still ongoing. Ships burned all around them, sending thick plumes of dark smoke into the sky. Men screamed from the ships, from the water. A burning flag went fluttering from a mast, the ministry's red banner and white circles lost from view as it fell behind the black hull of its ship.

The Hangman's war ship had taken most of the damage from the enemy catapults, men visibly bailed water as fighting was still ongoing at its bow, holes dotted everywhere. Maddox's ship had pulled alongside an enemy ship flanking the Hangman and figures choked the deck, but the two Sun Isles ships pulling in behind the enemy would soon overpower the soldiers on deck.

They sailed close to the Hangman's warship, the leader of the alliance standing just beside the helm, guarded by a dozen men holding shields, and he gave her a wave, which she returned. The fighting further out looked fiercer, not as many of those ships had been hit by the Skyfire, and the tribespeople's boats veered past enemy ships as the Hangman's pirates fought on deck, the tribespeople using spears and arrows to thin out the enemy numbers.

"It seems the Skyfire was just as deadly as the Order told us," Axilla said, also looking at the now sinking hulls, which hissed and steamed as the cindered beams sank below the surface. "Bless the Gods for their aid. If we had lost our warships, I don't believe the outcome would have been as favourable."

Birdie nodded to Maddox's ship, where tribesmen were climbing up the stern of the enemy ship. "They might be just as deadly as Skyfire."

"My people are renowned for their fighting prowess," smiled Axilla.

"You're from the Sun Isles?" asked Birdie.

Axilla nodded. "And let's pray that after this day, we may once again live in peace."

Birdie gently touched her tender nose and nodded too. "That sounds... pretty nice right about now."

Chapter 39: Nothing Personal

Kye watched as the battle went from a sure thing to a complete disaster. After realizing every barrel of Skyfire had been stolen, he'd soon put a name to the deed. The Order of Mist must have joined ranks with the Hangman and his black alliance. Kye's ships had been ordered to aim solely for the Hangman's great warship, its hull making an easy target for their catapults. But no matter how many rocks they'd sent tumbling down onto its crew, how many holes they poked into its hull, the damn thing remained floating.

He'd hoped the loss of their leader might make them lose heart, but when the Sun Isles ships appeared on the horizon it was his own men who became nervous. That and the barrel of Skyfire which had then exploded against one of their masts.

Kye had just enough time to dive from the ship before the liquid caught fire to everything below, and had once again been forced to abandon his sword and armour to that darkness that is the deep sea.

As he kicked water and tried to look for a nearby ally or place to hide, he could only feel that some power of the deep was desperately trying to claw him down, angered at the empty shells he'd sacrificed instead of true flesh and bone.

His thoughts turned to more close-to-hand things, like getting out of the water, and a nearby ship just got close enough for him to be thrown a rope, which he clung to desperately, dragging himself hand-by-cold-hand along and up the side of the ship, where soldiers pulled him aboard.

He was soon forgotten as enemy ships closed in around them, the tribespeople flinging their spears bound with ropes over the rail, trying to impale people and make a more sinister grappling hook. Onto the deck they swarmed, wearing masks covered with paints, weapons crudely made but gleamingly sharp.

Kye kept to the back of the fighting, waiting until he could steal a sword from a fallen soldier. He helped stifle the flow of enemies at the stern, but more appeared on the bow, and soon their ship was overpowered. Kye and five armed men with spears stood below the helm, surrounded by at least a hundred blood-thirsty savages.

They crept closer, about to surge at them, when a voice rang out.

"Leave them!"

A man appeared on board.

"Maddox," growled Kye. "About time you showed your face, you damned traitor."

"How could I ever have betrayed a black-hearted bastard like you, Kassova?" Maddox pushed his way through the throng, followed by more pirates and a red-haired woman dressed in the armour of House Vanderholm.

Kye only let his shock show for a moment.

"Hello, Kassova," smiled X.

"I should have known..." Kye bared his teeth. "You were working alongside the Alliance the entire time."

"My name is Ariss, and yes. But we had fun, didn't we?"

Kye ignored her, looking back at Maddox. "You left Anne behind to die alone. You betrayed her and the rest of your family. For what? How much was she worth?"

Maddox shook his head. "You've no idea what you're talking about..."

"Don't lie to me!" shouted Kye. "I sent you a warning, giving you all enough time to escape... But you abandoned her!"

"Your master killed her. Nefaro was up there that night, in the spire. He shot her while she was holding your damned child, I might add." Maddox laughed and shook his head. "You really didn't know? She *ordered* me to leave her there! Anne had me and Bella swear to take the baby and run, to keep her safe."

Kye steadied himself on the railing. "What about my daughter? Where is she?"

"I never planned to give her to you. She's not a bargaining chip, Kassova. She can decide if she wishes to speak with you before the Hangman decides your fate." Maddox disappeared back into the throng the way he'd come.

Ariss smirked. "Even one handed he'd still crush you, War Monger. Thank the Gods he's more merciful than I." She turned and followed Maddox, shouting over her shoulder, "bring him to the Fortress, alive! Kill the others!"

The tribespeople moved in, and Kye readied his weapon.

He would fight to the death. Kassova Kye, War Monger, Sword of Mala, would not go quietly, he would—

A pair of arms grabbed him from behind, another grabbed his arm holding the sword, more grabbed his legs. The remaining soldiers of his crew were turning against him!

"I'll have your heads for this," he screamed, before they bonded his limbs and gagged him.

One of his men had the decency to at least give him a sad expression. "It's nothing personal."

A large hand came down, swinging a baton.

The world went dark.

Chapter 40: Embracing your Demons

The metal door groaned open, releasing a familiar odour wafting out from inside the cell. Old sweat, shit, musty bedding and fear—the prisoner's aroma was the same the world round, she guessed. Birdie stopped herself from shielding her nose, nodding her thanks to Axilla as she entered the cell.

"Just call me if you need anything," said Axilla, as she shut the door behind her.

Kye sat in the corner on a bare stool, looking out a barred window at the churning sea. He spoke without looking at her. "I was wondering if you'd show up." He chuckled. "I apologise for my appearance but my standards for hygiene have drastically fallen. I'm sure the executioners won't mind, though."

"I didn't come here to talk about your lack of sponges," Birdie said through gritted teeth.

"Hah." He shook his head. "At least I won't have to worry about drowning anymore. A noose is highly preferable to a watery grave."

"My aunt always said dead was dead." Birdie leaned against the wall.

Kye looked at her. "She raised you well? You... were happy?"

"I would have been happier not hiding away for most my life. But it wasn't so bad."

"I never wanted for your mother to get hurt..."

"Storming her home with armed men is a funny way of showing that!"

"I tried to get her away!" Kye clasped his hands together, looking down at his feet. "I sent a message, telling her and her family of a hidden passage—"

"How did you know about the hidden passage?"

Kye shrugged. "I spent my younger years in the Clerics Palace, much younger than any of the other novices. Nefaro allowed me access to the archives, saying my mind was keen for learning and he wouldn't hinder it. Along with many other shreds of information, I found one tome with blueprints inside of it for the spire in Mala. After committing the map to memory, I burnt it and in my free time I wandered the spire, exploring the hidden passages. Then I saw your mother in their gardens, and was entranced. Every chance I got I would watch her, too afraid to approach."

Kye smiled. "Years later, after returning from training in the Palace of War, I built up enough courage to speak with her when she was alone. She recognised me from the court proceedings when I occasionally accompanied Nefaro. Weeks passed to months and we grew closer. We loved each other. And then all of a sudden she vanished." Kye clicked his fingers. "I spent weeks waiting in that garden, hoping, but she never came back."

"And then she was killed," said Birdie.

Kye nodded. "And then she died, yes."

Birdie pushed herself away from the wall. "How can you remain loyal to Nefaro? The man responsible for her death."

"Loyalty's all I have left." Kye looked away. "This close to the end, it doesn't make sense to change."

"People can change. You need to plead for mercy, swear to join the Alliance and spend the rest of your life fighting against Nefaro. If you beg for mercy, then I'll know you truly regret your actions. That there really *is* something worth saving deep inside of you. I still won't forgive you for what you've done, but I'll ask my uncle to plead your case."

Kye glanced up at her. "Why?"

"Because whatever my mother saw in you, it wasn't... *this*." Birdie shook her head. "It's for her alone that I'm giving you this chance. No matter what you and your master think of the Alliance, we're not black-hearted monsters."

Birdie walked over to the cell door and knocked on it.

"I would never have guessed a daughter of mine could be so... kind-hearted."

Birdie narrowed her eyes. "Don't mistake my mercy for weakness. If you're given a chance and you fail." The cell door opened. "I'll kill you myself."

Kassova Kye stood alone in the chamber, surrounded by a circular table of darkly polished wood, staring up into the vaulted ceiling. Two armed guards stood to either side of him, and Birdie hadn't seen him so much as fidget, instead standing cool and collected as the leaders of the Alliance spoke amongst themselves.

Long gone was the confident rogue storming into the planning room the day before battle. Now his pale face, stubble dotted cheeks, tousled hair and eyes surrounded by dark shadows made him look a shadow of that man. A week spent in a cell not knowing your fate would do that to a person, Birdie guessed.

The doors opened and the Hangman entered, wearing a white robe lined with gold trim. On his chest was an emblem of a golden trident, the Aquaria family emblem, once ruling family of High Shoals. He took the chair between Ubba and Maddox, eyes settling on Kye without emotion. The room had fallen silent and waited, and for once even Ubba showed no sign of ingesting silver dust, instead glancing from the Hangman to Kye.

The Hangman's voice was strong when he spoke, reflecting none of the strain his illness caused him. "Brothers and sisters of the People's Alliance, we gather to decide the fate of an enemy to our cause. War Monger Kassova Kye has been a constant malice to the freedom of every citizen of our nation. For decades he has done Nefaro's bidding without question, taking innocent lives, crushing any shred of independence, strangling the life and hope from the people that should be protected by his master.

"We have risen from beneath that oppression. Once plans made in secrecy are now exposed for the people to witness. Once a scattered force hidden away behind high walls have now become something for our oppressors to fear. But before we can begin the final act of justice, we must decide what's to be done with a champion of the enemy. Should we grant him a quick death, or something more fitting his long reign of terror? Whatever the decision, we must decide as one mind, and all opinions will be heard."

The chamber filled with voices as people shouted angry oaths to kill Kye with their own hands. After a few minutes the Hangman waved down the noise.

"Mostly for justice, but a few scattered indifferent minds, I believe. We understand that Kassova Kye wishes to address the court?"

"I do," Kye bowed. "I beg the people's forgiveness. A kindness shown to me by my daughter has lifted a fog shrouded over my mind since the death of her mother. A woman I dearly loved. I beg this court to allow me to right those wrongs. To use my skills to bring justice onto the man responsible."

"You'd turn against your master?" asked the Hangman. "How are we to know you're not lying? That you won't flee back to Nefaro and help him as soon as possible."

Kye bowed lower. "All I can do is swear it on the Gods and hope you'll see the truth in my oath."

The Hangman whispered with Maddox and Ubba for a long moment, then nodded and sat back.

Maddox stood up and cleared his throat. "My niece has just as much reason to want justice on this man than the rest of us. Because of Kye and his master's actions she has lost her mother and was forced to flee, living in hiding for most her life. But she has chosen to show mercy on him, believing that he can be trusted."

Maddox looked at her and gave a sad smile. "But I don't agree." He pointed at Kye. "This man should be shown *no* mercy! He deserves nothing more than a slow death. But for my niece's sake, I'll ask we offer him a fair chance. To be judged by fate alone. I ask he face a trial-by-combat, and that I be given the honour of facing him."

The Hangman nodded. "All who agree raise their hands."

Birdie looked around in horror as every person at the table lifted their hands.

"You promised me you'd give him a chance," said Birdie, trying to keep up with Maddox's pace, pushing their way through the crowd of people moving through the hallway.

"And I'm giving him as much a chance as he deserves." Maddox strode through a door at the end of the hallway, crossing a narrow bridge, headed towards his room. The trial had ended and people were relaying what decision had been made regarding Kassova Kye, many clapping Maddox on the shoulder, wishing him luck in the trial that would take place tomorrow morning.

"I asked you to give show him *mercy*, not kill yourself while you're at it!" growled Birdie. "I don't want to see you get hurt."

Maddox stopped midway across the bridge and turned around. "You don't think I'll win? I can beat him."

"It's not about who's going to win." Birdie pointed back at the direction they'd come. "You could've let him prove his trustworthiness in other ways. Ways that didn't have you or him shedding blood. All you had to do was ask the Hangman to give him a chance!"

"And why would I do that?" Maddox growled. "All my life I've wanted revenge on that silver-toothed fuck and the rest of his ministry. Now we're *so* close, you'd have me let him *join us*?"

"I'd ask that you're at least honest with me. Don't tell me you'll do something and then go and change your mind! How am I supposed to trust you after this?"

"Birdie, you're young! You don't know what it was like back then! That bastard doesn't deserve mercy. He doesn't deserve to see another sunrise! But you'll have one more night to speak with him, that's as much kindness I can offer."

"I won't forget this, uncle."

Maddox put his hand on her shoulder and she shrugged it away. "I'm doing this for the both of us, Blackbird. He'd only hurt you." Maddox turned and walked away.

Birdie clenched her fists and kicked the stone railing, stubbing her toe. "Fucking shit-balls!" she grunted, hopping on one foot. Sitting down, she leaned against the rail.

There was no way she could help Kye now. Giving him a chance had not only felt right, but it seemed the logical thing to do. Why hadn't they seen how useful letting Kye free and gambling on him turning against his master might be? It would cost them *nothing*, and might have paid them back ten-fold. But instead her uncle was letting his emotions guide his actions.

She didn't think she could face Kye now. What would she say?

I'm sorry for giving you a false sense of hope. But hey, at least we're even now...

Or

Yeah, I know I said I'd get them to give you a chance, but I lied... But hey, here's a sponge!

Birdie groaned and held her head in her hands.

Someone whistled lightly, and Birdie looked up to see Leek waving at her from across the bridge. Leek smiled as he crossed and offered her a hand up. "Sorry to disturb the moping around and self-pity, but I think you might want to see this."

"See what?" Birdie took his hand and stood up.

Leek smiled wider. "Oh, just you wait. I'm a bloody genius..."

"You're a damned lunatic," said Birdie, stepping away from it. "But definitely a genius!" she smiled and couldn't help but clap him on the back, shaking his shoulder.

"Genius, insanity... just two sides of the same coin." Leek pulled the cover back over the glass sphere of Skyfire.

"How'd you get it?" Birdie checked the fuse was intact and was delighted to see everything was in working order. Leek had hidden it away in one of hundreds of storage rooms beneath the Fortress.

"I'm a thief, it's what I do." Leek leaned close. "But we can't trust anyone else to help us."

"Help us?"

"Yip, help us break out your father." Leek put his hand on hers. "I don't owe anyone else my loyalty except you. You say we bust out the War Monger, then one War Monger busted out you get."

"Oh, Leek!" she grabbed him and pulled him in for a tight hug. "Thank you."

Leek's face was as red as his hair. "It's nothing you wouldn't do for me."

Then Birdie noticed something also covered in canvas. "What's underneath that one?"

Leek's smile faded. "Best not look under there... No, wait!"

Birdie stepped closer, intrigued. "Wait, what's that smell? Oh, by the Gods, Leek! What's a body doing down here?" The last statement was made after she had pulled up the canvas, revealing a bloated body.

"Found it floating in the water when I was getting a boat ready."

"You worry me sometimes, Leek. Wait, a boat?"

"Yeah. I have it anchored by the Bone Wall. I'm not sure where the hidden ladder is, but you can figure that out."

Birdie nodded. "Let's wait until its dark to move the barrel. I've got a plan beginning to take form."

Leek looked relieved. "That's good, because getting the Skyfire and body was all I had."

"Leek, did you make any of those sleeping draughts Maddox showed you?"

He reached inside his cloak and pulled out two small vials filled with a dark green liquid.

Birdie nodded. "Good, here's what we'll do..."

"Sure is," smiled Leek, as the three guards outside the cell licked their lips, and then quickly put their tankards back for another sip. He waited until they'd drained the ale inside before offering them the platter, taking back the empty tankards.

"Tell 'em thanks, and good luck in the trial tomorrow," said one of the guards, and Leek said he would, before leaving them to retake their seats at the table and continue their card game. Birdie waited for him around the corner, and it wasn't long before they heard the first body fall. The two guards laughed, making fun of the lightweight youngster, until the next man fell. The last man growled an obscene sentence before he took three steps and collapsed.

"Nice work, but they'll be fine tomorrow, right?" asked Birdie, as she carried the sphere of Skyfire around the corner, past the unconscious guards.

"Sure, sore heads, but that's it. That mixture will wipe their memories of the last few hours. Won't remember a thing."

They took the key from one of the guards and unlocked the cell. Kye stared wide-eyed at them as they entered.

"What's going on?" he asked Birdie.

Birdie held up the key for his chains. "If I give you a chance, I'll need you to swear to me you won't ever help Nefaro again. You'll never aid the ministry."

"Of course!"

"You swear it on my mother? Of the love you once had for her?"

"I-I swear it!"

Birdie unlocked Kye's chains, and he rubbed the red marks on his wrists and above the ankles. "What now? I'll never make it out of here."

"Leave it to us," said Birdie, leading them out of the cell. Leek carried the Skyfire inside the cell, and together they pulled the three guards around the corner of the hallway, out of harm's way. Kye didn't say anything, but the look he gave her was a mix of curiosity and amusement.

After hauling the body to the cell and getting it onto Kye's pallet, Kye pulled Birdie back as she went to light the fuse.

"What about my teeth? They'll know it's isn't me."

Leek smiled crookedly and opened the corpse's mouth, revealing a full set of silver teeth. "Way ahead of you."

They shut the cell door behind them, rushing around the corner just as the ground shook. Skyfire erupted inside the room, filling the hallway with hissing noises and smoke. Birdie led them through a door and down a series of stairs, ignoring the shouting coming from all around them. Through one final door they passed, along one more hallway, and stopped midway. Voices came from around the corner, shadows appeared on the walls, as Birdie found the hidden opening her and Ariss had used, and pulled the tunnel's entrance wide.

"In!" she hissed, following Kye and Leek inside and shutting it closed behind them.

"Now what?" Kye's face was barely visible in the dark.

"Now we get you out of here," said Leek.

"And you keep your word," said Birdie.

They rushed through the tunnel, leaving behind the muffled footsteps and shouts on the other side of the wall. Once they swam through the submerged tunnel, using rope for Birdie to guide them, they climbed the Bone Wall and back down the other side.

At the bottom a small rowboat was anchored nearby, its hull very much like the one Maddox used to use. At Birdie's expression, Leek smiled.

"It was hidden beneath the Fortress," shrugged Leek. "And no one seemed to need it."

"I don't know what to say," said Kye, and he offered his hand to Leek, who looked at it for a moment, before turning and diving into the water.

"I like him," nodded Kye, watching Leek swim away.

"Say you won't make me regret this." Birdie took out her dagger and pierced the skin of her palm. "By my mother's blade, and my mother's blood, swear you'll take this boat and never be seen again."

Kye took the dagger and done the same, and they clasped hands. "I swear it, Birdie. I'll never help Nefaro again."

She let go and washed the blood away in the water.

"I don't think I can leave you, though, knowing now you exist." Kye had tears in his eyes when she looked back at him. "You're just like your mother, you know. You have the same eyes."

"I might have wanted a father once, Kassova." Birdie looked away, to Leek, who was kicking water by the wall. "But that time is long past. The least you can do for me now is to disappear. Make a new life somewhere, and maybe do some good for once. Prove I wasn't wrong. If you can do that, then I can live with my decision."

"I just want you to know... for all it's worth... I'm proud of you." Kye took an awkward step closer. "Your mother would be proud too. She had a good heart. I see much of her in you." Kye went to put his hand on her shoulder, but then hesitated. Instead he held out his hand to shake hers. "Until we meet again, then... In this life, or the next."

Birdie looked at the hand and bit her lip, one part of her wanting to turn and leave, and the other...

She took a step closer and put her arms around him, not even realising she was doing it until she could feel the warmth of him, feel his own arms tighten around her as he hugged her back.

What must have been mere heartbeats seemed to stretch into hours as they embraced, and before she knew it, she was back on the wall, fighting the urge to look back, telling herself it was the cold stinging at her eyes.

Chapter 41: How the Mighty Have Fallen

"Dead, what do you mean *dead*?" said Maddox to the soldier in the hallway, who looked like he was about to faint as he leaned against the wall, which had been splashed with a small lake of water to stop the Skyfire melting through.

"I don't know what happened, Lord Black. We woke up and the place was in chaos, people lugging water, smoke filling the hallway. Then we saw the body lying on the bed."

Maddox growled as he pushed past the guard and into the cell, which was not a cell anymore but a giant melted gap in the side of the Fortress, big enough for a score of men to climb through abreast. The burnt remains of the once scourge of the Sea of Circles, War Monger Kassova Kye, lay smouldering on the pallet, almost unrecognisable as a human body at all, more a twisted pile of charcoal. But when he wiped them, the teeth revealed silver beneath.

One of his greatest enemies was dead, albeit not by his own hands—hand, but dead was dead, as Bella had always been fond of saying.

"We should display his body for the men to see."

Maddox turned to see the Hangman standing in the narrowest gap of the melted remains of the wall.

"Yes, I guess that would serve some purpose." Maddox stood back from the body.

"A shame you didn't get your chance for revenge, Maddox, but the gods seemed to have served their own justice. I'll take care of arranging the body for display. You should begin preparing the next plan of action..."

Maddox took one last look at the body, before turning and leaving the cell, to begin the journey back to Mala.

"It's fine, honestly," said Birdie, after Maddox had told her. "I mean... It wasn't you, was it?" and she continued to speak when Maddox just looked confused. "You weren't the one who done it? Kind of fitting, really, burning him the same way many of our own family were burnt during the purge."

Maddox putt his hand over his heart. "I swear, Blackbird, I had nothing to do with this. But I'll find out what happened if it's the last thing I do."

Bless Leek's big, clever, slightly unnerving brain for thinking of casting molten silver over the corpse's teeth, is all Birdie could think of as her uncle left the room. It disturbed her how at ease Leek had been in moving a body and then modifying it to appear to be Kye. But only for him either her father or her uncle would now be dead. Perhaps both.

Maddox spent the day organising a ship to Mala, and grudgingly stopped the interrogation of the three guards, admitting that they knew nothing. The next morning Ariss, Birdie, Leek and Maddox brought their equipment and supplies to the docks, where a familiar small ship was anchored, the same one they used to sail to the Hangman's Tower,

"I had it brought down from Breccia," grinned Maddox as they boarded.

Leek helped her across the gangplank. "One of your daggers is missing," he noticed.

Birdie nodded. "Yeah, think I dropped it in the tunnel diving back through the water. I'm sure there's more back at the castle stronghold. I'll miss it, though. It was one of my mother's."

The weather was chilled, but the wind favourable as they left Mount Lena, headed south-west. Days spent returning to their routine of life on board was broken by nightly feasts and mornings spent fishing. The wind changed then and it took them the best part of a week to reach Mala's Bone Wall, but Birdie wasn't complaining.

They approached and anchored near the secret entrance, each lashed together with rope, Birdie going first, quickly ascending the ascent. The four of them worked well together, quickly getting down the other side and making their way towards the mountains to the east.

That first night spent beneath the stars on the outskirts of Mala was strange, as Birdie couldn't help but feel a sense of excitement knowing who her father was, and that he was out there somewhere, alive. She also felt a sense of guilt at having tricked Maddox, but didn't regret it.

Finally, the mountains went from shadows to shapes, and they entered the narrow valley, the decrepit shack still huddled against the cliff. Maddox activated the portal and the dark rock came to life with blue veins swirling through the stone, transforming to pulsing liquid.

They held each other—hand-in-hand—as they stepped through the portal. But this time the feeling of fear and anxiety that had passed over Birdie at her first passage through the portal was now replaced with warmth in her heart. A reassuring net of safety closed around her as they were sucked in together—she was going home, at long last.

Kassova Kye was not a man that feared death. He had bravely awaited his fate in that cell, and had welcomed the duel with Maddox. But after being freed by his daughter, he now wondered would he have been better off taking his chances with the sword.

Water stretched across the horizon, a far more daunting foe than the Black Shadow. Waves pushed him this way and that, emptying his stomach of the bile inside. Shades of iron grey and foamy white swirled around him, soaking through his thin clothes, seeming to penetrate his very soul.

But then something had knocked against him, and looking up a ship had suddenly appeared out of nowhere. And then he'd recognised the ship, and Kye abandoned his boat, being sucked down into that horrible, familiar nightmare beneath the waves. The darkness below drew his gaze like an open wound. The vast abyss threatened to swallow him whole, and Kye decided he would take his chances with the ship.

He broke through the surface and screamed for help. The faces watched from over the rail, then ropes were lowered, and soon Kye found himself on deck, surrounded by men he least wanted to see right now.

"Hello, Kassova. Welcome to the Misty Wave," said Brother Orlot. "We've a lot to talk about, you and I..."

The Gods truly had a cruel sense of humour...

Captain Vines stood on the dock and watched the ship materialize from nowhere. One second he'd been looking at a mostly empty bay, besides the distant trading ships and patrolling warships further out, and the next a small ship was bobbing right beside the docks, dropping anchor.

His masked men mumbled uncomfortably as the brothers of the Order of Mist crossed the gangplank, escorting the familiar but somehow totally changed figure of Kassova Kye. The smile the War Monger gave lacked its usual gleam of razor-sharp edge, and Vines couldn't help but take in the new lines on the man's face, the deep shadows.

"Vines, what a sight you are!" Kye approached and embraced him in a firm hug, before letting go and looking up at the towering spire above the city. "I suppose we'd best not keep the Supreme waiting, lead the way!"

"Of course, Lord Kye. This way."

Kye couldn't count the emotions bubbling through him as he was escorted up into the spire. Happiness at returning home. Sadness for so much having changed. Comfort, knowing that if Nefaro killed him, he'd still live on in Birdie. And a bitter slice of self-indulgent pity, as no one had even noticed the man being escorted through the city's thoroughfare.

So much for being the hero they loved and adored.

He couldn't believe he'd ever cared.

Nefaro waited for him at the top of the spire, and Kye noted the new fortifications in place, large siege crossbows had been installed in nearly every corridor, archers dotted the towers like an anthill.

Kye stopped at the balcony, Nefaro leaning against it, hands on the parapet. Nefaro waved Kye's escort away, and Kye gave Vines a brief nod before the big man left.

"You have nerve, boy, showing your face here after failing me again." Nefaro turned to look at him. "But you never lacked nerve, hmm? No, just the other essential qualities—competence, leadership, loyalty—"

"I have *always* been loyal to you."

"Don't you dare talk back to me!" shouted Nefaro, taking a step closer to Kye. "You've failed me one too many times now. You'll spend the rest of your days overseeing the mines in Stadarfell. The next time you leave that damned island the only thing you'll use a sword for is a bloody crutch!"

Kye watched as the old man barked at him, pale face slowly filling with colour.

This was the man who had raised him, but at such a cost.

A large part still loved him somehow, though.

"And you can forget about your titles. You're no longer War Monger, I revoke it, as well as your official status with the Clerics Palace! You're nothing now."

"I'm sorry," muttered Kye, bowing, and he could sense it coming. Nefaro swung at him, and Kye caught his hand just before it struck his face. Kye smiled then, looking up into the old man's eyes, feeling a shred of that old, icy coldness inside of him.

He looked deep into Nefaro's eyes, ignoring the orders, which turned to growls, to threats. Kye reached into his trouser pocket, through the hole, to the hilt of Birdie's dagger strapped to his leg.

"What are you doing, Kassova? Let me go!" Nefaro saw the long gleaming stiletto as it slid out of the pocket, his eyes widening as he realized the truth of the situation. "Guards!" screamed Nefaro, but it was much too late for that.

Kye plunged the dagger through the old man's chest, piercing his heart. He pulled Nefaro in for a final embrace.

"For Lillith," he whispered into Nefaro's ear.

Kye let go and flung Nefaro back, who stumbled and toppled over the parapet, an expression of shock on his face as he disappeared from view.

Kye closed his eyes and listened to the silence.

That ball of anger had vanished from inside of him.

Minutes passed until someone cleared their throats. Kye turned around and saw Brother Orlot standing in the doorway. "Brother Kye, you'll want to see this."

Chapter 42: Just a Dream

On that night first night back at the castle stronghold Maddox dreamed of his sister, Anne. She was in her domed tower, her white nightdress illuminated with moonlight, her pale face turned towards Maddox and smiled. No words were spoken, but Maddox felt the love and gratitude radiate from her like the morning sun.

The tower faded and Maddox was stood atop the spire, looking out over the city of Mala. Ariss was beside him, resting her head on his shoulder. Her hand was in his and they held each other as they watched the sun rise over the mountains in the distance.

"You must protect her, no matter the cost," Ariss whispered to him.

"No matter the cost," muttered Maddox, turning to see that Ariss had vanished and he now faced a swirling fog surrounding him.

She belongs to us. We belong to her.

The voices whispered through the swirls, and multiple shadows appeared.

Maddox raised his hands against the advancing dark figures. They wore ancient looking armour. Maddox stepped back and fell from the spire, falling, falling...

She is ours. You must return her to us!

Maddox woke in his room covered in sweat. He gasped in air as he stumbled out of bed and took a drink of water. Turning back to his bed, he found Anne and Ariss standing in front of him. They raised their hands and pointed at him with blackened fingernails, their flesh grey and corpse-like.

"She must be returned," they droned. "Or else the world will crumble into darkness... return her to us!" And they tilted back their heads, screaming as they erupted into flames.

"What's wrong?" asked Birdie, running into her uncle's room. Ariss sat beside Maddox, clutching him tightly, daubing his brow with a damp cloth. She'd heard his screams from her own tower.

"Just a dream, nothing to worry about," Ariss smiled at her.

"The real nightmares lie in the world of the living," Maddox croaked as he sat up, giving a faint chuckle. "Always the philosopher. I'm fine."

But he didn't look fine. He looked pale, eyes wide with panic.

"You want me to make you something?" she asked, but Maddox shook his head, waving her away.

"I'm fine, go back to bed."

Birdie reluctantly left the room, but soon had a potion ready just in case he needed it. She went back to her tower and got back into bed, but couldn't sleep.

The nightmare had been too realistic for comfort. Hundreds of blackbirds had been falling from the spire in Mala, aflame.

Birdie shivered, looking up at the bright twin moons above her domed roof.

It was just a dream.

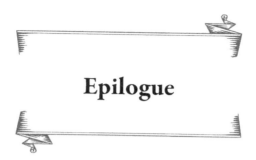

Epilogue

The city of Mala was on fire.

Maddox stood on the bridge, beckoning her across to join him and Ariss as they looked at flames engulfing the spire. Leek ran to join them, still holding a thick tome in his hand. Smoke filled the sky, flames spat and hissed, falling down from the spire as it slowly melted, raining death onto the city's inhabitants. Leek had tears in his eyes as he put his arm around Birdie, watching as the city in the space of an hour was engulfed in flames.

Birdie looked at Leek, a sharp fear cutting inside of her chest. He seemed to read her thoughts.

It couldn't' be him. Kye would keep his word, wouldn't he? *Wouldn't he?*

Birdie held her head in her hands as tears fell, knowing all too well the truth to her questions.

It had been her selfishness that'd caused this. He'd betrayed her trust. Had taken advantage of her mercy. Perhaps it had been weakness after all. And now innocent people were suffering for her mistake.

No.

Kye was the one who'd made a mistake.

Birdie looked up, her heart filling with something far more volatile but just as useful as pain and guilt. It welled up inside her like a ball of thorns, blocking out the doubts.

Anger took hold of her.

Her arm tingled, and Birdie lifted her sleeve, revealing a dark mark on her wrist. The same mark Maddox once had.

The bird gently glowed, revealing golden veins running beneath it.

Birdie frowned as she looked back up at the spire, clenching her fists.

I will find you, father. No matter how long it takes, I will make you pay for this.

I will gain my vengeance.

The Sea of Circles

Breccia - City of Thieves. Ruled by the Hangman and his swarm of pirate officers.

Trask – Powerhouse for Druids and Witches. Bones of the Twelve are a highly valued commodity in their culture due to their magical properties.

Mala - Closest city to the mainland port. Flanked by High Shoals and Stadarfell. These three islands can sever supply routes to the other allied cities at will. Many call these *The Unholy Trinity*.

Dogesk – Home to the War Mongers, trained at the Palace of War.

Isle of Bones – A fishing and whaling island. Shares strong blood-ties with Seandra.

Mount Lena - the Fortress.

Seandra –Seandra's navy is regarded as the best, but small, due to Nefaro's restrictions.

Ki Helm - Home to the Order of Mist. The Order make the Blasted Tower their seat of learning.

High Shoals – Some of the most talented artists and jewellers call this city home. It is a city of culture.

Stadarfell – A prison island where inmates work in the iron mine.

Tore – City of Dreams. Ruled by the Red Bastard, Lord Scarlett.

King City –Ruled by the Powder King, Ubba.

Sneak Peek of Song of a Feather!

Turn the page for a sneak peek of the sequel novel, Song of a Feather!

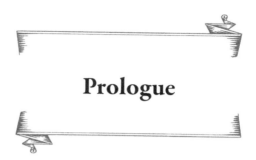

Prologue

The Sea of Circles is in turmoil.

The Hangman, leader of the pirate fleet and People's Alliance's health is failing.

His lover, Ubba the Powder King, has lost grip on reality and his mind is spiralling out of control. He grinds horns against Lord Scarlett, who fitting his self-centred personality has chosen to throw a tournament on his island of Tore, inviting the greatest warriors in the world to answer his call, promising wealth, fame, and fortune to one winner.

Supreme Nefaro has been slain by his protege, Kassova Kye, who now rebels and seeks to destroy all remaining footholds of the Ministry of Faces.

Plague has swept through the city of Mala, wiping out families in their dozens and a floundering Maddox Black tries in vain to stifle the disease's hold.

All the while Birdie Black remains in her castle stronghold, training, resentful towards her father and uncle for both their betrayals in her trust.

A year goes by, and the situation worsens, her contact with Maddox is slim-to-none and she decides to travel to the mainland with her close-friend, Leek.

And lurking in the corners of the Sea of Circles is a shadow, awaiting its chance to strike...

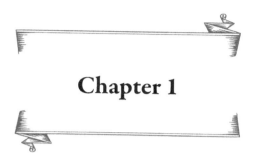

Chapter 1

The ship's dark blue hull rocked through another wave, sending the spraying water up into the woman at the helm's face. She kept her expression placid as the man struggled up onto deck, trying once more in vain to find his sea legs.

"Much further?" he shouted over the tumultuous roar of the water, wiping the long red hair from his eyes. It rather suited him, Birdie thought.

"Another hour, maybe two depending on the wind."

"We really should've chartered a ship instead. You didn't have to sail, you know."

"Where's the fun in that?"

The sails fluttered in the wind above, canvas and hull the same camouflaged hues. Leek gripped onto the railing tighter, as a large wave came rocking toward them.

"I forgot how much I hated this." He wiped away the spray once more.

"Here, you take the helm!" the girl moved aside, and Leek had to jump to grab and stop the helm from spinning out of control, as a rogue wave came at them.

"You're just like you're damned uncle!"

The woman pinched his arm in response. She slipped out a wineskin from inside her cloak. Birdie offered it to Leek, who also took a swig.

"Thanks." Leek looked sidelong. "Isn't that Maddox's favourite wineskin?"

"Sure is."

"Won't he mind you stealing it?"

"He sure will."

"Oh."

"He'll be OK."

"Um-mmm."

"Not like he'll be at the castle or anything anytime soon."

"Sure."

Birdie stoppered the wineskin. "I mean, he's been gone to see Ariss for weeks now." She pushed a few loose strands of hair from her eyes, flicked the long black braid over her shoulder. "Between him overseeing Mala and seeing Ariss, we never bloody see him anymore."

"I guess you're right there."

"How hard would it be to spend a bit more time with us?"

"Not hard at all, considering he has you training night and day."

"Exactly." Birdie hid the wineskin back underneath her cloak. "To be honest, since the situation with Kye he has barely spoken to me."

"To us," reminded Leek.

Since they'd freed Birdie's father, Maddox had been dropping hints that he knew they'd freed him. The previous Sword of Mala had made no attempt to hide the fact he still lived, having been around the Sea of Circles many times, bringing the proverbial sword down on all those still loyal to Nefaro's old regime.

The Ministry of Faces once ruled Mala, Stadarfell and High Shoals with an iron grip, but no longer. Kye had single-handedly brought down the Unholy Trinity of islands and since tossing the old tyrant off the spire the threads Nefaro worked so long to hold together had totally unravelled.

The Clerics Palace had once again taken control, as much as they could with the alliance breathing down their necks, and the Black Shadow, namely Birdie's uncle Maddox, constantly checking in and making sure no one attempted to return things to the way they were before.

And good riddance, she supposed. Things had been horrible in Mala. She had the scars and nightmares to prove it.

"Copper for your thoughts?" asked Birdie, looking sidelong at Leek.

"Just thinking back to the way things were."

"In general?"

"Namely Mala."

"Ah."

"I wonder what it's like there now."

"Not good, I heard."

"I mean, Paste, you know my friend I told you about?"

Birdie nodded.

"Well, he was able to get a note out to me every once in a while. I won't forget your uncle and what he's done for him since the plague struck the city. With the quarantine on going, it's been hard for him. People are dropping like flies, those that survived the spire burning, I mean."

Birdie's hands tightened on the railing, making the blood drain from her fingers.

After freeing Kassova Kye from the prison cell in Mount Lena, Kye had been found by the Order of Mist and had made his way back to Nefaro. But at least he'd kept his word about not returning to help, instead plunging a knife through the old man's heart, and tossing his body off the spire for good measure.

If Kye had left it at that Birdie would've bloody applauded him. But instead of leaving and never showing his face like he'd promised her, he'd set fire to the spire with barrels of the dreaded Skyfire, burning many in the upper sectors of the city.

"It's not your fault, you know?" Leek gave her a smile.

"It is, Leek. All those people who died that day died because I was too weak to leave my father to his own fate. I should've left him to fight Maddox. One life, no matter how painful it might've been to lose, was much better than losing hundreds of innocent people."

"But you couldn't have known what he'd decide to do."

She shook her head. "I was a fool to trust him. A mistake that I won't make again. I'll make him pay for what he's done, no matter how long it takes."

"And what does Ariss think about all this?"

Birdie looked at him.

"I... just noticed you've been sending each other letters."

"Did you read any?"

"No!"

"I know how curious you get."

"I swear, I didn't."

"Good. A woman's mind is her own to know. Ariss and I deserve some privacy, instead of always being questioned and annoyed by you and Maddox."

"But you haven't spoken to Maddox."

"He annoys her. You annoy me."

"We've been pretty much locked away together in that castle for a year. Bound to annoy each other eventually."

Birdie gave him a scolding look.

"I meant sometimes. Annoy each other *sometimes*... Not always."

"Shut up, Leek."

Maddox entered the hall and was surprised to find it almost empty. Only Ariss occupied the long marble table, seated at the head chair. He sat next to her and took her hand. She looked up from holding her head in her hand and smiled.

"Tough day?"

"Tell me about it." Ariss groaned as she sat back. "I thought things would get easier once we defeated Nefaro and his lackeys. But it's had the opposite effect."

"My father always said the best captains always got the longest voyages."

"What?"

"You're doing a great job, is what I'm trying to say."

"Oh." Ariss took a sip of cordial. "Because right now it feels like I'm bailing water with a thimble."

"Things will get better."

"Will they?"

Maddox noticed then just how tired she looked.

"I mean, the Hangman, or Joshua, isn't getting any better. And once he dies, who's going to keep things in order between his pirate crews? They're a bunch of lawless rogues at the best of times. I'm afraid they'll turn to their old ways once he's dead, and who will keep the navy in check then?"

"I know." Maddox nodded. "Without supplies from the mainland and other islands we'll be cut off."

"We need him. Without him we're finished. And now Ubba's ran off to King City, getting ready for this tournament with Lord Scarlett." She groaned and put her head back in her hand. "I mean, is it the more powerful the man, the more childlike the mind?"

"I think I'm quite mature, for a young man," smiled Maddox.

"Shut up, you old fool." Ariss leaned in and kissed him. "You've been great though, I must say. Without you by my side at the council meetings I feel like I'm just shouting at blank walls."

Maddox squeezed her hand. "Take a break. Once Birdie and Leek return from their trip let's go and relax at the castle stronghold for a few weeks. It will do you some good to get away from here for a while."

"Maybe."

"No maybe about it. We're going."

Ariss sighed. "I wonder how they're getting on."

Maddox looked around the room and grimaced as two officers entered carrying stacks of correspondence. "Better than us, I dare say."

The ship docked into the mainland port. Birdie left Leek to tie off the ship and speak with the dock captain.

It was strange, as the last time Birdie had gone through this port she'd been in cuffs and had got abducted for her trouble almost right off the pier. But now, handing in her papers with the actual real name on them and not the thousand aliases her uncle had created for them all, it was surreal in a way. Not to be hiding.

It was... nice.

"What're you smiling about?" called Leek, as she made her way back along the pier and helped Leek load up a cart they'd hired.

"I was just thinking of how much has changed."

One of the stevedores bobbed their head to Leek as he took the bags and loaded them onto the back of the cart.

"You can say that again. I'm not used to this treatment. I'm more used to being ran after and shot at." Leek laughed. "Though I prefer this much more than the latter."

Birdie helped Leek haul up a crate. Peeking inside she found about ten tomes Leek had 'borrowed' from the castle stronghold. He'd turned out to have a penchant for studies and had impressed Maddox with the concoctions he could create the last time her uncle had visited the castle stronghold. He not only could create potions now that would knock out a whale, but also remedies that surpassed the ones taught to Birdie by her aunt Bella.

Bella.

Birdie's stomach lurched at the thought of her.

How long had she longed to return to the woods? To visit the cottage and just... *be* there.

"I can't wait to get there." Birdie finished helping Leek load the cart and they climbed onto the driver's seat.

"Yeah, me too." Leek wiped back his hair. "I wonder if my mother's still there."

"It will be good for the both of us. We'll get some closure."

"M-hmm." Leek shrugged. "You're more hopeful than me, Birdie. I just want to be able to say I went, and nothing was there and now I can move on with my life."

"Me too."

Leek gave her one of his withering stares. "Birdie, I bloody *saw* the blueprints for the cottage you're planning on rebuilding. You have me wondering if you're even planning on coming back."

"Of course, I am. I don't plan on building the new cottage just yet. But one day."

"You really miss the woods, hmm?"

Birdie picked up the whip and set the two horses going with a flick. "Kind of. I guess the training has me drained. I can't wait to get some fresh air and just... breathe. You know?"

Leek smiled and reached back, pulling out a tome and flicking it open to the bookmark.

"You're bloody hopeless, Leek. Do you know that?"

About the Author

Rory .C.J. Dwane is an author and artist living in the midlands of Ireland. He writes in many genres and has numerous books self-published for different age groups.

His two upcoming stand-alone novels are scheduled for release in 2023, titled 'Knox of the Bloom' a Fantasy/Romance, and 'Empire of Sin' a Fantasy/Crime/Noir genre.

When he is not writing, he enjoys music, food, art, and hiking in the woods.

You can follow him via e-mail at his website, at https://rorydwaneart.wordpress.com

Or on his Indie Literary Press Facebook page, Crumpled Papers.

Also by R.C.J. Dwane

For Adults:
The Burning Tree: A Novelette
Blood Roots: A Novella
An Odd Anthology
Black Tales
For Younger Audiences:
The Adventures of Ominous Crane
Borris the Cabbage-Corn Kid

CPSIA information can be obtained
at www.ICGtesting.com
Printed in the USA
BVHW042255310123
657600BV00003B/10